JUN 1 1 2001

ELK GROVE VILLAGE PUBLIC LIBRARY

3 1250

P9-CCW-870

ELK GROVE VILLAGE PUBLIC LIBRARY
1001 WELLINGTON AVE.
ELK GROVE VILLAGE, IL 60007
(847) 439-0447

DISCARDED
Elk Grove Village
Public Library

SHARK RIVER

ALSO BY RANDY WAYNE WHITE

Sanibel Flats
The Heat Islands
The Man Who Invented Florida
Captiva
North of Havana
The Mangrove Coast
Ten Thousand Islands

NONFICTION

Batfishing in the Rainforest
The Sharks of Lake Nicaragua
Tarpon Fishing in Mexico and Florida (An Introduction)

RANDY WAYNE WHITE

SHARK RIVER

G. P. PUTNAM'S SONS   NEW YORK

WHI
White, Randy Wayne.
Shark river

This is a work of fiction. Names, characters, places, and
incidents either are the product of the author's imagination
or are used fictitiously, and any resemblance to actual
persons, living or dead, business establishments, events,
or locales is entirely coincidental.

G. P. Putnam's Sons
Publishers Since 1838
a member of
Penguin Putnam Inc.
375 Hudson Street
New York, NY 10014

Copyright © 2001 by Randy Wayne White
All rights reserved. This book, or parts thereof, may not
be reproduced in any form without permission.
Published simultaneously in Canada

Library of Congress Cataloging-in-Publication Data

White, Randy Wayne.
Shark river / Randy Wayne White.
p.   cm.
ISBN 0-399-14729-2
1. Ford, Doc (Fictitious character)—Fiction.   2. Marine biologists—
Fiction.   3. Bahamas—Fiction.   4. Florida—Fiction.   I. Title.
PS3573.H47473 S53   2001   2001016244
813'.54—dc21

Printed in the United States of America

1   3   5   7   9   10   8   6   4   2

This book is printed on acid-free paper. ∞

Book design by Victoria Kuskowski

With love, respect and admiration, this book is for my son, Rogan White, upon his graduation from high school—a great Third World traveling companion, a superb organizer, navigator, waterman, fly fisherman, a good man to have at your side in a tough spot, and one of my dearest friends.

The nervous system of the Herring is fairly simple. When the Herring runs into something, the stimulus is flashed to the forebrain, with or without results.   —WILL CUPPY

Technology is the knack of so arranging the world that we do not experience it.
                                                                —MAX RISCH

ACKNOWLEDGMENTS

Sanibel and Captiva islands, and the Koreshan Unity at Estero, Florida, are real places, though used fictitiously in this novel, as are certain actual businesses, marinas, bars, and other places frequented by Doc Ford and his friend Tomlinson. The same is true of Horse Eating Hole on Cat Island in the Bahamas, a place to which islanders will not stray because they fear the dragon. The lake and the legend attached to it are accurately described. I know because my friends Captain Mark Keasler and Captain Andy Fox were the first to sound and dive that lake, and find the caves there. I was lucky enough to be with them. As eighty-one-year-old islander Gaitor Ishmel told us on that day: "That lake a very bad place. If the creature don't eat you, it 'cause he down there sleeping."

In all other respects, this novel is a work of fiction. Names, characters, places and incidents are either the product of the author's imagination or are used fictitiously. Any resemblance to actual persons, living or dead, or to actual events or locales is entirely coincidental.

The author would also like to thank the following people for research assistance and for providing valuable contributions to this novel: Captain Peter Hull and Dr. John M. Miller of Mote Marine Laboratories; Craig Watson, director of the Tropical Aquaculture Laboratory for the University of Florida, Department of Fisheries and Aquatic Sciences; Ms. Jessica Lewis of Panama; Ms. Sue Williams; Ms. Sara Weber Rea for her help with the Koreshan Unity; Dr. G. B. Edwards of the Florida Museum of Natural History; Dr. Thaddeus Kostrubala, M.D., for insights into the brain's chemistry and effect on human behavior; Debra White for her unfailing support; and Ms. Laura Cifelli at Lee County Library. These people provided both guidance and information. All errors, exaggerations, omissions or fictionalizations are entirely the responsibility of the author.

Randy Wayne White
Cypress House
Key West

1

THE DAY I met the Bahamian woman who claimed to be my sister, and less than an hour before I was shot during the attempted kidnapping of a diplomat's daughter, my eccentric friend Tomlinson said to me, "Know how desperate I am? I'm thinking of having Elmer Fudd tattooed on my ass. Seriously, the cartoon character. You know who I'm talking about? The chubby guy with the red hunting cap, the one with the shotgun."

My eccentric, drug-modified friend Tomlinson.

I was lying in a hammock, leafing through a very old issue of *Copeia, Journal of the American Society of Ichthyologists and Herpetologists.* It contained an article on Gulf sturgeon, written back in the days when the occasional sturgeon was still caught in saltwater south of Tampa Bay. I paused long enough to straighten my glasses and stare at him. "You're kidding. From the Bugs Bunny cartoons? Even a regular tattoo, I've never understood the motivation. Something like you're talking about, I just can't comprehend."

"I told you about the . . . difficulty I've been having."

Yes, he had. Over and over he'd told me. Which is why I thought: *Boy oh boy oh boy, here we go again.*

"I *did* tell you, didn't I?"

"Yes, and I don't care to hear any more about your personal problems. It's sunset. In your own words: The Mellow Yellow Hour. I'm trying to relax before I change shoes and run. Don't screw with the molecular harmony—again, your words."

"I know, I know, but this is serious."

"So you keep saying."

"*Anything* that concerns Zamboni and the Hat Trick Twins is serious. They're just not theirselves, man."

Zamboni and the Twins—my friend's private name for his private equipment.

He explained, "The inflatable monster has finally turned all control over to my brain's moral guidance system, which is like a stone cold downer." He made a fizzling, whistling sound. "Sooner or later, it happens to every man, right? . . . *Right?*"

It was the fourth, maybe fifth time he'd asked me that question, but when a friend fishes for reassurance, you must reassure. "Of course. Very few exceptions."

"Okay, so you at least have a minor understanding of the motive behind the tattoo. Picture it"—Tomlinson created a frame with his huge, bony hands—"Elmer Fudd on the cheek of my ass, aiming his shotgun toward the shadows and he's saying, 'Come outta there you wascally wabbit!' Lots of bold color, reds and greens, but still . . . *tasteful*. Something that lightens the mood but also makes a statement."

I was nodding. "Yeah, choose the wrong shades, a tattoo like that could seem almost frivolous."

"Sarcasm. My equipment hasn't worked dependably in more than two months, yet my *compadre* offers sarcasm."

"Only because it's such a ridiculous idea. I still don't understand the motivation. Or maybe you're just joking."

We were on the second-floor veranda of a tin-roofed house, eye level with palm fronds and coconuts. Looking downward through the palms, we could see clay tennis courts, a swimming pool, sugar-white beach, and bay. Florida's Gulf Coast has a couple of exclusive, members-only islands. Guava Key is the one you read about occasionally, always associated with the very rich and rigorously private. The island is south of Tampa, north of Naples: a hundred acres of manicured rainforest and private homes centered on a turn-of-the-century fishing lodge built on an Indian mound. It is an island with no roads, no bridges, no cars and no strip malls, so it has the feel of a solid green raft at sea—boat and helicopter access only.

We were on Guava Key as guests of management. Tomlinson, an ordained Rinzai Zen Master and Buddhist priest, was there to teach a mon-eyed few members a course called "Beginner's Mind," which, I knew from our long association, has to do with Zen meditation and breathing techniques. I have no interest in meditation, nor do I feel the need to take vacations. Life in my little Sanibel Island stilthouse, collecting marine specimens to study and sell, is sufficiently satisfying. Plus, I tend to fret about my fish tank and aquaria if I'm gone for more than a few days. In them are delicate creatures that interest me, such as immature tarpon, sea anemones, and squid—fascinating animals that require a lot of care. Even so, he'd pestered me about tagging along until I finally lost patience. I told him enough was enough. Unless he came up with a good and practical reason for me to leave my work and go to Guava Key, drop the subject, damn it!

I should have learned by now never to refuse one of Tomlinson's invitations by invoking a preferred alternative. He's probably right when he says that I'm obsessive. I'm almost certainly right in my belief that he's manic. When the man becomes fixated, nothing can untrack him.

What he did was hunt around until he came up with a gambit that was professionally compelling and made too much sense for me to say no. It turned out that the state required Guava Key Inc. to file periodic fish counts from adjacent waters, all data to be assembled by an accredited marine biologist—something to do with past zoning variances. As owner and lone employee of Sanibel Biological Supply, I am an accredited, independent biologist for hire. He'd contacted management, and management had offered me a generous figure, all expenses paid, for myself and a guest. Jeth Nicholes had already assured Tomlinson that he and his girlfriend, Janet Mueller, would keep an eye on my stilthouse and feed my fish, so I had no choice but to accept.

Finding an appropriate guest, though, turned out to be more difficult than you might imagine.

The first person I called was Dewey Nye, the former tennis star. Dewey and I are old friends. For a time, we were on-again, off-again lovers. On-again, off-again until we both realized that the chemistry was wrong, quite literally. Mostly, though, she is my all-time favorite workout partner. By telephone, we agreed that, after the holiday season just past, a couple of Spartan weeks on Guava Key was just what we needed to shed a few pounds and cleanse our systems.

"Every morning," she told me, "we'll do a long swim, then a kickass run. Really push the envelope. Finish everything at P-squared."

I had to ask. "P-squared? What's P-squared?"

"I keep forgetting what an out-of-touch old hulk you really are. So I'll be delicate. It's jock for 'Upchuck pace.' Only, the first P doesn't stand for upchuck."

"Ah."

"They've got a health club? So we lift weights heavy every other day, then limit ourselves to two, maybe three cocktails in the evening. Our own little basic training retreat. After New Year's in New Jersey—it's been gray and sleeting for like twenty damn days in a row—after a couple weeks of this, shut up indoors with Rita, her poodle and her aluminum Christmas tree, I'm not sure who or what's gonna die first: my holiday spirit, or that damn yapping dog. What I need is a serious dose of Florida heat."

But five days before she was to fly in from Newark, Dewey's roommate, Rita Santoya, suffered an all-too-familiar bout of jealousy. Latin men are said to be possessive. It's an unfair generalization, yet Latin woman, apparently, can be just as bad as their clichéd counterparts. After a series of quarrels, Rita issued an ultimatum: If Dewey visited me in Florida, there was no need for her to come back.

As always, Dewey acquiesced.

"Maybe next time, Doc, when Rita feels a little more secure in our relationship. Don't worry, we'll get together again."

I told Dewey, any time, lady, any time, knowing there would probably never be a next time.

Male or female, the possessive ones never feel secure. Nor do their mates.

So I went through the short list: Dr. Kathleen Rhodes, but she was back in the Yucatán, doing field work. Nora Chung was available, but now had a romantic interest in a solicitous, sympathetic physician and didn't want to risk burdening the relationship so early in the game. Erin Bostwick was already scheduled to work the late shift all month at Timbers; Sally Minster (formerly Sally Carmel) was in the process of divorcing the neurotic abuser she'd married, but didn't feel right about slipping away with me until the legalities were complete.

She was disappointed. "I've had a crush on you since I was, what? Eight years old? Since the days you were living with your crazy uncle Tucker Gatrell, the dear sweet man, on that funky little mangrove ranch of his. So now you call."

Here's one of the ironies of male-female association: With women of sufficient character and humor, it takes only a few weeks to forge an intimate relationship, yet their well-being remains a matter of concern even years after parting. Their dilemmas still squeeze the heart.

One night, I found myself in my little lab, sitting beneath the gooseneck lamp, making a list of desperate last-minute replacement ladies. Thankfully, I caught myself. I've reached a stage in my life in which the little social interaction I have is guided by a simple maxim: I'd rather be alone than with people with whom I feel no emotional connection. That includes women.

Solitude is much preferred to the more disturbing isolation of sharing loneliness with a stranger.

I made no more telephone calls.

WHEN I TOLD Tomlinson that Dewey'd backed out, he lost none of his enthusiasm. "You're batching it? Perfect! Two weeks of island living. Fresh air, fresh fruit, plus lots and lots of cold, clean alcohol. It's just what the doctor ordered. We'll each have our own cottage, so the vacation ladies can choose for themselves. With the problem I've been having, escape may be the only sure salvation."

Even then he was obsessed with his perceived problem.

Now he was sitting in full lotus position, balanced strangely on the roof next to the veranda where the hammock was strung between rafter and rail. We'd been there for nearly an hour in silence, listening to the ambient bird-and-breeze sounds of a day so warm, during a winter so tropical, that jacaranda trees were already flowering bright as lavender parasails on this late February afternoon.

"Joking about having Elmer Fudd tattooed on my ass?" he said. "I wish to hell I were joking. You refuse to hear the details, even though I've made it clear that I need to vent. I've got feelings, man. Listening is one of the things that friends are supposed to do."

"I'm not a psychologist, for God's sake."

"You think I'd waste any more of my time with shrinks? Hey, let me tell you something, amigo . . . no, let's put it this way: If psychiatrists gave frequent flier miles, I'd have my own charter service to Fumbuck Egypt. Half my shrink friends call *me* for advice. The other half worry about the possibility that I snuck off and slept with their wives—which I did in way too many cases. People in the mental health professions?

They've got the horniest wives in town. Not that I'm in a position to help them these days."

Tomlinson was pulling at his stringy hair, biting it nervously. I noticed that his hands, which often had a slight tremor, were shaking more than usual. "It's not a physical problem. That much I know. The other morning, I woke up with a piss hard-on, and the damn thing nearly knocked the wind out of me when I rolled over too fast. My problem's spiritual, man. The fucking wheels are coming off my Dharma nature and my *daishinkon* faith is way back on its heels. I need to talk."

I had no idea what he was saying, but his tone told me it was important. I sighed, folded the magazine, and swung my feet onto the deck. As I did, I had a peripheral awareness of two young women below, jogging the footpath southward. One was blonde in a heavy blue sports bra and white tank top. The other was all legs and long chestnut hair, ponytail swinging like a flag.

I glanced at my watch, even though I knew the time: 5:30 P.M. plus or minus a few minutes, on a Wednesday, seventh day of February.

Every day for six days straight, an hour before sunset, I'd watched these two pass beneath our veranda, always headed the same direction. I'd seen them often enough to know that the blonde would be on the left, ponytail to the right and a half-step ahead. Blonde was the chatty one with a cheerleader stride and the bold, dominant voice. Ponytail was stoic, tomboyish, quiet, the apparent subordinate member.

I'd never exchanged a word with them, yet I knew their pace and I knew their schedule, just as I knew that half an hour later, near the island's grass landing strip, I'd see them once again on the little dock at the end of the nature boardwalk that trailed through mangroves.

The girls would be standing at the rail in a citrus-colored afterglow. They would watch the sun vanish before turning homeward, offering me the vaguest nod of greeting as I clomped up onto the dock, completing my second run of the day.

I am a creature of routine.

So, obviously, were they.

From old habit, though, and having once lived a life that required necessary wariness, I still practice a very simple precaution: I always vary my route and my routine. You never know who might be out there watching, logging your movements, waiting. I was never officially attached to any branch of the military, but I endured enough military training to have certain behaviors stamped so deeply that they have become part of the autosystem.

More than once when I saw them, that same ambient awareness noted the rich-girl genetics, knew the wealth that membership on Guava Key implied, and a secret little room in my brain sounded warning bells. It was an ancient alert, warning how easy it would be for a predator to become aware of these two women, track their movements, isolate them and take them.

As it turned out, I wasn't the only one who'd noticed.

There seem to be more and more predators these days.

TOMLINSON GESTURED TOWARD the swimming pool. "See the woman on the beach chair closest to us? The one with the Egyptian skin and hair down to her waist? Don't tell me you haven't noticed."

Oh, I'd noticed. I'm not a gawker; not the sly woman-watcher type, but there are certain females who move with such animal grace, who exude such a fertile sexuality, that it's impossible not to react. It's also impossible not to follow them with the eyes.

Through palms, the pool was a gelatinous blue. A dozen or so Guava Key members, mostly women, soaked or dozed in the late sunlight. Some day, a brave sociologist may write a paper that explores why a high percentage of very attractive women will predictably interact, socially and sexually, with only a tiny percentage of wealthy men.

It would be an unpopular paper, indeed, with the disingenuous and politically correct types.

These were the beautiful ones: women with sculptured hair and nails, wearing Saks straw Bahamas hats and boutique poolwear, women whose bodies illustrated the discreet attentions of plastic surgeons and silicone implants, and of hours spent laboring with personal trainers.

There was something different about the dark woman, though. She possessed a girlish reserve, a muscle and bone indifference that set her apart.

Now she lay on her back, one arm thrown behind her head, eyes closed, breasts flattened beneath their own weight, body a-glistening with oil. Her bikini consisted of three white napkin swatches connected by string. In contrast, the white fabric turned her skin a deep and vivid mahogany.

"Takes your breath away, doesn't she?"

I said, "She reminds me of women I saw on the Ivory Coast. Something about the cheekbone structure. Or maybe North Africa, with those legs."

"Her mother's from Senegal; her father's Saudi Arabian."

"You know her, then."

Tomlinson's voice had a sad, rueful tone. "Oh, I know her all right. Remember last year when I spent two weeks in Aspen at the International Bodhi Tree Conference?"

I nodded, suddenly more interested than before. I'd forgotten the name of the conference, but I remembered that he'd gone to Colorado.

Thus the increased interest.

Tomlinson was, apparently, much in demand at such events. There are very few westerners who are Rinzai Zen masters and *roshis*—a Japanese word for teacher. The man has his accomplishments but also his quirks. He can be infuriating, but he possesses an amazing intellect and his intuitive powers are the best I've ever witnessed. More important, he makes me laugh.

He said, "Nimba flew into Aspen via Paris and enrolled without her husband. That's her name—Nimba Dimbokro. It was a very confusing and painful time in her life. Her husband, supposedly, is a Saudi prince, but he acts more like some abusive camel-jockey redneck. You've read about vaginal circumcisions? He's exactly the sort who advocates that sort of thing.

"He's rich, of course. His family's made billions in oil. I mean literally *billions.* They have private jets; they own politicians in several countries; they have homes all over the world. Whatever she wants, Nimba gets. Except for one thing—freedom. Happiness. A couple of the biggies, huh?"

"I hope you're not telling me you slept with one of your students. What is she? Twenty-two, maybe twenty-five years old?"

Tomlinson's tone seldom approaches anger, but now it did. "Please tell me you're joking, then apologize. You think I would violate my moral obligations to a student?"

"I'm sorry. I apologize and withdraw the comment."

"I should hope so. Nimba came to the retreat in absolute emotional turmoil. She went through 'Beginner's Mind.' She learned how to sit, how to count her breaths. All very basic stuff. I was working with the advanced students, holding *dokusan* three times a day, and serving as monitor at *sesshin*s, so I wasn't her teacher. We had no interaction at all at the retreat."

I said, "Then you *were* lovers."

He shook his head. "Through karmic intervention, we met coincidentally at a ski bar. A place called The Slope."

"I'm familiar with the bar," I said, looking at him closely.

"The place happened to be holding a limbo contest that night. You may remember what a superb limbo dancer I am."

I shook my head. "Un-uh. The last time I can remember you limbo-ing was at the marina. It was almost a year ago at the Friday cotillion, maybe longer. You were wearing that red sarong you like, nothing else, so I left. Walked out on the docks, along with most of the other people there. Some things, you just don't want to see."

"Then take my word for it. I'm one of the all-time great limbo dancers. It's like a gift from God, the rhythm, the balance—actually a very delicate form of levitation if done properly. The great poet Basho wrote about it once. Metaphorically, of course—he didn't use the word 'limbo.'"

I said, "Ah." I'd returned my attention to the woman. She was lying there with her eyes closed, stretched out in the winter heat. "So you met her at the bar. Then what?"

"We danced. We laughed. We drank. As you know, people tend to trust and confide in me quickly."

"Yep, that I can certainly confirm."

"Before I knew it, she was leaning against my shoulder, crying. She told me the whole long, sad story. She'd been holding in the hurt for so long that, clinically, she was on the verge of a complete breakdown. I couldn't go off and leave her alone. No way. That night, she slept in my bed. But I didn't touch her—not in any romantic, sexual sense. She was much, much too vulnerable. Sometimes, being a moraled man in an immoral world is a gigantic pain in the ass."

"I couldn't agree more," I said, smiling. "You were on your best behavior. But somehow the relationship changed."

"Not then. We were together for the next three nights. Gradually, I talked her into a more peaceful frame of mind.

"We've stayed in contact since, and she's finally worked up the nerve to leave her asshole husband. She agreed to meet me here—not as a student, but for a few days of rest and relaxation. That was coincidental, too. I'd actually invited someone else, a woman I've never seen face to face. It was someone I really wanted us both to meet. But she backed out at the last minute."

There was something odd about his tone, but I didn't inquire.

Now, as his head turned toward the pool, his expression became a slow description of frustration and sadness. "Nimba arrived three days ago, the afternoon of my last Beginner's Mind class. You wondered why I haven't been here for the last few sunsets? I've spent all three nights in that gorgeous woman's duplex, and I couldn't perform. I tried and tried, and I just couldn't. The little bastard's turned traitor on me. Not that I'm so little," he added quickly. "Let's face it. Everybody at the marina knows. No way to hide the damn thing. I'm hung like a bull dolphin."

I said, "Very famous with the island women, no question about that. How'd she react?"

"Not good. She blames herself, of course. That abusive husband of hers has absolutely destroyed her self-confidence. Then I come along and add to her pain." He looked at me. "You understand now why I want to get that tattoo on my ass?"

"I think you're making too much of it. You say the problem's not physiological, so you need to back up a couple of steps. Take your own emotional survey. Figure out what's going on. Are you feeling any unusual amount of stress? Depression, maybe?" I hesitated before adding, "Or guilt? From what I've read about the brain's chemistry, guilt can be a very powerful inhibitor. Affects all kinds of behavior and body functions. Because of certain chemicals released, and there's another one—serotonin, I think—it creates a shortage of serotonin so there's a direct physiological reaction."

He wasn't looking at me as I added, "Or maybe it has something to do with all the dope you've been smoking and alcohol. Seems to me you stepped it up a few notches in the last six months or so."

Tomlinson was nodding, thinking about that. "Could be, could be. The source of all *karma* bondage is delusion, and there's a very fine line between being seriously fucked up and fucked up seriously. Now that you mention it, I *have* been having an unusual amount of werewolf mornings." When I didn't respond, he explained, "A werewolf morning, that's when you wake up, look around the room hoping not to see blood because you can't remember what happened the night before."

I said, "I'm no physician, but I suspect that's not a good sign. Once again, maybe you need to take that survey. Depression or guilt. Something's going on up there in that great big brain of yours, old friend."

He sighed. "Doc, some of the things I've done in my life, I'd give my left nut to change. Know how, on a computer, you can drag down, highlight, then hit delete? I'd trash a couple years of my life, no problem. Maybe even a whole decade, I was such a crazed asshole. Some mistakes, though, there's no going back. You just keep paying and paying. The masters teach that there are five deadly sins, and one of them is destroying your own Buddha nature. Maybe way back, that's what I did. And wouldn't you just know that my dick would be the first to show symptoms."

I told him, "Most people, the honest ones, would like to go back and change a few things. Some of the dumb things we do, some of the idiotic things we say. I'm talking about myself, by the way. You've got your demons, who doesn't? Don't be so hard on yourself."

He turned to face me. "You mentioned guilt, man. It's like you just tuned right into my brain frequency. Your intuition, it just keeps getting better and better, which, if you don't mind my saying, is a good thing for someone who started out with no more emotional sensitivity than a meat thermometer. No offense."

I was smiling again. "None taken."

"But this guilt thing . . . what might be bothering me, is some of my old screwups have come back to mess with my brain. Like in my dreams. Bad stuff I did, I mean *really* bad stuff. Just in the last few months the memories have come back, so yeah, maybe that's what's taking the lead out of my pencil. Doc . . ." I watched his fingers search and find another strand of hair to tug, the tremor even worse. "Doc . . . there's something I've been wondering about, but never had the balls to ask."

"Ask away."

"I've always kinda wondered if . . . well, do you know about some of the shit I got involved with? A long time ago, I'm talking about. It worries me that you've always known, and I've never taken the time or had the courage to try and explain."

I don't often lie, particularly to friends, but sometimes it's necessary. "Nope. I don't know what you're talking about, and I don't want to know. Whatever you did, whatever you think you did, all the good you've done for people—all the good I've seen you do—that should more than make up for it."

Beyond the tennis courts and the palms, I made peripheral note of two yellow Scarab-type high-performance boats idling in the direction of Guava Key's small back dock. I recognized the boats as being from the Mercury engine test center at Placida, fourteen miles north. All day long, those yellow boats could be seen flying up and down the Intracoastal Waterway, logging hours on experimental engines. Why were they out this late in the day? And why were they now idling into Guava Key?

Another little alarm bell went off in my head.

I stood and said, "It's time for my run."

"That's it? No more advice? No encouragement?"

I smiled. "I encourage you to take the lady home, sit her down and tell her exactly what you've already told me about your so-called problem. If she's as bright as you've described, she'll understand and she won't blame herself and she won't blame you, either. I then encourage the two of you to drink a bottle or two of wine and have fun—whether your equipment works or not."

I stepped through the French doors into the master bedroom, where I changed to shorts and Nikes. I stretched for a couple of minutes, then headed out along the island's conch-pink sidewalk. From above me and behind, I heard Tomlinson call, "Hey, I almost forgot—did you get your message from the front desk?"

I turned to see him still balanced cross-legged on the roof, a curious scarecrow shape, sitting as if he were, indeed, levitating. I answered, "I didn't get any messages. But then, I don't expect any messages so I never stop to check."

"Exactly what I figured. I was at the office this morning and the lady gave it to me to give to you. Someone called from the mainland—wanted to come over on the boat taxi to see you. The island's got to give permission, you know. Someone named Ebanks."

I said, "Ebanks? I don't know anyone by that name."

"They left a number to call."

I told him, "Maybe when I get back," and jogged away.

2

GUAVA KEY IS contoured by high hills and valleys, which are really the remains of pyramidlike temples built of shell by contemporaries of the Aztecs, a people known as the Calusa. After a couple hundred years of neglect and detritus rot, the shell base was now covered by loam and trees and designer landscaping.

I jogged down the highest hill through a grove of citrus trees, limbs heavy with tangerines and little yellow Spanish limes, then north along the beach. Ran past rows of modern vacation homes that were careful imitations of tin-roofed Cracker houses, and so thereby emphasized their newness. Where the pink sidewalk looped and ended, I cut toward the bay side of the island, picking up the pace as my lungs seemed to expand and become more efficient.

Guava Key once had a grass airstrip on the narrow, southern point of the island, but it had been recently closed and platted for building. On an island where property values are astronomical, a half-mile strip of open land was an impossible indulgence. I turned south on the strip, running hard on the straightaway. On either side was mangrove fringe. Through hedges of black limbs, I could see patterns of shadow and light and the brassy gold of water at sunset.

At the very tip of the island, ahead of me but not yet in sight, was a canal for small boats and a boardwalk that wound through the trees to a dock. It is the only deserted part of the island. No houses, no golf cart trails, too many mosquitoes for foot traffic. Yet, I knew that if I followed the boardwalk to the dock, I would find the girl joggers I'd seen earlier, the two of them standing there, cooling down from their run, watching the sunset.

I also knew from our few previous encounters that the blonde's greeting would be slightly cheerier, more inviting than Ponytail's grim nod.

I am reluctant to impose on anyone's solitude, so I'd decided to do what I'd done for the last two evenings: turn around at the boardwalk, thereby avoiding the women.

But, as I ran, something happened that caused me to change my mind. Nothing dramatic. It was a very small thing, indeed. What happened was, ahead of me and to my right, a flock of parrots flushed out of the mangroves, screaming and cawing their way into clumsy flight. Parrots aren't indigenous to Florida. Birds escape, meet, breed, reproduce, then tumble around in groups like feral outlanders. From my years in Central and South America, however, I am very familiar with the warning alarm that parrots make, and that was the sound I heard as the birds flushed.

Someone or something was in those mangroves.

Not that I suspected anything sinister. I have an orderly mind that naturally seeks explanation for the unexplained. This was an oddity, a small incident that did not mesh with the expected pattern of cause and effect. A mangrove fringe is an inhospitable area. Those swampy borders stink of muck and sulfur. They're a breeding ground for mosquitoes. People avoid mangroves for good reason.

So what had spooked the birds?

AS I APPROACHED the boardwalk, still running, I heard a voice call, "'Scuse me, mister big man. Hello? Could you maybe give me some information?" A female voice with the breezy, singsong rhythm of the Bahamas. When she said "maybe," I heard "maw-be." When she said "big man," I heard "beeg mon."

I glanced to see a tall, coffee-brown woman pulling a canoe up onto the bank of the little canal. Late twenties, early thirties, wading-bird legs, heavy breasts without bra that swooped and strained, defining themselves. She wore a tie-dyed T-shirt, scarlet and blue, over canvas shorts that emphasized her legs and muscular rump. I noted that her hair was braided cornrow-style with red beads at the ends and her gaunt, chocolate colored skin stretched tight over athletic cheeks, bones and jaw. A striking figure.

I held up an index finger—"Back in a minute!"—and mounted the boardwalk, ducking beneath mangrove limbs, feeling my own weight in the vibration of wood.

The boardwalk tunneled through the mangrove fringe for more than fifty meters, then made a sharp right toward the bay. When I made that turn, I saw what had frightened the parrots. I also knew immediately that the two runners, blonde and ponytail, were headed for a very nasty fall. Not that they realized it. Nope, not yet, and not surprising. Targets who are about to become victims seldom see it coming.

Ahead of me, the boardwalk became a low dock on pilings that poked a couple hundred feet out into the bay. The girls were at the end of the dock, leaning against the railing, faces toward the parachute-sized sphere that was the setting sun. The sky was a lucent indigo streaked with citrus and peach. The bay was glazed with molten gold.

Between the shore and the girls were two men. The men were walking toward the end of the dock, backs to me. Each wore blue coveralls, the legs of the coveralls showing fresh mud stains up to the calves.

They'd just waded through the mangroves, flushing birds.

Another telltale indicator: Both men also wore ski masks.

Except for 7-Eleven clerks and the occasional bank teller, we don't see a lot of ski masks in Florida.

My first reaction was surprise: damn! Then, as my brain translated the visual data, my reaction changed to: oh-h-h-h-h *damn,* because some kind of involvement was now impossible to avoid.

The men had some bulk to them and moved with a disconcerting confidence. One carried some kind of semiautomatic pistol in his left hand, the bottle-sized sound arrestor pointed downward, as if to hide it. The other man carried what looked to be a walkie-talkie or cell phone. On the south side of the dock, the yellow Scarab hull was idling in for a landing, its engines making a slow, thunderous rumble. It looked to be pretty close to thirty feet long and had the Wellcraft logo on the side. The other boat sat off several hundred yards, as if waiting to see what happened.

In panic situations where events unfold rapidly, the brain sometimes processes those events in what seems to be slow motion. That was the way my brain now reacted. It was as if I were viewing a film run at half-speed. My eyes suddenly enjoyed absolute clarity in which I seemed to see everything at once, interpreting and understanding what was happening and why.

Clarity is not always an aspect to be envied.

What I saw were professionals who'd done their homework. It is what the really good ones must do to succeed and survive. They learn their target's habits, their target's routes.

There's a very good reason for that.

All routes have a chokepoint—a section of road or walkway the target *must* take to reach his or her final destination. The most suitable chokepoints also possess a contained area that can be easily sealed and controlled by the assassin or his accomplices. That precise place where the hit will be made is known to people in the business as the X-spot.

What I had stumbled into was an attempt to murder or to kidnap one or both of the women runners. The shooter would shoot, confirm his kill, then escape in the yellow boat. Or the men would wrestle one or both of the girls into the boat, transport them at speed to another vessel or waiting car, kidnapping complete.

The second yellow boat could be there to serve as a decoy in the event someone gave chase, or as a backup. The boats were stolen, of course. Choosing Mercury test boats suggested a level of professional sophistication that was unsettling. They were fast boats but a part of the common seascape, boats that always followed the same Intracoastal route, so very easy to anticipate, track and take down.

Steal a couple high-performance boats, then abandon them when done. That was probably the plan. The actual escape vehicle would be nearby, a boat or a car on some island or maybe a chopper.

Unfortunately, in those few moments of clarity, I didn't process the wisest course of action. Charge into a group of armed men who were being assisted by other men, who were, presumably, also armed?

Suicidal.

I should have turned, tucked my tail and lumbered off to the nearest phone.

My instincts are usually pretty good. Not this time, though. This time, my poor judgment nearly got me killed.

THE ENGINES OF the boat now lying aside the dock were rumbling at idle, the vibration so loud that it radiated through water and wood. The noise masked the sound of my heavy feet.

There was another man in the Scarab, standing at the helm, his face covered by a bandana. Three men in all, two on the dock, one aboard, and their attention was laser-focused on the women who were their targets.

That was encouraging. It seemed to give me the extra few steps I believed I needed.

The women had finally noticed the approaching men. I could see the expression on Blonde's face change from surprise to puzzlement and then to fear when she correctly interpreted the only reason why men would wear ski masks in the late winter heat. I saw Ponytail's expression change from indifference to an emotion that may have been anger. Her reaction certainly wasn't passive.

As always, Ponytail was wearing a gray belly pouch strapped around her waist. I watched her reach into the pouch with her right hand as she threw her left hand up, palm out as if to hold the men away. Heard her yell, "Freeze! No closer!" as she drew a chrome, short-barreled revolver from the pouch, probably a .38, crouching as she lifted the weapon into the classic combat position.

Surprise, surprise. The lady jogger was armed.

I was sprinting now, seeing everything in articulate, slow detail as it happened. I watched the man with the big semiautomatic raise his pistol in the same instant. Watched his left hand bounce with the recoil of firing. Heard two distinct th-h-wap-waps as Ponytail's revolver flew high into the air then banged its weight upon the deck. I expected her to fall, but she didn't. I expected to see blood, but there was none. The woman wasn't hit. She was stunned, probably, and spasmed by shock.

There was no way the shooter could miss at that distance, so he'd fired intentional warning shots. The scene provided me with inductive information. The attackers weren't assassins. They were kidnappers. Or maybe the shooter had simply suffered a moment of indecision. It's not like the films and cheap television shows. Squeezing a trigger exacts a price. For most people, it's not easy to initiate the destruction of a breathing complexity never better defined than by the look of terror in a stranger's eyes.

Unfortunately, I know that truth better than most.

The shooter, though, was reconsidering.

I watched him swing the sausage barrel toward Ponytail's face. Heard Blonde screaming, "Don't hurt her! Don't hurt her!" as he leaned slightly as if to fire again, but then hesitated, perhaps hearing me for the first time. I was only a few strides behind him and pushing a lot of air ahead of me as I sprinted.

Both men began to turn slightly. I got a glimpse of dark eyes through holes in the ski masks. Both sets of eyes grew wide just before I impacted, running low and hard, generating a lot of torque. I hit the shooter in the lower back with my right shoulder. I heard a sickening sound, like a green limb snapping, and he screamed as I drove through him. Caught the second man with my legs as I tumbled past in a cross-body block. Heard him give a whoop of pain as he went down.

My glasses went flying when I hit the dock hard with my shoulder. I rolled, and came up on my feet, already in mid-stride, face-to-face with the two now-blurry women. They were still frozen, not understanding any of it, standing there, letting it happen.

I heard two lightning-bolt explosions—gunshots from a different weapon. No sound arrestor, and a volume of air sizzled past my left ear. I ducked reflexively as I caught Blonde in my left arm, Ponytail in my right, lifting them off the dock, still running. I'd hoped to tumble with them over the railing at the end of the dock, but great balance is not one of my gifts. Instead, I caught my shoe on something, stumbled badly, still holding the women, and crashed back-first through the dock's side railing, all of us smacking into the water, splinters of wood showering down from above.

As I surfaced, I heard one of the men yell in Spanish, "Shoot him but don't kill the girl!" which is why I pulled both women to me, forcing them underwater, all of us sinking to the bottom.

Blonde struggled. Ponytail was muscle-tight but still. She seemed to understand.

The water was murky with diatom bloom. I had to guess the direction and the distance to the dock. My feet found the muck bottom and I pushed away hard.

I misjudged the distance badly and smacked face-first into a barnacled piling. We all surfaced at once.

I was aware of men yelling in Spanish. I heard another lightning-bolt explosion as I grabbed each of the women by the back of the neck and pushed them beneath the dock, out of sight. I said into Ponytail's ear, "Stay under the dock, get back to shore. Run!"

The woman looked at me, a streak of blood on her cheek. She nodded, didn't hesitate, pulled the blonde after her, already moving from piling to piling.

I had to create a diversion, had to keep the three men occupied, to give the women time to find their way to the mangroves and escape.

And then what?

Look into the barrel of some indifferent weapon and experience the final white flash?

Nope, no way, not me. We never accept that eventuality. Not really. It goes against all our superb coding. I would do the impossible. I'd keep dodging bullets. I'd think of something. I always had, hadn't I? Unyielding expectation is our only buffer from the existential.

The big Scarab was to my right, bow pointed out, engines still rumbling. As I pushed toward it, someone began to shoot randomly down through the dock's heavy planking. I submerged, came up yards away, nose to face with a man's head and upper torso. He was leaning down from above, ski mask in place, semiautomatic in hand. My unexpected surfacing surprised him as much as he surprised me. I knocked the pistol away, locked his neck against my chest, turned abruptly and submerged again.

I was surprised that his spine did not snap. Instead, he fought back in a frenzy. He scrabbled and clawed at my face until I couldn't hold him anymore. I kicked him away, paused on the bottom, still underwater. Then I swam with long, slow strokes in the direction of the boat. I found the bottom of the Scarab with my right hand, touching the bladelike chine of the starboard side. I paused, then crossed underneath the hull of the boat and came up, eyes wide, on the other side.

The man who'd been at the wheel was now holding a submachine gun that looked to be an Uzi.

He had his back to me, still expecting me to surface near the dock. I could hear him shouting to the man I'd dragged into the water. His voice had interrogative inflections. Where the hell was I?

The Scarab had a partial dive platform mounted portside, off the stern. Not a lot of room back there with the twin outdrives. I got my right foot on the port corner of the platform, found a cleat with my left hand and vaulted up into the boat. I heard the man scream out a warning, lifting his weapon to fire as I lunged across the deck to the controls and jammed the single gearshift and both throttles full forward.

Scarabs are built for speed, and this one must have been loaded with some heavy-duty experimental racing engines. Two massive Mercury inboards were back there beneath the cowling. When I buried the throttles, there was a momentary hesitation, as if the engines didn't know what to do with the sudden infusion of fuel. It was in that mini-instant that a weapon fired and, simultaneously, I felt as if I'd been slapped beneath my left arm with a baseball bat.

In the aftershock of any serious injury, the brain scans immediately for answers: How bad is it? Has the vehicle been crippled for life? Will the vehicle survive so that the brain can survive?

I had no time for even a moment's reflection, however. The roar of the Scarab's engines was more like an explosion, and the boat seemed to rocket skyward. The bow lunged so abruptly into the air that it was as if I was on a rearing horse, or a plane about to take flight. I fell and grabbed the base of the helm seat with my one good arm, holding tight against the sudden rush of g-force, some part of me aware that the boat's stern line must still be tied to the dock. That's why the boat was tilting nose-high.

Not for long, though.

There was a terrible rending sound as part of the dock ripped away. Or a cleat. Or maybe the thick line they'd used to tie the boat. Then we were free, gaining speed like a dragster, the hull flattening itself over the water, bow-slapping like a dolphin.

I looked toward the back of the boat where the man with the Uzi had been thrown. He was crawling around on his knees, trying to fight his way back to his feet. He'd lost his bandana. I looked into dark, Indio eyes set in a Castilian face, a man in his mid-to-late thirties. He had a mustache and a pointed goatee. The blue coveralls he wore added a military inflection.

The Uzi was now sliding around on the deck, closer to him than to me. I watched his eyes focus on the weapon, then swivel toward me, gauging who would get to the submachine gun first.

I wanted no part of that kind of race. As he crabbed across the deck toward the Uzi, I got up shakily, my left arm feeling weirdly electrical, nearly numb, and pulled myself into the helm seat.

The Scarab's control console looked like something out of a science-fiction film, or the command station of a spacecraft. It seemed to have everything but what I was looking for—a built-in VHF radio. There were rows of high-performance gauges with matching bezels, and lines of toggle switches aside a steering wheel fitted with built-in trim-control buttons. Both throttles and the gearshift were low and to the right, everything within easy reach, the entire station done in ivory white.

When it comes right down to it, though, nearly all power vessels operate basically the same. And I have spent much of my life driving boats.

I glanced behind me to see that the man with the goatee was looking at me as he reached for the Uzi.

I scrunched down in the pilot's chair, backed the throttles slightly, then turned the wheel full to the left as I accelerated. The boat turned so fast and hard when the port chine bit that it nearly threw me out of the seat.

I glanced over my shoulder again to see that he'd been catapulted into the starboard coaming. The trouble was, the gun had been catapulted right along with him.

I backed the starboard throttle, banking us into a wide right turn, then shoved both throttles full ahead and watched the speedometer climb to a hundred and ten miles per hour. I was ducked down behind the scimitar windshield, but Goatee was not. He was getting the full force of the wind shear, his cheeks and lips fluttering. Even so, he was still struggling to get his balance; he wanted to get his hands on the weapon again.

We were headed north, now, into Charlotte Harbor. Continue on that course and at that speed, and we'd be off Sarasota in less than half an hour. Not that I had any intention of going to Sarasota, nor would I be able to. Off to the west, I could see the second yellow Scarab moving on a fast line to intercept us. Maybe one of the kidnappers back on shore had contacted them. Or maybe the erratic course of our boat had alerted them that their plans had gone terribly wrong.

Either way, they knew. I had the blurry image of two men standing at the helm of that smaller boat, coming hard at us on a collision course, their hands at an odd angle, holding something.

Weapons, of course. They'd be armed. Once they realized the wrong guy was at the helm, would they start firing? Maybe. No . . . probably. What was to stop them?

I made a sputtering noise of frustration, feeling a dizzy wave of unreality sweep over me. Had I really been dropped into the middle of this mess, or was it some kind of nightmare?

I looked at my left arm, blood dropping. Nope, it was all too real. And if I didn't find a way to put some distance between myself and them very, very soon, it was going to get much worse.

One thing I knew was that the men pursuing me wanted to get away as badly as I did. If not, they weren't very smart. Like fleeing an assassination, escape from a kidnapping must be effected quickly and without interruption to be successful. Screw up for a minute, and the entire oper-ation is compromised. Screw up for several minutes, and the operation not only fails, there are jail cells waiting. I was cutting deeply into their hopes of escape, and they had to realize that.

They didn't get the girls. Now they had nothing to lose and every-thing to gain by eliminating me quickly.

Time was the only weapon I had.

My left arm was getting some feeling back. There was a black smear of meat and blood in the fleshy area beneath my tricep. It was bleeding freely, but not spurting, and my left hand had enough strength in it to control the steering wheel. All very reassuring.

I glanced over my shoulder again. Saw that Goatee was up on his hands and feet, scrambling across the deck like a bear toward the Uzi. I cut the wheel hard to the right, and back to the left, then I accelerated to full throttle as I spun the wheel to port, once again, sling-shooting us back and forth through the water. The g-forces were terrible, like being in a centrifuge.

At the peak of the last turn, I heard a shriek and looked back to see that Goatee had managed to stay aboard, but just barely. His head was over the side, but his fingers were locked into the starboard coaming. I watched him gain his balance before I had a chance to make another turn. Anticipating the turn, he collapsed flat on his belly, and began to crawl toward me.

I wanted to shake him, needed to shake him. I wanted to make the guys on the other boat stop and have to waste time fishing their accom-plice out of the water. I needed to give them a good reason to abandon their pursuit of me.

I made three more sharp, accelerated turns in quick succession but couldn't lift him off the deck. It was like he had suction cups on his fin-gers. He was up on his feet now, a very wide stance, seemed determined to get his hands on me.

The other Scarab was still bearing down on us. I had to make a decision whether to fight or run. Would they risk firing randomly into our boat?

The Plexiglas windshield shattered before me, then shards of fiberglass began to explode in a firecracker series, from the transom to the cockpit. I ducked, then ducked again.

They were shooting already. Full automatic.

Suddenly, the decision was very easy. I'd have to fight. The question was: *How?* Maybe stop the boat, wrestle goatee for the Uzi, then shoot it out with the other Scarab?

I didn't like the odds. I wasn't at full strength, plus the guy with the submachine gun didn't seem very fussy about who he hit. If Goatee put up any kind of struggle, we'd both be exposed and easy targets.

I'd have to try something else. I remembered an old instructor of mine, years ago on an island far away, forcing us to repeat by rote what turned out to be a pretty fair dictum for the way to live a successful life: When surrounded by overwhelming opposition and defeat is inevitable, there remains only one practical option—*attack.*

Because I had no other options, that's exactly what I did.

With the approaching Scarab less than a hundred meters away, I brought our boat to a stop so sudden that goatee came tripping toward me. I timed it right and, with my good elbow, caught him once just under the chin. It knocked his feet from under him and he landed hard on the deck. He was groggy but still conscious.

Ahead of me, the Scarab immediately slowed, apparently interpreting my decision to stop as a gesture of surrender.

I waited, watching them idle toward me: at least two men aboard, both showing automatic weapons. The man at the steering wheel had a huge pumpkin-sized head with hair dyed punkish blue—the Latin rapster look.

I ducked low, not wanting to tempt them into shooting again, got down on my knees briefly, dripping blood all across the deck, reached and retrieved the Uzi. It had the standard thirty-round magazine and a collapsible stock. I looked to see that the bolt was closed, ready to fire, the selector switch on full auto. When Goatee tried to grab me, I swung the barrel toward his chest and said in Spanish, "Jump."

He shook his head, pretending not to understand.

I shifted the selector switch from auto to select as if in preparation to fire. I said, "So I'll try it in English. *Jump.*" Then I motioned toward the back of the boat, which was out of sight of the approaching Scarab.

Goatee didn't hesitate. Keeping his eyes on me, he rolled off the transom, into the water.

I ducked back to the helm, where I checked the boat's trim tab controls. They were on the steering wheel. Lower the tabs, and the stern of the boat would ride higher, forcing the front of the boat down. It's a handy option, a good way to compensate for an unbalanced load.

I checked the buttons to make certain the tabs were raised completely. Then I found the outdrive toggles, and raised the propeller arms about halfway. I wanted the front of my boat to, once again, rear high at full throttle, and that combination of raised trim tabs and outdrives would, hopefully, cause it to do just that. Then I held the Uzi in the air, waving it until I was sure the two men saw me. When I was certain I had their attention, I threw the little sub gun high over the bow into the water.

A final gesture of complete submission.

Which is just what I wanted them to think.

I watched the men lower their weapons. Saw Blue Hair speak into what was a walkie-talkie or cell phone. Waited until he finished talking and began the slow turn to come alongside my Scarab, where and when there was a good chance they'd shoot me, no questions asked.

I cupped my hand over the twin throttles, thumb tapping at the gearshift, breathing easily, hunched down and standing motionless until their boat was directly in front of me. I watched them continue to turn and waited . . . waited until the smaller Scarab was exactly broadside to me only about forty meters away. I waited another beat or two until the nose of my boat was pointed a few feet aft of their cockpit.

That's when I attacked. I jammed both throttles forward, steering directly at them on a collision course they couldn't avoid. Engines screamed and my boat lunged crazily forward, the sudden acceleration driving me back, pinning my head against the helm seat so that all I could see was the control panel and the orange sunset sky.

I saw both tachometers redline with cavitation and watched the speedometer jump from zero to fifty. I was still gaining speed when I felt the jarring impact of fiberglass on fiberglass. Something else they'd taught us at the combat driving course in the hills of West Virginia: When two objects collide, the object that maintains its velocity receives far less shock than the object not in motion. So I held the throttles forward as my boat careened wildly skyward, airborne, riding up and over the smaller boat, using it like a ski ramp.

I felt a second jarring impact as my boat's outdrives banged free. Then I seemed to hang suspended in air for an incredibly long time before smashing down back into the water, shipping a wave over the bow, soaking the entire boat and myself.

But my engines were still running. Amazing.

Behind me, the smaller Scarab was still moving, too. But not fast. Its windshield was gone and a chunk of some kind of wreckage lay on its stern cowling. At first, it didn't look as if anyone was still aboard. But then I saw movement. Saw Blue Hair reappear, then the second man. Watched Blue Hair move to the helm again and stand at the controls.

The boat began to turn toward me, moving faster.

I thought about making another pass at them, ram them one more time. I gave it a moment's consideration before deciding I'd pushed my luck as much as I possibly could. It was time for me to get back to the island and put all the space I could between us.

Guava Key was now more than three miles to the southeast. In the sunset's angular light, the island's white houses appeared to be varnished with lucent gold; trees on the high Indian mounds looked black. Soon I could see the small dock where the girls had been ambushed. It poked out into the bay from what was called the back side of the island. There was still someone standing there. As I got nearer, I could see that it was actually two men, one kidnapper holding up the other. Probably the kidnapper I'd shoulder-blocked hard from behind, the one who'd done the shooting. Apparently I'd caused some damage.

Injured or not, both were still mobile and probably armed. I thought about using the Scarab as a weapon again. Point the bow at the dock, roll overboard as I punched the throttles and give them a reason to jump. Then I glanced at my bleeding arm and thought, *No way.*

When presented with the option to run or fight, running is almost always the wisest choice.

I checked behind me to see that the other Scarab was up and making way again after stopping to pick up Goatee. Moving fast, too, steering a direct course toward me and the dock.

I turned sharply away from the dock, hoping to hell they wouldn't follow; would instead rush to pick up their two remaining team members and escape.

Over my shoulder, I watched the yellow boat bank momentarily in pursuit of me, then swerve back on course toward the dock and its comrades.

It seemed as if I hadn't taken a full breath in a long time. Now I did, steering north toward the other side of the island and safety.

ON THE EAST side of Guava Key is a service dock built heavy enough to handle the construction needs of an island where everything must be delivered by boat. I idled down well short of the dock, trimming my outdrives as I steered into shallow water, then killed the engines before vaulting off into waist-deep water.

My arm was still bleeding, T-shirt and running shorts were soaked black and I didn't want to draw a lot of attention by parading up the dock in full view.

I stepped into the gloom of the mangroves, moving fast over the roots. Exited out onto the island's pale pink sidewalk, now running, wanting to get to the two women I'd rescued before the law enforcement people got to them.

I figured they owed me a very simple favor—tell no one what I'd done. In any instance in which shots are fired and a person is wounded, there is a detailed series of investigations mandated by law. I didn't relish the idea of spending the next three weeks answering questions from cops.

But there were other considerations, too, more important ones. I keep my life and my past private for a reason. Tomlinson was exactly right when he said that there are mistakes for which we never stop paying. We all make them. I've made my share, which is why I can't afford to put myself in a position where someone might go snooping around into my past. If my arm needed surgical attention, I had several physician friends who'd be willing to take care of it quietly.

Holding my left arm tight against my side, I ran at long-distance pace down the sidewalk where it exited through mango trees and oaks adjacent to the old airstrip. I almost stumbled and fell, I was so surprised, when the tall, black woman I'd seen earlier stepped out unexpectedly from the trees to confront me. I moved to brush past her, but stopped when she held up her hands—whoa!—and said in her Bahamian lilt, "I saw 'em, I saw 'em shoot you, man!"

Surprised that she was there, I said the first thing that came to mind. "That wasn't me. You didn't see anything."

"What, you crazy, man? You feelin' okay? The gun goes bang and I see the blood fly, then you take off in the go-fast boat! I watched the whole business."

Said, "Nope, you're wrong, and I'm not talking about it," while thinking grim thoughts about strange timing, bad luck.

"You mister cool-and-calm, that's what I'm talkin' about. Man shoot you, it like it no big deal."

"No one shot me. Just forget it, okay? Forget you ever saw me. Please."

I moved to leave, but she touched her hand to my shoulder. "You hurt, man. You bleedin' bad. Your arm, and your face all cut up, too." In a much softer voice, she added, "Why you bleedin', if you didn't get yourself shot? Why you want me to lie about that?" Then she added, very softly, "My brother," looking into my eyes.

My ears heard, *"Yooo hurt, mon. You bleedden bod."*

I didn't want to listen to any more. I told her, "I cut my arm on the dock. There's nothing to lie about," and jogged away from her up the hill.

3

TOMLINSON'S BUNGALOW WAS down the pink path past the old fishing lodge, a white clapboard duplex built at the turn of the century and named after a nearby island, Gasparilla.

It was gray dusk now, just past the pearly interlude after sunset. I alternately walked and jogged on the shell road behind the houses, not wanting to be seen. Came up the back way beside his bungalow, and stepped onto the porch.

As usual, the French doors and windows were wide open, music playing on the stereo. Jim Morrison and the Doors, the thunder-and-rain passage from "Riders on the Storm."

The volume was uncharacteristically low, low enough that I could hear Tomlinson making strange noises, speaking strange phrases from inside.

Heard him say what sounded like, "Doin' the hokie-pokie-okee-dokie-Doctor-Billyboombah." Heard him say, "You white desert wench, you're the princess of my harem! Make me bark like the hound I am!"

I stepped through the French doors onto the wood floor of the living room; I could look past bookshelves into the next room where Nimba Dimbokro knelt at Tomlinson's feet, both of them naked, glistening beneath the ceiling fan, the woman's black hair screening the focus of her oral attentions.

I entertained more depressed thoughts about the continuation of my bad timing. I felt almost lucky to have lost my glasses.

I averted my eyes and stepped back as I heard, "Ali Baba and the forty thieves, yes-s-s-s! . . ." Then, in an accelerating cadence: "I think I can—I think I can—I think I can—I think I can—I think I *can*," as if reciting the children's story about some little red train.

After a silence, I heard the woman whisper, "Shuuush. Someone's in the living room, Tommy. I heard the door make that sound it makes. The spooky sound?" Very Americanized syntax with a Middle Eastern accent.

Tomlinson was already talking: "Dear Jesus, you're stopping now, doctor? The patient was just beginning to respond. A little more oxygen, that's all he needs, a little more oxygen and, damn it, he needs it *now.*"

"Tomlinson, *please.* Someone came in the house. You know why I'm worried. If he knew . . . honest, I heard footsteps."

"Footsteps?" He chuckled his relief. "Oh hell, that's just Doc. I heard the same noise. Unmistakable. When he walks, he sounds just like a great big Labrador retriever. Anything you can do in front of me, you can do in front of him. We're *compadres,* for Christ's sake!" Then he called out, "Hey, Doc, you there? Come on in. Honest, it's okay. Nimba, you mind Doc sitting for a spell? Let him give me some moral support. Knowing I got a buddy right here pullin' for me just might be the little extra edge I'm looking for."

I heard her ask, "Your large friend with the wire glasses?"

There was the sound of bedsprings and a woman's soft laughter before she crossed the door space, showing her body, flushed and swollen, hair swinging across buttocks, taking her time, certain that I was watching, but not turning to look at me. Her voice took on an added silkiness. "I've never done such a thing, but if you would like your friend to watch, I will say nothing. Or join us if you wish. Does he like to play the game you showed me, the silk scarf game? Three could play very easily if you'd like me to teach him."

The silk scarf game—apparently, another one of Tomlinson's strange pastimes, the details of which I did not care to hear.

But the woman seemed very willing. Years of repression had, apparently, expanded her boundaries of sexual interest.

I heard Tomlinson call to her, "He's the one says it's not your fault that Zamboni has the wilting disorder. Says it happens to every woman. Says you shouldn't feel the least bit responsible. Doc says that—" Tomlinson poked his head around the corner, tangled blond hair and black goatee showing. "Doc says that—" He stopped and gave a soft whistle, looking at me, and said in a strained voice, "Holy shitzkee! What the hell happened to you?"

I was still holding my arm, trying to stem the bleeding. "You've gotta get rid of the girl. Sorry."

He stepped out, holding a towel around him. "Doc . . . sit your ass down right now. You're white as a sheet. You cut a vein or what?"

I said, "Make the girl leave and I'll tell you. We have a lot to do, and I don't have a lot of time."

"I can see that," he said, turning to find his clothes.

BEFORE REPRESENTATIVES FROM the FBI, Florida Marine Patrol, and the local Sheriff's Department crowded into my little rental bungalow, I sat in a wicker chair looking out onto a bay glazed with tendrils of blue light—reflections of a winter moon through palms.

We'd moved to my place so I could get fresh clothes and spare glasses, and because I didn't want anyone to get the impression I had a reason to hide or be evasive.

Tomlinson was still working on my arm, cleaning the wound. At his side was a basin of hot water and a white washcloth that was already rusty with blood. He'd washed the wound with water and Betadine, then had to go door-to-door to find a roll of gauze, antibacterial creme and surgical tape for a dressing.

He'd returned with the first-aid supplies and some information, too. "The two women, they've already talked to the cops by phone, so it's probably not a good idea for you to ask them to change their story. Vince up at the Inn told me. They're sending a boat over to pick them up. Bring the cops out to the island, I mean."

"You didn't mention to Vince that—"

"Hey man, you don't need to tell me; I've been breaking laws all my life. I know how to keep my mouth shut. Something else he told me, the woman you saved? The blonde. She was probably the main target. Turns out she's some rich guy's daughter. Lindsey Harrington, that's her name. The other woman, the dark-haired one, she's either a friend of the family or works for the family, Vince wasn't sure. Maybe a bodyguard. He's wondered about that before. But lots and lots of new money."

It was no surprise that at least one of the women came from money. Everyone on the island had money. The thing that struck me about the attempted kidnapping, though, was that it had an administrative feel to it, the way it was set up, the two-boat backup plan, they way they'd obviously invested some time and tracked her movements before trying to snatch her. Money, of course that would be a part of it. Always is. But it seemed probable that there was more to it than that.

To Tomlinson, I said, "I didn't hear them say much, but one of them had a Colombian accent. That I'm sure of. If all you're after is ransom money, why make it more complicated by picking a target outside your native country?"

"Maybe they live in the States now. Were looking to score big and decided on Guava Key. This place is very famous, man—for the same reason you didn't want to come in the first place. The guys from AC/DC, Mick Jagger, that former vice president—lots of very heavy hitters come here."

"I know, I know, but it still doesn't seem like a natural fit. People tend to choose crimes the same way they choose a place to live. The surroundings need to be comfortable, well known, usually in an area where it's easy to interact without standing out. The desperate ones rob the restaurants where they used to work, kidnap the children of people they know. See what I mean? What happened this afternoon was more like international politics."

He said, "See? Now that makes sense. Politics, that's just what Vince told me. He knows the girl's father. They play tennis together, fish occasionally when he comes to the island, which isn't often. He's got some kind of government appointment, like an ambassador's deputy or something. One of those things that takes a big political donation to buy. Only Vince thought it was Peru, not Colombia."

"Both countries have their problems," I said, "so the political component, that's a possibility."

"But that's not where the girl lives. He said she's always been sort of on her own, allowed to run wild, 'cause her mother was killed in an accident way, way back, and she's spent most of her life at boarding schools. Last couple of years, though, Vince says she's been driving her dad nuts, some of the stuff she's been doing. Drinking, speeding tickets, political protests, that sort of thing. Whatever her dad's for, she's against. Kids, huh? Then she got involved in drugs, cocaine, crack. The serious amateur shit. Ended up in rehab, dropped off the screen for nearly a year. They sent her here as a kind of halfway-house deal."

Something else that the island's manager told Tomlinson was that the media were already calling. Already sending reporters and TV trucks to the ferry landing on the mainland. Not good news for me, but not unexpected from the way local law enforcement was reacting. For the last hour, I'd been hearing choppers, seeing their spotlights pan through trees in tubular columns of white.

Old familiar sounds. An old, familiar sight.

Tomlinson patted more blood away; tossed the gauze into the trash. Said, "Move your arm a little closer to the light. I need to get some more Betadine in there or you're going to end up with an infection."

The wounds weren't too bad. Just barnacle scratches on my face. The bullet had skinned a neat little ruby furrow off the underside of my arm. A black-and-green hematoma had already begun to radiate outward toward my biceps.

A very close call, indeed.

Two inches more or less to the left and I'd have been shot through the chest. Maybe through the heart.

It's something I've learned: No matter how secure our lives may seem, day after day, we live by degrees and survive by inches.

Tomlinson asked me, "So how you feeling now? I've got those pain pills if you want 'em."

"Kind of weak and shaky. All that adrenaline, all the emotion—it leaves you feeling like hell. Sick and depressed."

"Hum-m-m-m. It's not like you to feel much emotion about anything. Maybe you're beginning to evolve spiritually. Play your cards right, you could be more like me—an elevated being."

"If this is what it's like, you can have it. I feel like I might vomit."

"Then this is your lucky day," he said. "I got just the herb for that one, too."

THE MAN IN the gray suit, the one asking most of the questions, said to me, "Do you know anything about the drug cartels in South America? Colombia, I'm talking about. Or maybe a group called the Shining Path?"

He meant Sendero Luminoso, a terrorist organization founded by a Maoist university professor, Abimael Guzmán, in Peru's mountain state of Ayacucho. Sendero had exported murder and mindless violence throughout Latin America. Over the years, in a previous line of work, and in what now seems to be a former life, I'd had more than one run-in with Guzmán's unfortunate prophets.

I said, "The drug cartels, sure. They made a couple of movies about them awhile back, didn't they? They're like gangsters, lots of shooting. The other thing you mentioned, though, the Shining something? I don't think I've heard of that, but maybe it's because I don't have a TV and I don't read the papers."

I was still sitting in the same wicker chair, feet propped up, in the main room of my rental bungalow. Behind me, at the lunch bar, Tomlinson sat listening. Lined before me, on the couch and in a kitchen chair, were two men and a woman, all of them staring at me as if from a panel or court bench. The woman wore a green deputy's uniform, her leather gunbelt creaking each time she moved. Same with the guy from Florida Marine Patrol, only his uniform was black on gray.

The man in the gray suit said, "The reason I mention the cartels and the Shining Path is because the men who tried to kidnap Ms. Harrington this afternoon could've been from either one of those two groups. Or from a half-dozen other terrorist organizations that operate in South America. Tupac Amaru, there's another example. There're lots of them.

"We're not sure yet who they are, but we'll find out. The point being that Ms. Harrington's father apparently does have some political influence in that region, so he's bound to have powerful enemies. They're not going to like the idea of someone like you screwing up their plans, which is why you need to cooperate with us. You need to tell us the truth, then let us help you."

To Gray Suit, I said, "I don't doubt that you mean it—offer me protection, whatever it is you think I need, I believe you. I *understand*. You don't have an easy job, I *understand* that, too. But how can I make it any plainer? I don't want your help. I didn't do anything to need it. Or earn it."

"You keep telling us that, Doctor Ford. So I'm going to try one more time. Maybe speak a little more plainly, lay it all out. Here's the deal, doctor: You need to drop the act, come clean, and tell us what really happened out there. You don't have anything to fear from us. We're on your side, not theirs. I don't care what you did. You're the good guy, like the cowboy who came riding in on the white horse. You may have saved a couple of lives today. *They're* the bad guys. The kidnappers. Four or five punks against you, and you ran them off. Hell, we'll try to get you a reward, if you want. Why is that so hard to understand?"

I glanced at Tomlinson. "I guess he has to keep pushing, huh? Like those interrogators in the movies. Thing is, I'm getting tired of him implying I'm lying. It's not my imagination, is it? That *is* what he's doing."

Tomlinson was right with me. "Big time, man. Abso-fucking-lutely."

To the officer, I added, "The irritating thing is, you've done it several times in the last hour. We invite you in here, agree to cooperate in any way we can, and you keep pressing me to make up a story. Sorry. I'm not going to let you manipulate me into saying something that's not true. You either believe me or you don't."

I watched him purse his lips, glancing at the others. Gray Suit's ID badge, which I'd read carefully, said he was Doug Waldman, Special Agent for the FBI and a liaison to the U.S. State Department's Office of Counterterrorism. The badge was clipped to his breast pocket, displaying a fingerprint, a voice/larynx print and a complicated hologram.

The woman deputy leaned forward, her belt making a saddle leather sound, and said, "Just for the record, what I'm going to write in my report is the individual in question, this gentleman I'm talking about, he may or may not have given a truthful account. But I get the impression he's, you know, *intentionally* giving us an incomplete statement, which my captain in Major Crimes Division isn't going to like. What I can't figure out is, Why? Here he is, Joe Citizen, got a chance to be the big hero, get his picture in all the papers, see himself on TV, maybe even get paid by some magazine to tell how he beat off the perpetrators and saved the victim. But he refuses to submit full cooperation."

Cop words and sterile cop sentence patters—"perpetrators," "statements," the "individual in question"—speaking as if I wasn't in the room.

She turned to Waldman. "This individual's behavior seems kinda suspicious to me."

He nodded. "Very odd. That's my point." Showing his respect by listening to her.

THE DEPUTY SAID, "What I'm thinking is, maybe the interviewee had some trouble with the law before. Maybe doesn't want his picture spread around, worried someone will recognize him, or it's like a child support thing. I think we need to hold him 'til all our computer checks come back. The Florida Department of Law Enforcement is going to get involved."

The Florida Marine Patrol had changed its name into the more complicated and meaningless bureauspeak: The Florida Fish and Conservation Commission, which almost no one acknowledges. Neither, apparently, did the officer investigating from that agency, a man named McRae, since he was wearing his Marine Patrol uniform. He hadn't said much, but now he spoke. "Doctor Ford's got a pretty solid reputation around the islands, almost anyone who works on the water can vouch for that. But look, I've got to agree with Deputy Walker, Doc, I think you're leaving out big chunks in your story. You jog out onto the dock and see men wearing ski masks, at least one of them armed, and you just happen to knock the two women into the water and help them get away? That's not easy to believe. I'm sorry."

They were pressing pretty hard, but I had no choice but to keep stonewalling. Like I said, I couldn't afford the scrutiny that would come with admitting my involvement.

I let them see how exasperated I was becoming. "Isn't that what I've been telling you all along? I didn't save anyone. I've described what happened over and over. When I saw the guy fire his pistol, I panicked.

Somehow, I knocked the women into the water when I tried to jump over the railing. Hell, maybe I *did* grab them. But it wasn't intentional. I was trying to save my own life, not theirs. So then those guys keep shooting and the only thing I can think to do is climb in their boat and get the hell out of there. Which is just what I did."

Waldman's cell phone began to ring, and he left the room to answer it as I added, "I told the women to run to the mangroves, and I would've done the same thing if I could've. They were still shooting and it was scary as hell."

"How many shots?"

"A couple. Several. Lots. I didn't count."

"All those rounds fired and you managed to dodge every one of them. You must be quick as hell."

"I've already answered that question too many times."

McRae said, "When you got in the boat, was there anyone else in it? How'd you get control?"

I said, "I just climbed in and hit the throttle and their guy went flying off the stern. I was in a panic. You ever have anyone shoot at you before?"

"And one of the rounds hit you in the arm."

"No. Absolutely not. I'm not going to explain it again."

"Um-huh. Your arm and your face, they both got cut up on the dock when you fell?"

I nodded. "Maybe I need to write it down so you'll remember. I keep repeating myself, but you don't seem to hear. The whole thing's a blur. I'm not sure what happened when. I must have sliced my arm open when I crashed through the railing on the dock. Banging into the pilings with my face, that much I *do* remember. I was probably in shock. Probably still am in shock. Men in ski masks shooting guns like out of some crazy movie. It's not the sort of thing I'm used to seeing."

McRae now wore a soft smile. "Then I've got to ask you one more time—mind if we take a look at that cut on your arm?"

"Nope. I unwrap it, it might start bleeding again."

"That's what I figured. One phone call to the right judge, and we can have a deputy bring a court order out and place it in your hands. A piece of paper that says you've got no choice. We can make you take that bandage off and show us. Isn't that right, Officer Walker?"

As the woman nodded, Tomlinson interrupted, not bothering to disguise his outrage. "Hold on there, Dirty Harry. First you call him a hero, then you threaten him like he's a criminal? Very uncool, man, very, very uncool. That is a very serious conflict of vibes."

McRae looked at him for a moment before he said, "What did you call me?"

Tomlinson has a longstanding and irrational dislike of people in law enforcement that's gotten him into trouble more than once. He does not share my belief that most people in the emergency services tend to be better at their jobs than most others.

I cringed a little as he said, "Dirty Harry. That's what I called you. As in 'Dirty Harry, you can kiss my ass on the county fucking square.'"

McRae's expression changed, became a flat mask. "In my notebook, I've got you down as"—he flipped through a few pages—"I've got your occupation down as a Zen Buddhist monk and sociologist consultant. That's pretty foul language for a monk, isn't it, sir?"

"Well . . . normally, yes—when I'm on duty, I mean. So . . . consider this like a spiritual coffee break. I'm taking a little time off from being the Buddha incarnate to tell you that you're coming off like an asshole. Accidental or not, my buddy here just saved two women. Give him a little respect. Catch where I'm coming from? Can you relate?"

"No, I don't relate and I don't want to relate. But here's some advice: Drop the Dirty Harry references, sir, or maybe Doctor Ford won't be the only one we check out. Lots of times, you counterculture types have something old and interesting in the files. Outstanding warrants, possession charges from other states."

I thought that would make Tomlinson uneasy, but it didn't. He turned his palms outward, as if amazed. "First the guy threatens you, then he threatens me. Right here in our own private whatcha-call-it, our own private domicile. What's the use of staying on an exclusive island if it's not exclusive?"

I was deciding whether to reply or not when Waldman reentered the room. He said, "You folks mind if I speak to Doctor Ford alone? It'll take just a few minutes. I'm going to try one more time to convince him that he should cooperate. Tell us what really happened, then let us talk to the U.S. marshals, see what we can do about protection."

Tomlinson was still angry. "There he goes, calling you a liar again."

Waldman looked at him, no emotion. "A few minutes with Doctor Ford alone. Then I think we're done here."

4

FBI SPECIAL AGENT Waldman took one of the kitchen chairs, turned it, straddled it, then folded his arms over the backrest, his face very close to mine. He said, "Okay. It's just you and me now, Ford. Private, no one else listening. Your very last chance. So tell me what the hell happened out there today. At least give me some interesting version of the truth. Just a little something I can work with."

I shook my head. "Waldman, this is really starting to get tiresome. I collect fish for a living. I operate a tiny, one-man business. I've got a three-page catalog. I can send it to you. Want a hundred horseshoe crabs? Or a whelk egg case in preservative? I can collect it and sell it to you. Or brittle stars or octopi or unborn sharks with their veins already injected. That's what I do. That's what I'm good at. Not dealing with kidnappers or rescuing women."

"That's the way you want to leave it?"

"The truth's the truth."

He sighed, looking at me with careful appraisal. "You need to understand that, when you leave this island, whoever you screwed over out there on the water this afternoon may come looking for you. The girls say you knocked the hell out of the one guy. Said they heard a loud popping sound, like you maybe even broke his back. Depending on who it was, how bad he's hurt, who he's related to, they're not going to let something like that slide.

"With the drug cartels, it's business. A matter of pride. You hurt a member of their family, they're going to double the hurt on you. With people like the Shining Path, they're zealots, lunatics. What they enjoy is hacking someone up with a machete as a political statement. Not that you'd be a top priority. If they do check back and ID you, though, you'd be a very easy guy to find. Depends on whether or not you make it under their radar. Personally, I don't think you ought to risk it."

With the two of us alone now, Waldman's manner was less official, his tone more reasonable. There was a time when the FBI hired only CPAs and attorneys, and he had the bookish, librarian look of a man who enjoyed the clarity of numbers, but who also got out and played golf or tennis on weekends. His hands and fingers told me he'd been married to the same woman for many years, didn't smoke, didn't do manual labor, was left-handed and possibly dipped snuff judging from the orange stain on his thumb and middle finger.

Probably a good, dependable man. We might have become friends under different circumstances.

Even so, I wasn't going to accept his help. Also, I thought it was extremely unlikely that cartel people or an organization like Sendero would waste time and money on an insignificant marine biologist who just happened to be at the wrong place at the wrong time. But I also had to admit to myself that Waldman might be right about one thing. Revenge is a compelling motivator. There was a lot of adrenaline and mass combined when I put my shoulder into the shooter's spine. If he was badly injured, if he *did* have the right connections, he or his family might send someone after me to even the score.

It was a possibility.

The more information I had, the better chance I had of anticipating any move against me, so I decided to ask Waldman a few questions of my own, just in case. I said, "Off the record, you mind telling me why you think they targeted the girl?"

"We don't even know who 'they' are yet, Doctor Ford."

My expression was one of pain and tolerance. "Come on now, Agent Waldman. Wait a minute . . . know what? After nearly two hours together, we should be on a first-name basis, don't you think? Call me Doc or call me Ford. Okay?"

He nodded, and waited for a moment before he said, "Sure. You're Ford and I'm Doug. Just two guys talking, so talk away."

"Doug, what I don't understand is, you dropped the shields there for a little bit. Now, the first time I ask you a question, you raise the shields right back again. It's pretty obvious you've been in your business awhile. What's your title? Special liaison to the U.S. State Department's Office of Counterterrorism? You must have an opinion. Like you said, it's just you and me in here. So why not tell me what you think?"

"Are you offering me information in exchange?"

I said, "I think I told you everything, but I might be able to remember a few more details. I'll try. I really will."

"Okay. Why not?" His was a careful, formal smile. "I'll risk it. Lindsey Harrington's father is one of those behind-the-scenes diplomats, the kind you never hear about but who apparently has a lot to do with steering U.S. policy. He's got some very powerful connections. I say 'apparently' because the moment the Agency got word Harrington's daughter was almost taken down, the director ordered . . ." He paused, rethinking it. "Let's just say that certain people in the director's office made it very clear that this case is a priority. We've got people on the island doing the crime scene, standing guard over the girl, all of us reporting back with updates every hour."

I said, "They wanted her for political reasons? I'm not asking for the official position. Just your personal opinion."

"Why they tried to kidnap her? Political, sure, without a doubt. But is it drug cartel politics or political ideology? That's what I don't know. But we'll find out. We've got people working on the stolen boats, the rental van, the motel they stayed in at Englewood. They wanted the girl, but they really wanted to leverage Harrington."

"The girl's father, he's that important?"

"I've never heard his name before tonight. In the three years I've been attached to Counterterrorism, I've never heard the name Harrington mentioned. His official title is Consulting Ambassador, Latin America— a small-time political appointment. He works out of the U.S. Embassy in San Jose and he's got some kind of villa or condo outside Cartagena. In international politics, it's hard to tell who really does what. But Harrington, he's so far behind the scenes that we had trouble coming up with a fast, full dossier on him."

I told him, "Here's something I may have left out. One of the guys on the dock, he was yelling in Spanish. He had a Colombian accent. They speak a very clean dialect, particularly in and around the cities. Bogota, maybe, but I'm just guessing."

"Finally, you offer me a little scrap of useful information." He chuck-led, but it was a timing device, not laughter. "Colombian accent, huh? To pick out accents, you must be fluent. Spent some time down there in South America, have you Ford?"

"Several years. Traveled all over." Interpreting the expression on the agent's face, I added, "It had nothing to do with the drug trade, trust me. I was studying bull sharks. I've been researching them for years. The work took me all over South and Central America. All over the world, really."

"Really? Who funded it? Who paid for all that travel and research?"

"I got some grants. But mostly private corporations that have a finan-cial interest and see a potential for profit in certain sea products."

"Fascinating." His inflection said: *Bullshit.*

"You know anything about bull sharks?" I waited for him to respond, but he didn't. He sat there leafing through his notebook. Finally, I continued, "A bull shark will swim hundreds of miles up freshwater rivers for reasons that we still don't understand. It may have something to do with ferromagnetic crystals in their nervous system. Directional devices built right in, or perhaps it has something to do with the way their tissues deal with salt. Whatever the reason, they're a very unusual animal. The Zambezi River shark? The freshwater sharks of Lake Nicaragua? *Carcharhinus leucas.* The same, aggressive animal. Because of that shark, I spent a lot of time working in the jungle."

"That part of the story, I don't doubt," he said.

I wondered what he meant by that, the suggestive tone, but said nothing.

He said, "Okay, so you picked up on the Colombian accent. About six months ago, Lindsey Harrington's father—Hal Harrington, that's his name—attended a summit in Cartagena, along with representatives from several other Latin American countries. The U.S. has given them in excess of a billion dollars a year for the drug war—what they call a war, anyway—and the summit was to outline operational methods and long-term goals. That much is in the dossier. Maybe Harrington did something to piss them off. Maybe he bucked the Colombian establishment—it's one of the most corrupt countries on earth. Whatever he did, he made someone mad enough to go after his daughter."

"That's it? It's really all you know?"

"Yep. Pretty thin so far, but it's early. You haven't exactly been a fountain of information yourself. What I should tell you is . . . here, let me point out something that you may not realize, Ford. Something you haven't thought much about. Right now, you're safe. So's Lindsey Harrington. For the next twenty-four hours, two different federal agencies are going to keep this island secured while we finish collecting evidence. We have lots of video to shoot, lots of photos to take. Where you are right now is one of the safest places in the world. But you can't stay on Guava Key forever. Sooner or later, you're going to have to get into your boat and go home. So what are you going to do if those punks come calling again? You really feeling that lucky? That's why I'd like you to cooperate. If they put you on their personal shit list, it'd be nice to grab them when they come to grab you."

"Stake me out like a goat, huh?" I shook my head. "Sorry, the timing's bad. I'm too busy. I've got several research projects going on right now."

He parroted my words with a flat sarcasm. "Research projects. Like what that's so damn important?"

"I'm working on sturgeon, too. Not just bull sharks. I've got current projects, old projects—but sturgeon are what I'm doing right now. I'm working with some biologists from a lab not far from here, Mote Marine." All true. When Waldman didn't respond, I proceeded to tell more than he wanted to know about our sturgeon project, aware that a good way to deal with interrogation is to bore your interrogator. I informed him there'd once been a booming sturgeon fishery on Florida's Gulf Coast, all because of the profitable caviar market. I described the fish to him, with its scale cover of primitive bony plates and rows of bony scutes on its body. Told him that the sturgeon is a freshwater species that migrates into saltwater, and is very easily netted—which is why the sturgeon was so quickly decimated north and south of Tampa. I added, "Now you mention sturgeon to a coastal fisherman and he'll look at you like you're nuts. No one even remembers that they were here. So we're working on raising them in captivity, then releasing them into the wild. Problem is, they grow so damn slow."

Waldman stared at me, bored, not letting the details register. "You're not going to tell me a damn thing, are you?"

I said, "Nope, Doug, I'm not. I don't want any trouble. I really don't. I live a quiet, private life, and that's the way I want it to keep it."

He stood, hunted around in his jacket pocket for a moment and pulled out a tin of Copenhagen snuff. He flapped the can with his thumb, opened it, and pushed a big pinch of tobacco between cheek and gum. "I kinda figured you'd be a tough one to budge. That call I just took—when my cell phone rang a few minutes ago?"

"What about it?"

Waldman walked to the kitchen sink, spit and flushed it with water. "Our people in D.C. and Virginia have now had"—he checked his watch—"they've now had slightly more than four hours to come up with a dossier on you. Know what they found? And I'm talking about the best-equipped, most computer-savvy security agency in the world. Nothing," he said. "They found nothing interesting at all about you. Zip, zilch. Know what, Ford? From the information we got back, it's almost like you really don't exist."

I began to feel uneasy, but made it a point to take a deep breath, relaxing in my chair. "You're saying there's something wrong with not being in some crime computer somewhere?"

"You're in no computers *anywhere*. Nothing but the barest stuff, anyway. Harrington was tough to get information on. You're even worse. Any idea why that is?"

I told him no, hoping he'd drop it, but he didn't.

He leafed through a couple of sheets of paper and said, "Here's what we've got on you. You've got a six-cylinder Chevy more than twenty years old. I've got the block number and the registration number right here. Another thing? When you were still in high school, you took the battery of Armed Services Vocational Aptitude tests. Damn near aced them all. Not the highest scores ever recorded, but way, way up there. Then you vanished for seven years. Not a trace. No military record, no nothing. Next thing that shows up is that you're in California, graduating with a B.S. from San Diego State and then you get a masters a year later from Stanford. No record of where you lived, no record of credit cards, no student loans or a checking account. Nothing at all that indicates you were actually at those places and attended classes. But the degrees are legitimate. I made our people check. Your doctorate from the University of Florida? Same thing."

"That's weird," I said. "They don't give degrees unless you attend classes. Maybe it's because I've always been kind of a loner. That, and I've always tried to pay with cash. Saves on bookkeeping."

His smile told me that he knew that I was lying. "I've done background checks on grade-school teachers that turned up more data. Oh, by the way—our people did dig out one little interesting tidbit of information hidden away. Came from an old file in Pitkin County, Colorado. Aspen, that's a town you might know there."

It seemed to please him that I didn't react. "Seems that more than a decade ago, a guy by the name of Marion W. Ford was a prime suspect in the abduction and probable murder of a political radical who lived in the mountains out there. A guy who specialized in bombing military installations. The cops detained you—this guy Ford, I'm talking about—but nothing ever came of it. Once again, you just vanished. Marion W. Ford vanished, I mean."

I stood, not comfortable with the direction the conversation was leading. I said, "I think the computers have me confused with someone else, Doug. That was a long time ago, but I'd certainly remember something like that."

"I'd think you would, too. Know what the really sad thing is, Ford? Okay, here's what I think. The sad thing is that you should be given an award for what you did today. Or a bounty. Instead, maybe because you're nervous about certain things you did or didn't do in your past, you feel like you have to lie about it. Or maybe you just don't want to be put into the bureaucratic machine, deal with all the bullshit details."

I said nothing, waiting.

"There's something else that pisses me off, too. Something not directly related to you or what went on today, but there's bound to be a connection. Sooner or later."

I raised my eyebrows—what?

"It's those punks you chased off. Bigshot drug people when they have weapons, or political freaks like the ones who came looking for Lindsey Harrington. Sooner or later, if we don't take them down, respond with lethal force whenever we get the chance, the day will come when they score big. I mean really, really big. They're going to murder a bunch of us. They're going to make a great big pile of bodies. Just watch. When it happens, the so-called peace-loving members of this society are going to be outraged all to hell. They don't like it when their government plays rough. They won't vote or allocate the money for us to maintain a serious defense, but they'll sure as hell demand some answers. Why didn't we stop it from happening?"

I put my chin on my fist, listening.

"Want to hear a very likely scenario?"

"Sure. Friends keep telling me I should pay more attention to what's going on in the outside world."

"You and a couple hundred million others. I wish to hell everyone in the country would get the pacifiers out of their mouths, grow up a little, and take a look down the road at what's waiting for us out there. We presented the whole scenario to the Senate a few years ago, and the media didn't even blink. Hardly a word went out. Okay, here's the way it goes: A terrorist with the Shining Path or Hezbollah, or Islamic Jihad or Hamas tapes a standard one-hundred-watt lightbulb to the track of a New York City subway station. Minutes later, a passing train crushes the bulb. Contained in the bulb are spores of anthrax, one of the deadliest toxins known to humanity."

"Very simple," I said. "Very plausible."

He answered, "Plausible? It's inevitable. Or some equally nasty variation—sarin gas, for instance. Within hours, subway ventilation fans circulate the poison throughout the entire system. Then commuters begin dying. By the thousands they start dying, a hundred thousand or more for starters, and horrible deaths at that.

"It would cripple the nation. Bring everything to a stop. You can't bury anthrax victims. You have to burn their bodies. There would be funeral pyres throughout the city.

"There are millions of fine, patriotic, law-abiding Muslims and politically active Latins in this country, but there are also a handful of very well-financed zealots on the loose who really do believe that we are the Great Satan. They will do absolutely anything to destroy us. People who kill in the name of God or political ideology are, by definition, without conscience. To get those boats from the Mercury Test Center? They threatened to shoot the seventy-five-year-old security guard and his grandson, who just happened to be there, hanging out. Threatened an old man and a kid, and I think they would have done it. You think they're going to hesitate if they get another chance at you?"

I stood at the door and opened it. "I hope you're wrong."

Waldman surprised me by reaching to shake my hand. "Me, too, Ford. Judging from all the computer files that don't exist on you, I suspect you've had an interesting life. I wouldn't mind hearing about it some day."

As he turned to go, I hesitated before I said, "Hey, Doug? There's one other thing."

"Yeah?"

"The two women, Lindsey Harrington and—"

"The bodyguard's name is Gale Storm. Honest. After some old Hollywood actress. They both want to stop and thank you, by the way. Tonight, if you don't mind."

I looked at my watch and shrugged. It was nearly eleven. "It's probably already obvious to you, but I want to make sure. Someone had to be charting those women. Their habits. Someone here on the island. Their routine wasn't hard to nail down because they never varied it. Still, someone had to be on island, watching."

"We've already checked. There was a Colombian maid who didn't show up for work yesterday or today. She lived in a trailer park on Pine Island, and her trailer's been cleaned out, too."

"Same with the Mercury Test Center," I said. "They stole the two Scarabs right after it closed. Isn't that what you said?"

"Yeah. They used duct tape. Tied up and gagged the guard and the kid. Jumped the fences, climbed in the boats and off they went. Everyone just figured they were doing some special testing."

"I think they had to have someone on the inside to have two high-performance boats all fueled and ready. Or maybe they bribed an employee for the testing schedules. It'd probably be pretty easy to do. Claim to be from the competition—Yamaha or OMC—and buy off one of the staff people."

Waldman was listening, thinking about it. "The false flag gambit, yeah. But why? Those yellow boats don't run every day?"

"You'd have to live here on the islands to know it's unusual. Not two Scarabs out at the same time. I've seen them running in tandem before, but rarely. Nothing someone could count on. I think they probably had to pay some money to make sure it happened."

He opened his notebook and scribbled a few words. "That's useful. We'd have checked it out sooner or later, but now I'll push it toward the top of the list. Anything else?"

"Nope, just that I'm glad I don't have your job. The kidnappers, whoever they are, whatever their cause, you have to give them credit. They seemed to think of everything."

That brought a wry, ironic smile to his face. "Well, not exactly everything."

I said, "Oh? What'd they miss?"

There was a knock from outside as he said, "They missed you, Ford, that's what they missed. They didn't anticipate someone like you being here," as he turned and opened the door.

STANDING ON THE porch were the two uniformed officers with the dark Bahamian woman in the middle, her red-beaded cornrows swinging, clacking like miniature dominoes. Tomlinson was in the background, pacing—not reassuring because he's not the type to pace.

I felt my stomach muscles tense when Deputy Walker said, "Sorry to interrupt, but I thought it might save you some time. This woman says she saw the whole thing. Found us and volunteered herself. Says she was standing right out there at the edge of the mangroves, close enough to see and hear it all. Her name's . . . Ransom Ebanks? Is that correct, miss? That's an unusual name, particularly considering the circumstances."

The black woman nodded. "May be unusual to you but it ain't to me. Ransom R. Ebanks, that always been my name."

"Ms. Ebanks says she came here to do some sightseeing, just over from the islands, and walked right into the middle of the kidnapping. She eyeballed at least three of the perps, saw this guy, too. But that's all she'd tell us until Doctor Ford was present."

Ebanks, why was that name familiar? I remembered Tomlinson telling me someone by that name had contacted the office and left a message for me. But why? I'd never met her before in my life, and now here she was. I tried to keep my expression bland and amused as Waldman looked from me to the woman, then back to me. "Is that true, Ms. Ebanks? You witnessed the kidnapping attempt?"

Her soft, articulate accent seemed to add credulity. "Oh, that's the natural truth alright. I saw the big man there, watched what he did, runnin' from those men in the masks while they shot their guns."

Waldman pointed his finger at me. "This is the man you saw?"

She nodded.

"Why wouldn't you tell Deputy Walker what you saw unless Doctor Ford was present?"

She didn't answer right away. Instead, Ransom Ebanks locked her eyes into mine, trying to communicate something, but what she was communicating, I wasn't immediately certain. I expected her eyes to be dark but, in the porch light, they were a glittering, lucent blue. Quite a surprise looking into her African face, seeing those blue eyes. Their focus seemed intense, meaningful.

Was she waiting for me to say something first? Perhaps. Or maybe that's what I wanted to believe. Even so, I spoke quickly. "Probably because she wanted to make certain I was the guy she saw cut his arm when I fell through the railing and took the two women with me."

"Hey! That's enough." Walker took a step toward me, showing her no-bullshit cop expression. "He's leading her, telling her what to say."

The Bahamian woman's tone was suddenly just as tough. "He ain't leading nobody, lady. You quiet your mouth for a second, I tell you what happened."

Waldman said soothingly, "Now, now, let's stay calm, do this in an orderly fashion. It's getting late, we're all a little tired. Ms. Ebanks? Take your time. You say you saw Doctor Ford running while the men shot at him?"

I listened to her say, "Isn't that what I just tell you? Yes, the big man, the man standing right there with the bandage on his arm. What happened was, he so scared, he went and run away. First, he fall into the water, him and the two pretty girls. When that railing break? Then he jumped into that go-fast boat and man, he gone."

Waldman didn't seem convinced. "Really? You say the men were shooting at him while this man . . . you actually saw this man get away in the boat."

"That's right. I saw 'im."

"Why didn't you run away, Ms. Ebanks? A man his size was frightened; why weren't you afraid?"

"'Cause the men with the guns, they didn't see me. I back in the trees watching."

Waldman was still suspicious. "In the trees, okay. You just stood there watching while they shot. How many shots were fired? Any idea?"

"Four, maybe five. I don't know. I was watching with my eyes, not countin' with my ears."

"Not counting with your ears. Very amusing. Okay, they began to shoot at him. Then—take us through it step by step—after they started shooting, what happened?"

She was still staring into my eyes, trying to read something from me. Finally, she said, "He bang into the two pretty girls, like I tol' you, and he so big the railing break and they go splashing in the water. That how he cut his arm. Musta hit the dock or somethin', I'm guessing."

Deputy Walker said, "That's what he just told her to say. He was leading her, like I said."

Waldman gave her a warning look. Then to Ransom Ebanks: "You saw him cut his arm on the dock? No offense, miss, but how can you be so sure one of the bullets didn't hit him when the men were shooting? You say you did see them fire shots."

She was nodding, suddenly very self assured. "'Cause I saw just the way it happened, that's why I'm so sure. He went kinda trippin' and stumblin', holding them two women, and they all went crashing through the railing. That's where I saw him catch that arm on a nail or something—I can't be sure what it was, but the blood was flying. Then I watched them women run away into the trees while he go flyin' off in the boat."

"Was he alone in the boat?"

"That somethin' I don't know. But tell me this, Mr. Po-lice-man. This gentleman"—she used her hand to indicate me—"does he look so dumb to you that he just stand around while men's shooting at him?"

Then she laughed, showing pearl-white teeth, but her eyes were still focused on mine.

It suddenly became clear to me, the meaning of the direct eye contact and her intense expression. While she lied to the cops, she was also speaking nonverbally, looking through the lenses of my eyes, saying, *You owe me.*

5

THE BAHAMIAN WOMAN said, "You actin' like it don't hurt none, man. Like it no big deal. Almost like you used to getting shot, my brother."

What my ears heard was: *Yoo actin' lie it doan huurt nawn, mon. Lie it no big dill . . .*

An accent that fit her physiology. Look at the cinnamon skin, the bone structure, the braided hair, the gaudy golden ring on her right hand, and you saw twenty generations stylized by coconut palms, coral islands in a re-mote sea, and the patina of isolated British influence on African rootstock.

She was what? Probably in her mid-to-late thirties, but looked much younger, which is why I'd misjudged her age so badly the first time I saw her. Maybe forty, judging from the fine lines on the backs of her hands and at the corners of her eyes. A middle-aged woman, but very fit and in control of her body.

The cops were gone. Waldman had listened to her story patiently, asked a few questions, then said, since it was so late, would Ms. Ebanks be willing to give them an official statement in the morning?

She told him, "Yeah, man, but I got no place to sleep out here tonight. Maybe you ask the people at the fancy restaurant, up on the hill, they give me a free dinner and a place to stay, seein's how I'm agreeing to help you. Get me a nice room with fancy pillows, but I'd like the bed be pointed north, you doan mind. That the only way a person get his directions in a foreign land. Sleep w'his head pointed north."

She was a negotiator, maybe a manipulator, that much was becoming clear. The island girl wheedling herself some space among the rich Americans, already knowing how to do it, but seemingly unaware of how obvious she was and how naïve she came off. Speaking of superstition as if to educate others.

It didn't seem to bother Tomlinson at all, though. She'd already impressed him—that was easy enough to read. When he's interested in a woman, his face assumes a concerned, spiritual glaze that attempts, but fails, to camouflage carnal interest.

"Ms. Ebanks," he said, "you are most welcome to stay in the guest room of my cottage. We'll point the bed any way you want. And food, well . . . let's see, the restaurant's already closed, but I can fix you a late supper. A nice Camembert with red wine? Or I'll throw a salad together, spinach, asparagus and tomatoes. Put some music on, pound some alcohol or—you're from the islands?—we can burn something herbal, whatever you like."

The law enforcement people exchanged looks—*Can you believe this guy?*—but she seemed to like the sound of it and smiled at him. Told Tomlinson to call her Ransom, just the way she said it, running it all together, Ransom Ebanks. She said, "I'll stay in your house, Mr. Hipster man, but don't be getting the wrong idea. I'm not going to be a thing for you to be bouncin' on in your bed."

"No worries, no worries. Hasn't been a problem lately," he replied.

NOW THE COPS were gone and we were still in my bungalow, Tomlinson and the woman sitting together on the couch. I sat there listening to the two of them chatter away like old neighbors, still feeling weak, queasy and a little restless, thinking she'd bring it up, but she didn't. So I finally said, "Ransom? I hate to interrupt another one of Tomlinson's fascinating tales, but I need to get to bed. I'm exhausted, but there's something I want to ask you first."

"You ask me anything you want, my brother."

Why'd she keep calling me that?

I said, "You telephoned the front desk from the mainland and left a message for me. Why? We've never met—I'd certainly remember meeting someone like you. Then you show up here and tell the police that story about how I cut my arm when I fell off the dock. The whole thing very convincing. I couldn't have asked for a better . . . a more useful statement. So my question is—"

"Your question is, why'd I lie for you? *That* what you askin' me."

I made a hushing motion with my hands. "Let's keep our voices down. The whole chain of events, I don't understand any of it. For one thing, what're you doing here? They said you were here sightseeing. That makes sense, but why contact me? So, yeah, maybe that is the question: What'd you have to gain by lying?"

"Nothing to gain, man. I lied 'cause you wanted me to lie, didn't you?"

"I . . . it's not that I wanted you to lie. No, I wouldn't use those words. What you probably don't understand is that, the way the law's set up, if I admit that one of those bullets nicked my arm, I'd have to spend the next several weeks answering questions from police. I'd be testifying and filling out forms—the whole thing would be a mess. My picture in the papers, reporters sniffing around—ask Tomlinson, it's the sort of thing I hate. Which is why I'd prefer that they didn't hear details about certain parts of the story. That's all."

"Um-huh, um-huh, meaning you wanted me to lie. I knew that, that's why I did it. It not a thing hard to figure out, man. Down by that little bay, I watched you jump out the boat and wade ashore. First thing you tell me is I didn't see you get shot. But I *did* see you get shot. Then you tell me I was imagining things. Man, your shorts was still drippin' water when you say it to me. That's how I know you want me to lie." She tapped her index finger to her head. "I nobody's fool. On the island where I live, the people, they all say I very quick, man. Very fast in the brain."

I was beginning to believe it. Said to her, "It's not that you did anything wrong. Or I did anything wrong."

"'Course you didn't. But that don't make no never mind to me. I lie for you today, I lie for you tomorrow. That's what family people do for each other."

I said, "Huh?"

SHE WAS LOOKING at Tomlinson now, the two of them smiling, sharing some inside joke. Apparently, she'd already told him something she hadn't confided in me. I listened to her say, "It take me two weeks to track you down, Mister Doctor Marion Ford. Flew over on Air Bahamas, Nassau to Lauderdale, then took a big Greyhound bus across the Everglades to Sanibel. But you not there either, so I had to ask around, ask around. Everybody on that island, man, they all know you and like you. They tell me, 'Oh yeah, that Doc Ford, he a good man.' Man, that make me feel good and proud to come all this way just to surprise you. Wanted to see how your face looked when I told you the news."

Was the conversation making me dizzy, or was I still feeling the effects of blood loss? None of what she said made sense. I said, "What news? What the hell are you talking about?"

Her smile broadened as she stood and leaned, taking me in her arms even though I tried to pull away. I felt her skin against my face, as I heard her say, "The news is, I'm the sister you never knowd you had, man! My big ol' handsome white-skinned fella!" She stepped back, holding me at a distance, beaming, while I sat there feeling mild shock. "Hello, my brother!"

I was trying to hold her away. "Look, lady, I don't know what you're trying to do here . . . where you got the idea . . . but it's absurd, just plain silly. Believe me, I am *not* your brother."

"'Course you are, only Daddy never tol' you. Last month, the lawyer man, he sent me Daddy's secret papers. Got them right here in my backpack, you want to see your name and picture for yourself. Big ol' smiling picture of you and Daddy Gatrell. Know what else? He hid some money away for us. Now you and me, we going to go find that money and split it right down the middle."

"Daddy *Gatrell*? My name isn't Gatrell. Gatrell, that was my mother's maiden name—" I stopped as my brain made the slow translation. Then I said, "That pathetic old fool."

Tomlinson seemed very cheerful about it all. "Ransom is Tucker's daughter. All you have to do is look at her eyes to believe it; the same sled dog blue. You agree?"

I didn't want to look, but did and had no choice but to nod. They were just like Tuck's, the same crazed color of blue. Unmistakable, once I thought about it.

"So what happened is, about three weeks ago, Tucker's lawyer sends her these papers Federal Express, including a letter from Tuck that claims you're his son. Hilarious, huh? She's already let me look through the package; some interesting things in that black bag of hers, Doc. That Tucker, he was a character, wasn't he?"

I put up a warning palm—whoa. It was too late at night and I was too tired to listen to it. Not then, hopefully not ever. I stood and stepped toward the door, meaning it was time for them to leave I said, "Oh yeah, that old man was something."

My insane old uncle, the late Tucker Gatrell.

THE LIVING ROOM of my bungalow opened out onto a screened porch that sat above the ground on three-foot pilings, looking down across a little sand and mangrove beach to the bay.

I was sitting on the porch alone, finally. I had walked Tomlinson and the woman partway to his cottage, just to make sure that she didn't change her mind and come back.

Told her I'd listen to the whole story, read all the papers she'd brought, but tomorrow.

"I bet you're surprised to find out you got a sister like me!"

She kept saying that. She seemed very excited and wasn't the least bit deflated by the several times I replied, "I'm not your brother. Trust me, I'm not your brother."

If she was, indeed, Tucker's daughter, one thing that she had not inherited was his natural cynicism. I found her reaction touching but also frustrating. "But why would Daddy Gatrell lie to his own daughter? I saw the man seven, eight times in my life, and he loved me. That much I know. He not the kinda man to go tellin' crazy lies."

I thought, *If you only knew,* but said nothing.

I felt emotionally and physically drained, but too restless to sleep. So I opened a midnight beer to celebrate the sudden absence of people after spending the last many hours listening and talking.

Not that I felt celebratory. What I'd suggested to Tomlinson was true. Participation in violence opens all the adrenal reserves and dumps in way too much adrenaline way too fast. Especially violence that seeks the lethal existential. Violence has always produced a grayness in me. It seems to extract light and validity from those things that provide the scaffolding for what I normally see as a useful, productive existence: the chemical/mathematical order of biology; interaction with friends and lovers; days of solitude and open water.

Violence is a vital component in natural selection and the hierarchy of species, and I view it unemotionally in all conditions but my own, which is the human condition. Violence debases us. It sparks the dark arc that refutes all illusion. In the instant it occurs, humanity seems reduced to the most meaningless of fictions, nothing but a hopeful fantasy created by primates who aspire to elevate themselves.

I don't know why it affects me so, but it does.

Perhaps it's because inflicting injury on a person also inflicts an equal and opposite proof, the proof of one's own mortality.

As I moved from kitchen to porch, I kept reviewing the series of events over and over in my mind, wincing at my own stupidity, my own clumsiness, cringing at the *whap* of a bullet that passed much too close and at the sound of a man's spine snapping.

We are frail creatures, indeed. Contribute to the debility or death of another human and, if you have any conscience at all, you will find yourself standing on the lip of the abyss, peering downward, into your own black reflection.

No, I wasn't celebrating. But it *was* good to finally be alone. I took the Bud Light I'd opened, and poured it in a glass over ice with a wedge of lime. I had a book to read and a floor lamp for light. Had my portable shortwave radio at my side, dialed into Radio Quito, Voice of the Andes, on the 49 meters band, the English-speaking newsperson reading articulate government disinformation and sharing static with Papua New Guinea Radio and the BBC.

Waldman was exactly right. It was time for me to start paying attention to the world outside. Time for me to poke my head up and take a look around. I'd become way too comfortable in the tiny, safer world of boat and fish and my lab back at Dinkin's Bay Marina.

The book I was reading was an instructional pamphlet. I'd just taken delivery of a new telescope, a really superb Celestron NexStar five-inch Schmidt-Cassegrain, and now I was tutoring myself on some of the finer points of operation. Program it with latitude and longitude, then point it at Polaris, and by punching in the proper code, the telescope would swing automatically to the Great Nebulae of Orion or show you the polar caps of Mars or locate any of 1,800 deep-space objects already programmed into the little handheld computer.

Amazing.

I sat there reading in the soft light as a sulfur moth fluttered around, casting a pterodactyl shadow on ceiling and screen. Moonlight and the smell of night-blooming jasmine filtered in on dense air, as if fanned by the moth's wings.

I had the little telescope on the table in front of me, following the instructions, experimenting with the computer and clock drive.

I don't consider myself an amateur astronomer. I'm not knowledgeable enough or active enough to be worthy of the title. I do, however, enjoy applying what little I know about the science. Spend an evening viewing objects in deep space, and your own small problems and tiny life are given healthy proportion. Plus, as Tomlinson is continually pointing out, there is an unmistakable if unprovable symmetry and repetition of design shared by the marine creatures that I collect and the visible structure of the universe.

The rays of an anemone and the plasmaic traps of certain hydroids appear as micro mimics of starbursts and celestial protoplasm. In narrow passages between two islands, eddies created by a running tide swirl in patterns similar to nebulae and whirlpooling comets.

It's an interesting phenomenon, one I don't pretend to understand. So I've always had telescopes, and recently decided to trade in my old and simple refractor for this high-tech replacement. The Celestron has the added advantage of being very light—about twenty pounds, plenty small enough and light enough to carry around on my boat or in my truck.

I'd figured that Guava Key would be two lazy, uneventful weeks, with plenty of peace and quiet in which I could learn the scope's entire system and do some stargazing.

As Tomlinson says, "Want to give God a good laugh? Tell him your plans."

Even so, my previous days on the island had been sufficiently quiet, with good, dark nights and clear skies. I'd used the scope nearly every night, and was particularly pleased because a celestial oddity was occurring that week: The sun and six of the planets were lined up like cosmic billiard balls, an event that happens about every twenty years and unfailingly inspires an assortment of weirdos and prophets to predict global chaos and destruction.

Like the stars, the Earth's prophets don't seem to change much over the years.

So I was sitting, reading the manual, futzing with the little handheld computer. Venus, Jupiter and Saturn were easy enough to find on my own. But had the little scope been programmed to locate Mercury and Mars? I was following the guide through a slow step-by-step, looking from the page to the digitized screen . . . and that's when I stiffened in my chair, listening. I heard a twig break, then a rustle of leaves as the silhouette of a person moved across the porch screen.

I was so overly sensitized and paranoid from Waldman's warnings about drug runners, terrorists and revenge, that I was about to throw myself backward, out of the chair in an attempt to roll away from any potential line of fire, when I heard a woman's voice call, "Doctor Ford? Is that you?"

An unusually girlish voice; it sounded like a teenager who'd yelled herself slightly hoarse at some school function.

I stood and opened the porch door to see Lindsey Harrington standing on the sidewalk in a white T-shirt that hung to mid-thigh, no shorts showing on tanned legs, blond hair fanned over her shoulders.

I heard her say, "I hope I didn't startle you."

I answered, "Not at all," even though my heart was pounding.

I stood in the doorway looking at her. It seemed like she'd just gotten out of bed. Her smile and her wry tone implied apology as she said, "First thing I wanted to do was thank you. But the two women from the Sheriff's Department wouldn't let me leave our cottage. So now they think I'm sound asleep in bed, which is the way I always worked it when I wanted to sneak out, back when I was living with my dad." She used both hands to rope her hair back and stretched slightly. "Truth is, I can't sleep at all after such a crazy day. Mind if I come in?"

I pushed the door wider and said, "You want a beer?"

6

WE SAT, SIPPING our drinks, and took care of the uneasy formalities of strangers newly met. I listened to her thank me over and over again, and deflected her apologies for stopping by when it was so late.

Then we both began to relax a little as our exchanges became more personal and personable, her recounting what had happened that afternoon, the way she felt when she first saw the men in ski masks, me not saying much. When I could, I asked questions. I was interested in who she was, why the kidnappers had targeted her.

I sat and listened, then, as the diplomat's daughter told me, "My father was in D.C. for, what? Like sixteen years and spent eight working in the basement of the White House, part of the staff, so I got to know three presidents pretty well. Two of the three, you couldn't ask to meet nicer men. I mean, really cool guys. The kind you'd trust for a father or a grandfather. The third one, though, he was a pompous asshole."

"Your father worked for all of them?" I'd switched off the lamp and sat, alternately, looking at the water, then at her. Lindsey Harrington's blond hair looked satin white in the peripheral light, her face, delicate, pale, very young. The moon, low on the horizon, created a corridor of color on the water, silver and brass.

"No, just two of the three. He did, like, political analysis stuff, administrative stuff. I've never really been sure. The way he puts it is, picture the White House as a major corporation—which it is—so my dad would be like the equivalent of a department head in one of the smaller departments. He does it 'cause he loves it. It's not because he needs the money, that's for sure."

I watched the girl sipping at her beer, combing bangs back with nervous fingers while she told me about Hal Harrington. She explained that, back when her father was still in his late twenties, he'd gotten a job with one of the early computer companies as an unskilled laborer. He'd done the grunt work, unloading boxes, muling bundles of electrical conduit and parts. In his spare time, though, he'd studied the whole field, the way it was headed, liked what he saw and began to invest right there on the ground floor. Not only that, he invented what Lindsey described as a "little doohickey," a plastic sleeve that was a docking device for computer chips.

She told me, "Dad got the thing patented, and every computer company in the world uses it, so he was, like, a multimillionaire before he was twenty-five. Then, somehow, he got interested in politics, began to finance certain candidates, and ended up working in the basement of the White House for no salary. He moved me to D.C. with him. We had this really awesome suite at the Willard Hotel, and I attended this, like, really hotshit private school, Sidwell Friends, and hung out at 1600 Pennsylvania, when I could, which is how I got to be friends with all those presidents. Except for one of them, who was a creep, a genuine self-important dick, and his wife was even worse. This one time, we were in the state dining room, which is by the colored rooms, and my boyfriend—"

I interrupted. "Colored rooms?"

"Yeah, near the South Portico, the rooms are named after colors—Red, Green, Blue, Vermeil. It really is a cool place. Particularly if you are, like, totally into history, which my father is, so he made me study it, which could be a drag, but sometimes I actually enjoyed it. Anyway, we were at this boring-as-hell dinner, and my boyfriend went looking for the head. He opens a door by the colored rooms and catches the First Lady sneaking a cigarette. She, like, totally lost it, was screaming, swearing; almost had him arrested.

"Her famous brat younger sister was right there; witnessed the whole thing. And her famous neurotic poodle. Spend any time at all around the White House, and the first thing you learn is don't judge anyone by their politics. As my father likes to say, 'D.C. is the only place in the world that has assholes on both sides of the crack.'"

We were sitting at a white wicker table, drinks in hand, looking at a cusp of waning moon that was encircled by rainbow colors, the upper stratosphere showing ice crystals. She had her keys and cell phone before her on the glass top.

These days, it's impossible for me to look at a frail moon without feeling wistful and a little lonely. It reminds me of a long-gone friend.

It was nearly 1:00 A.M. I'd been listening to her talk for an hour, but was relaxed and enjoying it. She was one of the troubled ones, a person driven by family demons, but still cognitive and aware, and she had a self-deprecating sense of humor that I liked. Remembering that Tomlinson had mentioned she'd had a substance abuse problem, I'd amended my offer of a beer, saying maybe she'd prefer water or a Coke? But no, beer was just what she needed, she said, and with a rueful laugh added, "I'm a crack addict, not an alcoholic."

I said, "There's a difference?"

"Oh yeah. No one's ever tried to steal a vase out of the West Wing to trade for beer."

I COULDN'T GET used to her voice. She looked twenty-two, twenty-three—I really can't tell ages anymore—but she sounded sixteen or younger. It didn't mesh with consistent patterns of articulate thought and her world-weariness. She had a way of sighing, of looking off into space, that suggested emotional scarring and a loss of resolve or of confidence that originated in the marrow.

What surprised me most about Lindsey Harrington, though, was this: I liked her. Liked her despite her age and mall-girl vocabulary.

Initially, she'd hoisted a couple of red flags by saying, "I noticed you the day you got here, the first day you showed up on the island. You and that sweet old hippie with the really kind eyes. But you're the one who really caught my attention. It's not just that you're so big. Kind of wide and rangy and bearlike. It was, like, I don't know, something about your face and those wire glasses. Like if I was going to choose an ideal professor? You'd be the model. Real bookish and safe, but with enough testosterone flowing through that body to make it interesting."

Transparently ingratiating, I thought at first. Not just in speech, but in body language. Sitting there in the weak light, braless in her thin T-shirt, breasts swinging and showing cleavage when she leaned toward me to laugh or lift her glass, nothing else on but running shorts, looking into my eyes with her sad, rich-girl face, not caring what I saw.

When strangers who happen to be female are so obviously demonstrative, I'm quick to retreat.

But, no, that's the way the girl was, apparently. She spoke spontaneously, no editing whatsoever. Had nothing to hide, so nothing to fear. Same with her appearance. The rainforest humidity had made her hair wild as a lion's, ribbed and curled, but she'd done nothing to try and contain it.

At one point, she said, "At the White House, some of the staff would go fucking nuts when I refused to wear makeup or a bra, any of that crap. Lipstick's the only thing I like because it comes in flavors. To this day, you mention my name to the basement drones and they'll roll their eyes. It got so I felt like I wasn't welcome anymore, so I stopped going. Then my dad got assigned to foreign service, and that's the last time we lived together. That was six years ago, so I was . . ." She had to think about it. "Sixteen or seventeen."

I asked, "Are you still close?"

She chuckled, toying with the cell phone. "We were never close. My father's one of the world's greatest men, but the only time he ever shows, like, real emotion or, you know, like, concern, it's when I do something that he thinks is outrageous. The men I choose to sleep with, some of the causes I support, it drives him crazy. Know why I think it is, Doc?"

I said to her, "The reason you choose to do outrageous things? As of now, I've got a pretty good guess, but you tell me."

"What I think it is? It's, like, I've spent so much of my life having to associate with fucking fakes and political con artists that I've become, like, militantly natural. I want to live in a mountain cabin and grow my own tomatoes and curl up with my dogs by the fire. I want to walk around naked and take showers in the rain. If I never see another man wearing hair spray and a vote-for-me smile, it'll be just fine with me." She looked at me through the light for a moment before she added, "Know what my new motto is? Give me a man who prefers blow jobs to blow dryers. Catchy, huh?"

Another warning flag—and unexpected, despite the gradual and increasing hand and eye contact between the two of us. She was a patter and a toucher. I was surprised that I'd misjudged her intent.

I stood and said, "I think I'll get another beer. You ready?"

Her eyes hadn't wavered from mine. "Yeah. I'm ready. That was my point. But somehow I just offended you."

"Nope. Just surprised. And thirsty."

I CAME BACK with a Diet Coke but didn't sit. I said to her, "I think it's late, and it's been a very tough day for both of us, so it's time you headed home. Grab your stuff, and I'll walk you back."

She reached and took my right wrist in her hand, stopping me, swinging hair out of her face, eyes tilted upward, looking out from beneath pale eyebrows, "Mind if we spend the next couple of minutes talking like adults?"

I said, "That's what we were doing until just a moment ago, Lindsey. I'm curious. I was enjoying the conversation. You've got a good brain; a quirky, funny sense of humor. Why'd you decide to make such an obvious pass? Is it some kind of test?"

She was still holding my wrist. "I'm too obvious? Maybe you don't like it when the woman is the aggressor. Some men don't. Is that the problem, Doc? Or maybe you're hung up on the age thing."

"Nope. The body ages a hell of a lot faster than the brain, so it's neither one. Problem is, we don't know each other and we don't have a relationship. So there's nothing to be aggressive about."

She nodded and said, "Ahh-h-h-h," releasing my hand. "The moral, prudish type. I don't meet many of you."

"Lindsey, my friend, suddenly, we're both doing a very bad job of reading one another. And we were getting along so well."

"So maybe you just don't find me attractive."

"Let's see, you're five-seven, five-eight, great body, great face. So what's not to find attractive? I'll tell you the problem if you want."

She sat back and gave a pouty sigh. "I don't have anything else to do. Go ahead."

"Okay, it's simple. When I meet a man or woman whose behavior crosses normal boundaries, it scares me a little. I start asking myself, *Why?* So what I do is stop, take a step back and analyze. Slightly more than six hours ago, a man in a ski mask took a shot at a woman who was standing right beside you. Could be he was taking a shot at you; who knows? Maybe you're still in shock. Maybe you feel like you owe me something. After what you went through this evening, there are so many valid reasons for you to be vulnerable, fragile and not yourself that I'm not going to risk imposing."

"Imposing on me. *Right.*"

"Sorry, but it's the truth. Not for your benefit, it's for mine. I've got rules and I try to follow them. I need to be selfish that way." I thought for a moment, and took a sip of Diet Coke before I added, "My conscience has more than its share of scars, Lindsey. It can't tolerate many more. I like you. You've made me smile a couple of times. But I'm not interested. Not now. Probably not ever. And do us both a favor—don't push it, please."

She sat in her chair, looking out through the screen, drink in hand. She turned her head toward me briefly, and in her little-girl voice said, "You're serious. You really are."

"Yeah, I'm afraid I am. I'm flattered. You've got all the great genetics, all the soft and interesting parts in the right places. I look at you sitting there, your hair, the way you look in that white shirt, and it's . . . well, let's just say that you have an impact. The way you look, I mean. I can feel it in my stomach."

"A Boy Scout," she said. "Jesus Christ."

"I'm no Boy Scout. Believe me. Anything but."

Once again she reached out and touched her fingers to the back of my hand. I'd already noticed that her nails were short, no polish. "It's not like I'm bragging, but I've never had any guy say no to me in my life. Ever."

"I don't doubt that for a moment."

"Want me to tell you what the attraction is? To you, I mean. And you've absolutely fucked it up, by the way. You have zero chance as of now."

"Sorry to hear that, but I'm still interested. Why?"

I could feel her fingernails moving over my skin, but then they stopped and clawed down, her brief punishment. "This afternoon, when we'd finished our run, Gale and me, out there on the dock, uh, I've had such an absolutely shitty year. The only times my father came to see me was twice back when I was in rehab, and that was because someone overheard me talking about committing suicide. Not that I was really thinking of it. I wasn't. It was just talk, you know?

"But these four weeks on the island, I really think it was starting to change me. Maybe the discipline. Running, lifting weights, working my ass off every day. Eating right, getting in shape, talking to my shrink on the phone every single night. I started to feel some pride in what I was doing. Some confidence, too. Things were starting to seem okay to be me. Like I'm not such a goofball fuckup after all."

She scratched her check absently, thinking about it, looking outward but staring inward, processing the experience. "For the first time since I was a little girl, the world was starting to seem like a pretty good place. A safe place. When Gale and I were standing there watching the sunset, that's exactly what was going through my mind. The world really *is* a cool place."

I said, "Then all of a sudden, you look up and see two men in ski masks, one of them carrying a weapon."

She nodded. "Exactly. The world didn't seem so safe anymore."

She went on. "What I felt was so weird. Like fear so strong it was almost . . . umm, like getting an electrical shock, but slower with the feel of the electricity moving through my spine. Or like someone'd squirted ether up my nose. I was frozen, couldn't move. You know those terrible nightmares where you try to run but can't? Same thing. I wanted to run but couldn't, wanted to scream but couldn't, and then the guy shoots at Gale and I felt my bladder go. Standing right there, I pissed my own pants. That really . . . really—" She stopped momentarily, her voice breaking, sighed heavily, looking away from me so I couldn't see her face. "It really did something to me. For the first time in my life, I felt like a piece of meat. Something that could be . . . I don't know, it was like those news videos you see after a flood. All the dead and dying animals. Like I could be killed and left to bloat in the sun. I was no longer the eccentric daughter of the great man. I was a female animal and about to die—and that's when . . . that's when . . ."

She stood and stepped to me, weeping softly now. Placed her hand on my shoulder as she said, "That's when I saw you, Doc. Looked and saw you charging like one of those football players on TV. You had this expression on your face, complete focus, and it was like I was looking down from way up high, totally in slow motion, and that's when I stopped being scared. I had urine dripping down my leg, but I knew everything was going to be okay. I don't have a clue why, but that's the way I felt. You looked a hell of a lot bigger and meaner than the guys with the masks, but it was more than that. Like I told you, I noticed you right away, your face, big and safe-looking, and I knew you were going to save us. I just knew it and I was right."

Her hand had moved to the back on my neck, massaging it, and I let her. In her small voice, she said, "So you want to know my motives? Real simple. I came here to thank you in the best way I know how. I wanted to take you to bed and do absolutely anything you want me to do, then put you to sleep with my body still on you. You saved my life, and I don't think I'll ever be the same again. Maybe you've got to experience your own death to realize how much you really do want to live. For all that, I figured I owed you a big favor. Figured that now it was your turn to feel safe and protected."

I stood slowly, feeling her fingers slide down my back to my hips and stop there. I took her by the shoulders, squeezed, leaned and kissed her on top of the head. She was still weeping, her body spasming softly, and she fell comfortably against my chest, my right hand patting her rhythmically between shoulder blades. I said, "A generous offer, lady, but a bad idea. You need to go home, get some sleep."

She buried her nose and face against me, then into me. I listened to a muffled question. "You sure? Last offer. They're flying me out tomorrow first thing. They haven't even told me where."

My fingers were still drumming on her back. "Sorry, yeah, I'm sure. I may kick myself in the morning, but I think it's the right thing to do."

"You know, they say that the way you're patting me right now? It reminds us of our mother's heartbeat back in the womb, so it comforts us when we're scared. If I promise to be good, and if I promise not to hurt your bad arm, you think we could lie down on the couch for maybe ten minutes? I could use some comforting. Something important happened to me today, and I'm not sure what. It's maybe the only way I'm going to be able to sleep tonight."

As I held her, I glanced at my watch: 1:45 A.M., nearly moonset over the Gulf. Two more days until the new moon. "What will the deputies do if they check your bed and you're gone."

"I left a note just in case, told them I went out for a walk. This'd be the last place they'd think of checking."

"Ten minutes and no more," I told here. "But the couch in there isn't very comfortable."

WHEN I AWOKE, the porch screen was a black scrim of drooping palms and stars, no moon. Lindsey was cupped against me, back to stomach, like a spoon, air whistling softly through her nose when she breathed.

Somehow, my left hand had slipped up under her T-shirt, my fingers spread to hold the warm weight of her left breast.

I told myself I should take my hand away, but I didn't.

Then I told myself it was alright not to remove my hand because my left arm was finally comfortable, no longer throbbing, and it was medically permissible not to move my hand as long as I held her in a friendly, nonsexual way.

I lie to myself so often and so successfully that I'm amazed that I even bother to continue to try to live up to my own flawed values.

I lifted the palm of my hand away from her skin, leaving only my fingertips to touch her softly, feeling heat and perspiration on the heavy underside of her breast. Then my thumb and middle finger found her nipple, first tracing the denser skin of the aureole, before rolling the nipple gently, feeling it react, the tip of it growing, becoming erect and slowly heated in my hand.

I felt Lindsey stir, then press her hips back into mine, rotating slowly and pushing, exploring me with her buttocks.

Thus I knew she was awake.

Heard the little-girl voice say, "Hey, buster. You're no carpenter, so what you doing with a hammer in your pocket?" She had a furry, sleepy laugh.

I removed my hand from under her shirt immediately, got up on my good elbow and said, "Sorry. I was being stupid there for a minute. Which means you need to get off this couch right now because—" She flopped over to face me and pressed her hand to my lips before I could finish. "You think too much, Doc. Know that? Shut off your brain for a little while. Put it on autopilot. Your body knows what it wants to do. Stop being such a nerdy pain in the ass."

Then she put her hand behind my head and pulled my face to hers, touching my lips with her tongue, moistening them, searching, as her free hand moved downward over chest and abdominal muscles. Her fingers found the elastic of my shorts, then they found me, moving to explore, her fingers spreading as wide as they could to hold me, her thumb moving in slow rotary massage.

"Do you like this?"

"Yes."

"I'm not hurting your arm?"

"My arm? I'm not thinking about my arm right now. No, you're not hurting my arm."

"What about this? You like this?"

"Oh yeah."

She stood suddenly in the gray light. I watched her step out of her shorts, then strip the T-shirt over her head. She was ivory-colored in the darkness, sculpted white and hard, skinny-hipped with ski-slope breasts and very long nipples. She shook her yellow hair free as she leaned to help me shimmy out of my shorts, then used her left hand to hold me erect and perpendicular as she mounted me, sliding slowly down onto me, wincing as her body stretched to fit itself.

She sighed, shuddered, eyes closed, her hair long and breasts hanging down as she began to lift and roll, her pubic bone moist and hard, seeking friction with mine. I heard her whisper, "The astronaut position. I like this."

"Huh? Astro-what?"

"You're the astronaut, laying back in your seat. You get to reach up and play with all the knobs and buttons you can find."

More than an hour later, in the master bedroom by now, the sheets soaked with sweat, when we both thought we'd done everything possible to one another and given everything twice over, the girl, whose feet were beside my head on the pillow, removed her mouth from me, poked her head up with prairie dog surprise and said, "Houston, this is Apollo. We've got liftoff *again*."

I HAVEN'T HAD much experience with the morning-after awkwardness of a one-night stand for the very simple reason that I rarely, rarely do one-night stands. Fortunately, though, there was very little awkwardness. Not between Lindsey and me, anyway.

I walked her home in the silver, predawn dusk amid tittering birds and the seawind rustling of morning palms. We hadn't gotten much sleep, but she was energized, full of fun. Seemed to be completely at ease. She kept her voice low, chatting about the modern ceremony we had to complete: exchanging phone numbers, cell phone numbers, e-mail addresses.

Guava Key's paths are illuminated by moon-globe lamps that create little islands of light along the paths. In the light of one, she allowed me to see her theatrical expression of shock when I told her I didn't have a cell phone. "My God! When you're shopping, or cruising the malls, how can you make calls?" and shook her own cell phone at me.

She had that unusual gift for satire and self-deprecation.

"Know something, Doc? Yesterday was a hell of a complicated day, but I feel better than I've felt in a long, long time. I'm not sure why. I'm glad we met, that much I can tell you. Not just because you saved our asses, either."

I told her, "Why do I have to keep reminding you? I didn't save anybody. That's your official response, okay?"

Her laughter was a whispered sound and private.

"Whatever you say, Ford. But I'm glad you did."

I was feeling much better myself. Our lovemaking had been unexpectedly comfortable; a mix of tenderness and passion that left us both panting, then laughing. Usually, when I do something that breaches my own code of behavior, I get a niggling case of the guilts. Not now, though. I felt energized and content. The gray, residual depression caused by my run-in with the kidnappers had been swept away.

I wrapped my arm around her, steering her down the dark path. For some reason, something she said came back; I remembered her telling me, *Maybe you've got to experience your own death to realize how much you want to live.*

Oddly, as if prompted by my own thought chemistry, Lindsey told me, "The reason I feel the way I do—it's a kinda fresh start feeling, like nothing I've experienced before. I really could have died yesterday, but I didn't, so this is like the beginning of my new life. Used to be, I always had this urge in me. Destructive, you know? It was like an itch, something I had to scratch or just go nuts. But I don't feel it now. That weird urge to piss people off and fuck up my life. Anger, I guess. Contempt for everything, but now it's gone. Like it was never there.

"Then being with you in bed, it was like, wow! Not because you were great—don't get me wrong, you were just fine—but because it was like my first time, only better. What I felt, all those sensations, I really appreciated them, you know? They meant something. It was *fun.*"

"I'm happy to play even a small role," I said wryly.

She gave me a slap on the butt. "You did more than just play a role, come on. In fact, you may be a big part of the reason I feel so good. It's more than knowing I coulda been killed. What it may be? It may be because I've had lots of lovers, and I've had a few really close guy friends. But I've never been with a guy who was both. I think that maybe, just maybe, you're going to be the first."

I thanked her, but was thinking, *Slow down, lady. Slow down.*

I GOT A couple hours' sleep before the phone beside my bed rang. I picked it up to hear Lindsey say, "Hey, Ford? They're making me leave already. Shit! We just figure out what parts go where, that they make a nice fit, and we've already got to say good-bye. I'd ask you to come along, but they won't even say where they're taking me. Bastards!"

She sounded disappointed but not surprised. Like that sort of thing had been a part of her life before. She told me the whole operation, chopper and all, had been arranged by her father, and would I mind meeting her at the helipad because the cops weren't going to let her out of their sight even for a few minutes.

While I was brushing my teeth, the phone rang again. It was Tomlinson. It must have been a good night for him, too, because there was renewed energy in his voice. "Marion, holy moley! that sister of yours is something. Has an absolutely fabulous spirit, man, lots of heavy mojo vibes. No sex; didn't even try. But she has a real godliness about her, plus she is built like a brick shit house! We got in the hot tub. She brought this little, tiny, tiny bikini, and we stayed up talking until five. Smoked a couple fatties, drank some wine—you know, really getting to know each other, exploring each other's heads. That woman is smart, she's funny, she's unspoiled—got what we Zen folks call 'the crazy wisdom.'"

I said, "Crazy, huh? Then at least the two of you have something in common. And Tomlinson? Please don't refer to her as my sister."

He hooted. "Lighten up, Doc! We need to get together so you can go over these papers Tucker left her. I've read through them a couple of times. Kind of interesting, really. Old Florida stuff, from back in the cowboy and rumrunner days. The feel of it I'm talking about. Hey, Doc, I don't remember—when the old man died, did he leave a will?"

I said, "No. Tucker died intestate. His ranch, most of it he'd already sold off to residents of a trailer park down in the Glades. Nice people— you met them a couple years back. They've really fixed it up from what I hear. The ranch house and the barn went to me because I was his only heir. Supposedly his only heir, anyway. I've never even gone down to look at the place. The trailer park people take care of maintenance. In return, I pay them a fee."

The tone Tomlinson used was as close as he can come to being businesslike. "Okay, then I think one of the letters Ransom received can serve as his actual will. If someone decides to get attorneys involved, I mean. It's a handwritten instrument, and it's kind of fun, really. What it amounts to is, Tucker left some money for you two, but you've got to find it first. He hid it because he was paranoid about this old enemy of his, an island dude named Benton, beating you to it. Sounds just like that wild old gunslinger, doesn't it?"

Oh yeah. Trying to manipulate people from the grave—that sounded just like Tuck.

I told him, "Trouble is, Tomlinson, I don't want anything to do with it. I think you know why. So do me a favor and tell Ransom that the money's all hers. Whatever it is he left. And I'll give her the house and barn down in Mango, too. You think we ought to take her word that she's Tuck's daughter? Or maybe I should ask her to do a DNA before I transfer the papers."

"If those eyes of hers aren't proof enough, the conversation I had with her last night was. Isn't it weird how people from the same family have similar vocal inflections, move and walk and even write like one or both

of their parents? She wrote her address for me—Cat Island in the Bahamas. Used Tucker's sloppy, curvy block print."

I didn't think there was anything weird or unexpected at all about genetics determining characteristics and behavior, but I said, "Oh yeah, the
similarities can be eerie."

"Believe me, *compadre,* she's Tucker Gatrell's daughter."

"Okay. Then she can have the house if she wants. I've got the deed in
the fireproof box in my lab. But I'm not going on any of Tucker's snipe
hunts. I still have that fish count to finish up"—I glanced at my left arm;
it was throbbing again, but not bad—"and I'm not in the best of shape."

"She's counting on you, Doc. The woman's got enough psych-up energy for ten people. The way she looks, the way she acts, can you believe
that she's got two kids? She was a middle-aged housewife, for God's sake,
before she kicked out her good-for-nothing husband and took her life
back under control. What I'm saying is, she's strong, man, very strong.
In other words, partner, I don't think she's going to take no for an answer.
And keep in mind, she really did come through when you needed her
yesterday. If you catch my drift."

I said, "You're not suggesting that she'd try to leverage me, are you?
Threaten to go to the cops and tell them the truth?"

Listened to Tomlinson say, "Probably not," but I was thinking: *Of
course she would. She's Tucker's daughter.*

THIRTY MINUTES LATER, standing, waiting on luggage to be stowed
aboard an orange, multipassenger Bell helicopter, I perceived an unmistakable chill from the two women deputies who'd stayed the night on
Guava Key and stood guard over the girl.

Well, they'd supposedly stood guard.

One of them was Deputy Walker, who hadn't exactly been my advo-
cate during the interrogation the night before. I'd avoided her questions,

true, and we certainly hadn't struck up even a conversational friendship, but that didn't explain her behavior or the behavior of her fellow officer.

As Lindsey and I approached the helipad, they seemed to make a point of ignoring me, and when I asked, "Is Waldman still around?" Walker shrugged and turned away.

I'm not a stickler for mindless social ceremony, but neither do I allow rude behavior to go unquestioned.

I moved close enough so she couldn't ignore me. "Maybe you didn't hear my question. Is Doug Waldman still on the island?"

There was something in her expression and her tone akin to contempt. She braced both hands on the gunbelt around her waist and said, "Why? You had your chance to cooperate last night."

I took a couple of slow breaths before I said, "So maybe you got a lumpy bed and couldn't sleep. Or the husband and you had a fight over the phone. What I'll do is give it one more try. Is Waldman around? I want to ask him something about the investigation."

The deputy told me, "We can handle it, believe me. We don't need your assistance," and walked away.

I received the same strange, inexplicable animus from Gale Storm, who touched me on the shoulder and, when I turned around, said, "Thanks for the help yesterday. I appreciate it." But her tone said she wasn't thankful and her quick, limp handshake told me she couldn't wait to get away.

"No need to thank me," I replied. "From what I saw, you handled yourself pretty well in a situation most people can't even imagine. You've got nothing to be ashamed about."

That seemed to infuriate her. "Ashamed? Why the hell would I be ashamed?"

I was tempted to say because she froze and lost her weapon, but instead I said, "Exactly the point I was making. No reason at all." My shrug tried to tell her, *How would I know anyway?*

But she wouldn't drop it. She was wearing navy blue shorts, gray Izod shirt and a golf visor, plus the same little gray belly bag. She'd either retrieved her weapon from the dock or she'd found a backup. She removed the visor, wiping her forehead, as she said, "Look, before I went into the private sector, I graduated from the FBI academy at Quantico and three or four other schools you wouldn't even know about. If there's one thing I don't need it's some fisherman trying to insinuate that I somehow blew an assignment. So please don't."

Was everyone on the island in a foul mood? Or maybe Storm had received some kind of royal ass-chewing from Lindsey's father. No way of knowing, but this time I wasn't going to let it pass. I said, "One thing I can say for you, Ms. Storm, is you'd be a great train engineer." When she raised her eyebrows quizzically, I added, "You're always on time and on schedule. Your afternoon runs? I could set my watch by them. Plus you never varied your route. Not once. Just like you were on tracks. Very dependable. And predictable. I guess I wasn't the only one who noticed, huh?" then I looked into her face until she turned away.

Then Lindsey was beside me. She grabbed my hand and began to steer me away toward a hedge of hibiscus that separated the grassy landing area from the bay. She said to me, "I don't care how shy you are, how proper, I'm not leaving without a good-bye kiss."

I let her pull me along, saying, "What the hell's wrong with these people? Yesterday I was a hero, today I'm poison. Even your bodyguard—what did I do to make her mad?"

"Gale?" Her expression said it was unimportant, why waste the energy? "Don't worry about her. Gale's always pissed off about something. It might be that she's jealous."

"She's jealous because of me?" I smiled. "I don't think so. She hasn't shown the slightest interest. But I'm flattered you'd think that."

"Not *you,* you big dope. She's interested in *me.* She's been wanting to come on to me for, like, the last month, but couldn't work up the nerve.

Too professional, probably." She turned to face me, laughing. "That's hilarious! Gale interested in you? She's gay. Man, are you out of it sometimes."

"Yeah, I don't doubt that, but the question's the same: Why would she be jealous? Unless you told her about last night. Which you didn't . . . did you?"

"I don't tell her anything. She always, like, goes straight to Dad." She paused for a moment. "Now that you mention it, though, um-huh, she is acting weirder than usual."

Lindsey was still thinking about it. She stood close enough to speak confidentially. "Or it could be because of dad. Yeah, that might be it. My father spoke to her this morning on the phone and had her close to tears, he was, like, yelling at her so much. I was in the next room and could hear him. That's how pissed off he was.

"Same with the two women cops. With them, what happened was, my dad did a conference call this morning. Them and their boss at the Sheriff's Department, Dad's point being that they hadn't done what they were paid to do, which, when you think about it, they didn't. . . ." She let the sentence trail as we were approached the bushes. She turned to me again, made herself as tall as she could be on tippy-toes. Held my right hand to her chest as she kissed me gently, then harder. "I like you, Ford. We need to get together soon. Real soon."

"It's something to think about."

She kissed me again. "No, it's not. You think way too much. That's your problem. Like the shoe commercial: Just do it."

Smiling, I used my good hand to hold her away momentarily. "Okay, sure, you've got a point, so we'll get together. But you know what I'm thinking about right now?"

In a torch singer's smoky voice, she answered, "If it's the same thing I'm thinking of, we've only got about five minutes, so drop your shorts and let's get started," then laughed at her own parody.

"No, what I'm wondering is how'd your dad know the two women cops screwed up? They were assigned to guard you, but you snuck out. How could he know that? That's my point."

She made a face and shrugged. "I've never figured out how my dad knows all the things he knows. I quit worrying about it long ago. He's always watching me, always finding out stuff."

I experienced a slow, uncomfortable dawning. "You mean he knows and the deputies know where you went last night, where you stayed? That we were together?"

"Maybe not but it's possible. They usually keep track of me every damn second of the day. The bodyguard I had before Gale, she was like that, then Gale, and always because of Dad. They bug my room, bug my phones, tail me when I'm out. Because of the drug thing, only that's not going to be a problem anymore. I'm serious, Doc, I feel like I've changed."

"Phone?" I said, thinking of the cell phone she'd carried with her. I was aware of a satellite surveillance system, controlled by the National Security Agency, known as Echelon. An NSA operator could sit at his little screen in Fort Meade, Maryland, tune in on a cell phone conversation on the other side of the earth. Could also use the conversation as an effective direction finder; laser in on the precise location, know what street they were on in Singapore or Perth, know if the person using the phone was turning right or left. It was that exact.

Lindsey said, "I don't know how he finds out all the stuff he does, but don't worry about it. Plus, who cares? The only thing I really care about right now?" She gave me a slowly lingering kiss, then a slap on the butt. "All I care about is you calling those numbers I gave you, letting me know when we can get together again. You promised, so don't forget, damn it."

I was nodding, still considering the probabilities. "Yeah, it would have to be the cell phone. You wouldn't even need to add a mini-transmitter into something like that. Just dial in on the phone's preprogrammed number. Or . . . yeah, maybe they would have to install one more little chip."

"Ford! You *are* going to call me. Leave a message at the numbers I wrote down, let me know where you are. I'll call you here on the island, just as soon as I get to wherever in the hell it is they're taking me. But if they won't let me call, don't think it's because I don't want to." She had gray-green eyes with flecks of gold on the iris. Looking at me, her expression became affectionate, her eyes intense. "I like you, Ford. It's nice not to feel that itch. That destructive itch. I want to stay in touch."

I became certain that someone had eavesdropped via the girl's phone a few minutes after I watched the chopper bank away, swinging northward, gaining speed, when I was summoned to the island guests' services desk.

Someone had called my room three times; left the same name, the same number.

The first two message slips were blank, but the third read, "Hal Harrington wants to discuss recent Apollo mission. Call immediately."

7

RANSOM EBANKS ASKED ME, "Why would our daddy lie about somethin' like that? About you and me being brother and sister? You look at the papers I've been trying to show you, the ones back on the island, then you understand."

In Tomlinson's bungalow, in a small black backpack, she had a manila envelope filled with papers. Letters mostly, some legal documents and photos. I'd glanced at them long enough to notice that there was a drawing of some kind, too.

I said, "Tucker would lie because—" I almost said Tucker Gatrell lied because he was a fraud and a pathological liar, but caught myself.

Tomlinson was right. The genetics were unmistakable. The eyes, the vocal tones, even the way she turned her head and paused before speaking: all characteristics that reminded me of Tuck. Not that it was surprising my bawdy old uncle had sired a daughter down in the islands. He'd spent a lot of time in Cuba, the Bahamas and Central America, drinking and carousing. I reminded myself that daughters tend to be sensitive and protective about their fathers no matter who they are. It wasn't Ransom's fault that she was Tucker's daughter. No need to be cruel, so I started over.

"Tucker would lie because he was . . . let's just describe him as an unusual person. He was theatrical. Prone to exaggeration, almost like an actor. That's one way to describe him—the man would have been a decent actor. Which is what he was doing when he told you I was your brother. Exaggerating. Acting like it was true. His little way of having fun. Isn't that right, Tomlinson? Tomlinson knew the guy. Oh, he was wild about Tomlinson."

I was being facetious. Tucker's common greeting when he saw Tomlinson approach was, "It'll be a couple hundred more years before you hippie bastards should be allowed to mate with human beings. But that doesn't mean I won't let you buy me a beer."

"Wild about me," Tomlinson echoed. "Describes our relationship perfectly."

I said, "My mother was Tuck's younger sister. Much younger. She and my father were killed in an accident a long time ago. But you and I are fairly close to the same age. So see? It's impossible. If we are related, Ransom, you'd be my cousin."

She turned away then paused, that familiar cowboy actor pose. Toyed with the big gold ring on her right hand, thoughtful, then shook her head.

Why was it so difficult for her to accept?

WE WERE ABOARD my twenty-four-foot trawl boat, dragging nets and culling the catch so I could finish my fish survey. Tomlinson and the woman had agreed to help because I was temporarily one-handed and couldn't operate the trammels alone.

It was a winter-blue morning with a light chop out of the south. The breeze was balmy, scented with jasmine and mown grass. We were less than a hundred meters off Guava Key, both outriggers down, nets in the water. They created a brown swale that, if seen from above, would be an expanding vortex contrail as I steered us in wide circles and the rollers pressed themselves along the bottom.

I hadn't called Harrington yet. For one thing, I dreaded it. Talk to a man about a one-night stand with his daughter? For another, my work took precedence—or so I told myself.

My trawl boat is a specialized vessel, built to drag shallow water, and ideal for collecting on the flats around Sanibel Island and the Gulf littoral. It is made of cedar planking and painted gray on gray, with a gray wheelhouse.

No, it is not built for style, nor is it maintained for looks.

I'd bought her used in Chokoloskee a couple years ago and single-handedly chugged up the inland waterway past Mango and Naples and Fort Myers Beach, and put her to work. It'd paid for itself in less than a year. When a university or lab sends me a big order for a species of plant or animal that I can't collect by hand at low tide, or with a cast net, I fire up the net boat and rumble out into the bay.

"Rumble" is the appropriate word. It is powered by an old standard six-cylinder engine. The name brand is Pleasure Craft but it is actually made by Ford. Plugs and points, and no computer gizmos of any kind. In the little pilot house is a wheel, a throttle and the minimum of gauges— water pressure, oil pressure and temperature. Above the pilot house, folded like the wings of a pterodactyl, is a complicated rigging of wires and steel booms to raise and lower drag nets, port and starboard. On the stern, a plywood culling table runs across the transom, with a twelve-volt light system so I can work at night. There are two huge live wells and a storage hatch on the port side built the size of a bunk, so I've got a place to doze if I get sleepy or just choose to lay out late, looking at the stars.

The trawler is slow, dependable and about as graceful and easy to maneuver as a floating slab of cement.

But it's functional—all I care about—and easy to use.

Tomlinson had been out with me enough to know how to set the nets while I steered. Ransom stood next to me in the wheelhouse, talking, not wanting to believe that I was telling her the truth.

She illustrated a component of the human quandary: When you have wholeheartedly accepted one vision of reality, it is very difficult to have that reality challenged, then replaced by another.

She was still shaking her head as if perplexed. "Whenever he mentioned you, I could hear the daddy sound in his voice, him telling me about the brother I had back in Florida. Like the sun rose and set on you. Tell me about how you so smart and big and strong, jes' about the best at everything you did. From what I saw out there on the dock yesterday, the way you handle yourself with them bad men, sweet Jesus, he tol' me the truth, he did. Get yourself shot and you act like, hey, it no big deal. Like you knew exactly what to do, zoomin' around out there on that fast boat."

That was surprising to hear. Tucker was prone to criticize and denigrate, particularly when he was drunk—which he usually was.

I said, "No matter what he told you, what he said, it doesn't change the simple fact that I am not your brother."

"Uh-huh, that what you keep sayin' only I don't understand the reason. I saw my daddy six, maybe seven times in my life, but I know he cared about me, and I know he cared about you. What so hard to believe?" She thought for a moment, making a show of it. Swung her braids for effect, red beads rattling, then touched an index finger to her face. "Maybe it because of my color. Yeah, maybe that the thing. Daddy, he used to tell me, 'I got me a big ol' 'Merican boy and a sweet little Island girl. Some white folk, they don't like that. That the reason? You fault daddy for lovin' a black woman, my brother?"

I groaned. She was as maddening as Tucker had once been, and seemed to have the potential to be as transparently manipulative. I said, "Oh, *please*. Tomlinson, would you explain it to her?"

He was standing, watching the trail of the nets, alert for unexpected snags. Hook an unseen engine block or sunken tree, and the entire superstructure could tumble down if you didn't back the throttle.

He made a noncommittal wave with his hands—don't put me in the middle of *this*. "Doc, all I'm going to say is, you two have exactly the same eyes. You and her both, the same color, just like Tuck's. You didn't realize that? Hah! No, I can *tell* you didn't. It's true. Take a look in the mirror, *compadres*. But a racist? Nope, Ransom, the label doesn't fit. Racism requires lots and lots of dumb emotion, plus a dose of stupidity. Doc has a first-rate intellect, and the average rock has more emotional sensitivity. Your brother just doesn't have the tools."

"You're so helpful," I said. "Thanks a lot."

Tomlinson nodded toward her. "Maybe you haven't noticed, but this happens to be one of the rare, spectacular ones. Living proof that a controversial assertion of mine is accurate: The most beautiful women in the world are always over thirty-five. *Always.* Why? Because, like great art, beauty requires fabric and depth. When it comes to beautiful women, Doc, you know my motto: Ingratiate yourself any way you can, then do whatever it takes to win them over." He touched his fingers to his lips. "You are stunning, Ms. Ebanks."

That earned him a dazzling smile. She said, "Thank you, Mr. Thomas. You a very nice person and speak lots of pretty words," before she returned her attention to me. "Know what you should do? When we get back to land, you read Daddy's letter like I asked, then you understand. The one sent me last month by that attorney man, the one Daddy Gatrell used. Judge Lemar Flowers, he the one. When I stopped at the marina, your place on Sanibel, them friends of yours knowed right away who Judge Flowers was. He famous around that island. Took one look at the letter, the handsome man behind the counter, the one who got the stutter, he told me where to find you."

She'd taken a Greyhound bus north, then sat around on the mainland, awaiting permission to board the private ferry to Guava Key. After several hours without a response, she'd borrowed a canoe and paddled the five miles alone.

Her determination, at least, was impressive. And Tomlinson was right: Ransom was physically spectacular, no doubt. She had a sprinter's long legs and dense muscularity, but her body was unmistakably, sensationally feminine. This morning, she wore the same yellow canvas shorts, but she'd traded in her tie-dye for one of Tomlinson's black, sleeveless Harley Davidson T-shirts. The black shirt lengthened her and lightened her skin, so that she looked as if she was made of very, very firm and sculpted pale chocolate. But I'd already identified too many of Tuck's mannerisms and genetics to see her now separately, as her own attractive entity.

"I'm very glad I came to find you, my brother. The thing that surprises me, though, is you be so very stubborn."

I sighed, held my hand up—we needed to stop talking while I did my work. Behind us, I could see that the catch bags at the end of the otter trawls were already engorged, which meant that she and Tomlinson had to help.

I said, "Time to bring in the nets."

I shut down the engine, and used my right hand to crank in one otter trawl while Tomlinson cranked in the other. The nets were each eighteen feet long; woven funnels with heavy wooden doors at the mouth to keep the nets open, galvanized chain on the bottom to keep them down, plus rolling sea grass guards so they wouldn't tear up the grassbeds. The rig was designed to shepherd everything in the boat's path to the rear of the net, an expandable ball that was kept closed by a simple knot.

As I cranked, I listened to the steel cable creak with the weight of resistance, and watched the pod at the end of the net trail in and grow larger. Once I had the release-sack winched into the air, I reached up and, by hand, swung the boom over the boat. It hung there like a giant balloon, pouring seawater onto the deck, a hundred pounds or more of croaking, clicking, squeaking, popping sea life.

Anyone who says that the underwater world is silent has never been underwater.

As many times as I've hauled in trawl nets, I've yet to lose the feeling of anticipation and expectation before dumping that first strike from new bottom. You never know what might be inside.

I told Tomlinson, "Leave your net in the water. We don't want to kill anything. We'll cull mine, then yours."

I pulled the string, and out gushed a wriggling, scampering mass of living protein. There were hundreds of fish, dozens of species: grunts, pinfish, flukes, cowfish, file fish, immature sea trout, croakers, gray snapper, lane snapper, thread herrings, immature female groupers, skipjacks, box fish and southern puffers, the last two making rapid-fire inhalations as they inflated their bodies like miniature footballs. There were blue crabs and calico crabs, arrow crabs and hermit crabs. There were shrimp and sea horses, sea urchins, hydroids and stingrays all buried among grass and gumbo that smelled of iodine and fresh sea bottom, which is one of the most delicate and compelling odors I know.

Ransom commented on how much we'd hauled in—"Man, I didn't know that many kinds of things lived down there!"—then surprised me by adding, "What we got right there, them sea urchins, man, they something sweet to eat."

I was rigging a tarp to protect our catch from the sun. Along the transom, made of PVC, was a raw water sprinkler to keep everything wet and cool. I said, "Help yourself, but you need to eat while you help me chart. We want to get everything back in the water as fast as we can."

I'd already familiarized her with the four clipboards I had hanging in the wheelhouse. On each was a paper on which were listed many dozens of species by their common names. As Tomlinson and I called out animals and released them, she was to make a mark in the appropriate box.

I watched her grab a salmon-colored spiny urchin, crack the bottom with a knife and scoop out the golden eggs. "Ummm, man, we shoulda brought a lime with us. Lime and sea urchin, that a very nice thing. A cool beer to drink, that make it better."

I said, "If you want, we'll put a few in the live well. You can eat them later."

"Can we keep a couple of them horse conchs, too?" she asked. "I slice it up and pound it tender, then fry it real hot. It more peppery tastin' than the queen conchs, but it something good, man. Down on my island, the Vitch people—the voodoo people, I'm talkin' about. The vitch people, they say a man got trouble with his short leg, all he got to do is eat some fresh horse conch raw. That make him stand up strong. Like a stallion horse, you understand?"

Tomlinson said, "Short leg?"

Ransom had a busty, bawdy laugh. "The little god 'tween your legs I'm discussin'."

Tomlinson stood motionless in thought for a moment, then I watched him bend and lift two mahogany-colored horse conchs out of the pile, turn and place them elbow deep in the wells of aerated seawater where I store animals I need to transport alive.

He dried his hands on his paisley surfer shorts, saying, "Sounds delicious."

SPEAKING RAPIDLY TO Ransom as I dropped fish overboard, I said, "That makes five . . . six . . . seven French grunts . . . yeah, that's all of them. So now we'll start on file fish and sea horses. There might be a couple of pipe fish in there, too. That should be . . . Clipboard C. Ready?"

She was looking at the chart. "No, man, no, you wrong, that make nine French grunts. You miscounted, plus there's one right there by Mr. Thomas' knee. I can see the tail."

Tomlinson and I were down on the deck, using our hands to cull through the thigh-high piles of grass and clumps of tunicates, searching for more life. My left arm was feeling pretty good. The more I used it, the better it felt.

"She's right," said Tomlinson as he held up the candy-colored fish. He slid it back into the water and watched it swim away. "Nine French grunts it is."

I told her, "Good job, way to keep track. Tell us when you're ready for the sea horses. That'll leave the tunicates and the soft sponges, then we're finished for the day."

Not finished with the survey—my contract called for three seasonal replicates, all to be done with cast net and otter trawls like the two I was using. I refuse to use three-panneled trammel nets anymore because they are too deadly, too destructive and there's too much chance of them being lost, sinking and killing fish for years afterward.

Over the years, I've refined my own survey technique: Count the number of fish and the number of species from several specific habitats around an island—I'd already documented 237 different species around Guava Key. Calculate respective totals. Then use aerial photos to measure the various acres of habitat in the adjoining water space, and multiply acreage by the number and species of animals found in similar areas.

Much of it is subjective judgment. You have to make considerations for mechanical biases: The size of net mesh, the speed of the boat. For instance, my slow trawler with its large meshed net is never going to catch a mature tarpon nor a microscopic tarpon larva—but that doesn't mean they don't both live in the waters around Guava Key. They certainly do.

Once I consider all the data I've collected and match figures from other regions, it's not difficult to make an objective summary about the health of a body of water and its sea bottom.

From everything I'd seen over the last week, the bays around Guava Key were still healthy enough to be productive, but there were some danger signs. The water seemed unusually murky for February—it had a green turbidity, not the tannin-amber color normally associated with mangrove back country.

Curious, I'd checked the local telephone book. There were more than a hundred public and private golf courses listed in the county that adjoined the bay. My Florida atlas was more specific: Of those one hundred courses, more than a dozen of them were boundaried by brackish water rivers and creeks that flowed directly into the bay.

I'd thought the numbers must have been a misprint until I called several fellow biologists around the state. It turned out that most coastal counties in Florida have at least that many courses, and some of the bigger, tourism-driven counties have far more.

Nothing against golf. I've played enough to appreciate the artistry of a well-designed course, and I wish I had the coordination to be good at the game. I also agree that golf courses are correctly considered green space preserve areas by state planners—but the problem is, what does it take to *keep* them green?

In Florida it takes fertilizer. Tons and tons of inorganic nitrogen and phosphorus. Much of that fertilizer is not absorbed by fairway grasses. It washes off into water hazards and the water hazards drain into creeks, the creeks into rivers, and rivers drain into bays. In all brackish and saltwater live, suspended, myriad species of microscopic plant life, or phytoplankton. Microscopic plants react to fertilizer in the same way Bermuda grass does—they turn a bright, rich green.

That's great for a golf course, but terrible for a bay. When water turns murky, the depth that sunlight can penetrate is reduced. If sunlight does not reach the sea bottom, sea grasses cannot grow. Sea grass is the perfect habitat for the shrimp and crabs on which game fish such as sea trout, redfish and snook depend. Filtering species such as tunicates and sponges also use sea grass as a necessary anchor.

If murky water kills the sea meadows, then shrimp, crabs and fish are eliminated as well, along with the very filtering animals required to make the bay clear and healthy again.

It is a hugely destructive intrusion that needs to be taken seriously, yet state bureaucrats spend far more time and money thwarting private homeowners from building docks (which provide excellent underwater habitat) and trying to implement such pointless boondoggles as manatee idle zones. The idle zones can't be enforced and, worse, will have negligible effect on manatee fatalities because of the simple fact that the draft of a vessel is often more problematic than a vessel's speed.

There are many fine, intelligent state-employed bureaucrats and biologists working in Florida, but the mandates they receive, and the objectives with which they are charged have, historically, been tragically shortsighted or misdirected.

The woman said, "We get back, I'm gonna fry up some of that conch, what you men think? Catch me a nice snapper, I'll make that, too, with johnnycakes and some good fish gravy." Ransom was talking while she studied her clipboards. Apparently, she was adding up numbers without having to be told. I liked that.

Tomlinson was still shoveling his hands through mounds of grass. "How 'bout you let us buy you lunch at the Tarpon Lodge? That old restaurant on the hill."

She smiled, still calculating. "Oh man, I like the sound 'a that, but I don't have no clothes for a place so fancy. I got me a pair of jeans, a lil' ol' black skirt, but nothing good enough for rich man's place."

Tomlinson said, "Oh, baloney—excuse my language. See what I'm wearing?" He touched the sleeve of his tattered, hibiscus-pink Hawaiian shirt before plunging his hands back into the pile. "We're on an *island*. This is considered formal wear. Pair of flipflops and cutoffs, you can go anywhere but a funeral, which they don't have out here anyway. They don't have funerals because the rules don't allow members to die while on club property. So when we get ashore . . . awwww-OUCH!"

Tomlinson's scream was oddly high-pitched, so feminine that I would have laughed had he not tumbled hard over onto his side, holding his right hand as if he'd been stabbed.

The woman and I were both immediately beside him, helping him up. He was breathing hard; seemed a little dazed and was still holding his wrist. "I just got the shit shocked out of me! Like there's a fucking 220-volt line in there!" He was staring at the last pile of grass and gumbo, but wary of it, keeping his distance.

I looked at his hand. No puncture wounds, no blood, but it was streaked with red.

"Damn, that *hurt!*"

I was on my knees again. I had the little wooden-handled dip net, searching through the grass. At first, I thought he'd grabbed a saltwater catfish or stingray—unassertive animals with painful defensive systems. A stingray's spine has serrated edges and two groves that run the length of it, venomous glands in each. A thin layer of skin called the integumentary sheath covers the spine, and a complicated proteinous toxin is released when that sheath ruptures upon penetration. I stepped on a small stingray once, and it took all my resolve not to sit down and bawl like a baby.

Saltwater catfish are almost as bad. Their dorsal and lateral fins are serrated like double-edged saws, and the slimy venom secreted from axillary glands in the sheaths of their spines is an extremely painful protein-based poison. Because there was no puncture mark on Tomlinson's hand, though, I figured he'd grabbed some kind of jellyfish—the stinging nematocysts of a Portuguese man-o'-war, in sufficient number, are potent enough to hospitalize a grown man.

I saw that it was neither. Lying on the deck, beneath the gumbo, was a banjo-shaped animal that was a little less than two feet long. It had the round body of a ray, but the truncated tail of a fish. Its milky gray body was covered with peculiar triangles, circles and semicircles that were suggestive of military camouflage or some weird alien, computer coding. An unusual and highly adapted animal.

"What the hell is that thing?"

I touched it gently with the tip of the wooden handle. The fish moved ever so slightly, its black eyes indifferent, gill clefts moving rhythmically, secure in its own defense system.

I said, "It's an electric ray. We don't get a lot of them around here, but when we dragged along that sand beach? That's probably where he was." I used the handle to lift it slightly, then amended. "Sorry, where *she* was. The way you tell is, they're kind of like a shark. The males have elongated claspers."

We were all three crouched over it now. I turned the misting water spray on the ray to keep it cool, and still it did not react.

Tomlinson's eyes were wide, very excited. "Its skin was really smooth when I first touched it. Then it was like he flipped the power switch. Zap! Serious voltage that went straight to my brain, then arched down to my toes. Awesome! Like a bright red light flashed on behind my eyes and I could see a wiring schematic for my entire nervous system. Far out, man!" He paused; was looking at the ray, thinking about it. "Hey . . . what happened was, it hurt like hell, yeah, but it also gave me a kind of weird high. It wasn't just painful, it was . . . *interesting.* In a chemical-electric way, I'm talking about. A really far-out sort of rush."

Ransom said, "Lordy, Lordy, some pair, you two white men. My brother, he have a bullet cut his arm, it don't even bother him. Mr. Thomas get a shock, he like the feeling."

"No, no, what you don't understand is, I am a scientist, Ransom, a very dedicated karma explorer. Pain and pleasure—they're not that far removed. Or maybe I . . . what it could be is, I've been desensitized by some very high voltage." He lifted his hair and pointed to the tiny lightning bolt scar. "Mother nature zapped me once. I also spent a couple weeks doing a little table dance which some Freud-geeks used to describe as electroshock therapy. Didn't have much choice about either one, but this, yeah, it wasn't too bad."

I said, "This is what they call a lesser electric ray. It's got chemical tissues"—I pointed without touching—"there and *there* on its body which can generate something like forty volts. Maybe not even that. But it's got a relative in the Atlantic—I've found a couple in the Gulf, too—an animal called 'torpedo ray,' maybe because of its shape, but probably because it packs such a jolt. A torpedo ray can knock you on your butt. It'll produce a lot more than a hundred volts."

Before I could consider stopping him, Tomlinson reached out and touched the ray again, then looked at me, still holding his fingers to the fish, breathing fast and shallow. I watched his expression transition gradually from pain to exhilaration and then studious delight as he began to speak as giving dictation. "Not bad . . . not bad . . . whoa, got a little surge there! Yes, a very natural high. Yep, beginning to move through the cerebral cortex down into limbic Happy Valley. There . . . there . . . yes! My plumbing's now on-line! Doesn't really hurt, man, once you . . ." His eyes widened. "Oooh-lah-lah! Man, this is like a neurological cleansing!" He yanked his hand away and sat back heavily. "Phwew!"

He was suddenly concerned. "I didn't hurt the fish, did I? Like drain it or something?"

I began to lift the ray by the tail—it couldn't shock from the tail. "No, it's fine. They spend all day cruising the bottom, shocking sand worms, then sucking them out whole. Long pink worms almost exclusively, I can't remember the Latin name. Shocking things is what they do."

"You're going to release it? Doc, why don't we keep it? You study the fish, then I'll drop by every now and again and I'll let the fish do little experiments on me. When I was touching it? I could feel every part of my body come to life. *Every* part of my body—if you catch my drift."

I lowered the electric ray into the water, skated it back and forth a few times to make certain it was healthy, then watched it flap away with birdlike grace. "He's always joking around, Ransom."

He threw his hands up—the ray was gone. "Man, I wasn't joking!"

The woman was kicking dead turtle grass and goop toward the stern, cleaning up to go. Same as with calculating the clipboards—she knew what to do without having to be told. I was already starting to like her despite the fact I didn't know her and had been convinced I didn't want to know her.

"You two coconut-headed men, it gonna be fun going with you and getting daddy's money."

She'd asked and asked, but I'd yet to give her an answer.

"We'll talk about it," I said. "I'll look at the things Tucker sent you, then come up with a solution that's acceptable. Something to make you happy."

"Uh-huh, that good, man. What I want right now, though, is to get myself cleaned up. Gonna bathe myself, put on my little black skirt and let you buy me that expensive lunch just to celebrate."

I told her, okay, but first I had a phone call to make.

8

CALLING FROM THE portable phone in the master bedroom of my cottage, I listened to the fourth ring, hoping no one would answer. I felt like some guilt-ridden adolescent schoolboy who'd been caught misbehaving and who dreaded a confrontation with the principal.

I was on the verge of hanging up, when a man's voice said without hesitating, "Okay, so we finally get a chance to talk, Dr. Ford. And if I sound a little agitated, it's because I've been waiting all morning for your call. I asked them to make it clear the message was urgent. The woman at the desk didn't tell you that? Do the lady a favor and *say* she told you it was urgent. I'm on the island's corporate board."

Caller ID is one of the minor irritants of this digital society.

He sounded middle-aged, no older. He had a very deep voice, lots of testosterone, just a hint of southern accent but an articulate airiness that told me this was a man who was used to giving orders, not taking them, a man accustomed to sitting back and listening, an intellectual counterpuncher. Oddly, his bullying threat—*I could have the lady fired*—seemed forced, overly theatrical. Something about it didn't ring true.

When I didn't respond immediately, he said, "This *is* Doctor Marion Ford, isn't it?"

I answered, "There—that's maybe not a polite way to begin a phone conversation, but it's at least acceptable. Yes, my name is Ford. Thanks for asking. And you're Hal Harrington."

"Of course!"

"I wasn't sure. Last night an FBI agent told me that you're a diplomat. I guess I expected you to be diplomatic."

Which caused him to stumble, interrupted his timing, and he became momentarily formal. "You're right. You're exactly right. Especially when the first point of business should be to thank you for saving my daughter yesterday. I mean it. Thank you very much, Dr. Ford."

"No need."

"As far as I'm concerned, there is. The people who tried to abduct her are of the very slimiest variety. Lowlife opportunists. Small-time drug people who hate my stand on a particular issue, and're looking to make a big jump in the cartel community. No one else would have tried anything so risky. They'd love to have a major bargaining chip, and I don't doubt for a moment that they'd have killed Lindsey if they'd succeeded. Bargaining wouldn't have saved her. I'm very thankful you were there and decided to get involved."

"Read the reports, Mr. Harrington. I didn't save your daughter. She saved herself."

"Nonsense. You mentioned my occupation? In my line of work, an important job skill is . . . well, let's put it this way. I deal with liars and equivocators on a daily basis. If I couldn't get a little edge here and there by recognizing what's true and what isn't, I wouldn't be very effective."

I told him, "Okay, we're both glad your daughter didn't get hurt. Let's leave it at that. But there's nothing urgent about calling to say thanks. So something else is on your mind."

"Yes, very true. You're an insightful man. There *is* another subject I'd like to discuss. Actually, what I'd like to do is share some information, then ask a favor. You'll find it interesting; probably find it informative. The subject has to do with your past, Dr. Ford. And your future."

With the phone wedged between shoulder and ear, I moved out onto the veranda. Through the palms, the swimming pool was a Caribbean jade. There were four or five women in lounge chairs, baking themselves black. Overhead, circling in a pale winter sky, was a pair of osprey hawks, screaming their ascending whistling call as if outraged by the intrusion of these dozing women. I watched the osprey as I said, "My future? I thought the reason you called would have something to do with your daughter."

Harrington's tone became both amused and accusatory. "Oh, it does, it does. This has a lot to do with her—and I find it odd, by the way, that you should refer to her as 'my daughter' instead of 'Lindsey.' Maybe one of those Freudian things, huh? You two had yourselves quite a time last night. A girl nearly young enough to be your own daughter."

"Mr. Harrington, if you surprise loved ones by spying on them, shouldn't you *expect* to be the one who's surprised? The way you spend your nights, your private time, how'd you like her to know every detail?"

"I do whatever it takes to keep track of her, and I don't apologize a damn minute for that! I stay informed. I've got to, her recovery requires it. Don't try to turn it around, Ford. You two sitting around chatting away like adults, then on the couch. I've got the entire transcript on the desk in front of me. Playing astronauts, for Christ's sake! Every word you two said, at least every word before you hauled her upstairs to the bedroom."

I'm not always conversational, but I am seldom at a complete loss for words. I now was.

"Are you still there, Doctor Ford?"

I finally found voice. "Yes. I'm listening."

"Know what I find most offensive? The way you manipulated her. That pious act of yours: 'Lindsey, Go home because it's the right thing to do.' Here, let me read a sentence or two back—"

I said quickly, "Nope, we're not going to do that. I choose not to listen to a review of our private conversations."

"Oh, I don't blame you for not wanting to hear it. The girl's a drug addict, Doctor Ford. She's emotionally unstable. She's spoiled, immature and, let's face it, Lindsey's not extremely bright either. Two generations ago, back in Houston, my grandfather would've shot you down like a dog for doing what you did."

A father ridiculing his daughter—how do you react to something like that? True, I hadn't been on my best behavior with Lindsey. True, it was understandable the man was furious. If Harrington wanted to vent, okay. I'd stand there and take it. But I was quickly becoming irritated by the man's cruel characterizations of the girl.

"Doctor Ford, tell me something. Is it your normal course of habit to take advantage of young women who've been recently traumatized? The girl was nearly killed, for Christ's sake! Then you hustle her off to bed and treat her like some damn floozy from a Caracas whorehouse. Unfortunately, I've got to admit, and it pains me to say it, Lindsey tends to *act* like a whore whenever she gets the chance—"

Which did it. All I was going to listen to. I raised my voice, interrupting him and said, "Harrington? Has anyone ever told you that you're an ass? Because you are. You use a word like that to describe your own daughter? In my opinion, Lindsey's the one with the brains in the family. And the maturity. You've got my number. Call back when you're calmer. Or acquire a little class."

And I hung up.

I WAITED FOR all of twenty seconds before the phone rang. I was still on the porch, looking at the pool. I noticed Tomlinson and Ransom approaching. They'd showered, were wearing fresh clothes, Ransom in a short black skirt and green blouse, Tomlinson in a tank top and a green sarong wrapped around his waist.

The happy couple in matching colors, immersed in conversation.

Sharing a joint, too, from the way it looked. Tomlinson holding fingers to his lips, head tilted as if in analysis, then exhaling slow smoke—all distinctive—then handing the cigarette to Ransom, who was using her hands to talk, right at home with the process.

When the phone rang, I punched the button to hear Harrington say, "Okay, so you passed the first test. Congratulations. I'm relieved. You should be relieved, too."

I said, "Pardon me?"

"I apologize for doing it, but I needed to know. It was important. I had to find out how you really feel about Lindsey. Do you respect who she is?—a very gifted and complicated person. I had to find out before going any farther. A simple test of character. Would you defend her? Would you tolerate someone speaking badly of her—even her own father?"

I said, "You've got to be kidding."

"Not at all. In the last eighteen hours, I've learned a great deal about you. But I have no idea what kind of man you are. I had to make a quick assessment, and there was no better way—"

I interrupted him again. "Harrington, I stopped taking tests years ago. Most of us do when we become adults. So call me when you want to have a mature conversation—"

"Don't hang up on me again, damn it!"

I wanted to. I came close to putting the phone down and walking away. But there was something in the man's tone, an edge of worry and desperation that made me pause. So, instead, I took a couple of breaths, controlled my anger, and said, "No more tricks, no more devices. If you want to talk, we'll talk. But no more manipulating."

He seemed relieved. "Okay, okay. You have my word. But you have to understand my thinking. Why I need to be careful. I don't apologize for wanting to find out if you have genuine respect for my daughter. You could have used her very easily. Many men would have jumped at the chance. She was indebted to you. As much as I love her, I also know that she doesn't always think before she acts. Plus there are times when she'll do absolutely anything to make me angry, because she knows—"

I finished the sentence for him. "Because she knows it's the only way to get your full attention. We discussed that—but then, you already know. You have the tape, don't you?"

"I've known it for a while—and regret that it's the truth. I mean, it *was* the truth. But not now. In the past, it wasn't easy for her to get my full attention. I admit it. You're exactly right. I also admit I haven't been a very good father. I know that, too. Years ago, when Lindsey's mother died, something went out of me. Some emotional component—but you don't need to hear about that."

I said, "You don't want to tell me about how your little girl let you down? What was it? She either reminded you too much of your late wife, or maybe she didn't come close enough."

He gave a snort of self deprecation. "Pew! Cocktail party psychology, but you're a little too close for comfort. There's a Mayan maxim that goes 'Only through a stranger's eyes is our vision perfect.' Something like that, so maybe it really is that obvious to outsiders. From the time Lindsey was three, she was the mirror image of Linda—that was my wife's name. I didn't realize the truth. Or wouldn't admit it. It hurt too much to be around my daughter, and we tend to avoid the things that hurt us, don't we? I screwed up. I was inattentive, and maybe figured out the problem way too late. But I adore my daughter, Ford. Please do not question that. Don't even insinuate it because I won't tolerate the suggestion."

Harrington's tone was returning to normal. The forceful administrator, in charge once more.

"There's a reason why I'm telling you this."

"I'm sure there is, Mr. Harrington."

"Hal. Or just Harrington."

"Okay."

"I want you to help me. But I don't want to discuss it on the phone. Not these phones, anyway. It's personal and confidential. Do you understand my meaning?"

What he meant was that the phones might be tapped. With the FBI investigating an attempted kidnapping there was that possibility.

I said, "If you're saying you want to meet in person, I don't understand the point. I don't see how I can possibly help you."

"I worded it badly. I want you to help Lindsey."

"Lindsey? I'm more than willing to help Lindsey in any way I can. But how?"

"You can start by granting me a small favor. Take the island ferry to the mainland. It leaves every half hour. Walk or drive to any pay phone you want and call me. I'll expect to hear from you by . . . say, two P.M. Is that clear?"

I've met a handful of men in my life who had sufficient presence and confidence that when they issued an order, it was as if they were speaking in the past tense, as if the order had already been carried out. Harrington had that quality. On the other hand, I've taken enough orders in my life to know what's required of me and what isn't.

"I've got friends expecting me to join them for lunch. Sorry, Hal. You tell me a little more. Give a few more details so I know where all this is headed. Now. On this phone or not at all."

I listened to several seconds of silence before Harrington said, "It's a small thing to ask, Ford. Believe me, it's much to your advantage if you do what I ask."

"Oh?"

"Or do it for Lindsey. I love that little girl more than anything in the world. From some of the things she told you last night, it sounds like you maybe made a difference in her life. I approve of that, Ford. I wholeheartedly approve. Maybe you can continue to make a difference. She wants to change her behavior, I'm sure of it. I think you can help her, and I *know* I can help you, too. That's what I need to discuss. How we can help each other. But privately."

When I still demanded to hear more, his voice acquired an impatient edge as he said, "Let's try another approach, then. Back when I was working in the White House, one of my tasks was to cross-reference old security files. Really top secret stuff. The thing that struck me as funny was, in the most electronically advanced nation on earth, I had to dig through a couple of boxes of carbon paper that were found locked away in the hidden safe of a former President's personal secretary."

Harrington said the name of the President, then continued, "The secretary died about the time the President left office, and then the President died. In all the moving around, the safe was somehow overlooked. Three years ago, they were remodeling, ripped up the floors, and there it was. One of those floor safes that fits in flush. Because reviewing old documents for security designations was part of my job, the safe was brought to me. Inside were some very interesting documents, Ford. No . . . that's an understatement. Explosive documents—that's a word the media would use if they found out. Which they haven't. But they could, if I choose to release the information. Care to hear more?"

No, I didn't want to hear more. But I had to listen. Had Harrington really stumbled onto something? I said, "I don't see what any of this has to do with me, but it's interesting. Sure, I'm listening."

"I thought you would. What I found in the safe were manila folders and envelopes sealed with thumbprinted wax—old-time security measures for stuff that was never, ever supposed to be opened. The President's secretary, you may remember, was in her nineties when she died. She'd worked in the White House forever, way before World War II, and she still used the old ways to protect herself and her Presidents. In this case, the President she was protecting was the one I mentioned. He wasn't the only one who needed protecting, though. There were other men involved, all of them highly trained and absolutely anonymous—until I opened those files."

I felt an empty, rolling nausea in my stomach, and my voice sounded hollow when I said, "That means nothing to me."

Harrington had become increasingly confident. "Of course it doesn't. Just interesting reading, that's all. So make up your mind. You really want me to continue discussing it on this phone line?"

I looked at my watch. Tomlinson and Ransom would be sitting in the Tarpon Inn, waiting. They'd have to eat without me.

I told him, "Give me half an hour. I'll call you from a pay phone."

INSTEAD OF TAKING the ferry across to the mainland, I fired up my little yellow Maverick flats boat and flew across Charlotte Harbor at sixty miles per hour, blasting a geysering rooster tail as I trimmed the Yamaha outboard, crossing ankle-deep bars and flats, translating my irritation into speed.

I'd call the man, but from a place he wouldn't expect. It was way too easy for someone with the right connections to bug or place surveillance on every pay phone within several miles of the ferry landing.

So, instead, I ran across the bay to the little island village of Boca Grande, tied up at Mark Futch's seaplane dock and walked the quiet tree-bordered streets downtown. I found a pay phone just across the street from the Temptation Restaurant and watched through the window as Annie served beers to a bar full of fishing guides.

I straightened my glasses and dialed the phone. Harrington answered immediately. He seemed much less formal, no longer on guard. "You on the mainland, Ford?"

"It's what you told me to do, isn't it?"

He chuckled. "Once again, bullshit. I'd be disappointed if you could be bullied that easily. But you *are* at a pay phone. That's my guess. You're too smart to call from anyplace else."

"I'm flattered."

"Not that I don't believe you, but with all the technology these days, who knows? I've got a scrambler here on my office line that converts our voices from analogue to digitized, then back again. But know what I think? If I can have it electronically converted one way, any hotshot with the right computer program can have it electronically changed the other way. Which is why I maintain faith in the basics. Are you at a wall phone or in a booth?"

"It's bolted onto the side of a building with chrome shielding."

"Try to peek into the conduit that comes up from the ground. There should be a wire in there. An insulated wire, probably beige-colored."

I looked and said, "A standard payphone, yes. A crème-colored wire comes up into the back." I knew why he was asking, but made no comment. The man seemed to know his business.

"Plain old-fashioned telephone wire, something that's easy to understand and monitor. Let me check my meter." There was a pause. "Okay, my line's secure here, and no trace of resistance on yours, no drop in voltage according to this little computer of mine, which means we can say anything we want about anybody we want and it goes no farther. Just between you and me."

I replied, "Guess I'll have to take your word for that."

I was still watching the fishing guides through the window of the Temptation, but I was also maintaining a peripheral eye on the street, too. Watching for slow-moving cars. Watching for men moving on the tops of buildings.

If I'd been set up, I wanted to see it coming before it was too late to react.

There wasn't much for me to see. It was a nice, balmy winter day with the smell of frangipani drifting above warm asphalt. A few blocks away, beyond the beach at the end of the street, was open ocean. A quiet afternoon. Boca Grande doesn't get a lot of traffic. It's way off the regular tourist track. A rich little tropical outpost with the atmosphere of a Vermont village.

Harrington started by saying, "If you're the man I think you are, you have an impressive record, Doctor Ford. Or should I call you Commander Ford? If they gave out medals to people like you, I suspect there'd be a couple of important ones on your uniform. If they allowed people like you to have uniforms."

Was he fishing, or did he really have proof? I said, "Then I'm not the man you think I am. What I don't understand is, you said something about helping Lindsey. But you're not talking about Lindsey. So what's the point?"

"The point? The point is an operation called Sky Hook. Ever hear of it?"

The words jolted me. I hadn't heard them spoken in years. There was now no doubt that Harrington had found some hard-copy files. Absolutely no one outside our small team was supposed to know that name.

I felt a deflating sense of the inevitable. Thought to myself, *It's finally happened,* as I said, "I have no idea what you mean."

"Then let me tell you all about it. Really fascinating stuff. An international spy ring, deep cover reconnaissance, espionage, sabotage, political terrorism—and at least three successful assassinations. You probably don't know anything about those, either."

He was wrong about the number of assassinations. There'd been at least seven, probably more.

I said, "It sounds like one of those movies. Something they dream up in Hollywood."

"Oh, it gets much, much better. I'll give you all the details if you want—maybe jog your memory about a few things. Later, when I'm done, you can decide if you're willing to do a couple of favors for me. And Lindsey, of course. She's my main concern."

"Is this supposed to sound like extortion? Because it does."

"No, what it's supposed to sound like is diplomacy. You said yourself, that's what I do. In the real world, Doctor Ford, this is the way diplomacy works."

Harrington told me a few things I already knew, but much I didn't know or even suspect. He said that Sky Hook was one of many operations successfully carried out by an illegal team of intelligence operatives. The organization was the brainchild of a President who figured out how to take the law into his own hands without really breaking the law. Harrington seemed to admire that. Said that sooner or later, they all try it. But he was one of the few smart enough to get away with it, plus he had staff members loyal enough to protect him afterward.

"In his memoirs, even on his deathbed, the President never gave away the secret. To give up the secret was to sentence certain people to death. He knew that. Clearly, his Chief of Staff knew it, too, because he's the man who administrated the operation. Same deal. Took the secret to his own deathbed. Just like the old secretary. As far as I know, except for the file here on my desk, there is absolutely no other written record of this illegal organization."

Standing in the pale February light, feeling the breeze freshening from off the Gulf, I thought about the papers locked away in my safety deposit box on Sanibel. Locked away in the bank just down Periwinkle Way from the Timbers Restaurant and Bailey's General Store. Harrington was wrong. Other written records did exist. For my own protection and security, I'd kept several original documents and copies of others. Mostly orders and directives I'd received. They were never signed, of course. Ever.

I said, "I'm still listening."

"It was in the second year of the President's first term. He believed, and not without cause, that certain subversive groups inside and outside the country had become so powerful that there was no quick and legal way to deal with them. He thought the Republic was in real danger— and let's face it, he was probably right. The President had also developed a mistrust that bordered on hatred for the media. Way too many leaks from some of the highest branches of government. So he did something very bold and very smart but absolutely illegal.

"The President came up with an idea. Why not create his very own team of intelligence operatives? Provide those operatives with the finest training this nation had to offer, but fund them through the private sector. That way, there would be no money trail. There was no legal obligation for him or any of his staff to make the existence of his team a matter of public record. This still doesn't sound familiar?"

Actually, it *was* news to me. I'd never known for certain how the organization had gotten started. I said, "This is the first I've heard any of it."

"Funny thing is, Doctor Ford, my diplomat's instincts say you're telling the truth—for once. Which maybe isn't so surprising. The way they set it up was, they created a classic series of isolated, working cells, all on a strictly need-to-know basis. From all I've read in those files, I'm convinced that many if not most of the men involved never really did know who they were working for."

The phone to my ear, still watching the fishing guides through the window, laughing, joking about something. I thought, *You've got that right.*

Listened to Harrington say, "The President's closest friend and adviser was one of the wealthiest men on earth. They had the same political views, the same fears. *Presto,* instant financing. The President had earned the respect and devotion of the chairman of the Joint Chiefs of Staff. That gave him immediate, unquestioned and clandestine access to all military records. So those three men—all dead now—decided to go ahead with the plan on an experimental basis: Create a super-select special warfare, intelligence-gathering unit that operated at the President's pleasure and answered only to his administrators. Here—you want me to read the unit's covenant statement? One sentence, it defines what the team was designed to do and the methods it could use."

I said, "It's an interesting story so far. Go ahead."

"Okay, this is from an unsigned White House directive: 'This civilian organization shall be established to serve and protect the best interests of the United States of America through the use of any and all means the group's members deem beneficial to the well-being of the nation.' How's that for telling the legislative and judicial branches to go to hell? 'Any and all means necessary.' Are you sure you've never heard any of this?"

Actually, there'd been a period in my life, while working in Asia, that I'd kept a coded version of that mission statement in my pocket day and night; carried it around like a good luck charm, or a declaration of absolution. "Nope, Harrington. But, like I said, it's a good story."

"Hal."

"Okay, Hal."

Harrington told me how the President and his men had set it up and made it work. Listening to him was like listening to an unexpected biographer describe unknown components that designed my life. The men who created the organization had a name for us: The Negotiators. They later changed it to Negotiating and Systems Analysis Group as a cover, but they continued to refer to us as The Negotiators in private correspondence.

They took it very, very slowly. They decided that a top priority for members of their new organization would be intelligence. Brain power was an imperative. So what they did was, they reviewed results from the Armed Services Vocational Aptitude Tests. Then they coupled those results with IQ scores from high school or college. Because they had a service pool of several million men to choose from, they came up with a lot of good, bright prospects.

Without much trouble, though, they narrowed it down to a couple hundred candidates. The people they went after didn't even know they were being considered. That's when the real culling process began, according to Harrington. Men with wives were immediately eliminated. Same with men who had large or interactive families. They wanted men with few family ties. Men who could disappear for many months, or maybe forever, and not have pissed-off mothers or sisters asking embarrassing questions.

He said, "Athletic aptitude was another major consideration. The training the candidates had to go through was extremely physical. So was psychological stability. The sensitive, artistic types were dropped right away. There's a note in this file from one of the government shrinks, a kind of protest letter. Want me to read it to you?"

I'd never heard any of this before. I'd always wondered why they'd selected me and how they'd selected me. I would have loved to come right out and ask to read through everything he'd found, but I couldn't risk that. Instead, I told him, "I'll listen to a little more, but it's getting old."

"Okay, how about I read just a couple of key sentences? The shrink wrote, 'I feel I should point out that the candidate template you describe is a man without conscience, or at least one who has the ability to repress emotions that many believe are key to a healthy, well-adjusted human being. It's my feeling that such individuals, depending on their training, could become extremely dangerous.'"

Harrington said, "See there? That's the kind of man they wanted." He told me that, in the same letter, the psychiatrist used the phrase 'cold-blooded analysts' to describe an ideal candidate, which caused the diplomat to chuckle. "Somehow, that doesn't sound like the man who wrestled around with his conscience before taking my daughter to bed. Maybe you've matured, Commander Ford. Or softened up a little."

He was enjoying this too much. I wondered why. As for me, I was tired of the implicit drama that he seemed to be prolonging. I was tired of waiting, tired of the low-grade anxiety I felt while he continued to avoid the obvious: Had he or had he not found my name in those files?

It was time to put an end to it. I said, "Why are telling me this? Are you suggesting that I was somehow a part of some kind of illegal army? Or whatever the hell you would call something like that?"

He laughed. "Haven't you been listening? Of course I am! Are you denying it?"

"You found my name in one of those files? Because, if you did find my name, there must be—"

"Relax, Ford. That's what you've been worried about the whole time. I'm sorry. I was being cruel. The obvious question: Are you mentioned by name? I think you'll be relieved. Nope, you are not mentioned. There are no names in the file. The administrators did a superb job of protecting their people. Your code number's in there and your code name. Lots of other bits of telltale information that helped me pick you out. But no, the name Marion W. Ford is not included, which is why I've never had to pass the files along to my superiors. If we don't know who you and your teammates are, there's no one to prosecute. And you *could* be prosecuted—there's no statue of limitations on murder, as I'm sure you know."

I felt a sense of relief so great that, when I noticed one of the Sanibel guides, Alex Payne, waving at me through the Temptation's window, I grinned mightily and waved back. I said to Harrington, "Names or no names, I don't know why you're bothering me with all this cloak and dagger business. Aren't we supposed to be discussing Lindsey?"

"You'd be a pretty fair poker player, Ford. You just did a good job of hiding the new little bounce that's in your voice. And relief. You're one of them, alright. The people in your team have become a very private and personal hobby of mine. Very impressive. They cross-trained you with every branch of Special Operations—the SEALs, Green Berets, Marine Recon, passing you off as members of Studies and Observations or the real NSA, but you belong to neither the military nor the Department of Defense. Ingenious, because who's going to know? You guys certainly aren't going to talk—there were fewer than, what? Two dozen of you?"

I had no idea how many of us there were. I'd met only the six men I trained with. But I said, "How do you come up with crazy ideas like this, Hal? Comic books? Late-night television?"

"About you? One thing that tipped me off is your profession, a marine biologist. But wait—the way I *first* made the connection was, I get a report that the guy who saved my daughter apparently has all kinds of surprising combat skills, but he refuses to take credit for what he did. I thought, *That's weird. He won't admit he's a hero?*

"Then they tell me that even the FBI computers can't find any information on you. Even weirder is, they tell me you clearly hate the idea of media attention. No interest at all in having your fifteen minutes of fame or doing the talk show circuit or signing a big book deal. These days, people will do anything to make money or get attention, but not you. It made no sense. So a little light went on in my head. Could you be one of The Negotiators? That's where the marine biologist part comes in.

"What I did was, I went through all the bios. The FBI told me a local marine biologist had saved my girl, and I knew there was a biologist in The Negotiator files somewhere. I'd read them all, but I went back through them again last night. There you were. Assignments all over the world. Central America, Africa, Asia. Always under the guise of research. Extended stays and very deep cover."

I said, "I didn't realize I was so well-traveled," giving it a facetious touch.

"Oh yes. All of you covered a lot of ground but traveled in very different circles. You're part of an eclectic bunch for a reason—a doctorate and a real profession are great cover, and the President wanted his little group to drop real deep roots. There're a couple of CPAs, a couple of attorneys, one journalist, three physicians, several computer experts, a politician, even an actor. Plus you, the marine biologist. You can go anywhere in the world to study fish, mix with the scientific community, do your real intelligence work on the sly, then come home. That's how I made the connection, Ford. That's how I knew you're one of them. Something else you should be aware of?"

"I can't imagine."

"In your file, I also read about a mission that was assigned to you several years back. Something your anonymous superior called a 'Blue Light' mission. As in the last thing a person sees before he dies is a blue light, correct? It wasn't your first, but"—He began to chuckle—"I find it ironic that the target is now, apparently, a friend of yours. He was with you during your interview with the FBI. I found it shocking, I have to admit, but amusing, too. Sighurdhr Tomlinson—did I pronounce his name correctly?"

I said, "You seem to be threatening me with events I know nothing about."

"Really? I don't need your name to prove it's you in that file. There are all kinds of ways. What I haven't told you yet is that I've discovered the identity of another one of your teammates. He's become a very rich and powerful man. He'd be a real headline-grabber. It's quite a fun hobby, your little group. Prove one of you exists, it's an oddity. Prove there are two of you, the Attorney General's Office might decide they've got a case. I'd hate to have to make those files public, then have to give them all the other information I've collected."

I said, "Is this more of what you call diplomacy?"

"No. This is the way I ask favors."

"Let me guess. The favor has something to do with you being an obsessive, overly protective father."

He chuckled. "And revenge, too. Don't forget revenge."

It didn't take Harrington long to detail what he wanted me to do and exactly how he expected me to do it.

He wanted to use me as bait, plain and simple. He wanted to use me to lure in the men who'd attacked his daughter. He couldn't be certain they'd come after me, but there was a chance, and a chance was all he wanted. When I asked him, "Why not let law enforcement handle it?" he said, "Oh, I plan to. You think I'm suggesting vigilante justice?" He laughed. "That's more your department, isn't it? No, I just want to speed up the procedure, that's all. Find the bastards and put them behind bars now."

Why didn't I believe him?

He went on. "I'm not certain who targeted Lindsey, but I've got a pretty good idea. If it's the guy I think it is, he's beyond dangerous. He's a sociopath. Which is why I want to nail him as quick as I can."

I said, "Whoever planned Lindsey's kidnapping was no idiot. They did their homework; it was a very professional job."

"I didn't say he was stupid, I said he was a sociopath. I think it's a guy by the name of Edgar Cordero. Edgar, in my estimation, is one of the most ruthless men in Colombia. You want an example? A few years ago, one of Edgar's young lieutenants began to deal marijuana on the side. Not in any big-time way. Just to make a little extra cash and probably with his sights set on going into business for himself one day down the road. Edgar found out and went berserk. Literally.

"The young lieutenant returned one afternoon to find that his wife and daughter had been beaten to death with a baseball bat. Edgar did it all by himself. Went calling, found the two of them alone and went to work. It was an aluminum bat and he left it there. His little warning to every other man who works for him. Since then, he hasn't had any problems with his people selling product behind his back."

I said, "His enemies, when someone crosses him, he goes after their children. That's what you're telling me."

"Uh-huh, which is why I think it's Cordero. Like his personal signature. Something else—I mentioned that I think he's a sociopath? Listen to this. Edgar also has a fondness for cutting off the ears of adversaries. Before he kills them. They say he keeps them on a string behind the bar at his ranch up in the mountains. The ears, I mean. He shows them off to friends . . . or to people he wants to intimidate."

"I can see why you don't want a guy like that after Lindsey."

He said, "If it is Cordero, I'll know soon."

We discussed details for a while longer before I asked him if he had any kind of timetable in mind. He said, "My hunch is, the next couple of days, I don't think you have anything to worry about. They won't be ready yet. Today's Thursday? By Sunday, though, you better be on your toes. Sometime next week for sure. If they decide you're worth the effort."

I had a feeling Harrington would do his best to get them to think that I was. As I stood there listening, looking at the clear winter sky, looking at the guides drinking beer inside the Temptation, I felt a constricting sense of the inevitable that was nearly overwhelming. I had no options. As much as I despised what he was asking me to do, I had no choice. It was as if I had stepped onto a trapdoor and plummeted right back into the world I thought I'd left far, far in my past.

He had me, and he knew it. I couldn't refuse, which made me furious. But I could negotiate. At least, I could try to negotiate.

When he'd finished, I said to him, "I'll help—but only because I care about Lindsey. And I want a favor from you in return."

After I'd told him what the favor was, he said, "I figured it was something like that." His voice had a little smile to it when he added, "Sure. No problem."

9

RANSOM SAID TO ME, "You don't want me as your sister, okay. But here's what I don't get, man. Why don't you want to be richer? That's what I really don't understand. Ev'body loves money. And Daddy left us a nice chunk of it. Just out there waitin' on us to go find. So why you bein' so stubborn, man?"

A bunch of money. *Right.*

In his letter to Ransom, to be delivered only after his own death and the death of at least one of his many enemies, Tuck had written: "Follow my directions, and you and your big brother will find more than six thousand dollars cash greenbacks, which I got from the recent sale of fifty head of prime Brangus beef cattle. Along with the money, there's some old-timey letters and pictures I collected on the trail. You may get a hoot out of the stuff if, being an uneducated island girl, any American ever takes the time to learn you to read."

My sexist, condescending uncle. The letter was in his familiar block script; lots of phonetic spellings: *Fallow my directions & you and yore big brother* . . . Tucker implying that someone else was too dumb to learn to read and write.

The man never recognized nor admitted his own ironic view of the world.

He'd also written: "I'd leave the cash money to you the regular way, keeping it in a bank, but I don't trust no damn bank, plus there's some local talk of a white man and a big Indian robbing the Miami loan shark that stole money from them first. Being Italian and not trustful, this foreigner kept a list of serial numbers from every hundred-dollar bill he left out open in the till like bait to test his runners and pimps. Which is why it's a good thing I got your money selling prime beef and hid it away so's the wop couldn't prove it from that paper full of serial numbers."

Because I was making every effort not to speak badly of her father, I didn't tell her that the white man was obviously Tuck and the big Indian was Joseph Egret, a genuinely decent man who was my uncle's best friend and partner for many decades despite Tucker's constant criticism and racial insults. Why Joseph tolerated the old fool, I never understood. I suspected they stayed together out of habit, like an old married couple, and because they'd come to rely on one another during long and rugged lives spent mostly just outside the law.

Money, though, I could talk about. I tried to make her understand that her inheritance wasn't really that valuable—not easy, because she came from a section of the Bahamas where the average annual income was less than what an average American makes in two weeks.

Not an unusual disproportion in poor regions around the world.

I'd pointed it out before, and now I reminded her again, "Even if he did leave you six thousand dollars, which I doubt, it's not that much money. Not in the States, it isn't. Not most places in the world. If you had fifty times that much, you couldn't call yourself rich. Think about it. You come all the way to Florida from the islands, invest all the time and expense, you're not going to end up with much profit. Which is why I want you to have what money there is. All of it. Take everything you find, plus I'm going to give you what's left of Tuck's ranch. You arrange for an attorney to do the work; I'll sign the papers. All I ask in return is leave me out of it. Go without me. Take Tomlinson. The guy's brilliant when he's not falling down stoned. If anyone can figure out Tucker's directions, it's Tomlinson."

Ransom already trusted Tomlinson, I could tell. Not surprising. I'd seen more than one crippled bird or malnourished stray dog thread its way through a dockside crowd to nudge attention from Tomlinson's hand. Same with people. He attracted the shy, the damaged and the frightened ones. They were drawn to him like a lantern attracts moths, as if he provided a lighted safe haven. Abused women have haunted eyes, like a small creature peering out from a hole, and mannerisms that are nervous, self-conscious. Many times I'd watched Tomlinson work his magic on them. The soothing voice and kind words. Mostly, though, it was his touch. He would wrap their hand in his, or hug them, and you could almost see the fear and pain being drained from their bodies. You could watch the darkness pass from their eyes.

Not that Ransom was a damaged woman. No. She was strong-willed, smart, transparently manipulative and had a gift for turning arguments around to emphasize her opponent's guilt, which she then tried to use as leverage.

Now, for instance, she made a guttural noise of irritation, jammed her fists on her hips and said, "You're startin' to piss me off, my brother. My friend Mr. Thomas not here to speak for himself and you callin' him a drunk like he some bum you find in Nassau town, eating outta the garbage pails at the Straw Market. Then you call Daddy a liar, sayin' he never left us no money. If Daddy such a liar, how come I got this?"

She reached into her pocket and pulled out a worn gold coin about the size of a fifty-cent piece. Held it in the light so that I was staring at an image of some long-gone Spanish king struck deeply into the metal. On the coin's smooth field were the words FERDINANDUS DG HISP REX and the date 1751. Apparently the king's name from that period was Ferdinand.

Struck on the coin's back was a complicated shield and the words NOMINA MAGNA SEQUOR. My Latin is imperfect. Something about a name . . . a charter and . . . Sequor? I didn't have a guess.

It wasn't the first time she'd used a doubloon as proof of Tuck's veracity. Yesterday, after dragging the nets, and after my conversation with Harrington, she'd sat me down in the kitchen of Tomlinson's bungalow, and dropped four gold coins on the table—a theatrical effect that Tucker would have appreciated. One of the coins was smaller than the others, but all had a surprising weight and density to them. They were cool to the touch.

"In the papers the attorney man sent, our daddy told me where to find these nice things. They right where he say I find 'em. On my island, Cat Island, they hidden 'neath the stone cross in a monastery that were built by a crazy ol' hermit, Father Jerome. It sits up there alone on the mountainside, and Daddy Gatrell had to climb that mountain, then stuck them away. All four of 'em in a leather bag. You got any idea how much these baubles worth? Two of 'ems yours, but I sell my half, I could buy me one of them satellite TVs if I wanted. Or air conditioning for my little house on the island. Man in Nassau offered me three hundred dollars each for 'em. What I'm tellin' you is, he left more money out there. All we got to do is go get it."

Then she'd slid Tucker's letter in front of me, both sides of an old sheet of legal notepad covered with his handwriting.

I read the letter. Looked though the folder, at all the old photos, and I read the papers in there, too.

There was a photo of a much younger Tucker Gatrell holding a caramel-colored child on his lap, a stunning black woman at his side—Ransom as a little girl, and her mother.

There was also a photo of Tucker in his jeans and Justin beaverskin cowboy hat standing with me. I remembered exactly when it was taken, the uneasiness of him being there. It was a few minutes before the final match of the high school state wrestling championships, my junior year. I was wearing my singlet, the weight class sewn on the hip—189— white on green.

Looking past my shoulder at the photo, Ransom had said, "My, my, you still got the shoulders and that skinny lil' butt. But them glasses you wearin', the black rims, they make you look like a hooty owl with muscles."

She was surprised that I wasn't interested in the photo or Tuck's letter. Then she seemed stupefied when I refused to accept two of the four coins. She'd yelled, "Man, you don't want to help me? Then I don't understand why the hell I lied to help you!" and stomped off.

That night, I had dinner with her and Tomlinson at the Tarpon Lodge, but she'd recovered her composure. Didn't mention the subject once. Spent the evening holding court in the bar, telling funny stories, flirting with the waiters. Wearing that black skirt with her long legs sticking out and a white blouse that illustrated well why she didn't need a bra. Then Leo sat down at the piano bar while Ransom took turns dancing with every man in the room until jealous wives began to intervene and lead their husbands home.

Now it was Friday and we were in my trawl boat, skiff in tow, puttering home to Dinkin's Bay. Tomlinson had paddled the rental canoe back to the mainland at first light, then loaded his backpack onto his forty-two-foot Morgan *No Más,* along with Nimba Dimbokro and her five big suitcases for a farewell cruise to Sanibel before he called a cab to take her to the airport the next morning.

Our stay on Guava Key, we'd both decided, was over. For Tomlinson, it was because he wanted to help Ransom go find her inheritance.

For me, it was because of what I had been forced to promise Harrington.

When I said to Tomlinson, "Is Nimba mad because she has to leave a day early?" he shook his head, disconsolate. "It's gonna take me five hours to beat my way to the marina, and she says she's going to oil herself up naked and give me one last try. Then she's sleeping aboard, and I know damn well she's gonna try again. Ransom staying over last night brought out a competitive streak in Nimba that her Zen instruction didn't touch. The pressure, man, it's really starting to take its toll."

Meaning Ransom had to ride with me.

RANSOM SAID, "Know what the feeling is I get? From reading Daddy's letter over and over, I get the feeling he may have stolen that money, which is why he had to hide it. Him and someone else, the big Indian he mentions. The doubloons back on Cat Island? It took me awhile to admit it to myself, but same thing. Daddy stole that gold from a very mean man there, and had to hide it away in the monastery 'cause he couldn't get off the island with it."

For some reason, I found that hilarious, and had to fight back the laughter as I replied, "Tucker Gatrell a thief? Well . . . I guess it's something we have to consider . . . yes, as upsetting as it may be to you. That Tucker would send you off to find stolen money . . . now that you mention it, uh-huh, we have to admit it's a possibility."

Stealing money, stealing horses, pigs, chickens, small planes and the lyrics from country-western songs—there wasn't much that Tucker hadn't stolen at some stage in his life. I didn't share that with Ransom, but I was thinking: *Finally, she's catching on.*

We'd crossed Charlotte Harbor and left the Intracoastal markers off Bokeelia on Pine Island and cut in behind Patricio Island, running back country. Running doesn't seem like an accurate word to describe a rattling, rumbling twelve knots, but at least we were moving steadily over the bottom. It was one of those low-pressure-system lulls we sometimes get in winter. The air had a summer density but the sky was Rocky

Mountain blue. On the far curvature of earth and sea were borders of cirrus clouds. The clouds were a fibrous silver: crystalline illustrations of wind sheer, adrift, like sails.

We'd picked a good day for passage. In a chop, my flat-bottomed trawler pounds miserably. In a squall, it's borderline dangerous. Today, though, the bay had a gelatin texture, lifting and rising with the slow respiration of distant oceans and faraway storms. The air was balmy, scented by the tropics and syncopated with cool Midwestern gusts of wind that touched the face, then vanished.

From my elevated spot at the wheel, I could look down and see the bottom slide by. Could see the floury white sand pockets and meadows of sea grass—individual grass blades leaning in the tide as if contoured by a steady breeze. Could see crossing patterns of spooked redfish and sea trout, pushing expanding wakes through the shallows. Could see table-sized stingrays explode from the marl, could see the astro-shapes of sea stars and brittle stars isolated in their own paned universe. Could see anemones and comb jellies and drifting medusoids, their tentacles angling downward and behind, like storm clouds dragging sheets of rain. There is something intimate about sea bottom, when you have the opportunity to see what exists there, a sense of an unclothing, which makes it personal, private.

"Are you hearing what I jus' said?"

I answered, "Huh?"

Ransom was shaking her head, smiling. "I keep talking, I get the feeling you not listening, my brother. The fish and things, them sea creatures, you get a real happy light in your face when you look at them."

It was true that she'd been talking right along. Not the maddening, nonstop meaningless chatter of a neurotic. Talking with passion, though, about Tucker and his letters, which is why I wasn't listening. I much preferred to concentrate on the sea bottom.

She was sitting in the captain's chair beside me, barefooted, feet propped up on the bulkhead. She was wearing the yellow canvas shorts again, but with a pink tank top, on the front of which was printed:

KALIK

OFFICIAL BEER OF JUNKANOO

RUM CAY, BAHAMAS

Her beaded braids were tied back with a pink ribbon, and I noted that around her neck she wore strings of cheap red and white beads as well as beads of white and yellow. From my trips to Cuba and the islands, I recognized them as Obeah beads. Or Santería beads. Because to understand a people you must also understand their beliefs, I'd had to do some research for my work in those places. Obeah is a potent religious mix of voodoo, Catholicism and old African superstition. The beads would have been blessed or empowered by a priestess, known as a Babalao in Cuba or, on most of the islands, as an Obeah "vitch" or witch.

I couldn't remember for certain, but I thought that the red and white beads that Ransom wore honored the God of Destiny. The meaning of the white and yellow beads, however had stuck with me. They were worn only by women and invited grace from Ochun, the goddess of rivers and love and female sensuality.

I'd always found that a charming combination: river, love, sensuality.

Judging from the way she'd fondle the beads while in thought, I guessed her to be a true believer, which was not surprising. More so than most religions, Obeah and Santería both offer quick relief from emotional suffering without moralizing sermons. For every physical or spiritual ailment, for every lapse in luck or judgment, the priests can come up with a combination of herbs or spells or beads to make things right again. Obeah doesn't have much interest in morality or ethics. Among the world's poor, those two things can be an expensive indulgence.

"What I was telling you about was the bad man that Daddy Gatrell stole the gold from. You didn't hear a word, did you?"

"Sorry."

"I tell you one more time if you stop lookin' at all the fishes down there. Why you like them things so much, man? Down in the islands, we got those things, but we don't care about them. They just somethin' nice to eat."

"I like them because . . ." I let the sentence trail off. To describe what she considered food as a fascinating lineage of cause, effect and ruthless adaptation seemed pompous. Same with the philosophical imperative: The microcosm can be a perfect mirror of the macrocosm only if the source of creation is the same. So I finished, "I like them because it's always been a hobby. So tell me about the bad man again. I'll listen. Promise."

She put both her hands on my left shoulder. Gave me a little push, but not hard enough to hurt my arm. "Then you sit where I sit, and let me drive so's you can concentrate." When I hesitated, she said, "Man, I can drive a boat good as you any ol' time. Out here, what I gonna hit? An *island*?"

I shrugged and let her take the wheel.

THE REASON THAT Tuck's attorney hadn't contacted her until more than two years after Tucker's death was that he'd been ordered by Tuck to wait until the man from whom he'd probably stolen the Spanish coins had also died.

Ransom told me, "He a very dangerous man on my island. Man by the name of Sinclair Benton. I kept askin' myself: 'If Daddy got them coins honest, why'd he have to hide them? Why couldn't he take them off the island or just give 'em to me straight away?"

The reason, she'd decided, was that Benton kept a sharp eye on Tuck and Joseph when they visited, and an equally close watch on Ransom, whom the whole island knew to be Tuck's daughter. Seven or eight times,

Tucker had visited her during her childhood, and seven or eight times, island thugs had forcibly searched him before he left.

"I don't think Benton know'd for sure who it was robbed him, but he always very suspicious of Daddy Gatrell. That why it always too dangerous for Daddy to go back and get that treasure. Benton, he was a big ol' Obeah man, a gorilla man—what we call Mr. Bones, the Prince of Death. Benton, he a witch. A real witch who know all the spells and powders. Ev'body on the island scared of Benton, and Benton, he hated our daddy more'n he hated most white men, and that sayin' something. Probably 'cause my momma love Daddy Gatrell so much."

Just hearing that combination of words, "Daddy Gatrell" was still difficult for me to process because it was such an outrageous mismatch. I found the fact that he'd gone back to see his child surprising. I found the fact he'd actually remembered her in a will positively shocking. No one ever described Tucker as a thoughtful or sensitive man.

Ransom had one hand on the wheel, steering easily as she talked. "Judge Flowers, he was directed to wait until he got notice of Benton's death before he send me these papers. Daddy didn't want to put us in any danger, understand?" She pointed to the little storage box where her single suitcase was stored along with the papers that had been mailed to her. "That evil man died a month or so ago, and everyone on Cat Island was happy. Had us a big party, all the junkanoo bands, all the scrape-n-rake bands, we singin' and playin', dancin' and drinking that ol' rum. Two weeks later, these papers arrive from the judge, and I been searchin' for you, my brother, ever since."

At first, I thought she meant Cat Cay, a popular, highly publicized fishing destination. But, no, she meant Cat Island, a large, remote key in the middle of the Bahamian chain. The only reason I knew about the place was that a couple of the Sanibel guides had broken down while making their way along the islands and had to spend a few nights there. They'd told me it was one of the few places in the Bahamas that was pure, hadn't been touched by tourism yet. Only one paved road, a few cars, mostly fishing and agriculture.

Ransom said, "I don't know what Benton did to make Daddy Gatrell mad enough to rob him. I don't doubt there was a very good reason for it. But know what?" She had very white teeth when she grinned; they made her skin appear darker. "I don't much care the reason 'cause I got me the gold coins, and I got me more than that, too. Like I tell you before, I'm in the new part of my life. Many women my age, they look in the mirror, see their ass gotten big, their bubbies droppin' down, they kids all gone. So they think 'I ain't gonna fight no more 'cause my womanly life, it all done.' Not me, man! I done already told you about how I changed my-self. Or maybe you didn't hear that, either?"

Yes, she'd told me and I'd listened, impressed. Told me all about her-self in the first hour or so, riding along in that slow boat. She wasn't that eager to talk about herself. I had to keep asking. It is an old and favorite device: Keep asking the right questions, and there will be no need to talk about yourself.

Ransom was quite a bit older than she looked—thirty-seven. When she was fifteen, she'd married a Cayman Islander by the name of Ebanks, a turtle fisherman. She had two sons, one now twenty, the other, her first born, died when he was fourteen.

"The dragon got him," she told me. "The mangrove lakes on Cat Is-land, they ain't got no bottom. Flow right out to the big ocean, man, through caves. My son, Tucker—I named him after Daddy, under-stand?—my dear lil' boy, he went swimmin' in a lake we call 'Horse Eatin' Hole.' That 'cause it got a dragon living down in its caves that come out at night and eats horses. But my young Tucker, he just laugh when people tell him that. He say, 'That just superstition, man!' Smart? That lil' boy, he *was* smart! Readin' books all the time, collecting butter-flies and bugs to study. The islanders, they all laugh and call him a fool when he say they no dragon. So what that strong lil' boy do? He go to

Horse Eatin' Hole and swim at night just to prove himself. Went down in the black water, and he never came up. Lil' Tucker, he not a good swimmer and the dragon got him sure enough.

"That night right there almost kill me, too. It were the worst night of my life. When they come tol' me, I don't remember nothing for three or four months afterwards. Nothin' except my throat hurting from the sound of my crying."

I found that story touching on several levels, and not only because tears welled in Ransom's eyes as she told it.

A woman who believed in dragons. A woman who believed in taking control of her own destiny and beginning a second life—her Womanly Life, she called it.

Which is exactly what she decided to do.

Looking at Ransom, it was difficult to imagine her fat and soft. No . . . it was impossible, looking at those legs, that hard body. According to her, though, the death of her son was the beginning of a physical decline that nearly ruined her. "I had me a job waitressing at the little restaurant down at New Bight. I'd drink goat milk shakes and eat sweets all day long, still always so tired I could barely make myself walk home to bed. Got so, my husband, he wouldn't touch me. I strip my clothes off, man, he look the *other* way."

It got worse. On Cat Island, mail is delivered by slow boat, which works its way down the Bahamian chain. During one mail call, she'd had to deliver meals to the crew. As they ate, she overheard them laughing and joking about a man named Ebanks who had wives on at least three neighboring islands, lots of children, too. The reason it was so funny was because the postal service couldn't keep all the Ebanks women straight.

"That a very dark period for me," she said. "A time come in a woman's life when we got the choice to give up, start living like we old and not womanly no more. Or we can fight back. Givin' up, that the easy thing to do, 'cause you just keep sliding and sliding like you got no control 'til the end. That what I learned, my brother! People, they not afraid of dyin'. Dyin', that be easy. What we really afraid of is that we not strong enough to make our living a success."

Ransom decided to take the risk, find out if she was strong enough. Ironically, her pivotal moment was catalyzed by Sinclair Benton, Tucker's old enemy.

Now, over the noise of my trawl boat's burbling engine, she said, "That the part I didn't tell you, but that Obeah man, Benton, he had somethin' to do with me choosing to change what I'd become. What happened was, I was waiting tables at the restaurant when the big witch walk in. Sinclair, he always got two or three bad men with him, and he scary enough by his own self. They all three sit down at my table and Sinclair, he grabs my shorts as I walk by, holding me by the rump. Then he looks up at me with those lil' berry eyes of his and he says, 'Back when you's a high yella girl, I tried to get you in the bushes many times even though you spawned by white trash, but you always run away. I tell you somethin' about how the world changes. You still high yella, but now you a high yella cow. These days, you try to get ol' Benton in the bushes, I be the one to run away!'

"Ev'body in the restaurant thought that very funny. They laugh and laugh. I laughed, too, on the outside. But on the inside, I felt something change in me. Something way down deep."

I liked the flint clarity of her voice when she told me that story. Liked the unemotional resolve. It had been the final indignity, which made even more understandable the course of discipline she chose.

"What I knew was, I'd already lived a life for other people—it what I call my Motherly Life—which is the same as saying I'd lived as a person that was only part me. I decided, fuck 'em man! It were time I lived my next years just the way I wanted. I thought of it as my second life. What I call my Womanly Life. Every time I got weak or scared, I'd jus' remind myself of Benton and all the others in that restaurant who laughed like I really was some ol' cow, and that's where I found strength."

It took her several weeks to build up enough momentum so that she didn't dread, day by day, her new routine of work and exercise. It was nearly six months before she came to actually enjoy it.

"That mountain where Daddy Gatrell hide the doubloons? I didn't even know they was hidden there at the time, but every day, I'd walk partway up that mountain, huffin' and puffin' like I had a wagon attached to my big brown ass. But I didn't quit and I'd get a little further and a little further each time.

"Something else I did was, we got a real pretty hotel on Cat Island at Fernandez Bay. It's Mister Armbrister's place, old British loyalists people, and the beach out front has water like glass over a bowl of sugar. I started swimmin' along that beach. Doggy paddlin' at first, kinda pulling myself along. It was just like climbin' the mountain. I'd go a little further each and every time.

"I walked every day and swam two, maybe three times a week. I stopped drinking them goat's milk shakes and eatin' them sweets, and I didn't smoke no more cigarettes, either, except for a lil' ganja now and then to give me a smile. Mrs. Armbrister, she figured out what I was trying to do, and she showed me a little outdoor weight bench they got there. So I started lifting weights, too.

"After a year, I'd walk by a mirror and didn't even recognize the strong woman I saw there. Man, I liked that woman! I could run up that mountain, clear to crazy Father Jerome's monastery. I could swim all the way down the beach to where the surf hits the cliff. Mrs. Armbrister, she had to send off to Lauderdale to get more weights, that's how much we was lifting.

"Only thing I didn't like was my bubbies still had a little sag, but one of the guests at the Armbrister's hotel, turns out he a famous plastic sur-

geon when he not sitting around drinkin' rum and fishin' for boneyfish.
I danced with that nice doctor three maybe four nights, and bring him
coconut drinks when he sitting out there under the palms. One night he
whisper to me, 'What you give me to meet you in Nassau and fix your
bubbies for you free?' I told him, 'Man, you so handsome and sweet, I
give you *that* anyway. But you fix my bubbies, somethin' nice I also do for
you is promise not to tell your wife.'"

She was Tucker Gatrell's daughter, alright.

"Getting that letter from Daddy Gatrell was a sign to me," she said.
"It hurt my heart not to know that he'd died, but it also made me feel
good knowing he cared. Benton, he wasn't the only witch on our island.
We got us a good witch, too, an old woman, Mizz Baker, who give me
these beads for luck, and fix me up some special gris-gris bags. You know
what a gris-gris bag is?"

She reached into her pocket and pulled out a little yellow pouch about
the size of two tea bags, sealed with string. Inside, she said, were herbs
and a magic potion that the witch had said a spell over, giving them
power.

When she handed the pouch to me, I bounced it light in my palm,
then held it to my nose. It smelled of turpentine and some kind of power.
We were off Useppa Island, another of Florida's exclusive, private islands.
I could see men in white shirts and shorts playing croquet. I could see
people eating lunch on the patio outside the Collier Inn. It was a striking
contrast: a voodoo talisman and a Obeah believer backdropped by modern America's affluent.

"That a gris-gris bag Mizz Baker made especially for good luck.
When she give it to me, she say, 'The letter from your daddy, that a sign
it time to go out and start your Womanly Life.' So that really why I'm
here, my brother. And why I'm giving this gris-gris bag to you. The
thing done already brought me good luck 'cause we together now. I hope
it bring you the same good fortune."

10

THE FIRST THING I did after securing my skiff and the trawler was check the shark pen, which is on the deep-water, sunrise side of my piling house. I stood on the top deck and watched three bull sharks, all thick as small ponies, swim a slow clockwise perimeter along the heavy netting.

Usually, they swam in just the opposite direction. Lately, though, it was clockwise. I've never understood why.

I checked their feeding chart—Jeth had fed them twenty fresh mullet that morning. That was the most difficult thing about keeping sharks in captivity—getting them to eat. They could be very fussy. But these three seemed to be doing okay. They looked healthy. One, a female, had a very deep mating scar on her back, which I'd treated with antibiotics. It looked to be nearly healed.

Standing at my shoulder, Ransom said, "Man, the way you look at them scary animals, I bet you got names for all three of 'em."

I answered, "Why would anyone name a fish?" and moved on.

Then I checked my fish tank, which is the primary storage unit for the plants and animals I catch and collect and keep alive.

The tank is actually a thousand-gallon wooden cistern, built like a whiskey barrel, that I'd cut in two, mounted on the widest part of the dock and then added a sub-sand filter and a hundred-gallon upper reservoir to improve water clarity. PVC pipe and a Briggs raw water pump kept it oxygenated.

The tank is so large that it's a miniature, self-contained sea biota, its own little saltwater universe, and so heavy that I'd had to have extra pilings jetted in beneath it for support.

In the tank are local flora and fauna: turtle grass, tunicates, sea hydroids and several common vertebrates, such as killifish, small snappers, immature groupers, several immature tarpon and snook, plus plenty of shrimp so the fish don't eat each other. There are also sea horses, whelks and tulip shells, and as many reef squid as I can keep alive and uneaten. I like to keep squid in the tank because they are delicate, and good indicators of an aquarium's integrity.

Ransom followed me around like a shadow as I checked the filters and water flow. She seemed amused that I would keep fish as what she perceived to be pets, names or no names. She was also very comfortable with my house—surprising, because it's a simple place. Not all women like it. It's two weather-bleached cottages, really, under one tin roof, built at the turn of the previous century on a plank platform over the water, and connected to the mangrove shoreline by ninety feet of boardwalk.

She looked at the cypress planking, the peeling gray paint and the outdoor, rain cistern shower. Looked at the Franklin fireplace, which is my only source of heat. Considered the little gas stove where I cook and the simple ship's refrigerator. Noted the single bed, the sparse furnishings, the worn throw rugs, and completely misinterpreted what it all meant.

"Man," she said, "I thought I was poor, living in my lil' house on Cat Island. At least I got me a portable heater for when the northers blow and a television set that gets two Miami stations and one outta Nassau. When we find that six thousand dollars, my brother, you keep it all. You need the money a lot more than this girl."

She didn't seem to understand or believe why I was amused by that.

"Why you smilin' at me? You think I'm joking? No, I mean what I'm saying—we use the money, buy you some decent furniture, then I take what's left over if there some money remaining."

Perhaps there is a sense of subconscious linkage due to familial genetics. More likely, it was because it was absolutely impossible not to like and trust this woman even though I'd tried to remain disinterested, indifferent. Didn't matter. She'd won me over and there was nothing I could do about it. Whatever the reason, I decided to give her a vague idea—a very vague idea—of what my income is per year.

After I told her, she said, incredulously, "You got to be kiddin'!"

No, I wasn't kidding.

"You got all that money, why you live so poor?"

I looked around my house, trying to see it through her eyes. "Money's got nothing to do with the way I choose to live."

She found that funny. "Man, money got everything to do with how a person live. You got money, you should show it off a little. Get a little flashy, man. Let people know."

I said to her, "Once they know, then what?" Meaning that, like giving a name to a shark, it made no sense.

I don't believe people who say they don't care about money and I don't trust people who care too much.

The acquisition of money is necessary to living a life of acceptable independence. The question, of course, is what is acceptable? And how much will it cost?

A couple of years back, after a beery night of philosophical discussion, Tomlinson and I had both decided to take an active interest in acquiring money. I saw it as a clinical exercise. He saw it as a spiritual experiment.

We both succeeded way beyond our expectations, but I feel no pride in what has been the steady accumulation of paper wealth because I had no emotional interest in it to begin with.

The same is probably true for Tomlinson.

Reason's simple: The credit belongs entirely to Mack. Mack, who owns and operates Dinkin's Bay, has a New Zealander's appreciation for thriftiness and a genius for the American stock market. Coincidental to that discussion, I'd just separated a very evil man from a sizable chunk of money, and I'd asked Mack to invest it all for me. I didn't care if I lost the entire bundle—indifference can also work as a very effective cleanser of ethics.

By the end of that fiscal year, had I not reinvested my dividend payments, profits would have far exceeded what I make collecting and selling marine specimens.

I already had a sizable cache of cash hidden away in foreign accounts, so I'd taken ten percent of what I estimated to be the total and had Mack invest that, too. Tomlinson did the same with his own sizable inheritance after the untimely death of his father. Without even trying or really caring very much, we'd both become men of means and perhaps even wealthy, depending on how the market went and whose standards of wealth you used.

I was checking a recent and already much regretted acquisition—a telephone answering machine—as I explained this to her.

She said, "You tellin' me you make all that money and don't even do no work for it?"

On a pad of paper, I noted that a Professor Steven Dougherty had called from Grinnell University in Iowa with an order for three hundred small horseshoe crabs preserved in formalin, as I said, "There's risk involved. Not as much now because the guy who does the investing for me—you'll meet him tonight, a man named Mack. This guy, Mack, he handles my investments, and he's done what they call diversify. What that means is, he's spread the money out into more dependable stocks, which are supposed to be safer. The marina has a big party every Friday night. In just a couple hours, right at sunset. Mack'll be there."

She was very interested, I could tell by her expression. "This man you talking about. This Mack? A man with brains like that, I bet he's married."

"No, but he's got a very complicated love life. If you're suggesting . . . if you're even considering the idea, what I should tell you is, if you want to marry a man with money, choose someone else. Marina people don't date each other. Not at this marina, anyway. Because of me, or because you're close to Tomlinson—either one of us—it's like you're living here. So drop the idea."

Staring at me, her nose flared. "Hey, man! Let's have us a little understanding here, okay? I won't give you no orders if you don't try to order me around. How's that sound? Besides, I ain't gonna marry no man anyway. If I do, it going to be for the size of his heart, not the size of his wallet."

She had Tuck's quick temper, too.

"Sorry," I said. "That was unfair. I could tell you're interested in Mack, though. I'm not wrong about that."

"I'm interested 'cause you think you're the only one who'd like to be rich? If I give this man a big chunk a' money, maybe he can make me rich, too."

Listening to the answering machine, I noted that a Dr. Picking had called from Waldron College in Michigan and wanted to place an order for a hundred medium sea anemones, fifty preserved octopi, and up to two hundred live goose barnacles if I could find them. A pretty good order, because all those things are easy to get in February.

As I wrote the order on a pad, I said to Ransom, "You can ask Mack at the party tonight. What you need to keep in mind, though, it's like I already told you: Six thousand dollars isn't a lot of money even if it does exist. Which I doubt. Invest a small amount like that and it's going to be a long wait until you can consider yourself wealthy."

"There you go doin' it again. Speaking mean about Daddy Gatrell. Besides, who knows? Maybe I be able to let this man invest more than just six thousand dollars. Maybe I saved up some big money from my waitressing. I'm a hard worker, man, make no mistake about that. A very hard worker. So, yes, maybe I have more money to invest than you thinkin', my brother. How about I had . . . and I'm just throwin' out a figure here . . . but what if I had, say, seventeen thousand dollars to invest. Or say that seventeen thousand dollars plus another three thousand? Your friend Mack, if he put that money in stocks, how long it take me to have enough money to buy me a nice house on Sanibel plus a pool, maybe? And a car? I want me a nice red car, one that's got power windows."

There was something in her tone—a duplicity of meaning—that made me uneasy. A specific figure spoken offhandedly, as if it were invented. The addition of $3,000—half the money she hoped we would find. There was something she wasn't telling me. The tone was too familiar, and so was the impression of divisiveness.

Where had I heard that tone before?

Why'd I even have to think about it? Tucker Gatrell, that's where I'd heard it before. Many times before. The same manipulative chord that signaled an unwillingness to trust a lesser human being with his actual plan. She was parroting Tucker's old trick. Holding back information because knowledge truly is power. Intentionally keeping her own agenda secret, which I found offensive as hell.

I was about to tell her exactly that. But then the final message on my machine caught my interest . . . then it captured my attention. I was surprised to hear the formal, diplomatic voice of Hal Harrington say, "Doctor Ford, I'm afraid I have some distressing news. The Latin gentleman injured on the dock yesterday? I've just received a report from a reliable source who's informed me that a man by the name of Amador Cordero was admitted to All Saints Hospital in Cartagena late yesterday evening. He was brought into the county via private plane, and rushed to the hospital. He was unconscious by the time they got him to the emergency room where it was determined that he had a severe spinal cord injury.

"Cordero is currently on a life-support system. The prognosis is not good. At best, he'll be a functioning paraplegic. Amador Cordero is the oldest son of Edgar Cordero. I've already told you about Edgar, and I can assure you that he is extremely interested in any information relating to you. I suggest you be alert, and be aware. Very alert. Very aware. If I learn anything else, I'll contact you immediately." He added, "My best to Mr. Tomlinson," and hung up.

I deleted the message and took the notepad across the room and out the door, Ransom following along, talking behind me. "He referrin' to the person in the mask you hurt yesterday, that's what that all about, ain't it? He telling you it worse than you think, he warning you. Something scary 'bout his voice, too, it so deep. Who *was* that? Maybe you better call the po-lice, my brother. Let them handle it."

It was an unsettling thing to contemplate a person connected to tubes, being inhaled by a machine, frozen in his own immobile body because of something I'd done. I had to stand there and think about it for a moment. Had to remind myself of Amador Cordero's behavior, his assault on two innocent women, before I answered, "I'm not calling anybody. Neither are you."

BY NOW, SHE'D followed me through the door into my lab, with its odor of chemicals and alcohol, old wood and ozone from aerators oxygenating the aquariums along the south wall. The aerators made comforting, burbling, Flubber-like sounds. She continued to press me to seek help from the police until I told her knock it off; I wasn't discussing it anymore. That what I wanted to discuss was her cryptic interest in investing a large sum of money in the stock market.

"You think I'm going to introduce you to Mack? No way. You're not talking to Mack until you give me the whole story. That figure you mentioned—seventeen thousand dollars? Where'd that come from? You pull a figure like that out of the blue?"

"It just a number that come into my head."

"Don't do that to me, Ransom. I'm telling you right now. Tell me everything or I'm not going to waste my time talking with you."

"Just because I lied for you don't give you the right to call me a liar."

"See? That's exactly the sort of thing you do that really pisses me off. It's another one of your devices. I know you lied for me, but please don't try and use it to manufacture guilt. I asked you a simple question."

"You don't believe I could make that much money waitressing?"

"On Cat Island? Absolutely not. I'm not stupid. So tell me—if you really do have that much money, where'd you get it?"

Ransom was looking out the window, suddenly not so interested in what I was saying. Heard her say, "Uh-oh!" but very soft, like she didn't want me to hear.

I looked out the same window to see two large black men, one of them wearing a red, black and green Rastafarian headnet, the other with dreadlocks matted long and hanging down like a mane. The two of them were walking along the boardwalk toward my house. On their faces were forced expressions of neighborly confidence and familiarity—contrived since they certainly were not my neighbors. One of them used an ebony-handled walking stick. He wasn't limping. A walking stick in the hands of a healthy man is a weapon, not a cane.

"Do you know those men?"

"What men you talking about?"

I put my hand on the back of her head and forced her to look through the window that her eyes were suddenly now trying to avoid. "*Those* men. Tell me the truth. There's a reason I'm in a hurry, so don't screw around."

The reason was that if the two men had been sent so soon by Edgar Cordero, I needed to open the old locker from beneath my bed and dig out a firearm. I've dealt with enough drug people, and more than enough Colombians, to know that if men came all that way to take revenge, they'd fire without hesitating and shoot to kill.

Ransom was frightened. There was no mistaking the involuntary muscular tremor. She said, "Goddamn, man! What them two no-account Jamaican boys doin' here on this fancy island?"

Yeah, she knew them alright. I said, "Then tell me. Who are they? Why're they here?"

"That mean man I tell you about, the witch man. Sinclair Benton? He like the Jamaicans 'cause they so smart and they work so hard. Those two, one named Izzy, the bigger man, he named Clare. They worked for Mr. Benton. They at the restaurant that day he call me a cow, the day they all laughed."

The men were looking at the house now as they walked. Heard one of them call, "Yoohoo, Ransom girl? You got ol' friends come here to lay the visit on you. You in there, Ransom girl?"

I had her elbow now and gave it a squeeze. "But *why* are they here? Tell me."

She really was scared now. It was in her voice. "I'm sorry, my brother. If I'd known they'd come this far looking for me, I wouldn't a done what I did. Them Rastamans, they ain't supposed to like to *leave* the islands, man. They call a plane an iron bird, like it something bad."

Before I could ask again, she turned her face to me and said, "Could be, they think I stole something from Sinclair Benton. From his house after the man died. Could be that the reason they come to Florida looking for me."

I said, "Seventeen thousand dollars? Is that what they think you stole?"

She smiled, her blue eyes looking into mine. "Man, Daddy Gatrell, he were sure right about how smart he say you are. How you know that?"

Outside, the two men were coming up the steps to the top deck. I heard the same voice call, "Come out and see your friends, Ransom girl. Or we come in and see *you*."

As I went toward the door, she said behind me, nearly whispering now. "And a ring. They maybe think I stole a ring from that bad man, too."

I looked at the gold ring on her right hand. I'd noticed the ring because of its unusual size but hadn't taken a close look. "That one?"

She was twisting it off, in a hurry now to slide the ring into her pocket. "Could be," she said.

IZZY WAS THE talker, standing there with his big smile, golden stars on front incisors, his dreadlocks matted and waxed like combed wool hanging to the small of his back. Loose blue drawstring pants, white tank top that showed muscles and cordage and veins when he moved his arms, his skin very black except for his palms, which he showed often because he was a showman. He used big hand gestures. The palms of his hands, they were salmon-colored, nearly pink.

Clare stood beside Izzy, a step behind, his silence making him seem bigger, a man who filled his own space and spilled out into the space of everyone else. It was impossible not to be aware of him. He stood there listening in his knit Rasta cap, red, green and black, which was huge on his head, holding all the hair we could not see, Clare with his tiny black eyes set deep beneath his forehead, the frontal plate of his skull wide and very flat, leaning his weight on the ebony-handled walking stick. I noted that the handle was a death's head, another skull, this one polished bright, jaws thrown open, laughing. Or screaming.

What was Sinclair Benton's Obeah nickname? Ransom had told me. Mr. Bones.

Izzy said, "So that how we find you, my sister! It not so hard. We know you fly Air Bahamas to Lauderdale, and the Greyhound bus people, they very helpful. And you a girl who like to talk! You talk to the ticket lady, you talk to the bus driver, tellin' ev'body your plans. What Clare and me, what we don't understand is, we come all this way to see you, why you not happy to see some your old island friends?"

His speech pattern and delivery were much faster than Ransom's, his accent a rounder, Jamaican lilt. I heard, *Wha-we dawn unerstan-eeze, we cawm all dese way* . . . as I sat, leaning my hip against the railing, close to the front door of my house. Ransom was standing in front of them, face to face. She'd stepped out to meet them as if dealing with guests from the instant I said, "You fellas have a reason to be here?" preparing to tell them to leave. But Ransom had told me, "I'll handle this mess," and left me there to watch and listen.

Now she said, "First thing you should know, Izzy? I ain't your friend. Man, I careful about who I be calling my friends. And you two ain't among them."

It was the second or third time she'd skewered them with a barb. Now, as before, Izzy just laughed, turning to share the fun with an un-smiling Clare. He flicked his hands at Ransom as if to flick the insult away. "Girl, you spirited! That much I always know. Maybe you unhappy because we two island men, we remind you of the old times back at New Bight." For the first time, he directed his attention to me. "Mister? You maybe not believe it, but this fine-looking woman, she not always so fine-looking! No sir! Back on the island, she used to be what we call a cushion girl. A cushion girl, she someone who easy to lay on the floor and make for very easy pushin'. This girl, my sister Ransom, she had lots and lots of cushion and always ready to get down on the floor with 'bout any ol' bush boy that come along. Yes, she was!"

I didn't like the shrill laughter he used as a rim shot to his poor jokes. Didn't like the condescending way he called me sir, not meaning it, letting me know with his inflection that it was a veil for contempt. To Ransom, I said, "How well you know these two guys?"

She said, "It took me a day to know they both idiots, and took fifteen years to try and find a way to ignore 'em." I was heartened by her tone, her combativeness. She was right there with me.

I said, "Then I think I'm going to ask your island visitors to leave. This guy—" I swung my chin toward Izzy. "He's either very stupid, or he's very rude."

Clare spoke for the first time, opening his eyes slightly, as if I'd just awakened him. "What you just say, my man? You call my brotheren stupid? Man, that a very stupid thing for *you* to do. You insult my brother, you insult the Lion of Judah, you insult the Holy Piby. Man, you insult *me.*"

Rasta talk? Apparently.

I told him, "The only one I was trying to insult was Izzy. But if I nailed you and a couple of others, that's just fine. Ask Izzy to explain that as you leave. Which you're going to do right now, by the way."

Izzy held his hands up—hold it, hold it! Said, "Ransom girl, now I understand why you come to this rich Sanibel Island place. You make yourself so beautiful, you find you a nice big white gentleman to look after you. Protect you when you need it. That a very good thing. And sir? You got you a very good woman here. Nice woman who know how to work hard, treat her man right. I make you angry with what I say about my old friend, sister Ransom? Then I apologize. Yes I do. Clare and me, sir, we come from a lil' island far away. Don't know nothin' about behaving in a rich man's world like this. So please forgive me. Forgive us."

I said nothing, looking at his golden smile, at Clare's fuming glare, not certain if I was disappointed I had a bum arm or not. Clare had the look of muscle density and lots of fast twitch quickness. Maybe it was better to have an excuse. A reason to call the cops and ask someone else to make them leave.

Yep. Not much doubt about it. In a way, I was glad my arm was in a sling.

When I still made no reply, Izzy said, "Whether you accept our 'pology or not, sir, we got us a problem. Yes, we do. I very sad to say that. But it not a *big* problem if Ransom agree to cooperate. Thing is, Ransom, she went into the home of my former employer—his name Sinclair Benton— she go into Mr. Benton's home after the man die, and she helped herself to a pile of money there, and a ring. That ring, it very valuable, man."

"It not just any ring," Clare added, looking at Ransom. "You so ignorant in the ways of the Lord, you probably don't even know what it was you took. That ring, it a holy ring, girl. It the royal ring of Haile Selassie, the one made a present to him by the Ethiopian Church. That ring, it belonged to King Solomon, who give it to the Queen of Sheba, who give it to her son, Prince Menelik of Ethiopia. And that the way the ring be passed along for three thousand years 'til our Saint, Bob Marley, he lost it somehow on one of the small islands. But our employer, Mr. Benton, he get it back 'cause he know the proper way of certain words and herbs."

Ransom said, "You mean he a witch. That what you sayin'. Or Benton stole that ring from Bob Marley his own self."

"Don't you be talking about Mr. Benton, you know what's good for you girl. He dead but he still got power on Cat Island."

"I ain't on Cat Island no more. Big ol' fat witch man! He treat me dirty all my life."

Izzy was still using his peacemaker's tone. "We all know why that is, Ransom girl. It 'cause your white daddy steal a bunch'a gold coins from him long ago in the back years and Mr. Benton, he not a man to forgive a person easily."

"He call me a cow! You two boys right there to hear his words. Laughed right along with everybody at New Bight."

"That give you no right to rob him!" Clare banged his walking stick on the deck for emphasis, then said to me, "She take a stack of cash money, too. American money. Ten thousand dollars was in that box, girl.

Izzy, he just happen to count it before she come that night and get his brother so drunk on the cane rum and strip him naked offering to give him the womanly present."

Izzy cleared his throat uneasily. "Could'a been a little more than ten thousand dollars, my brotheren. I tell you, I count it very quickly 'cause I know it not my money to be touching. Maybe she stole more than ten thousand. That I not so sure about."

I smiled, seeing it now, understanding Izzy and Clare's interest. I said, "You're calling the lady a thief. What I wonder is, why don't you contact the police? Have her arrested if you're so sure it was her."

The reason they hadn't called the cops was obvious. It was because they planned on stealing the money and the ring for themselves. Not only that, something else was now clear: Izzy had lied to his partner about how much cash there was. Told him there was ten thousand when, apparently, there was nearly twice that. Lied to get a bigger split. But Izzy was staying calm, playing it cool. I listened to him say, "The reason we don't contact the magistrate, man, it 'cause we care about our island sister. Ransom a good girl. She a hard worker, don't make no trouble for nobody on the island." The dazzling golden grin returned. "Man, if'n I knew how beautiful she gonna turn out to be in her old age, I'd taken this woman into my bed years ago. So why should I get her in trouble with the authorities, man? You think I want to see this good woman in jail? That where they sure gonna put her if she choose not to cooperate with us today."

I said, "That's very kind of you, Izzy. You too, Clare."

"Your white gentleman friend, Ransom, he a very reasonable man."

I said quickly, "I wasn't finished. Thing is, when your employer died, I'm sure an attorney had to be involved in settling the estate."

"Oh yes, you exactly right about that. Mr. Benton, he a very wealthy man. Had him *two* attorneys and they make everything go real smooth. One of them come clear from Nassau."

"They handled Mr. Benton's estate."

"Of course they did. Everything fine and legal."

"Then they had to know about the missing cash, right? And the missing ring. Which means that the police are going to be after whoever stole it, no matter if you turn them in or not, Izzy. It's out of your hands."

Izzy puffed up a little, confident, very pleased with himself. "That where you all wrong, sir. What you don't know is, Mr. Benton, he a smart man. The way he get the ring and all that money, it his own business. So why should he pay the tax magistrate in Nassau for the fruit of his own labors?" There was the big grin, again. "Understand my meaning? There no official paper record of them things that was stolen. Which is why, if Ransom cooperate, the magistrate got no *cause* to arrest her."

I'd taken a few steps forward. Now I put my right hand on the girl's shoulder. "There's no record of Benton owning the ring or the money?"

"No, man! That's why your girl safe with only me and Clare knowing what she did."

"Really? Then I'm very confused now. If there's no official record of the ring and the cash being part of Benton's estate, how can you or anyone else prove the ring or the cash exists?"

I watched the smile fade slowly from his face as he began to understand my meaning.

"If you or the magistrate can't prove they existed, how are you going to prove Ransom or anyone else stole them? That's the part I don't understand. The cops can't touch her. So how're you doing her a favor not turning her in?"

The patronizing tone, the jollyness, were suddenly gone from his voice. "The favor we doing her, my man, is not treatin' her like the thief she is. The way we'd do it down in the islands."

"Oh? How do you treat thieves down in the islands?"

I was paying careful attention to the body language of both men, to the signals they gave off. Noticed that they began to move imperceptibly apart—the first feral indicator of attack formation. Noticed that Clare changed his grip on the walking stick, not even thinking about it. Noticed the jerky movements of Izzy's head, his eyes moving in fast surveillance—was anyone way over there at the marina watching?—as his feet moved him a few inches at a time to my left. Noticed his eyes freeze for a moment, looking down into the water beyond the railing of the deck. I saw the moment of recognition when he realized what those dark shapes were, swimming in slow circles below, and he said, "You got some big biters in there, man!"

"Bull sharks. That's right."

"Down in the islands, we catch a thief, what we might do is take 'em out to the deep water, where the color change, and chum up some them biters. Let the thief hang over the water while the frenzy goin' on. Maybe drop him in among the sharks a few times 'til they get smart and tell us where to find what they stole."

Which is when he lunged toward Ransom, his mouth telling his brain what to do as it came to him.

He had her by the hair, pushing her toward the railing by the time I got to him with my one good arm.

11

I HAVE NO idea what he planned to do once he got Ransom to the edge of the platform. Probably hold her there, threaten to push her in with the sharks if she didn't come through with the money. Izzy was the spontaneous type, making it up as he went along because he had nothing to fear from me. Him along with his buddy, huge, mean-tempered Clare, against a guy with his arm in a sling. He had the kind of dumb bully confidence that's seldom challenged and often gets people killed.

He had a fistful of red-beaded braids in his right hand, and had grabbed the back of her shorts with his left, controlling her that way as Ransom tried to battle him with her elbows, but she was unable to get to him because he hugged in close behind her.

You expect women to scream. She didn't. Furious, her voice became more of a growl. Pure outrage. She knew all the descriptive words and how to use them, as Izzy demanded repeatedly, pushing her toward the water, "Where the money, girl? *Where* that money?"

Clare moved to intercept me just as I got to Izzy, but not before I got a few shots in. I hit Izzy with a right fist deep in the kidneys, once . . . twice, then buried my fingers into his face, squeezing hard. I heard his muted scream as my thumb dug up under his jawbone and my middle finger found traction in his eye socket, my left shoulder in the small of his back providing a foundation for torque. I felt Clare's hands find my shoulders from behind, but I ducked low and under, then came up abruptly, driving my fist into Izzy's groin from the backside.

It's an ancient motor response etched in the primitive brain: If something strikes you in the nuts from below, you jump—jump as high as you possibly can, jump and lunge away. Izzy didn't have great leaping ability, but my fist provided all the additional power necessary to somersault him into the air and over the railing. The microsecond of silence was punctuated by his knowing scream just before he splashed into the shark pen.

I didn't see him hit the water because Clare was on me by then. On me, holding me, shaking me, suffocating me.

In the first moments of any fight there are certain things immediately known: Is your opponent stronger than you? Is he confident or is he operating on pure adrenaline and panic? Is he skilled? Is he vicious? Has he done this dance before?

With Clare, the answer was yes on all counts.

He wrapped his bearish arms around me, lifting and twisting so hard that I felt the vertebrae in my spine pop as my feet lifted off the ground. I elbowed him once . . . twice . . . three times in the stomach, and it was like hitting bone, his abdomen was so heavily muscled.

I tried to strike down on his instep with my heel. Missed because he was holding me so high off the deck. Tried to strike down on his kneecap with my heel, and missed there, too.

Meanwhile, Clare knew just how to work it. He used my every spasm and movement to work his forearm tighter and tighter under my neck, finding the left side of my throat with the sharp, upper edge of his radius bone. Then he used that arm bone to seal off my windpipe and to slow the blood moving through my jugular to the brain.

There is a strange moment, just before unconsciousness, when the ears begin to roar with the thudding, frustrated pounding of heart muscle, and light begins to dim slowly, slowly, like the dilating beam of a spotlight.

Through the slits of my eyes, I could see Ransom's mouth moving, screaming at Clare, probably, but I could not hear her.

I could feel the overwhelming constricting of the big man's arms; knew that he was killing me, but felt a sleepy indifference, resigned to the inevitable—death was not as painful as I'd feared. I felt a glimmer of hope when, for some reason, he loosened his grip, but that hope immediately vanished when I realized why: Instead of using his arm to choke me, he was now using the cane. He had both hands gripped on it as if to decapitate me. I used one arm to fight the cane away . . . then ripped my left arm out of the sling and used that too, operating on pure panic . . . and then, inexplicably, he stopped.

For an eerie moment, I thought I was dead. He'd beaten me, he'd won, so was it true? Had the terrible, crushing pressure on my throat really ceased?

Yes. He still had me in his control, but I could breathe again and my brain began to function again. I sucked in huge gulps of air, trying to clear the fog away. I lifted my chin to create even more breathing room, opened my eyes wide, and I saw why the man had stopped trying to kill me.

There stood Ransom in front of us, holding the golden ring in her fingers, showing it to him. My hearing had returned, too, and she was saying, "This the ring you want, Clare? Yeah, man, I can see in your face, this the ring you come all this way to get. This the king's ring, that what you say? Man, if'n I knew it was Haile Selassie's ring, I'd given it right back to your people 'cause I'm not the kind to show disrespect for someone's religion."

Clare was still holding me, but loosely, the way a cat whose attention has wandered holds an injured mouse. "Thank you, sistren. That the attitude I expect you to have. Praise most high to Ivertime, Him and Him, I and I. You give me the ring and the money, we go leave you in peace."

By tilting my head downward slightly, I could see Izzy thrashing in the shark pen below, fighting his way to the edge of the heavy netting, which was held in place by floats. He was gasping and shouting, "The biters's after me, man! Help me get outta here, man!"

Ransom seemed very cool, knew just what she was doing as she moved toward the edge of the deck, still holding the ring high. "You want this ring, Clare?"

"Ain't that what I jus' tell you? It for our people, Sistren."

"Then let my brother go."

That confused him. "Your brother? Your brothren, he down there fuckin' with the sharks. How I gonna let Izzy go?"

"No, man. *That* my brother. You let *him* go."

It took a couple of seconds for his brain to process what she meant, then he laughed, amused. "This fella your brother? I let him go, all right. I'm gonna throw him down there with the sharks, let them decide dark meat or white meat."

"No, you let him go now, damn you!"

"Don't be swearin' at me, sistren. You give me the ring, then I release this fella. As it say in the Book of Amos, 'Are ye not as children of the Ethiopians unto Me, O Children of Israel saith the Lord.' You do yourself righteous, my sistren. This your chance to please the living God of Abraham and Isaac, He Whose Name Should Not Be Spoken."

"You know your verse, Clare. That much I give you."

"Yes, I do. That from the Holy Piby. The one true Bible. Now give me the fuckin' ring!"

Ransom was looking at me, looking into my eyes as Clare pushed me toward her. She stood there holding the ring high as bait, telling me something. I listened to her say, "My brother? You ready for what I'm gonna do?"

Clare said, "What you gonna do when? Give me that ring, that what you gonna do right now or I'm gonna rip your boyfriend's head off. That exactly what I'm gonna do, my Sistren."

She was still looking into my eyes. "You want the ring, Clare? You want it real bad? Then you jump in there with the sharks and get it." I watched as she tossed the ring in a high arc into the air; watched the ring spin and glitter down, then implode like a bullet slug on the surface of the water.

"You crazy girl! You one crazy bitch!" Clare had made a clumsy, last moment lunge to intercept the ring, but didn't even get close. He'd taken his hands off me to do it, and I had to fight the urge to use the opportunity to spin away, jump down to the lower deck and escape to the marina. Leave Ransom there alone and run for my life.

I wanted to do it, but I couldn't.

Instead, I stepped in behind Clare and hammered him in the small of the back with my right elbow. Drove the same elbow down on the side of his neck when he stumbled. Then tried my best to duck under his arms when he swung around to grab me.

I wasn't quick enough, though and, once again, I was trying to battle my way out of the big man's stranglehold. I could hear Ransom screaming at him to stop, as the world began to grow drab and gray once more. I knew I had to find a way to break that hold, or probably die, so I let my body go limp and my head fall forward, as if I'd passed out. When I felt Clare relax his grip, keyed by my sudden weight, I didn't hesitate. I slammed my head backward and felt it strike a cartilaginous mass—his nose. Heard a phlegmy groan as I slammed my head into him once more. Then I dropped, turned and drove the pad of my open palm into his chin.

Clare's face was a mess; he was still stunned from the crushing blow to the nose. Even so, the shot to the chin didn't drop him. When he stumbled backward, I caught him by the throat; slid my thumb and forefinger in and nearly behind the delicate laryngeal. As I pushed with my hand, I tripped his feet out from under him, then held his entire weight against the rail above the shark pen. His eyes were wide, probably from lack of oxygen, but terror, too. He knew what was down there.

I held him, my muscles creaking with the strain, pretending as if his three-hundred-plus pounds was an insignificant mass, no problem at all holding him with one hand. I wanted him to look into my face and believe that I held his life in my hands. Wanted him to feel the same demeaning realization that I'd felt, knowing that whether I lived or died was his decision to make.

I counted on his not knowing the truth about sharks—that it's difficult to get them to eat even fish in captivity. That the only real danger of going into the water with them was the chance of being rammed if they panicked.

I held him there as he used both hands to try and pry my fingers free, squeezing, squeezing, and I said, "The way you're bleeding, those sharks are going to be all over you, Clare."

He could barely form words, his voice hoarse. "Don't let me fall, man. I do anything you want. Don't let me go there."

"They missed your buddy. I doubt they'll miss again."

"Please, man. Please. I can't even swim."

I said, "Can't swim? Good. Those sharks are bottom feeders," and pushed him hard over the railing.

His falsetto scream was terrible to hear—but oddly gratifying, too. He hit the water with the grace of a boxcar and came up blowing water out his nose and still screaming.

Clare was wrong about not being able to swim. Apparently, he'd never been properly motivated before. I watched him doggy-slap his way to the buoyed netting and throw himself over into shallow water where Izzy was already wading to shore.

"We ain't done with you yet, Ransom girl!" Clare was holding his face in obvious pain, his Rasta cap pouring water as he slogged across the muck bottom. "The Lion of Judah, He save me from the water demons, but He not gonna spare you!"

Ransom gave it right back to him. "You Jamaican trash—you come back to this island, the police gonna arrest you and put you *under* the jail!"

Which didn't seem like a bad idea. I had not the slightest desire to test myself against Clare ever again. To Ransom, I said, "You go in, call the Sanibel Police. Just dial 911, tell them it's for me. I'll stay out here and make sure they don't come back."

Now Izzy was yelling threats as Ransom stepped closer to me and said, "Call the police . . . man, you think that's a good idea?"

"Hell, yes, I think it's a *great* idea. You want those two creeps following you? Maybe jump you when I'm not around?"

"Yeah, but the police, man. They listen to what Clare and Izzy have to say, then maybe they come askin' about that ring. It down in the water, they *know* where that is. Or the seventeen thousand dollars. Then maybe they contact the Bahamian government, and I got to answer all kinds of more questions. Like how'd I get enough money to buy me one of them satellite dishes for my new TV, which I plan to buy soon as I get home. Or how'd I afford that fancy red sports car which I'm gonna buy, too. A car like that, on Cat Island where we only got a little piece of one paved road, it gonna be *seen.* Which means people gonna notice, man."

"You and Tucker," I said, disgusted. "Two of a kind." I was watching Izzy and Clare hurrying into the mangroves now, looking back and still yelling at us, but giving it less and less, eager to get the hell away. Probably convinced we really were going to call the police.

I looked at my left arm. The bandage had been ripped away and I was bleeding again. "You go inside. Over the sink, there's a little first aid kit. You get that, and I'll be right in."

"Where you goin'?"

"Is that ring really worth something?"

She shrugged and made a noncommittal face. "Man, I just thought it somethin' pretty 'til Clare tell me. But them Rasta people, they sit around at their reasonins, smokin' their herb and talkin' shit, I don't think they know what's real, what isn't. Haile Selassie, he the king of all the Rastas, they think he God. So, yeah, it could be worth some money." She looked from me to the water. "What about them big sharks, though?"

I said, "I'll get the ring; you get the first-aid kit."

TOMLINSON WAS LOOKING at the ring, holding it up to the light. I listened to him say, "What we might have here . . . what you need to understand first is, Rastafarianism has two important symbols. One's the Rastafarian bible, the Holy Piby. The other's the royal ring of Haile Selassie. Wait, make that three important symbols. There's also the Rasta colors, black, red and green, or red, black and gold. It varies. The red stands for the church triumphant, which is the church of the Rastas. Black as in black Africans. Green represents the beauty and vegetation of Ethiopia. The gold, it might have something to do with this ring. I did a research paper on the sect, back when Rasta was just beginning to spread from Jamaica to the other islands. I spent a couple months down there. Love the people, man. The kids jumped right into Rasta because it was a way of saying screw you to the establishment, particularly the white establishment. And let's face it, who can blame them?"

I have no politics, though I seldom share Tomlinson's indulgent view of human behavior, but made no comment.

I listened to him say, "The story behind the ring is, the Ethiopian Orthodox Church gave it to Selassie out of gratitude when he pledged loyalty to the church. This was back in the 1930s. Supposedly it belonged to King Solomon, who'd given it to the Queen of Sheba so that she, in turn, could give it to their son, Prince someone of Ethiopia. Menelik. That's the name. Menelik was the first Ethiopian king in a dynasty that Rastas believe lasted for more than three thousand years. It ended in 1975 with Selassie's death. Selassie wasn't much of a leader—his people starved, lived in filth and he didn't much care. He liked to dress up in uniforms and get his picture taken with young girls. Didn't matter. I don't know why it is, but failed kings make the best gods, which is what happened. The Rastas think of him as the second Christ."

"The Lion of Judah," Ransom said. "That what they call him. The way they paste their hair and rub it out, it supposed to look like a lion's mane. I grew up dealin' with the Rastas, that how I know. But how you know so much about them, man? Down there writing your paper."

I said, "When it comes to religion and illegal drugs, Tomlinson's IQ jumps about fifty points."

We were in the lab. My arm newly bandaged, I was sitting on the wooden roller chair by the Cabisco binocular scope. The marina's black cat, Crunch & Des, was in his familiar spot on the stainless steel dissecting table by the window, tail thumping. Every now and again, the cat would lift his head, reconfirm our presence with yellow eyes, then flop his head down, immediately asleep again.

Ransom said, "You think that really is the famous ring?"

I didn't. I'd already studied the ring under low magnification. I have no interest in nor appreciation for jewelry, but I don't think it would have impressed me anyway. It was made of gold that was worn and smoothed from handling. Inset onto the face of the ring, in oynx, was the head of a lion, the design of which I associate with British royalty. The lion had two tiny diamonds for eyes.

Stamped into the bottom of the band was a jeweler's hallmark: 18K. Inside the band at the top, just to the side of the setting, was the apparent place of manufacture: NEW YORK.

It wasn't three thousand years old, that much was certain. Had never been worn by King Solomon or the Queen of Sheba. It also seemed very unlikely that an Ethiopian church would have given their new king a ring made in America.

"You never know, though," Tomlinson said. "It's possible. For instance, say one of the archbishops or an Abun—one of the church's patriarchs—happened to be visiting New York and got the idea that a ring might ingratiate him with the new king. So he finds one with a lion's head or maybe had it made. Waited around spending church money in the Big Apple then sailed back on the Queen Mary. I can see it happening."

I said, "He plans to tell Selassie the ring's a couple thousand years old, but lets the jeweler stamp New York on it? That's a stretch."

Tomlinson made an open-handed gesture—*Who knows?*—and handed the ring to me. It had some weight to it. He said, "I can make a few calls, do some research. The important thing is, it doesn't matter what we think. The two Jamaicans think it's the real ring. Maybe there're others who think the same. Maybe hundreds of others, which makes it very dangerous, man. Screwing with people's religious icons is a no-no." To Ransom, he said, "The guy you stole it from, what was his name?"

"His name Sinclair Benton, but I never saw it as stealin'. That man call me names and treat me mean. Worse, though, he call Daddy Gatrell names. Probably made it hard for Daddy come see me sometimes. The way it happened was, I walkin' past the house of that ol' dead witch, and one of his boys grabbed me and tried to make me to do the jiggy thing. I let him get drunked up good on cane rum, got his clothes off him and let him pass out thinkin' happy times was comin'.

"That how I got the whole house to myself, but it spooky, man, 'cause of the feeling that old witch still around. I found me a box full of money and that ring laying on the desk, right out in the open. So I didn't see it as stealin'. It more like a payment to me from the good Lord, cause that devil-man Benton, he so evil. Besides, how can you steal from a thief?"

"Do you think Benton had the kind of power or the connections to get his hands on something so valuable? The ring, I'm talking about."

"Everyone through the islands know Sinclair Benton. Even the voodoo people in Haiti afraid of that man. And he rich. He charge people for the spells he cast. The more desperate a person be, the more he charge them. I know a woman in Arthur's Town who give Sinclair her house to drive the demons outta her sick son."

Tomlinson looked at me. "See, then it is possible. When Selassie died in 1975, the ring disappeared. Somehow it ended up in London a couple of years later, where, supposedly Selassie's grandson, Crown Prince Asfa Wossen, gave it to Bob Marley as a present. When Marley died . . . that was around 1981, I think. Anyway, it disappeared again. Some say it was stolen, some believe it was handed down to the next Rasta prince. What I'm saying is, even if no one else wore it or owned it but Bob Marley, it would still be valuable . . . and dangerous."

When I didn't respond after a few seconds, Tomlinson said, "You're not taking this seriously, are you?" Then to Ransom, he added, "Doc lives in his own little hermit world. Fish and test tubes and microscopes. I wouldn't be surprised if he didn't even know who Bob Marley was."

I knew. But I sat and listened to Tomlinson tell me the story anyway, tell me that Rastafarianism was never really popular in the islands until 1966, when His Imperial Majesty Haile Selassie visited Jamaica and converted Rita Anderson, who was Bob Marley's wife. That day came to be called by the brotherens as "Groundation Day," perhaps the most important day in Rasta history. Later, Anderson convinced Marley to convert to Rastafarianism and he and his reggae band, the Wailers, spread the teachings of Rastafarianism throughout the world with his music and lyrics. Everywhere, from Central America to Australia and the South Pacific, people listened. Not an insignificant number of the world's population took the lyrics seriously and were converted to Marley's religion. Selassie was the God, Bob Marley the psalmist and prophet.

Tomlinson said, "People think Rastafarians just sit around smoking weed, singing and dancing. That's a part of it, yeah, but it's not an easy religion to follow. Rastas aren't allowed to eat just any food. A true Rasta only eats I-tal food. That's food cooked but served as raw as possible. It never touches chemicals; it's natural, never canned. Lots of Rastas are vegetarians since eating almost raw meat isn't what you'd call appetizing. The ones who do eat meat can't touch pork because pigs are the scavengers of land. Same with shellfish, because they consider lobsters, crabs, shrimp, stuff like that to be scavengers, too. They can eat fish, but the fish can't be more than a foot long. Anything bigger is a predator, a danger to their spirit."

No wonder Izzy and Clare had not reacted calmly when introduced to the shark pen.

"I love the Rastas, love their spirit and their faith. The Holy Piby, man, I read it. The black man's Bible, that's what some call it. Inspired, some very powerful stuff in there. It was first printed back in the 1920s in the Ethiopian language of Amharic. It says that God and all of his prophets were black, and some believe it contains the lost verses of the Old Testament. The reasoning makes more sense than some people want to admit. The way it goes is, Ethiopian nobility always considered themselves direct descendants of King Solomon. They were black, so Solomon was black. If Solomon was black, then Christ had to be black, too. Which is very cool, I think.

"When I was in Jamaica, I lived with a Rasta group called the Twelve Tribes of Israel. For a time they were very heavy into the Black Power movement, which they needed to be, but in a very positive and peaceful way. Reform through education and political action. Some of the splinter groups, though, they believed violence was the answer. Still do. They were serious racists, too. Kill the whites—all whites—and there would no longer be oppression."

I had the ring under the binocularscope again. Nothing ornate about the typeface. Plain, very American: NEW YORK. Without looking up from the microscope, I said, "I remember that time. Kill without remorse for political gain. A lot of whites and blacks were doing it. Assassinations. Bombings. Overthrow the government at any cost. What was it Mao Tse Tung wrote? 'In the struggle for socialism, the death of a million innocents means nothing.'"

Tomlinson stood suddenly to leave. "Ransom? If I were you, I'd get in touch with some Rasta people you know and trust. Or I've still got some friends with the Twelve Tribes if you want me to do it. Tell them you have a ring, maybe Haile Selassie's ring, and want to give it back. Today, I mean. By phone. Before the rumors start to spread. Before more of the violent types come looking for you."

12

AS I WALKED with Tomlinson to the marina to get the mail, he said, "All that stuff with the Rastas reminds me of something I've been meaning to bring up, Doc. Lately, more and more, the older I get, the things I did in my past really bother me. Some truly shitty stuff, man. I'd like just the two of us to sit down one day and talk about it, you don't mind. About something I was involved with a long time ago, but it concerns you. I think it's a talk long overdue."

In some inexplicable and maybe perverse way, I'd been goading him when I brought up revolutionaries and bombings. I wasn't certain why. Perhaps it was because I was beginning to have second thoughts about the deal I'd made with Harrington. But I said, "Sure, we can talk. Another time, though. Getting beaten up, getting shot, arguing with Ransom about my uncle. Little stuff like that, I'm kind of pooped out for some reason."

"Okay. But soon."

"Yeah, soon. A couple of weeks, a couple of months from now, when we both have some time. If you can help me get this business with Ransom squared away, that would be a good way to start."

"Absolutely," he said. "No worries." He walked on in silence for a time before he spoke again. "I went through the stuff Tuck sent to Ransom. What a circus act that guy was. And what a romantic. He sent her drawings, which I know you saw, but also this cryptic letter."

I said, "You read it. I'm not going to waste my time."

"That's my point. You don't have to read it. I've already figured out where Tuck hid the six grand. It's at his ranch. We've got to meet a guy there and he's going to give us another letter. We can go get it tomorrow, you want. Or Sunday."

"Make it Sunday. I've got at least a full day's work in the lab, plus a lot of phone calls to make. The Aquaculture Lab at Gainesville has been working on reintroducing Gulf sturgeon south of Tampa Bay, and I've been doing research for the director. Then I've got to contact all the offshore stone crabbers I know and see if I can buy some of their old rope because of an order I've got for gooseneck barnacles. But first I need to check with Jeth, see how the fish did while I was away."

Tomlinson said, "What?" already preoccupied with private thoughts. When I repeated myself, he said, "Did you hear what happened to Jeth? Between him and Janet?"

Jeth was one of the marina's fishing guides, a huge, good-looking guy with a big heart and a slight stutter. Janet was Janet Mueller, who lived up at Jensen's Marina on her little blue Holiday Mansion houseboat.

"What happened?"

Tomlinson's attention had wandered again. "Huh? What happened to who?"

I stopped walking. Put my hand on his shoulder and turned him. "I gather that things didn't go well with Nimba, did they? On your trip back from Guava Key."

He laughed bitterly. "It couldn't'a gone worse, man. It was terrible. A faithful woman who finally decides to go out on her abusive husband, but the guy she chooses can't consummate the relationship. A woman with her religious background, it was like having God in the room telling her she was a sinner and damned to Hell. Like that was the reason He wouldn't allow me to perform. The moment we got back, she threw her luggage in the trunk of a cab and headed for the airport." He sighed. "I don't blame her, man. She worked and worked on me, the whole trip down. Zamboni tried to rally a few times but never really made it across the blue line."

"Maybe it's time you spoke to a physician. I hear they've got drugs now for that. Some kind of pill?"

"I'm way ahead of you. I talked to Dieter today when he got back from lunch. He's got his license to practice in the states now, which I really don't give a shit about, but it means the drug companies give him all kinds of interesting samples. He gave me a pill to try."

Dieter Rasmussen was a retired Munich psychopharmacologist who lives over on A Dock in his gorgeous Grand Banks trawler, *Das Stasi*. He's a big guy with a shaved head, good-looking—judging from the reaction of local women—brilliant, rich and he loves the kicked-back, happy life of Dinkin's Bay. I hadn't liked or trusted the man at first, but he'd done a good job of fitting in with the marina community, so now we played chess occasionally, or sat around on my deck at sunset talking science, genetics, natural selection—things that interested both of us.

"What'd he give you?"

Tomlinson was wearing baggy surfer shorts, no shirt, veins and ribs showing, his gaunt face serious beneath matted blond hair. He stuffed a hand into his pocket, and produced a small, blue, diamond-shaped pill in a blister pack. "Viagra," he said. "It's the only one he had left, but he's got so much respect for me as a fellow scientist, he said what the hell. I had no choice but to accept. You know how I hate to use prescription drugs, but I'm desperate, man."

He *sounded* desperate. He had the same air of preoccupation and depression he'd been projecting for the last several months. It's normal for Tomlinson's personality to vary with his moods. I've learned to recognize his highs and emotional lows. When he's down, in a funk, I know, for instance, to leave him alone, give him time and the black mood will pass.

But this mood wasn't passing and it was beginning to worry me.

"I wasn't aware that you had an aversion to any kind of drug," I told him.

It was a friendly barb calculated to make him smile, but he didn't smile. I listened to him say, "When it comes to pharmaceuticals, I'm an explorer not a commuter. You're not going to see me on many subways. But if I find a space shuttle available? Look out. Plus, with prescription pills, I worry about side effects. Like this pill. Some folks say it can blur your vision and give you a slight headache, too. Doctor Dieter tells me about all that and immediately I think, Jesus, what a dangerous drug. First it screws up your vision, then it gives you a hard-on." He made a sound of frustration and disgust. "But it's worth the risk. I don't have many options remaining. So tonight, after the marina's party, I'm going to test the little blue pill and see if my goddamn pecker has an ounce of manhood left in him. Fortunately, I've found two humanitarian-minded ladies willing to participate in the experiment."

That, at least, sounded more like the old Tomlinson. "Anyone I know? Or is it confidential?"

"You remember Barbie and Bobbi, the Verner twins who work at Hooters?"

I said, "Sure, the two redheads." Hooters was where we went for cold draft beer and chicken wings after playing baseball.

"Barbie and Bobbi, they are two smart ladies. Both're working their way through college, majoring in psychology with a minor in comparative religions, which is one reason we've become good friends over the last year. They're not kinky, they're not promiscuous, but those two girls have the instincts of surgical nurses. They're familiar with the problem; they know I need help. I called and spoke to both of them before I came to your place. So guess what? Didn't even hesitate; they both volunteered to get naked with me, bless their hearts. They're coming to the party, then we're going for a short midnight shakedown cruise on *No Más*."

I was laughing now. I couldn't help myself. "Then why are you so depressed? You ought to be grinning like you just won the lottery. You know how many men in this country who'd give anything to trade places with you? Two Hooters girls, for Christ's sake."

He shook his head from side to side, disconsolate. "They don't know about this pill. What if it doesn't work? If I can't make it with two Hooters girls, I might as well stick my dick in the dirt and use it as a tomato stake. The worst thing, though, man—and this is what's really bothering me—if the pill doesn't put serious lead in my pencil, I'll never be able to face those girls again. After something like that, where can we go to eat wings?"

DINKIN'S BAY MARINA is three hundred yards or so up the shoreline from my lab. If the mosquitoes aren't swarming, it's an easy walk along the shell road. If you want to get to the marina by boat, you head north under the Sanibel Causeway, then turn left just past the power lines and run in close along the deepwater of Woodring's Point. To get there by car, follow Sanibel's Tarpon Bay Road past Bailey's General Store, down the shell road, into the mangroves and through the gate to the bay.

Lots of people come by boat and car and bike because Dinkin's Bay is an unusual place.

Beyond the shell parking lot, there's a community of old wooden buildings that extends out onto the water via a latticework of wobbly docks. It is a welcome anachronism on an island known for tourism, busy beaches, thousands of real estate salesmen, reclusive artists, designer homes and elegant restaurants. There are plank tables for cleaning fish, a big wooden bait tank whose pump hisses twenty-four hours a day and picnic tables beneath a tin roof so visitors have a place to sit while they eat the marina's fried fish and crab cakes and chowder. There is a gift shop, too.

It's called the Red Pelican, and it smells of incense and imported cotton and silk. It offers blouses and dresses, sarongs and knickknacks from all over the world, plus paintings by local artists.

Next to the Red Pelican is the marina office and store. It's a two-story building. Stocky, pragmatic Mack, owner and manager of Dinkin's Bay, runs the office below. Jeth lives in the one-bedroom apartment above.

As I walked toward the office, I heard a woman's voice call, "Hey there, Doc! You coming to the party tonight?" I looked to see JoAnn Smallwood waving at me. JoAnn is part owner of the soggy old Chris Craft cruiser *Tiger Lily,* one of Dinkin's Bay Marina's gaudier floating homes. She's a skinny-hipped, busty woman who, along with her roommate and partner, Rhonda Lister, runs a very profitable weekly newspaper, *The Heat Islands Fishing Report.*

I stopped to talk with JoAnn for awhile while the other liveaboards worked or washed their boats, or carried grocery sacks or coolers along the docks, everyone seeming to move faster than usual. Nearly every person who passed me had to stop, say hello, and ask why my arm was in a sling.

To each and every one, I told them, "Fell off a dock."

To the few who said they'd met my sister, that she was gorgeous and charming and funny, I replied, "Funny's right. That's her little joke. She's actually my cousin."

It was Friday night, the official end of the workweek on the connected barrier islands of Sanibel and Captiva. Saturday and Sunday were the busiest days of the week, but Friday night is still the traditional gathering time for the liveaboards and marina employees, a brief quiet time before the weekend rush, when all the locals come together as a community to drink and laugh, to complain about the traffic and the tourists with no one around to offend.

It was nearly five P.M. JoAnn and Rhonda had hung Japanese lanterns on the stern of their boat, a sure sign that it was a party night. Music was already booming from inside the trawlers and sailboats and cruisers that lined liveaboard row. I could hear showers running; could smell the shampoo odor of soap mixed with the more common marina smells of diesel and rope and varnish. Could see that Mack and Jeth had already set out the big Igloo coolers filled with ice and beer. Could see Eleanor and Joyce and Kelly loading the picnic tables with food. Knew that, within an hour or so, Mack would walk out, close the steel gate and lock it, a necessary ritual that is also symbolic: The outside world could no longer intrude on our small marina stronghold.

Now JoAnn waved me closer and said, "Did you hear what happened while you were away? Between Jeth and Janet, I mean."

It's impossible to avoid marina gossip so I usually listen politely, then pointedly try to forget what I've just heard. I said, "Someone told Tomlinson, because he mentioned it. But no particulars."

JoAnn has short copper hair that now looked bright red, perhaps because of the satin sheer pink dress she wore or the yellow hibiscus blossom behind her ear. There was a pleasant bounce of hair and cleavage as she made the waving motion again. "Then come aboard. You're gonna need a beer after you hear it. It's that damn sad."

I looked at my watch: 5:10. Almost sunset time. Almost party time. It was the first day in weeks that I hadn't worked out, and I still felt sick and sore from my run-in with Clare.

"A couple of beers, maybe that's just what I need," I told her. "But then I need to go talk to Mack about something." I used my good arm to pull me up the old Chris's boarding letter, through the railing gate.

JoAnn said, "Jeth and Janet, we all know they've had their problems. But what do you expect if you date someone from your own marina?" She gave me a meaningful look, sitting there in her party dress, one chunky leg crossed over the other, a margarita in her hand.

A knowing look because we'd both felt a long-standing sexual attraction for the other. We had come close to acting on that attraction a few times, but had been smart enough to defuse it on each occasion. JoAnn wasn't beautiful or even pretty by general standards—which is to say the predictable and often perverse standards of New York advertising gurus. She had nice hair, a Rubensesque body and the kind of wide, plain face that I associate with cornfields and small Midwestern towns. But there was a commonsense sexuality about the woman that I felt on a bone-and-marrow, abdominal level. Apparently, she felt the same for me. So we took pains never to be alone.

We were in deck chairs, sitting on *Tiger Lily*'s stern, where we could look across the docks to the marina office and the shallow-water mooring where the fishing skiffs—the Bonefishers and Makos, the Aquasports, Egrets and Lake and Bays—sat motionless on their lines, big outboard engines tilted upward like the wings of old fighter planes on a carrier. Through their silence, the engines implied velocity and a certain competence.

She'd brought me my standard drink: Bud Light in a big glass over ice with a squeeze of lime. I now took a sip and said, "Yep. It's way too risky to date among the marina family."

"Exactly. Everyone agrees. But if anyone could make it work, it's those two kids. Janet loves the big lug so much, the first time they had trouble, you know as well as I do, that's why she moved her boat up to Jensen's. Thought the distance might help, and it did. Since then, they've been doing great. Jeth stays on her houseboat when he doesn't have a charter, and you know how often Janet overnights here. Hell, I think it's been good for all of us, because now everyone at Jensen's has gotten to be like part of our extended family. And they're such a fun, crazy bunch."

Jensen's Marina on Captiva is one of the last of the old Florida fish camps. Run by three brothers who also happen to be raving individualists, walking into Jensen's is like traveling back four or five decades. I said, "The guides up there, Dave, Bob Sabatino and Jimmy, when they clean a female black tip, they've been saving the unborn sharks for me.

And Janet, of course, she's one of the few people I trust to take care of my fish."

JoAnn nodded. "While you and Tomlinson were on Guava key, she was here every night helping Jeth. Until it happened."

What happened was, the previous weekend, Janet and Jeth had had some minor squabble. In all human pairings, sometimes varying with the situation, there is a dominant member. Janet was the more forceful of the two, but never in an overpowering, offensive way. She was more goal-oriented than Jeth, much better with details, and so she tended to control the relationship. The argument had something to do with Jeth's seeming lack of professional drive. How could he expect her to marry him, to produce a family for the two of them, if he continued working as a handyman around the marina and guiding only when he felt like it?

It was a serious subject as far as Janet was concerned. Marriage was important to her. It was her second try, and getting everything right was vital. There was a good reason. A couple of years back, Janet had come to Sanibel an emotional and physical wreck after quitting her teaching job in Ohio. She had had to quit her job because she was suffering anxiety attacks and depression so severe that she could no longer function. It took us awhile before she trusted us enough to tell us the story. It was not a happy story. Her first husband, the only man she'd ever loved, had been driving home late after work one snowy night. On the same road, coming from the opposite direction, was a woman who had no license because of her long history of alcohol abuse.

All that Janet could remember from that night, and the week that followed, was a highway patrolman coming to the door . . . and a nurse crying with her, at her bedside, because of the miscarriage she'd suffered.

It was a long, long time before she could bring herself to date anyone.

When she'd finally healed sufficiently, Jeth was a good choice. He has the looks and the build of a college linebacker, but he is one of the kindest, most mild-mannered men I've ever met. Even so, Janet's prodding had finally pissed him off and he apparently told her to go find another man if she wasn't satisfied with his professional aspirations or his income.

"That's how it got started," JoAnn told me. "It wasn't a big fight. Nothing serious—at least, that's what Janet told me, and she had no reason to lie, Doc. This was two days after it happened, and she was absolutely devastated. Broken-hearted. I don't think the girl's stopped crying all week."

Coincidentally, that same weekend, Janet had been invited to an all-night bachelorette party in Sarasota. She and her girlfriends were to spend the evening going from bar to bar in a limo. Lots of drinking and dancing and harmless fun.

"But it wasn't so harmless," JoAnn told me. "The last thing Janet did before she got in the limo was try to call Jeth at his apartment. She tried a couple of more times before midnight. He still wasn't home, which made her mad for some reason, so she stuck the cell phone in her purse and decided the best way for her to stop worrying about what Jeth was doing was to have a hell of a good time on her own. Which she did. There were five or six girls in the party. They went to a couple of bars, then to one of those male review strip clubs. That set the mood. Then, at Passe Grille, they happened to run into a bunch of local guys who were having their own bachelor's party. Great-looking guys all of them, and one of them started hitting on Janet.

"You know how shy she is, Doc. I think she's cute as can be but, let's face it, she doesn't have the kind of looks or the kind of body that guys tumble over. She wasn't used to that kind of attention from a man so smooth. Plus, all the other girls had matched up with one of the bachelors, and there was a kind of screw-it, let's-have-fun attitude. No one was gonna tell, especially the girl who was getting married 'cause it was her last night of freedom and she was behaving worse than any of them."

JoAnn noticed that my glass was empty. She stood and got another beer from the little on-deck fridge. Stopped to exchange pleasantries with two of the guides, Javier Castillo and Neville Robeson, then took her seat again, sipped her drink and turned her face toward me. Said, "We've had some great talks, you and me, Doc. Someone like you, I feel like I can say any damn thing that comes into my mind, and it'll be okay. One thing we've never talked about, though, it's something that most men don't know or even suspect about us women. It's not all the time, and the mood has to be just right. But it happens. What it is, when women get together in that kind of situation, sexuality can be . . . well, *contagious.* I've felt it myself plenty of times. It's like being part of a pack. You all get horny as hell at the same time, and there're suddenly no rules at all 'cause the whole group's doing it." She paused for a moment, considering what she'd just told me. "You're a scientist. You think there could be some kind of biological reason for feeling that way? Herd instinct, maybe?"

I didn't feel like smiling—intimate stories about friends told by a third party make me uncomfortable. But I smiled anyway. "I'd prefer not even to guess about something like that. So what happened at the party?"

Janet and her friends had drunk a lot and they'd kept drinking is what happened. Janet and the handsome guy she'd met ended up alone in the back of the guy's Mercedes. She wasn't too drunk to know what she was doing. It was consensual, it seemed safe and fun at the time, and it was very, very passionate. She'd never done anything like that in her life. Didn't think she was capable of doing something like that. I had a hard time believing it myself . . . but, in a way, it made perfect sense, too. Janet's one of the plain, doughy-looking ones. Round face, mousy brown hair, legs and thighs prone to heaviness. Very quiet and competent and dependable. Good with computers and bookkeeping. She's in her mid-thirties now. Probably seldom in her life experienced the overwhelming flattery of a certain kind of man who's very good in bars.

JoAnn said, "Janet told me it was like being temporarily insane, and I know exactly what she means. She wouldn't let the guy go all the way.

But they got stripped down and real sweaty. Completely dropped all her inhibitions probably like she never had before—"

I interrupted. "Please don't tell me she confessed all this to Jeth. I hope to hell she was smart enough and adult enough not to try and get rid of her own guilt by laying it all on—"

"She didn't confess," JoAnn said. "She didn't have to confess. Remember that cell phone she put in her purse? In the back of the Mercedes, every time they'd move a certain way, she'd squeeze up against that purse and hit the redial button accidentally. Jeth's recorder will tape messages up to three minutes long. He was out to almost two 'cause he had to tow in Duke Sells, who'd broken down about seven miles off the lighthouse. Got back to his apartment exhausted, got his first beer of the night and played his messages. Stood there and listened to fifteen minutes of his girlfriend making love to another man."

I felt sick myself just hearing it, and I didn't doubt it for a moment when JoAnn added, "When Janet got back the next night and realized what'd happened, she went to him and actually got down on her knees outside the door of his apartment and begged him to forgive her. Jeth wouldn't let her in. Never even opened the door. That was six days ago. He hasn't spoken a word to her. Says he never will again. I saw Janet yesterday. Remember the way she looked when she first came here? After her husband was killed in the car wreck? Shaky, gaunt, all the horror in the world in those pretty eyes of hers. Clap your hands behind her and she'd jump out of her skin. That's the way she looks now. She can't eat, can't sleep and can't stop crying. She thinks she's cursed. I mean, really *believes* it. Or that she has some destructive badness in her that keeps screwing up her life intentionally. I had the worst feeling when I left her houseboat—a feeling that she's not gonna make it this time. It's too much after all the stuff she's already been through."

I stood, placed my mug on the teak table. Said, "Mind if I use your phone?"

"What're you going to do, Doc?"

There was a wall phone on the control console bulkhead just to the left of the helm seat. "What's Janet's number? I haven't called her in awhile."

Now JoAnn was standing, her expression dubious. "Hey . . . wait a minute, big fella. You're way too smart to put yourself in the middle of something like this. Give them some time; they'll work it out themselves."

I held the phone away from my ear. "Do you really believe that?"

She sighed, thought about it, then sighed again. "No. No, I don't believe it. Not for a minute."

"You know how stubborn Jeth is. If he's been telling people he'll never speak to her again, you can bet that's exactly what he'll do. As in *never* again. You think she's strong enough to deal with that?"

JoAnn shook her head slowly. "Janet's at the end of her rope. That's what I believe. After something like this, she may end up one of those crazy hermit spinsters. A bag lady, who knows? I think she's about to completely lose it. But what the hell can we do to help them?"

13

I THOUGHT I knew the answer to that. The call didn't take long. A few minutes later, Mack said, "A cell phone? You went for how many years without even an answering machine, and now you've got a cell phone?"

I was inside the marina office now, and had just opened the FedEx package he'd handed me. There was no return address on the slip, but I knew who'd sent it.

I pressed the power button of my new cell phone, heard the phone's irritating beep, turned it off again and stuck the thing in my pocket.

Mack and Jeth were sitting behind the glass counter. Mack was wearing a safari shirt, the kind with pleats that he's partial to. He told me he favors that kind of shirt because it's the sort of thing his grandfather wore growing up in New Zealand. He had his Ben Franklin bifocals on to see because he was tallying up the day's receipts, a South Trust money bag bulging with cash within safe reach. Jeth sat behind him on a stool in the corner. He was leafing through a *Florida Sportsman* magazine, wearing his guide khakis. His expression was glum. His face reminded me of the way JoAnn had described Janet: gaunt, like some of the life had been leached out.

When I entered, I said, "Looks like we've got live music tonight, huh?"

Mack turned and glanced out the window briefly. The Jensen's Taxi boat had just pulled in, loaded with amplifiers and instruments and musicians.

"John Mooney's playing with the Trouble Starters. Jim Morris is back from Key West, so he's going to sit in. Danny Morgan, too. Ought to be quite a party."

I said, "I've got so much work to do in the lab, I can't stick around for long. But I'll be able to hear the music, no problem." I waited for a moment before I added, "You're going to be there, aren't you, Jeth?"

He grunted, shrugged, said nothing.

Mack ignored him. "Your sister stopped by. Said she could play the steel drum if we found one for her, so Jimmy Jensen scared one up. And that she'd get a limbo line going. I really like her, Doc. But you know what you might suggest to her? Don't use that outside shower of yours. Not during daylight, anyway. She was out there showering this afternoon and two of the rental boats collided. One of them's going to need fiberglass work. Plus old Mister Wells—the nice old gentleman who leads the Audubon tours? He fell off the dock and twisted the hell out of his knee. She's got some amazing body, your sister does. Isn't that right, Jeth?"

Jeth grunted again and held the magazine a little higher in front of his face.

I reached behind the counter, lifted a cardboard box full of my mail and began to sort through it. I told Mack, "She's not my sister, she's my cousin," before I said, "Hey, there's something I need to discuss with you guys."

I told them that, for the next couple of weeks, they should be wary of any stranger who came asking for me, of anyone who called and wanted to know where I was. To notify me right away. I told just enough about the scene on the dock with the Rastafarians, and Jeth showed some interest for the first time.

"I wish to hell I'd of noticed it going on," he said fiercely. "I'd'a beat the crap out of both of them. They come up here like they own the place and attack you like that? On *our* island, the bastards. Ca-ca-call me next time, Doc. I'll make them wish they was never born."

He had a lot of anger in there bottled up, no mistaking it. I'd never heard that intensity in his voice; had never guessed he possessed even the slightest potential for violence.

I said, "If you see them, notify me or call the cops. That's all you need to do. Or if anyone stops by or calls trying to find me. Give me a heads-up."

Mack seemed uneasy. He was a newspaper reader, a CNN junkie, but even if he had no interests beyond the borders of Sanibel, he would have known about the kidnapping attempt on Guava Key. News travels almost as fast as gossip among island people. Even so, he was prudent enough not to ask if there was a connection. "Thing is, Doc, I wish you'd told me earlier. This morning, I had two calls. Both from men and about half an hour apart. They wanted to know how to get in touch with you, where your place is. I saw no reason not to—"

I said, "Perfectly understandable, Mack. You didn't know."

"Well, what I was going to tell you is, one of them had an island accent. So it may have been one of the Rastafarians who paid you the visit. The other man, though, he had a Spanish accent. Cuban, I figured, but maybe not. I wouldn't know the bloody difference."

I didn't like the implications of that, but I made an effort not to let them see that I was concerned. "Did he identify himself?"

"Nope. Just asked about the marine biologist who lived here, mentioned your name and said it was important he contact you. I figured he wanted to place an order." Mack was done with the receipts. He folded his calculator and began to put everything away.

Outside, through the window, people were already beginning to circulate on the docks, freshly showered, drinks in hand. Ransom was out there wearing the kind of short, clingy dress that might be called a chemise—black satin material that hung from her shoulders on two thin straps, showing the inside of her thighs when she moved those long legs of hers. She was wearing white beads in her hair now. Had three . . . no, four men standing around her, all of them listening intently as she spoke, wanting her to see how interested they were in what she had to say. Three of the four had to be ten, fifteen years younger than her. Didn't matter. She already had her own little flock of admirers.

Time to go out and join the party.

Mack stood as he said, "You want, I've got a couple of spare bedrooms at my house. You're welcome to stay as long as you like. Or maybe we should get the chief of police over here. Invite him to the marina for a drink and ask if his people can keep a watch on your place."

I was shaking my head. I didn't want anything to do with involving the police. Not now. I told Mack, "I can handle it myself. But help me keep an eye out for anyone who wants to contact me for the wrong reasons."

"No worries, Doc. If we don't take care of our own, who will?"

"Exactly." I had my box of mail under my arm and said to Jeth as I was walking out, "You don't mind, I'd like to talk with you for a minute. About how my fish did while I was away."

He still had his face in the magazine. "There're fine. You had a seahorse die, a couple of pinfish, that's all. I dah-da-didn't miss a feeding. You know you can trust me."

"The stuff I want to ask you about is a little more detailed. Outside?"

"I don't see why I've got to go outside just to—" He looked up for the first time and saw the expression on my face. He folded the magazine with the reluctance of a difficult teenager. Said, "Okay. You've got questions about your fish. Whatever."

Jeth accompanied me down the shell road toward the path to my house, not wanting to follow but I left him no choice by walking as fast as I could, talking, asking questions at the same time, so it would have been rude to stop, and Jeth is never rude.

I kept him on the subject of my aquaria. Had he seen the sharks actually eat, or had he assumed they'd eaten? What about the largest of the immature tarpon in my tank? I'd noticed some scale damage on her. Had someone done something to spook her; caused her to slam into the wall of the tank? "You know how careful I am with those tarpon," I told him. Then I switched the subject to the netter who brought me fresh mullet and thread herring three times a week. Maybe there was a better, more dependable source over on Pine Island. Saint James City, maybe. Or Bokeelia.

"Might be a more cost-efficient supplier," I said.

I could see that he was bored with the subject. Didn't want to be there listening to it. Tolerated it only because we'd been friends so long. He did a lot of heavy sighing. He ended several sentences with, "That's about all I can tell you . . ." meaning he was ready to head back to the marina, probably his one-bedroom apartment where he'd spend the evening alone, moping upstairs in his room while the Friday night party raged outside.

I didn't let him. I continued to bore him with questions about my fish until we got to the locked gate, which is right next to the path through the mangroves that leads to my boardwalk. I stopped there, leaned my weight against the fence and looked at him for a moment before I said, "I heard about what happened between you and Janet."

"Boy oh boy, that's just what I thought," he said severely. "You didn't want to talk about your fish tanks. You got me out here alone to talk about her. But, damn it, I'm not gonna talk about that woman. Not to you or anybody else."

"At least listen to what I have to say—"

"Nope. End of dah-dah-discussion. Far as I'm concerned she doesn't even exist. Like she's dead. I don't want to ever hear her name again."

"Her name's Janet, and she's not dead. She's an important part of your life and you need to deal with what happened."

"You're starting to piss me off, Doc! Seriously. It's none of your business. I don't go asking you nosy questions. What the hell gives you the right to do it to me?" He folded his arms across his chest, eyes glaring. Defensive posture.

"Jeth, I'm asking you as a favor. You, Janet, me, we've all been friends too long to—"

"If you're my friend, you'll drop the goddamn subject! I not only don't want to talk about it, I don't even want to think about it! Which is why I'm gonna take my ass back to the marina and pretend like you didn't pull the tricky deal you just pulled." He turned to leave, but I caught him by the shoulder. It stopped him. Stopped him not because of the grip I had, but because I'd crossed a very dangerous boundary. With someone like Jeth, verbal manipulation is one thing, physical contact with the implication of force is another. He looked at me, his face turning crimson, then looked at my hand. "Let me go, Doc. Get your hand off me. Now."

"Nope. Not 'til we talk."

"I mean it. You're pushing way too hard. Don't think you're safe just because you got that arm in a sling."

"You want to hit someone, Jeth? Go ahead and hit me. But after I pick myself up, you're going to stand there and listen to what I have to say."

"That's enough!" He whirled and, in one motion, used his elbow to knock my arm away before he grabbed my shirt collar in both hands and jammed me hard up against the fence. "I warned you. I told you to get your fucking hands off me!"

I didn't fight back, didn't struggle. Let him hold me there, looking into his bulging face, his crazed eyes. Waited while the fury moved through him and slowly, slowly dissipated. Waited and watched as he took a big shuddering breath, then shook his head as if just awakening from some nightmare. "Christ, Doc. I'm sorry. But you just wouldn't quit. You had to keep pushing and pushing and . . . shit!" He yanked his hands away and turned his back to me. "I can't talk about it," he said miserably. "I won't talk about it. Not after what she did."

"Is what she did really that bad?"

"You're goddamn right it is! You didn't have to sit there like an idiot and listen to that phone tape. First couple of minutes, I couldn't even figure out what the hell was going on. It scared the devil out of me because I knew it was Janet, and I thought she was hurt or kidnapped or something, that's why she was moaning. Once I realized what the hell it was, though, I couldn't stop listening. It was like some sick thing in me wanted to hear. I still don't know why."

I said, "We all do things that, later, we simply can't understand."

He turned to face me again, eyes teary but some of the anger returning, too. "Don't make excuses for her. Don't you dare! The guy she was with—Mikey, that's what she called him, this guy she'd never met in her life before. I'd kill the sonuvabitch if I could find him. You know what the woman I planned to marry did for Mikey?"

"Knock it off, Jeth. I don't want to hear the details, and there's no reason to put yourself through it again."

His voice grew louder; had acquired the thin edge of hysteria. "You wanted to talk about it, so let's talk! You didn't hear the tape, so how else can you know? Janet and her new boyfriend, Mikey, on the recorder, they were both breathing and moaning and he says, 'Jan Ba-bah-baby, why don't you slide down there and make me feel really good.' And Jah-ja-ja-Janet tells him, 'Oh baby, I want to do that anyway,' and then I could hear what she was doing, the sound of it, and that's when I ripped the fucking phone out of the wall, ran it down to the docks and threw the goddamn thing into the water. Know what I did then, Doc?" He shuddered massively once more, pressed both hands to the sides of his head, eyes closed, as he said, "I vomited."

I hesitated, then stepped to him and put my hand on his shoulder. Gave him a little shake and said, "You need to talk to her. You don't have to forgive her. You don't have to make up with her. You don't ever have to speak to her again. But you need to allow her the chance to apologize.

Person to person, face to face. You know her past, what she's already been through. Yeah, I know, it's a bad time for you, but it may be a dangerous time for Janet. As in very dangerous. This time, she might not fight her way back. Grace is what she needs right now. Grant her some grace. She's a good person, a good woman. She's my friend and she deserves that."

"A good woman! That's a laugh."

I squeezed his shoulder, wanting him to listen. "I didn't want to have to use this, but I've got no choice. Three or four months ago, it was around Halloween. I couldn't sleep, so I went for a jog. It was way after midnight when I got back, and I saw you in your skiff. You and that little waitress, the new one from Boston who tends bar sometimes at Sanibel Grill. Mary Kate? I didn't come over for a close look, but it was pretty obvious what you were doing."

He raised his head, turned as if to face me, then thought better of it. "You . . . you were there? You never mentioned that to me before, dah-da-Doc."

"I'll never mention it to you or anyone else again. I promise. If you just cut Janet some slack."

"The little brunette who works for Matt. I . . . what I think we were dah-dah-da-doing was just talking. She stopped by the marina and it was kinda late."

"Hey—this is me you're talking to. You and the girl on the casting platform. Want more details?"

He shook his head, still not able to look at me. "Ah-h-h-h shit. I was hoping no one would ever know . . . that I could forget what an idiot I was. The night you saw us, I'd been at one of Duke Sells's all-day duck-and-oyster parties. I don't know how I ended up with her. She's always been kind of a flirt. Told me I had nice eyes. I bought her a couple drinks. After that, I cah-ca-can hardly remember what happened."

"I imagine Janet's memory is pretty foggy, too. Could be it's one of those if-a-tree-falls-in-a-forest deals. If no one's around to remember, maybe it didn't really happen."

"I was so drunk. That's what I mean."

I heard a car pull around the last curve of the shell road. I looked up to see Janet's little Ford pickup. I hardly recognized the woman inside. Janet's hair was a stringy mess, her clothes were wrinkled, her face sunken around the two dark and haunted holes that were eyes. I clapped Jeth on the back. I said, "So right away, you and your former girlfriend have something in common," as I watched her step out as if in a daze, eyes seeing nothing but Jeth. Then I gave him a little push toward her. Watched just long enough to see her walk . . . then run into his slow, reluctant arms, the two of them holding each other in a silence that was more like mutual shock, and then one, then both of them, were sobbing.

I turned and walked down the boardwalk to my stilthouse. . . then I began to run, too, when I heard the phone ringing.

I answered just before the recorder took over, and heard Lindsey Harrington's voice say, "Doc! I was about to give up on you, big boy. Man, do I miss that bod of yours!"

14

LINDSEY SAID IT'D been a crazy couple of days. She'd never been through anything like it in her life. That now she knew what it must be like to be President. Or a big-time rock star, the way they'd choppered her off the island, everything done in secret, to some airport she'd never seen before.

Hal Harrington had been there waiting, and flew her in a Learjet north, but her dad wouldn't even tell her where. Then it was into another helicopter, and finally a waiting limo which drove them for more than an hour or so, and by that time it was dark, so she really couldn't say for certain where she was even now. Didn't even know for sure what state she was in.

"Woke up yesterday morning," she said, laughing, "and I'm like, where the hell am I? Looked out the window and there were mountains all yellow and silver with aspens, and fresh snow on the ground like you see on calendars or Christmas cards. I mean, it's a totally awesome place. Like my own ski lodge with a rock fireplace that covers one whole wall, and I've got a bird feeder outside, which I'm keeping full so I can watch the cardinals. Because what else do I have to do except read or watch TV?"

The worst thing, though, she said, was that I wasn't there to share the place with her—she said it wistfully, in a way I found touching, a girl with a crush—and it'd be especially great having me around because she'd been alone since this morning when her father had to fly back to Colombia on business. Except for the two bodyguards her father had hired, of course. They were always around but kept their distance. "Dad thought Gale was a little too chummy, and that's not gonna happen again."

I was standing at the window, watching the band set up on the docks. I was using my home phone, not the new cell phone. I stood there watching the sky turn tropical fruit colors, from pale mango to orange to citreous yellow, then purple . . . the anvil shape of a spent thunderhead smoky gray in the distance. I could see Ransom tapping a steel drum experimentally, four men around her now, plus Mark Bryant's ancient golden retriever, Shadow, his tongue hanging out. There were probably fifty people out there, socializing on the docks, and Ransom was the only one who'd drawn a crowd. I turned my attention from the window for a moment and noticed a white envelope on the Franklin stove, with a note attached to it.

As I listened to Lindsey telling me about how weird it was, wearing a thong bikini one day, earmuffs the next, I saw that the envelope was the letter sent to me by my late uncle. A letter I'd seen but had yet to open and read. I saw that the note was from Ransom to me, the handwriting on both envelope and note very similar. I read the first sentence of the note, "My Brother, It's hurting my heart that you still haven't read Daddy Gatrell's letter to you. . . ."

I folded the note for later, as Lindsey told me, "The first thing my dad did, when he met Gale and me at the first place we landed—this was right after we left the island—he about squeezed the wind out of me, he was so relieved to see I wasn't hurt, then he took Gale aside and fired her ass. I don't know what he said to her, but you know how there's a type of person you can't picture crying?"

An image of Jeth popped into my mind. I checked the docks again—

he and Janet weren't out there. Hopefully, they'd gone off on their own to talk. I said, "Yeah, I know exactly what you mean."

"Gale was such a macho jock, Mr. Tough Girl, that I wouldn't'a believed she'd ever cried in my life. Wrong. I don't know what my dad said to her, but she was bawling her eyes out when she came out of that room with him. She'll never work for him again. Maybe never work in the security business again, he was so pissed off."

I said, "Your father would really do that to her? Ruin her career?"

"He said she wasn't very good at it."

"I agree. She was terrible. Still—"

"You don't know my dad, Doc. Nicest guy in the world—if he decides to make time for you. But don't cross him. *Ever.* And he's always been so protective of me, it's practically like being smothered. Want to make him mad? Do something to hurt his little girl. Me, I mean. That's the way he still thinks of me. The weird thing about Dad is, the madder he gets, the quieter he gets. That's how I knew he was furious at Gale. He smiled at her—but a different kind of smile—and kept his voice real soft and low, which told me, uh-oh, Gale's about to have her head handed to her on a platter. Which is what happened. She'd almost gotten me killed, that's the way he saw it, and she had to go. He's got this favorite saying. How's it go? Oh yeah: In diplomacy, getting even is the best revenge."

I told her, "I can hear him say it." I could, too. After talking with Harrington on the phone, I didn't doubt it for a second.

"But know what the great thing is, Doc? He actually likes you. First time maybe ever that he approves of a man I'm seeing. From just that talk you guys had. That, plus after checking you out through probably every file the government computers can access. He didn't tell you *that,* though, did he?"

"A computer check," I said. "No kidding? He'd have gone to all the trouble of running my name through a computer? It's surprising what some fathers will do." Through the window, I could see Tomlinson now.

He had the Verner twins following along behind him, Bobbi and Barbie, the two of them with big smiles, drawing lots of attention themselves, looking buxom and identical in navy blue warm-up pants and white T-shirts. They looked like they were dressed to run a couple of miles. Or to go for a sail with Tomlinson.

Through the phone, I could hear Lindsey ask, Was I kidding? Her dad had done background checks on everyone she'd ever dated. Then she said, "Why would that surprise you? *Hello-o-o.* He had us *taped,* for Christ's sake. When we were making love. Remember? Of course he'd do a background check. But it musta come out complimentary, 'cause know what he told me?" She changed her voice, made it deeper, imitating her father. "'That Dr. Ford, he seems like a good man. Lot of integrity. If you're smart, you'll stay in touch with him. He's not like the kind of losers you usually run with.'" She laughed at her own theatrics. "He even told me, after things die down, when he feels I'm out of danger, you and I ought to head off on some kind of trip. Can you believe it? Have a little fun. Jesus, he even referred to you as the astronaut, joking about it, which embarrassed the crap out of me. But Dad was like, 'Hey, no big deal.'"

Mindful of one of the promises I'd made to Harrington, I said, "I'll make a deal with you, Lindsey. You keep working out, stay healthy, I'll fly you to Florida and we'll spend three or four days cruising around, camping. Whatever you want."

"By 'staying healthy' you mean staying clean. Just come out and say it. No drugs, no cocaine."

"Okay, no drugs, especially cocaine. I like the woman I met on Guava Key very much. Don't go screwing up a winning combination. Plus, I meant the part about working out. Even without Gale there to push you. Keep the momentum, then we can start working out together when you get to Sanibel. I need a running partner."

"Sanibel," she said dreamily. "I've been there. What's the name of that big bird sanctuary? And I love the beaches. I can just picture us, waking up early and going for long walks. But Doc? Something that'll help motivate me is you calling. Every day if you can. Twice a day would be better. I don't want to be pushy, but it's already boring as hell here. The bodyguards are supposed to take me cross-country skiing tomorrow. But I'll have my cell phone. Hearing from you gives me something to look forward to."

Staying in touch with Lindsey was also part of my promise to Harrington. "A couple times a day," I said. "You got it."

I WORKED IN the lab until about ten. I had a stack of bills to pay, and a smaller stack of invoices to send out. Do business with any state or federally funded organization—which is about all I do—and you soon learn that the bureaucrats make even getting paid a complicated series of often meaningless, unnecessary, busywork hoops. Small people exercise their power in small ways.

I also had a little stack of personal mail to answer. The inexorable use of the Internet and e-mail has conferred a new and surprising power to handwritten letters, and I take care to answer the few I now receive. I had a long letter from Dewey Nye. She started out by apologizing again for her last-minute cancellation of Guava Key, which caused me to reflect on how certain small decisions may have a gigantic impact on our lives. I played the private little mental game of what-would've-happened-if. What would have happened if Dewey had ignored her lover and stayed with me on the island? What would've happened if she'd been running along beside me the afternoon I confronted the kidnappers? She might have been shot, not me. Might be badly wounded, might be dead. Or, instead of grazing my arm, the slug might have drifted a few inches to the left. Human existence seems a dichotomy of random intersections acted out on a precise biological framework . . . which may explain my passion for biology.

I answered Dewey's letter and a couple more. Kim and Mike from

Cabbage Key had gotten married and the happy couple had sent me a card postmarked Fiji. There was also a note from Captain Peter Hull of Mote Marine reminding me to contact him about the five-year research master plan they were contemplating for Charlotte Harbor.

I sat there writing in the perfect little circle of light provided by a gooseneck lamp. Then, because I hadn't eaten, and because Mack and the others tend to get miffed if I don't make at least a token appearance at their Friday parties, I showered, changed, locked the lab behind me and headed off for the marina.

I carried the mail with me outside. Stopped, listened, then slowed my pace where the path opened out onto the shell road.

Was there a car waiting, engine off, at the gate?

Yep. Lights off, too. I could see one . . . no, two dark figures sitting in the front seat.

I felt my heart start to pound harder as I stood there trying to decide whether to keep going or trot back to safety and call the police. I was still standing there when the car started unexpectedly, the passenger window rolled down and I heard a snatch of laughter, a teenage hoot, then peeling tires on loose shell.

Kids parking.

I berated myself for being unduly paranoid . . . then forgave myself immediately, remembering the way Clare's big arm had crushed the air out of me.

I had become a target, and I knew it. Which is why I had to be very, very careful. You're not paranoid if the bad guys really are after you.

And they were.

I readjusted the mail in my good arm, and walked it to the marina's drop box before joining the party.

The band was still playing: three men with guitars, another on congas, Tomlinson on harmonica and Ransom on steel drums. They were doing a Buffett song—*One Particular Harbor*—all six really into it, banging it loud, the crowd singing along, some of them dancing, too, maybe prompted by Ransom, who danced with Bahamian rhythm as she played.

I watched Tomlinson for a few moments. He was shirtless, his abs and veins demarcated by dock lights, his face invisible behind a screen of hair as he leaned his mouth into cupped hands, playing. He was barefooted, too, his knobby legs protruding from purple and yellow paisley surfer shorts that hung below his knees.

I stood there listening, enjoying it, looking out past the docks to the dark water and stars beyond. JoAnn brought me a beer, then Rhonda joined us, too, linking her arm into mine and leaning her weight against me, the three of us standing close as if slow dancing, me sandwiched between. Old friends.

"Shadow loves it!" Rhonda yelled. Mark's old retriever sat at Tomlinson's side, panting, eyes focused upward, as if expecting a treat.

Nearby were the Verner twins. Both had similar expressions on their faces. Same thing—expecting a treat.

I'd finished that beer and another by the time the band took a break. I had joined the guides at the picnic tables under the tin roof near the bait tank. That's where the food had been moved just in case of rain. I dropped a ten-dollar bill into the jar and filled my plate with shrimp, cracked conch and a slab of baked redfish.

I'm not a fussy eater; certainly no gourmet snob, but I rarely order seafood at a restaurant. The Timbers on Sanibel and the Prawnbroker on the mainland are exceptions. The restaurants on Cabbage Key and Useppa are a couple of others. I rarely order it for a very simple reason: The marina's seafood and the seafood I make at home are both always so far superior; why risk it?

Shrimp are a good example. Buy shrimp from any American market or restaurant and they can't compare, because commercial shrimpers give their catch a chemical soaking so the shrimp will smell milder, fresher and be a viable, salable product longer.

Not so at the marina. We buy the shrimp right off the boat from the bay shrimpers. Shrimp that haven't been soaked in chemical brine, so none of the delicate iodine flavor has been leached away.

Combined with that is the fact that Joyce, who cooks in the seafood market, uses a very simple recipe I brought back from Panama, compliments of some of my Zonie friends. Fill an empty wine bottle with virgin olive oil and a dozen or more chili peppers. Cork and allow it to age for at least a few weeks. In a large bowl, pour the chili oil over fresh shrimp, squeeze in the juice of two fresh limes. Not lemons, *limes*. Salt heavily. Add garlic, black pepper and, if you can find it, some Everglades Seasoning from LaBelle for a nice Cuban touch. Allow the shrimp to marinate for a day. Cook them on a very hot grill. The oil creates a lot of flame and sears them nicely black. It only takes a minute or two on each side. Overcook the shrimp and they're ruined—dry and tough to peel. Get them off just as they turn pink and you've got one of the world's great culinary experiences.

Which is why I'd heaped my plate high with shrimp. I sat there eating the shrimp, washing them down with iced beer, talking to the guides. Talking with the guides is a favorite pastime because they spend so much time on the water that any anomaly, any unusual experience, is immediately noted. Most light tackle guides are keen observers and have an even keener sense of humor—a necessity in their very tough business.

I sat there with Dalbert Weeks and Javier Castillo from Two Parrot Bight Marina, plus Nels Esterline, and big Felix Blane from Dinkin's Bay. They wanted to know about the attempted kidnapping on Guava Key, and I reduced the incident to three or four vague sentences, then spent the next half hour or so listening to their stories. Trolling offshore in twenty feet of water for king mackerel, Dalbert's party had jumped what he swore was a sailfish—extremely rare that close to Sanibel or that far from the Gulf Stream. But as Felix noted, "That's the great thing about saltwater, man. There are no gates out there and fish can swim anywhere they want. You know Sword Point up by the mouth of the river? Supposedly, way, way back, some guy landed a swordfish there and that's practically *fresh* water come the rainy season."

Tracking the same king mackerel run, Javier had found the flotsom of what he thought was a refugee boat. As a Cuban who'd fled his homeland during the Mariel boatlift, he'd examined the debris more carefully than most. "Inner tubes tied together, that's what I first see. Three in all, one of them got no air. That tell me something 'cause inner tubes, that's the way we used to fish off Havana. Paddle them out"—he made a twirling motion with his hands—"use nothing but hand lines right there at the edge of the Stream."

He'd also found a five-gallon plastic can with AGUA spray-painted on the side. The can was empty. "Those people dead," he said sadly. "Died of thirst, maybe went crazy drinking saltwater. Who knows. Over so many years, how many people you think that *maricón* Castro has killed in all?"

I noticed Ransom walking toward me, signaling me to come over, as I listened to Nels ask if anyone else had noticed that orange-colored cloud right at sunrise. He told us it was floating over the Gulf of Mexico all by itself, and was shaped perfectly like the head of a man.

"It looked like Mark Twain," he said, "with the long hair and moustache. Or maybe Albert Einstein. Wouldn't it be weird if it was one of their birthdays yesterday?"

Ransom was smiling, seemed real happy with herself. She was thumping her hands, playing an invisible drum, her hips swaying. I noted that she was wearing the golden ring once again, lion's head in black, as she said, "My brother! I *like* this marina where you live. People, they so nice to me. Ev'body come right up and talk real friendly jus' like back on Cat Island. An' they love you, man. They tellin' me, 'Your brother, he a good man. He do this for me, or he do daht for me. Your brother, he hold this whole community together.'" She hugged her arm around my waist. "That make me so proud. You know what I think I'm gonna do?"

What she was thinking about doing was moving to Sanibel. As I listened to her tell me about it, I noticed a commotion going on over near the rental canoes. It was Tomlinson and several people standing around watching. Tomlinson seemed to be playing tag with Mark Bryant's dog. He'd tiptoe up to the dog, lunge to grab his collar, and the dog would sprint away. The dog seemed to be moving faster than I'd ever seen an old dog move. He was amazingly agile for an animal his age. It had to be some kind of game, yet Tomlinson appeared to be getting frustrated.

I watched him continue to stalk the dog as Ransom said, "You know what I'd planned to do. I planned to go back to my island, buy me some property, build me a big house with a satellite dish so I don't have to go to the hotel bar no more to see my shows on the television. Maybe buy me that red car, too, and some air conditionin' for the hot days. But after just one night here, seeing how friendly the peoples are, I got me another idea."

I smiled as the dog began to sprint in crazy circles, really having fun, as Tomlinson tried to anticipate the dog's trajectory, strangely not seeming to be having much fun at all.

Ransom said, "So the idea I got into my mind, I was talking to some of the women about it. That nice girl, Joyce, who does the cooking and JoAnn, too—man, that woman got a sweet feeling for you! What those ladies think I ought to do is don't buy a house at all, but maybe buy me a little boat instead. See, that way I can live right here on Sanibel. You get sick or hurt or need somethin' done at your house, then I'm right here to help you. And if I get homesick for the islands? I'll just drive my lil' boat back to the Bahamas and work my way real slow down the chain 'til I get to Cat Island."

I heard Rhonda call, "Hey, why is Tomlinson chasing Mark's dog?" as Ransom added, "I already got me a little less than seventeen thousand dollars. That plus the three thousand Daddy Gatrell left me, that'll give me nearly twenty thousand. Now don't go tellin' me *that* ain't a lot of money."

I'd warned her before, and now I warned her again about Tucker's absurd jokes.

I watched her grin fade into a puzzled scowl. "Why you keep saying that, man? What else I got to do but show you those gold coins? Our daddy, he never told you he hid away money?"

Actually, Tucker *had* told me that he'd hidden away money. Often. He was always bragging about all the money he'd made; how much he'd pissed away on failed business schemes, whiskey and women; how much he had buried if he could just get to it. Tucker had been a tropical junkie. He'd loved the islands; he jumped at any excuse to hop a banana boat or a freighter and head south. The only thing I never doubted about him was that he'd wasted a lot of money. He spent much of his life working cattle in Central America and Cuba, and commercial-fishing the Bahamas. The man I knew never had a cent.

I told her, "Remember what I said about exaggerating? That's what he might have been doing. He exaggerates to make himself look more important than he really is. Than he really was, I mean."

The woman's tone became severe. "Don't you talk that way about Daddy. Way you speak, you didn't even like the man."

Truth was, she was right; I didn't like Tucker Gatrell. I had my reasons, too. Good reasons.

"Did you read the letter I left out for you? The one he wrote just to you?"

I told her I hadn't, and instantly regretted it when I saw the unhappy look on her face. I'd known her for only a couple of days, so why did I already hate the idea of disappointing her or hurting her? It wasn't rational, but there it was. I liked her as a person. She had an endearing honesty about her; seemed genuinely good-hearted, but it was more than that. "I'm going to read it," I added quickly, "tonight."

She was shaking her head. "Man, why you want to wait? You go read that letter right now, them come back and listen to us play some more."

She looked at my empty plate. "What's the holdup? You done stuffin' your face."

I chuckled, amused and penitent, dropped my garbage in the can, and told her that's exactly what I'd do if it made her happy. I walked around by the shallow water docks past the rental canoes to tell Tomlinson that I'd be right back.

The little crowd that had been watching him play tag with the dog had scattered. He stood there alone by the big sea grape outside the Red Pelican. He had his hands on his hips, sweating, breathing heavily. He motioned with his head when he saw me approach and said, "Look at that evil little son-of-a-bitch. And I used to sneak him Milk-Bones every time I had the chance."

I followed his gaze to see the old golden retriever standing at the edge of the parking lot, staring back at us. The dog's tail was curved at attention, head held high. "I don't get it," I said. "What's the problem. Why in the world are you mad at Mark's dog?"

"Because of them, that's why," he said, and jerked his thumb toward the Verner twins. They were now standing on the stern of *Das Stasi,* giggling at something Dieter Rassmussen had apparently said.

"Huh? I'm not following. Are you stoned?"

"No! That's another thing. There's so much on the line tonight, I didn't smoke at all and only had seven, maybe eight beers. I can't even feel it, man. Then that bastard comes along and spoils the entire gig."

Meaning the dog again.

Tomlinson faced me, his expression pained and said in a frantic whisper, "The fucking dog ate my Viagra, man! I took it out to show Mack what the pill looked like and dropped it. Before it even hit the ground, Shadow gobbled the damn thing down like the Milk-Bone piggie he is. Wouldn't give it back, either. So now I'm cold sober, plus I've got the Verner twins to deal with. How's *that* for a living hell on earth?"

15

I WALKED BACK to my stilthouse, picked up the envelope that was addressed DUKE FORD, SANIBEL, then tossed it back onto the desk and tried to ignore it. I neatened the kitchen even though it didn't need neatening, then fiddled with my record player, searching through albums for something to play. Finally selected an old favorite, Crosby, Stills, Nash and Young, and put it on, volume low. Listened to it while I avoided the envelope, marveling at my own immaturity. How could Tucker Gatrell, a man who'd been dead for nearly two years and whom I'd hardly really known, still continue to have a negative influence on my life?

I truly didn't like Tuck. That, at least, I could admit to myself.

As of a few years ago, I could also finally admit the real reason why.

It had to do with my parents.

My long-dead parents.

I'm not an emotional person. I have very little patience with sappy sentimentality or maudlin displays.

Still, there's bound to be some emotional attachment between child and parents—which is probably why I still resented what had happened many years before, and the role Tucker had played.

When I was eleven, both of my parents were killed in a boat explosion. They'd set out on a trip through the Ten Thousand Islands south of Naples in Tuck's homemade, cypress cabin cruiser. It took me more than a year to jigsaw pieces of that boat together and do what professional investigators had failed to do: explain why the boat had exploded.

There were accelerant pour patterns on what remained of the inner hull of the boat—arson wasn't a consideration, so there'd been a gas leak. Flames will spread fastest across the underside of boat decking or a bulkhead overhang, so the flooring adjacent to a flammable wall is the most likely point of origin.

On the cruiser, the fire's point of origin was just beneath and above the gas engine's starter motor. The starter motor was mounted low, under the big block's cooling jackets, only a few inches from the bilge pump.

Thus I isolated the fuel that had created the explosion and the source of combustion. But what had caused the gas leak? That took longer to figure out.

Tucker had always considered himself a brilliant inventor. He'd applied for and received a number of worthless patents. By going through his papers, I discovered that one of his "inventions" was a butterfly shutoff valve for fuel lines on inboard boats. The valve was made of PVC plastic and joined together by common plumber's glue.

Petroleum products—such as gasoline—neutralize plumber's glue, so his choice of sealant was not just idiotic, it was lethal. The glue had melted. The valve had leaked fuel into the bilge. A spark from the engine's starter motor had ignited the explosion.

Tucker never accepted nor admitted responsibility, though late in his life he did offer me a vague apology.

That's not the only reason I never got along with my uncle.

Tuck was more than a decade older than my late mother. He looked seventy when I was fifteen. By the time I was thirty, he still looked seventy and he still wore skinny-legged Levi's and pearl-buttoned shirts. He wore gunslinger clothes because he owned a mud and mangrove ranch in a backwater called Mango, a little tiny fishing village south of Marco Island where he kept a big Appaloosa horse and a few cows.

The last of the Florida cowboys, or "cowhunters" as they were known— that's what he fancied himself. Newspaper people loved the guy because he was always good for a colorful quote, and more than one writer said Tuck resembled an older Robert Mitchum, but that had more to do with his attitude than his looks. He had the Jack Daniel's swagger, the polar-blue eyes, the shoulders and scrawny hips and lots of stories.

The trouble with Tuck was, there was no way to tell which of his stories were true, and which weren't. Many of those stories were based on the fact that he'd spent a lot of years supplementing his income as a fishing and hunting guide. He'd started in his early teens and, with his natural gift for people and his knowledge of the backcountry, he actually did become one of the most famous guides in Florida. Tuck claimed to have fished such luminaries as Thomas Edison, who had a winter home in nearby Fort Myers; Colonel Charles Lindbergh; Harry Truman; Walt Disney; Clark Gable; Dwight D. Eisenhower; Dick Pope, who was one of Florida's first promoters; Ted Williams, Mickey Mantle and John F. Kennedy. Not only claimed to have fished them but to have been their friends—close friends with a few of them, which led to other outrageous assertions.

Tuck loved nothing better than to sit on his porch at sunset, chew tobacco, tell stories and get drunk. I know because, as an orphan, the court had assigned me to live with him. I did, too, for a couple of years, which was all I could tolerate before I moved out, still in my teens, and lived alone until I graduated from high school.

Something else I disliked about Tucker was that he was prone to sloppy behavior and indifferent to shabby living conditions. His house was always a filthy massing of clothes, spittoons, garbage and dirty dishes. Once, when Tucker's old horse, Roscoe, cribbed himself into colic, Tuck moved the animal inside during three days of rain, stepping over islands of horse manure as if they were nothing more than soiled socks or someone's old shoes.

Always orderly by nature, I retaliated by following my own instincts toward sanity. I became fanatically neat, driven by insistence on accuracy and a lifestyle that sought precision. It was the only way of creating distance between myself and the unfortunate genetic connection to my late mother's brother.

I was even less tolerant of his wild lies and self-serving schemes. They were crazed and so constant that I refused to acknowledge or play a role in any of them. Tucker claimed to have found the Fountain of Youth in his pasture, and sold bottled water to tourists until the state made him stop. He got it into his head that, while guiding Walt Disney on a tarpon-fishing trip, he'd given the famous Californian the idea for Disney World. He'd filed a claim for damages in an Orlando court and was laughed out of town. He tried to make it as a country music singer and failed. Because he'd run guns to Cuba prior to the revolution, he'd tried to get Fidel Castro to assign him a massive land grant in Pinar del Rio, but failed at that, too, and damn near ended up in prison on the Isle of Pines.

Tucker became the living symbol of all the things I did not want my life to be. He was random and maudlin, an obnoxious drunk with a terrible temper who could be on the verge of violence one moment, on the verge of tears in the next.

The only thing I liked about living with Tuck were visits from his old friend and partner Joseph Egret, an Everglades Indian of mild humor and gigantic stature. Why Joseph put up with Tuck and his constant racist badgering, I never understood. The two of them were dedicated to each other, which was the only valid endorsement my uncle ever received as far as I was concerned. I liked Joseph a lot, but he wasn't around enough to make a difference, so I left.

As punishment, Tucker tried to leverage me with guilt whenever he could, and he called me Duke, a nickname he knew I hated but used anyway.

What good would it do to explain the whole sad relationship, though, to Ransom, who really was the man's daughter?

THE BAND WAS playing again.

I worked around in the lab until there was nothing left to do, locked the door behind me, went into my house and switched off the turntable.

Through the screen window, I could see the lights of the marina casting saffron columns across black water. I could see the Japanese lanterns aboard *Tiger Lily,* lucent paper blooms of green, strawberry and blue. Could hear Danny Morgan singing another Buffett song: "Cowboy in the Jungle."

Appropriate.

It was a song that always conjured up images of a cowboy who'd spent a lot of his life in one kind of jungle or another—Tucker Gatrell.

I went to the table, picked up the envelope and opened it. Inside were two sheets of yellow legal paper covered with the man's sloppy block hand.

I opened a beer, poured it over ice, then cleaned my glasses. Finally, I took a seat in the overstuffed chair by the reading lamp along the north wall, and I read:

Dear Duke,

If you're reading this, it means I'm dead and so is that black-hearted son-uva-bitch Sinclair Benton. I hope to hell I had a chance to piss on the gold-toothed bastard's grave, but I got no way of knowing as I write this. So, if I didn't, please piss on his grave for me. I'm serious. Throw some seed around and try to get the birds to shit on his headstone, too, while you're at it. He's got it coming.

Something else it means if you're reading this is you met my little girl. Ain't she a dandy? I wanted to name her Roscoe after my favorite horse of all time, only her mama wouldn't stand for it and changed it to Ransom 'cause that's what the beautiful little girl was worth to her, a king's ransom.

Her mama's name was Rumer and she liked the letter R.

It ain't easy for me to explain how it was I come to father a child I never claimed openlike. Maybe it is all men got a secret little place in their hearts, a place where we keep all the little lives we live but ain't supposed to live. Not out of shame but because in some places we are one person and some places we are another, which is how men are. It was like that with me and Ransom. I only got to be with her eight times. The last five of them times Sinclair Benton and his goat-humpers tried to beat the fire outta me. I never had to break so many colored noses in my life but they weren't quitters, I'll give them boys that much, and they bout succeeded in killing me twice.

Didn't matter. I kept going back to see my little girl whenever I had the money and could.

Sinclair Benton, he and me hated each other.

When I met Ransom's mama, she was bout the most beautiful woman I ever saw, white or colored. Almost as pretty as Munequinta, my little Cuban girl. Smart, too. Rumer, she could cipher arithmetic and write and read almost as good as me. I loved that woman and she thought the sun rose over my head, and I don't blame her an ounce for giving up on me and marrying an islander, even if he was a no-account coconut-picker who spent most his time away and drunk.

Which is why it was easy for Benton to catch Rumer when she was all alone, no one to help, and do what he did to her.

Benton didn't take to the idea of her having a blue-eyed child, so he cast spells against her and when the spells didn't work and she wouldn't stop seeing me, he used his fists.

209

Understand now what I mean? Piss on that old witch's grave a couple times for a purty lady who cared for your old uncle.

Duke, there was only one way for me to hurt Sinclair Benton, and Joe and me worked it out slick as can be. We hurt him real, real bad. He knew it was me but could never prove it, which shows just what a smart plan I come up with and probably pissed him off every remaining day of his life. I surely hope so.

Trouble was, after that, it got real, real dangerous for me to go back to Cat Island. Even so, I was the best daddy I could be to Ransom. Sent her and Rumer money when I had it and little doodad presents. I thought more than once of having them two brung over to Florida, but quit the idea each time. It ain't no secret that I'm a rambling man, no husbandly good to any woman, but that's the cards I drawed. It's a short life and a dangerous world and as I told Joe more than once: Why'd the Good Lord give us tallywhackers and trigger fingers unless he expected us to use them?

Trouble is, when you live the life I've lived, you lose the folks you love. One way or the other, you lose them all. Rumer died last year and it nearly broke my heart hearing about it. Nothing makes you feel older and smaller than when a woman you loved and bedded passes from her own aging.

Here's the thing: With me dead, that little girl's got no one else in the world to look after her. Which is why I told her you're her brother. That ain't such a bad thing, is it? Why let someone feel lost and alone in the world if all it takes is a lie to make things sunnier?

One thing that ain't a lie, Duke, is that Ransom's gonna need your help. I've tried my best to protect that girl, which is what I'm doing right now, writing this letter and giving it to Judge Flowers. What I'm doing is setting it up for her to get her inheritance in a way that Benton's goat-humpers can't steal it from her. I can't risk them taking this letter or finding out in some easy way where it was I hid what I hid. There's gotta be a couple safety stops in there to make sure it's Ransom and you who find it, nobody else.

I'm begging you to do this, Duke. I'm dead now and you got no more reason to hate me for what I did even though it has hurt me and haunted me every breathing day of my life. I wished I coulda come right out and say what I'm saying now, but I'm a lowlife, stubborn son-uva-bitch and I admit it. Everytime I tried to do something good in my life I ended up doing bad. The worst thing I know is, I am the cause of my own dear sister's death, who was your mother and, if I burn in Hell for that, I will not feel no more pain than I did shouldering the guilt when I was alive. Please don't blame Ransom, who is your own sister, for that.

Good luck from the grave!

Tucker M. Gatrell

PS—I think my horse Roscoe's nuts have grown back because of water he drunk out of a spring that's here at the ranch! I'm going to call you and see if you still hate me, cause if you don't I could use some help to figure how much to charge for water that seems to have lots of strong vitamins in it.

I checked the top of the first page—it wasn't dated.
Typical.

I read one of the paragraphs several times before I folded the yellow paper and slid it back into the envelope. As I did, I noticed a smaller piece of paper inside that I'd overlooked. Took it out and saw that it was another handwritten note, but the handwriting was much different. It had the beautiful flowing loops and curvature that I associate with a people who learned to write before typewriters were common, a precise pencraft that is more like calligraphy. It was from Joseph Egret.

I read:

Dear Marion,

Your Uncle Tuck is drunk as usual and passed out, which took longer than most nights because it's after midnight. He give me this letter to address and send, so I decided to write you a letter of my own. I'm sleeping out in the barn and it is a real pretty night here on the ranch with stars over the water and the shrimp boats in close enough I can hear them and there are lights in the windows of those little houses down on Mango Bay where Sally Carmel lives. I know you remember how it was and always liked it when the two of us went out in the pasture and looked up at the sky at night and we could hear the little diesels of them shrimpers working in shallow.

Don't that seem like a long time ago?

Marion, I have been having powerful dreams. Most the frog-eaters I know would not understand but you were always different and might. My dreams tell me I am not going to be in this world much longer. I believe that I will be passing into the next world soon. This may be good because if it is an Indian afterworld there will not be so many frog-eater automobiles and I will be with people of my own kind. That is a good thing because I have become an old man and lonely. Your uncle has become an old man and lonely, too. We were partners all our lives and now we will soon share death, too, which may be the first time I ever heard Tucker quiet for more than a few hours.

That is why I write. Judge Flowers is supposed to send these papers to Tuck's daughter after Tuck and Sinclair Benton die. If my dreams have been wrong, and I am still alive when you read this, come get me right away so we can go straight to Cat Island, which will save you a lot of time. Your uncle cannot do anything the simple way. We both know that. This time he has a reason, though, and it's not just some crazy trick. At least I think he's got a reason and not just being tricky again. You will find out for yourself, and maybe we will find out together.

If I am dead when you read this, good luck. There are a couple of things I'd like you to know. You have met your cousin, Ransom, who has a strong heart. I doubt if your uncle told you that you also might have a cousin who lives in Cuba. He fathered a son there. Or I might have fathered the son. We've never seen the child enough to be sure, but the boy's mama was romantic with us both. That was often the way when we was on the trail.

Something else you don't seem to know is that Tucker Gatrell is like Ransom. He has a heart that is strong and good. He may be a drunken liar and half crazy but he is a decent man, plus my partner, and always will be. I hope you will honor his wishes, Marion. He's always felt real bad about how things turned out.

Sincerely, Your Friend
Joseph Egret

I stood when I'd finished Joseph's letter. Took off my glasses and cleaned them, smiling. Frog-eaters—Joseph's name for tourists and modern Floridans, white and black, because he knew them to eat the legs of Everglades frogs, something his people would not do.

I turned and went into the lab and filed the letter away before returning to my house and bolting the door behind me. I rummaged through the desk until I found the two silver keys on their ring, then got down on my hands and knees, pulled the fireproof lock chest from beneath my bed and opened it.

One key fits the door, the second key fits the lock on the drawer's false bottom, which I also unlocked and removed, thus revealing neat stacks of folders and notebooks, five bogus passports, some clothing, and other detritus from a life I thought I had abandoned long ago.

For a moment I was taken aback when I realized that two very important manila envelopes were missing. Over the years, I'd grown used to seeing them each time I opened the little secret compartment. One was labeled OPERATION PHOENIX, the other with the words DIRECCION: BLANCA MANAGUA written on a label in red felt-tip pen.

I felt a mini-moment of panic because, in a very worst-case scenario, they are my only wedge against potential legal problems from which no statute of limitations would ever protect me.

Harrington had been right about that.

Then I remembered that the envelopes were presumably right where they were supposed to be: in the bank's safety deposit box where I'd stored them several months before.

My notebooks were still there, though, and I removed them carefully, pausing to linger over the names I'd written in precise block print on their covers, each notebook catalyzing visual memories, some good, many bad.

Coast of Bengal
Borneo/Sandakan
Nicaragua/Politics/Baseball
Havana I
Havana II
Ox-eyed Tarpon/South China Sea
Masagua's Ridley Turtles and the Magnetic Mountain
Singapore to Kota Baharu (with 3rd Gurkhas)
The Hannah Smith Story

There were others.

All contained the carefully kept details of my most private life, much of that lifetime spent traveling alone through the Third World tropics, necessarily duplicitous years spent doing clandestine work as well as the work I still care passionately about: marine biology.

I set the notebooks aside and found what I'd unlocked the box to find.

I squatted there staring, for a time, at the nine-millimeter Sig Sauer P226 semiautomatic handgun that lay, in its shoulder holster, atop a black Navy watch sweater that I had not worn in a long time. I removed the Sig Sauer from the holster, feeling the weight of it. Popped the clip, flipped the slide lock and removed the barrel. The weapon had an industrial, black finish . . . the spring and metalwork, though, had gathered a couple of small spots of corrosion.

Why did I find the marring of this old weapon so distressing?

I took a can of WD-40 from the cupboard beneath the sink and polished until the rust was gone. Then I disassembled the entire weapon and cleaned every element to a mirror finish before I took up the clip again and layered in ten silver-jacketed nine-millimeter hollow-points, the slug of each round copper-bright and symmetrical. Each cartridge singular . . . dense.

I lifted up the sweater and found the brown case made of cowhide leather. Unsnapped it to see a six-inch custom-built sound arrestor resting on its own cradle so perfectly that it gave the impression of a surgical instrument.

I screwed the silencer onto the barrel of the Sig, aware of its frictionless threads and flawless pitch. Swung the weapon in a fast arc, the balance of it no longer as comfortable and familiar as it had once been. Recalled the amplified blowgun noise it made when fired.

Nothing comforting about that memory, either.

I stood and placed the weapon under my mattress. Hung the sweater in the closet. Then neatened everything and locked the door behind me before returning to the marina.

It was getting late, but the party was still spinning along. I noted that Tomlinson's sailboat, *No Más,* was under way, the little engine he seldom used straining to push the boat's mass toward the deepwater opening of Dinkin's Bay. I pictured him out there at the wheel, a Verner twin on each side, and wished him a silent good luck.

I had another beer. Mingled around listening to Ransom on steel drums, still playing with the band.

When she was done, I told her I'd go with her to find her inheritance. That I would help her if I could. First, though, I needed a couple of days to finish up some work. And that we couldn't travel together. It was too dangerous.

She kept asking why.

I didn't tell her why.

16

I SPENT THE weekend dragging nets, wading the flats, collecting specimens, then working in the lab. The biology professors at Grinnell and Waldron College would have been heartened. Maybe even proud. The thing is, I never receive an order without feeling an obligation to provide what I can as fast as I am able. It creates a specific, physical connection between my small lab and the wider world. For reasons I don't pretend to understand, that connection is important to me. The image of starfish and sea anemones taken from the Sanibel littoral sitting in heated classrooms, snow and cornstubble through the windows outside, is oddly satisfying.

No Más was back at its familiar anchorage, out in the bay, a short boat ride to the marina or to my docks.

No sign of life aboard, though. On Saturday, I tried to hail Tomlinson via VHF radio. No reply. I stopped by in my skiff and banged on the sailboat's hull. No answer.

Strange, because his little dinghy was tied off the stern, which meant that he was aboard. I could smell the cloying odor of incense and marijuana. I could hear the stereo playing the monotone Latin chants he always listens to when in a certain mood. Live at the same little marina with a person, and over the months and years you will come to know his quirks and react accordingly. Tomlinson wanted to be left alone—which suggested his voyage with the Verner twins had not gone well.

A couple of times that day, Ransom made vague references to Tomlinson and his whereabouts, before she finally said, "I like that Mr. Thomas, but he kind of a strange old hippie, ain't he? He just go off and disappear, never say a word to me about where he gonna be."

"You think he's acting strange now?" I said to her. "Stick around."

I listened to her tell me what I already knew—tomorrow the two of them were driving to the little bayside village of Mango, because, according to Tucker, he'd left something there for her to find.

If I knew Tuck—and I did—he'd try to bounce us all over Florida just for fun, which is why I wasn't going to join the hunt until my work in the lab was done.

I listened to her say, "I look into that Mr. Thomas's face and it like looking into the face of someone who were maybe an owl in a different life. Or one of them saints in an old painting like you see in church. He act so young, but his eyes, man, they old, real old, and filled with sadness. What the problem with that crazy boy, Mr. Thomas?"

Her tone suggested personal interest and warm concern. Maybe romantic interest. She was asking me for specific information in a sly way with her innocent, general questions.

After the third or fourth inquiry, I told her, "He's got a lot on his mind. Tomlinson, he's a very emotional guy with a strong sense of right and wrong. It could be . . . well, I think he feels a lot of guilt about something . . . maybe something that happened in the past. It's finally caught up with him for some reason." I told her I didn't know why. She'd have to ask him about it, not me.

I didn't like the niggling little surge of conscience my disclaimer produced.

I realized I not only didn't like disappointing Ransom, I wasn't comfortable lying to her, either.

RANSOM SAID, "Man you can't eat 'em. Why would anyone want to pay good money for something so ugly?"

She meant the five-gallon bucket of horseshoe crabs she'd collected. A horseshoe crab looks like a plastic, caramel-colored helmet with a spiked tail. The hairy legs beneath contribute a spidery effect.

It was still Saturday, the 10th day of February, the day of the new moon according to my almanac calendar. No matter what time of year, summer, winter or fall, tides on the new and low moon are called "spring tides" worldwide. Because the moon is in direct alignment with the sun, the combined gravitational influence of those two bodies has a substantially greater effect on water mass.

Not that tides are always dependable or predictable in the Gulf of Mexico. Ask any boater. They are not. Sanibel, Captiva and adjacent islands generally have semidiurnal tides, which means two equally high and low tides per day. Because the moon rises fifty-eight minutes later each evening, those tides usually peak nearly an hour later every twenty-four hours.

Usually.

Because the Gulf is not much more than a gigantic saltwater lake joined to a larger ocean, there is a kind of slopping-bowl effect. It's easily illustrated. Put water in a bowl, then tilt the bowl slowly and rhythmically, one side up, one side down.

Tilt the bowl to the right and water rushes away: low tide on the left edge. Tilt the bowl to the left, and water rushes back the other way: high tide on the left edge. But soon, very soon, the wave thus created will separate into two opposing waves. When those two waves collide, water in the bowl does not fluctuate much at all. Which is why, about once a month, tides around the islands do not seem to change.

One-tide days, we call them.

Weather over the Atlantic and Caribbean can also often override the lunar pull. Distant winds can push water into the big bowl or winds can slow the water from leaving the big bowl—"wind-forcing," in scientific terms.

Random—that's the way tides seem, at times. What is not random, though, is that on each and every spring tide, full moon or new, the bays and shallow water flats around Sanibel become livelier, more interesting places.

Which is why I almost always go out collecting on those days—lots of interesting stuff to see and find. The strong gravitational influence keys very predictable animal behavior, too. A good example is the horseshoe crab. Every Florida spring, on the highest tides of the month, female horseshoe crabs plow their way to shore and lay their eggs above the tide line, out of reach of lesser tides. In the same way, every Florida spring, on the full and new moon high tide, the eggs of those same animals hatch (often in concert with a storm, for reasons unknown to me) and the miniature animals plow their way back toward deeper water again.

I'd described that cycle to Ransom over coffee that morning, and she'd insisted on coming along. She told me, "Man, I grow'd up on the ocean, but it like my eyes wasn't workin' too good 'til I met you, my brother. I go with you and learn some more about what I should already know. Besides, Mr. Thomas, he don't answer when I try to call him on the radio."

Her mind on Tomlinson again.

I'D STEERED US out the mouth of Dinkin's Bay, then northwest on Pine Island Sound. I ran a mile or so to the back side of Sanibel Bayou, which is part of Ding Darling Sanctuary, a national preserve. On the bay side, there is a long sandbar that traces the mangrove fringe from Dinkin's Bay clear to Wulfert Channel, a sand bridge interrupted only by narrow creek entrances such as MacIntyre Creek, the Umbrella Pool and Hardworking Bayou.

It was 11:30 A.M., low tide. Pine Island Sound more closely resembled a flooded golf course than a saltwater estuary. The bar was exposed, dry and firm, a temporary peninsula ten meters wide and several miles long. On the Sanibel side, separated by a fringe of muck, were red mangroves elevated above the water on monkey-bar roots. On the bay side were hundreds of acres of turtle grass as green as spring wheat, that plateau of green pocked with sea pools and guttered by creeks.

Idling toward the bar, I could smell the salt and sulfur and iodine mix that is the smell of low tide, the odor of life and rot and the spermious musk of reproduction.

I anchored my boat in two feet of water and we waded in, both of us wearing white rubber boots and carrying five-gallon buckets. I had that order from Waldron College for horseshoe crabs, plus I needed sea anemones.

We had no trouble finding both. It was as if someone had pulled a plug, exposing a sea bottom alive with hundreds of species of wiggling, crawling, squirting, drifting plants and invertebrates. As we slogged along, I answered Ransom's questions if she asked about something; occasionally I would point out an animal I found unusual or interesting. She was quick and perceptive, but her interest in science seemed uneven, and her attention was prone to wander.

Mostly, we worked.

At the edge of the bar were hundreds of female horseshoe crabs. Some were nearly buried in mud, actively laying eggs. Others were in transit, drawing a half-dozen or more smaller males along behind, all of the males primed to deposit their white milt when the female was ready.

At one point, Ransom said, "You keep talking about their eggs like there's something to see. Back on Cat Island, we go out and collect turtle eggs sometimes. The green turtle and the hawksbill, they the best, but we sometimes eat them big ol' leatherback turtle eggs, too. Scramble them up with grunts and grits. Or maybe a nice piece'a pork if you can find it. Them turtle eggs, they something good, man. But I never seen no crab eggs."

We'd been collecting only male horseshoe crabs, but now I stooped and leveraged a female out of the muck and put her aside. Then I used my fingers to dig down a few inches through the sand until I felt the familiar globular mass. Waited until the water had seeped away, then pointed at the clumps of greenish-gray eggs. I told her, "Each female lays thousands of eggs. Maybe tens of thousands, I'm not sure. See how she buried herself down in the mud? At least six inches, maybe even a foot. That's so the eggs won't get washed away before they hatch. It takes about six weeks from the time a male fertilizes them until the eggs are mature enough to—" I stopped talking, looking toward the Intracoastal Waterway, which was just a mile or so away. Something had caught my attention. I could see two yellow Mercury test boats speeding southward, outward-bound from the test center, traveling fast.

Were the boats slowing now?

I stood watching them, aware of how unlikely it would be for those same test boats to be targeted again as escape vehicles, yet automatically calculating how long it would take for me to get back to my skiff, where I had the Sig Sauer hidden away in the little bag I used to keep towels and my handheld VHF radio.

"What's wrong with you, man? You look like you just see'd a ghost. Or maybe somebody walked over your grave. Or my grave."

I didn't respond. I watched until I was certain the boats weren't slowing. Watched them continue down the channel—normal routing, normal driver behavior.

"You gone deaf, my brother? You hear what I ask?"

I turned slightly toward her as I said, "Huh? Sorry. I lost the thread. What was I talking about?"

Ransom had her hands on hips, staring at me. "Crabs. You was telling me about their eggs and stuff, but I don't care nothing 'bout that no more. What I'm seeing right now, my brother, is you scared of something. Real scared."

I bent, returned the female crab to her nest. Said, "Crabs . . . right, I was telling you about crabs. What most people don't realize about horseshoe crabs is they're more closely related to spiders and scorpions than to true crabs. They have no antenna, no elaborate or oversize mandibles. The spiked tail? It looks like a weapon, but it's actually a leveraging device. They use it to right themselves if they get flipped over."

She was still looking into my face. "There's something you not telling me, man. Izzy and Clare, yeah, they two scary Rastamen, but it more than that. A man like you, them two not amount to much worry, so it somethin' else. Somethin' serious. What I see in your face just now, it scare me, too. It bad, man, it very bad. What going on in that heart of yours, my brother?"

Why did she keep pushing? I said, "You're exaggerating. And misinterpreting. You want me to tell you about horseshoe crabs or not? I know they look simple, maybe not that interesting, but they're really one of the great survival stories on earth. The crabs you're carrying in your bucket right now are identical to fossilized crabs dug out of the Alps. Two hundred million years old, that's how long they've lived unchanged—essentially perfectly designed animals. You don't find that interesting?"

"It's them Spanish men you're scared of, isn't it? Uh-huh, uh-huh, your eyes talkin' to me now even though your mouth saying something else. What you call them . . . Colombians? The Colombians, they after you and you know it, but you ain't saying nothing."

I told her, "I'm talking away, but you're not listening. You asked me why we're collecting crabs that can't be eaten, which is what I was getting at if you'd just listen. The thing about a horseshoe crab, they have a small amount of blue-colored blood, which is important to pharmaceutical companies. Research facilities, too. Their blood clots at the slightest contact with endotoxins, which are toxic byproducts of some bacteria. Endotoximia is a lethal form of blood poisoning, so what we're doing is important work."

"Blood poisoning, yeah, I know that a bad thing, but them Colombians, they something bad, too, which is what we should be discussin'. Why you don't want me to help? Maybe I got some methods you don't know nothin' about." She stepped to me and pulled the collar of my shirt open. "See here? Why you not wearing the gris-gris bag I give you? That good luck, man! Something else I can do for you, I can get some Goofer dust. Put a little on you, then pray over it every day for nine days. That and some blue stone mixed with amber and turpentine and salt to protect you from all harm. It very powerful. It what we call an Assault Obeah, a curse on your enemies."

I was shaking my head, amused by the irony. Me talking research and technology, Ransom replying with archaic superstition: an illustration of the diversity of two islands, an example of similar genetics from diverse cultures.

She straightened my collar and leaned closer. "I tell you something true now, 'cause I can see you're not a believer. That same Assault Obeah, I used it against Sinclair Benton. Nine days after my last prayer, that bad man was found dead in the same lake that kill my baby. I tol' you about that evil place. We islanders saw vultures, knew Benton was missing and sent a couple tourists to check. There his big body was, face down, out there like he was tryin' to find something.

"Sinclair drown in Horse Eatin' Hole, a man who couldn't swim a stroke in his life and had no reason to be at a place nobody on Cat Island have the courage to go near except my sweet brave Tucker. That how strong that spell is."

I picked up my bucket and began to walk along the bar again. I was walking in ankle-deep water, at the demarcation of turtle grass and sand,

and soon found a nice little pocket of sea anemones. It was in a slightly softer area where there were also dozens of nickel-sized siphon holes in the sand: a bed of angel-wing clams below.

I touched my middle finger to one of the holes. I could feel the angel-wing's siphon jetting water as the clam dug deeper, effecting escape.

Ransom continued to follow. "What I don't understand is, why you worried about them Colombians finding you way out here in the middle of the ocean? How they even know you're out in your boat, man? It what tell me you're very scared for a reason, 'cause you not the type to scare easy."

The Colombians could have known because that morning, on the phone, I'd given Lindsey a precise rundown of my schedule. Told her where I would be and when I would be there. Would do the same thing tomorrow morning and the next day and the next.

It was something else I'd promised Hal Harrington.

To Ransom, I said, "You're imagining things, again."

THAT NIGHT, A little after midnight, Tomlinson came sneaking up the boardwalk to my house, exaggerating his careful steps in an attempt to be quiet, and thereby made even more noise than usual.

I heard Ransom's happy giggle, the muffled lyric of voices, my cousin probably pretending that he'd surprised her.

There was not much chance of that, because I'd strung a hammock for her in the breezeway between the house and the lab. She'd told me she liked sleeping out there because she could look at the stars and hear the night sounds, plus the tin roof that connected the two little buildings kept the dew off her, so it was fine, just fine. Best place to sleep on Sanibel, she told me, and was probably right.

I was lying in bed reading *The Windward Road,* a classic by Archie Carr, the great Florida biologist, and listening to my shortwave, Radio Bogota. I had just heard a news reporter say in Spanish that Colombia's military had suffered casualties in three days of heavy fighting against guerrillas. Fifty-four soldiers and police were dead, and a United States–built army helicopter had been downed by suspected rebel fire. Another seventeen were feared dead or taken prisoner by the leftist Revolutionary Armed Forces of Colombia, FARC. According to the reporter, the rebels were reacting to a recent U.S. antidrug policy of interdiction by force. Some of the smaller producers were being put out of business.

That made me think of Hal Harrington. It also brought back some memories of Colombia, a place I love.

Colombia is one of the most beautiful little countries in the world and also one of the most tragic. When its economy flourished, then became dependent on the drug trade, the first casualty was Colombia's own legal system and the respect its citizenry had for that system and their republic. It started with marijuana, then cocaine. Now Colombia is the second largest producer of heroin in the world. The beautiful little country of rain forest and ancient stone cities just keeps getting dirtier and more ruthless as the drug whirlpool sweeps it around, dragging it deeper and deeper into the abyss.

If Colombian drug merchants had come to care nothing for the lives of other Colombians, they would not hesitate to kill me. Ransom was exactly right: I was afraid. Afraid for good reason. Somewhere beyond the night and across the Caribbean, Amador Cordero, oldest son of Edgar Cordero, was hooked up to tubes and hoses, a paraplegic. I was the cause and his father would have his revenge.

The only question now was when . . . and who would come looking for me?

I heard Ransom laugh louder, then the slap of Tomlinson's bare feet on wood. I saw his silhouette fill the doorway, told him to come in before he had a chance to knock, and there he was: Hair more matted than usual, eyes glassy, pupils fixed, completely naked. His lower body was caked in what looked to be gray mud, his torso painted red, his face streaked with tribal designs, black and yellow.

I said, "You get kidnapped by Indians or just showing off your artistic side?"

Behind him, wearing one of my T-shirts as a nightdress, Ransom made a clicking noise with her tongue and said, "He *all* man, that for sure. From the top to the bottom. Lordy! That something I no longer got a question about!"

Tomlinson was staring at the wall beyond me, maybe looking out the window . . . no, just staring. He seemed to be in some kind of trance, and weaving, too. I realized he was very drunk or stoned. Probably both. I listened to him say, "I spent all night, all day, praying and meditating about what to do. I pounded up leaves and drank the sacred Black Drink, what the Indian shamans used to drink when they were on a vision quest. The Calusas I'm talking about, here on Sanibel. That's why I'm here."

Still amused, an approving smile on her face, Ransom said, "You been smoking some herb, too, that what I smell. Smell very nice, too. That the bad thing about not having no pockets, you walking around naked like that. You got no place to carry a little present for your friends."

I crossed the room and found a towel. I wasn't wearing the sling now. My arm was still bandaged but it felt a lot better, no longer so stiff, although the bruise had darkened, spread and turned a sickly shade of blue-green.

Which was not much different than the shade of Tomlinson's face right now. The unpainted areas, anyway.

I said to him, "I think you should sit down before you fall down. Maybe some food would help. There's a piece of grouper in there from dinner."

He was shaking his head. "No, man. Not now. It came to me. In my vision. That I should come here and tell you how it was, what I did. Everything. We need to talk. I don't know why I put it off for so long."

"You want to talk now? This instant?"

"Damn right, amigo. I wait 'til I'm sober, I might lose my courage."
I tossed the towel to him. "Okay. I'll listen. But do me a favor first."

TOMLINSON SAID, "Nearly fifteen years ago, I was a member of a polit-ical activist group that was responsible for sending a bomb to a San Diego naval installation. It killed three people and injured another guy pretty bad. One of the people killed, he was a naval officer. I think he was a friend of yours. You didn't know? I've always wondered if you knew or not."

Instead of answering, I said, "A political activist group that sent a bomb? That seems like a pretty mild way to describe cold-blooded killers."

"Well, revolutionaries then. Or anarchists. That's more like it. This was back when I was a teaching undergraduate in Boston. What we really were—there were thirteen of us who were super-active; the core group of true believers, I'm talking about. Power to the people. Up the establishment. Death to the pigs. That's where our heads were at, but we were so young, man. So fucking young! Really, what most of us were was just a bunch of dilettantes who thought violence was like what we saw on television. Good guys and bad guys, cowboys and Indians. Like that."

I said, "A lot of people wouldn't have the courage to admit that."

Tomlinson said, "It's the truth, man. The truth. Back then it seemed like we were doing the right thing, trying to crash the establishment so we could start all over and make things better. You've got to know your-self, some things going on during that time period really sucked. Until I saw the film footage of the people we'd killed. That's when it got real, man. Way too real. I've never been the same person since."

I was sitting on the bed. Tomlinson was in the reading chair by the north window. Instead of wrapping himself in the towel, he'd borrowed a pair of khaki shorts. They were baggy. He had his forehead braced in both palms, looking at the floor as he spoke, not looking at me. The floor lamp above him made his hair seem a brighter blond, the shadow of his goatee darker, the tribal paint on his face surreal.

Through the window behind him and to his right, I could see black water and a fringe of stars. Out on Periwinkle, the island's main strip, bars such as 'Tween Waters and Sanibel Grill and at Casa Ybel were probably still going strong, but this side of the bay was given over to darkness and silence.

I'd asked Ransom to leave. She was outside somewhere. Maybe eavesdropping, maybe not.

It didn't matter.

I sat there and listened, saying nothing, as Tomlinson told me how it was. The rallies, the demonstrations, the late-night talks about civil disobedience and insurrection, discussions of violence becoming gradually more and more acceptable and extreme as the subject of violence became commonplace. Their words making it seem doable and real, the fantasy of their small unit making bloodless war, accomplishing good, changing the world. The women members into it, a communal feeling, sex and drugs and revolution. Like it could really happen and they, the elite, had a responsibility to *make* it happen.

Conditioning is one of the least appreciated dynamics of human behavior. Take a group, any group, and condition them to a philosophy or pattern of conduct one tiny deviant step at a time and, within a few years or less, you can convince them that such atrocities as mass suicide or marching one's own neighbors into ovens are both perfectly reasonable acts.

Tomlinson's group had found a book called *The Anarchist Cookbook.* It gave detailed directions on how to make bombs and detonators. They'd already rented a little farm. They began to experiment.

Amazing. The ingredients were easy to find, the bombs easily built. They actually worked.

BOOM!

For the novice, activating a weapon gives the illusion of power. They all felt that power and liked it.

The bombs they built became more and more sophisticated. Finally, one night, one of them said it was time to become part of the revolution, which was like a dare, and no one said no, and so they rigged a contact detonator to a six-volt battery, packaged it and sent it to the Naval Special Warfare base on Coronado Island off San Diego.

It was in early winter when Coronado's jacarandas are in bloom; whole streets lined with lavender trees from the country club clear to the Hotel Del.

Tomlinson told me, "About a week later, the FBI came calling. Interviewed us all. I don't know why they didn't make any arrests. I thought sure we were all going down. Nothing ever came of it, though. The other members, they were like, 'Hey, man, the pigs just aren't smart enough to catch us.' I didn't send the bomb, help make it, nothing. But I didn't stand up and tell them not to make that bomb, either. So there was blood on my hands. Blood on my hands just as sure as if I'd killed those three men all by myself. After that, the next year or two, I don't remember much. The guilt, man, seeing those smoking corpses on TV. I went insane. No other way to put it. My father finally had me institutionalized. Just to keep me safe."

The other members of the group didn't fare as well. Within two years after the bombing, six of the thirteen members had either been killed in freak accidents or badly injured. Two others simply vanished.

"I was with one of them when it happened," Tomlinson told me. "I'd just been released. I wasn't ready, was still woozy from the shock therapy and all the drugs, but I guess they figured it was time. So I hooked up with this old pal of mine in Aspen, a guy named Jeff. He also happened to be one of the original members of our group. The group that sent the bomb. We were in this bar called The Slope, and I went to take a whiz. Came back, and Jeff was gone. His car keys were still on the table, had a full beer and his cigarette was burning in the ashtray.

"His folks spent a fortune trying to find him, but he was gone, man.

Vanished. It was like there was some dark thing out there stalking us. Hunting us down. Taking revenge on us, one by one by one."

I was holding a can of Diet Coke. As I listened to him, the can began to slowly dent, then collapse in my hand. I told myself to sit back, relax, maintain an expression of indifference.

He sighed, paused, chewed at his hair for a moment, then went to the little fridge, opened the door and knelt to see in. As he did, he said, "That was the end for me. I couldn't take any more. I borrowed money from my old man and bought a sailboat. Headed out to sea. Offshore, a hundred miles or more out, was the first time in years I'd felt any sense of peace. Or safety, after what we did. It was a kind of spiritual rebirth, man. And a release, too. It's like I always say: I love being offshore because no one can hear you scream."

He stood, holding a fresh beer. He told me that after months of cruising, he began to recover. Began to study Buddhism, doing sitting meditation twice a day every day. He also began to research the families of the three murdered sailors, wanting to make restitution, and finally found a way. He pretended to be the administrator of a private organization that provided scholarship money to the children of servicemen killed in action. Every extra cent he made, he funneled into that fund.

"I interviewed all three widows by phone. I got to know them. Nice ladies, but only one of them had children, Cheryl Garvin. I talked to her several times. That's where I first heard your name, long before we ever met. A guy named Marion Ford, but everyone called him Doc. You were tight with her late husband, Johnny, and already sending her money to help out."

I sat listening, trying not to react, as he added, "When you showed up on Sanibel, I put the two together right away. I figured you'd come to kill me. I expected that all along. By then, a couple more of us had either died in an accident or disappeared. And look who's talking—me, the guy who always says there's no such thing as coincidence. You with your spooky background. Tell me the truth, Doc. If you'd been sent to kill me, I'd be dead, right?"

I nodded as if I had no idea what he was talking about, and, before I could think about it, heard myself say, "If I had that kind of background, yeah. Unless they failed to assign some kind of time frame. An oversight that left it entirely up to me when to do it."

He smiled for the first time. "I get it, one of your jokes. Like you still might *have* to pull the trigger. Uh-huh. But no, my point is, for us to end up friends is very powerful karma, man. It told me I was back on the right path. Maybe even forgiven. Two months ago, though . . . early December, it was the anniversary of the bombing, and it all came back for some reason. The guilt. The horror. You know why I pushed so hard for you to go to my retreat on Guava Key? Because I'd already arranged for Cheryl to be there, Johnny Garvin's widow, and I was going to tell you both the truth. Finally get it off my chest. But she had to cancel at the last minute."

I nodded and stood, feeling some of the old anger return, fighting it, then compartmentalizing it. I am very, very good at compartmentalizing emotion. I waited until I was under control before I said, "I'm glad she didn't come. It was a long time ago and why put her through it again? Just to make yourself feel better?"

I watched the words hit him and saw them hurt. I took no pleasure in that. It was true. It had all happened a long, long time ago, and several years back I had made a personal decision to leave it all where it belonged—in the past.

Once a decision has been made, emotion—any emotion—is wasted energy and a poor use of time.

As I opened the door, showing him out, I added, "One thing you maybe overlooked. From what I just heard, anyway."

"What's that, man?"

"It was a violent time. There were a lot of subversive groups around. Not just yours."

"Revolution, man. Yeah. There were tens of thousands of committed souls. The energy was so strong it came through the walls like heat."

I said, "Uh-huh. So if the FBI didn't arrest anyone from your little group, how are you so sure the bomb was yours?"

17

THEY DIDN'T DRIVE to Mango on Sunday, because Tomlinson was too shaky and hungover. Instead, he puttered around the marina with Ransom, the two of them drinking bottled water and sneaking off occasionally to smoke.

My guess, anyway.

He had to listen to a lot of jokes about Mark Bryant's dog, too. Good stories travel fast around the islands and islanders aren't shy about exaggeration. Sunday morning, Jeth told me that he and Janet had found the runaway retriever a few miles away from the marina only an hour or so after the party ended. Sunday evening, though, the story had grown epically. I ran into Alex Payne at Bailey's General Store, and he said he'd heard that the dog had assaulted half a dozen poodles on Captiva, then tried to swim across to Demere Key where, apparently, there was a female dog in heat.

"I heard even that big black cat you've got at the marina had to run for his life and still hasn't come back," he laughed.

Nope. Crunch & Des was in my lab, sleeping by the window, right where I'd left him.

Early Monday morning, Tomlinson came puttering up in his little dinghy, borrowed the keys to my pickup truck and took Ransom away with him. I gave him my new cell phone to use. I told him I'd been having some engine problems with the truck and he might need it if they broke down.

I waited until they were gone, then jumped in my boat and ran straight across the bay to Punta Rassa, where I'd already arranged for a rental car through the big resort and spa there.

I checked the contract twice to make certain I'd paid for full insurance coverage, no deductible. I checked to make sure it had a good emergency brake, too. Most rentals don't.

It was a Japanese car, white, common, indistinguishable from a dozen other similar makes, foreign or domestic.

Perfect.

I sat in the car at the boat ramp parking lot, watching traffic come across the bridge from Sanibel. I was waiting to see the cab of my old blue pickup come up over the rise, Tomlinson and Ransom inside, and planned to sneak into traffic behind them.

Earlier that morning, right on schedule, I'd called Lindsey at her snowy hideaway, which now she was fairly certain was in Colorado, although her dad wouldn't allow her to describe the little nearby ski resort where her bodyguards—Big Ben and Little Ben, she called them—now took her daily. I called her not just because I'd agreed to call her but because, I realized, I had come to look forward to our talks. Liked hearing her strong laughter. Liked hearing her energized plans for things we were going to do in the future. At one point, she'd told me, "Know what I'd enjoy doing? Coming back to Florida and just the two of us getting on a boat and going somewhere. Some place that's peaceful and quiet, but wild. Not one of those resort places. A place that's got some heart to it. After all this crazy crap is over and we know we'll be safe."

Something about the phrase "that's got some heart to it" brought a specific location to mind. I told her, "If you want wild and remote, there's an area south of here where the Everglades drains into Florida Bay. Nothing but mangroves and empty beaches and this river that runs clear back up into the sawgrass."

"Can we go there and camp? Promise?"

The last time I'd camped in that area was years ago, just after my parents were killed. I'd gotten in my little skiff and disappeared on my own, alone for more than two weeks.

I didn't tell her that. I'd never told anyone that.

"We'll get a houseboat," I said, and talked with her for a little longer before listing my plans for the day—driving alone to Mango—so that she could pass them on to her father, via telephone, as I knew she would.

It was the first time I'd ever lied to her.

THEY WERE BEING followed.

I wasn't certain at first. With Ransom driving, they came rolling over the high bridge, then east on the six-lane highway with its 7-Elevens and strip malls. I filtered in behind, keeping a car or two between us, but I could see they were so busy talking that there was no danger of them taking notice of me.

Ransom was an inconsistent driver. She'd speed up, then slow down, drifting back and forth across lanes. She probably didn't have much experience driving in traffic. Maybe she'd never driven in traffic before. What had she told me? Cat Island had one tiny little section of paved road, that's all. Everything else was shell or sand.

Florida attracts some of the worst drivers from around the nation and around the world. It had to be a white-knuckle introduction to life on the modern highway.

But she seemed relaxed, unimpressed. I could see her laughing and chatting away as she tailgated and swerved and cut off cars that she'd passed, indifferent to blaring horns and angry finger-grams flashed her way.

She and Tomlinson seemed to have more and more in common. They were both horrible drivers.

Because she was unpredictable, it took me awhile to spot the car that was following them. I noticed a green Ford Taurus with the plain, unadorned look of an inexpensive rental.

Had I needed to tail someone, it was the kind of car that I would have selected.

I watched the car pass my blue pickup, then linger until my truck had passed it. Then the Ford fell in behind, but in a different lane. When Ransom slowed unexpectedly to something approaching school-zone speed, the Taurus had to pass once more. When the car gradually reduced speed so that Ransom could again slip by, I knew I was watching a solitary surveillance. Had even one other car been involved, the Taurus would have handed her off and continued at speed.

Nope, it was a lone tail. And not someone particularly good at what he was doing.

MANGO IS ABOUT fifty miles southeast of Sanibel, and there are a couple of ways to get there. Like me, Tomlinson tends to stick to the slower back roads and I was pleased when I realized that he was doing the navigating. We went south on U.S. 41—an illustration of crazed manners and automotive chaos. In South Florida, melting pot driving habits are so unpredictable and dangerous that defensive driving is not enough. You must drive tactically. After fighting our way southward, we turned inland on Corkscrew Road, a two-lane asphalt. I dropped back a quarter-mile or so from the Taurus, then pulled up closer when a cement truck slipped out between us, providing me with good cover.

I drove and watched the scenery change from car dealerships and office condos to orange groves, Brangus cattle and phosphate pits; vast acreage interrupted by an ever-growing number of gated communities with names like Cross Creek Estates, Eagle Ridge, Jamaica Bay—names founded not in geography but at the desks of advertising agencies. The logos varied but the template was the same: little guardhouses, rolling fairways, stucco and spray-creted houses with red synthetic roofs pressed to look like real Spanish tile, lakes and palms in sodded lots, communal pool and tennis courts, and high, ivied concrete walls built to keep Florida out, thereby preserving inside the careful replication of a mid-western suburb.

We turned south, and the land changed again, from fertilized green to dry-season gray, cypress trees standing in sawgrass, limbs bare as winter maples, and black water that glittered on the distant curve of horizon.

A cement truck turned down a shell access road, leaving just the three of us on this isolated, narrow highway. My blue pickup, the Taurus and me, all of us separated over a mile of fast asphalt.

I decided it was time to make my move.

THE DRIVER OF the Taurus had Latino features, the black hair and coloring. He was wearing a collared Polo shirt and narrow, wraparound black sunglasses.

He drove one-handed, forearm draped over the wheel. Cool and very relaxed. He was focused on the pickup, and no doubt figured I was up there ahead of him. He hadn't done a visual ID, just assumed if the truck was rolling, I was in it. No problem. He'd stay right back there until it was time to make a move of his own. Or maybe call in for backup; just a messenger boy assigned to keep me in sight.

I came up behind him gradually, opened the glove box and placed the Sig Sauer on the seat beside me. Then I pulled the ballcap I was wearing down low, punched the accelerator and passed him. I got a pretty good look at the guy from his blind spot before I touched a shielding hand to my face, not wanting to risk him recognizing me. I pulled back into my lane after a safe distance . . . and then gradually, very gradually, began to slow.

I wanted to put as much space as possible between the Taurus and the pickup. Wanted to now do to him what, presumably, he had planned to do to me: separate me from traffic, isolate me, then strike.

He was a tailgater. He came flying up behind me with a road rage flamboyance. I watched in my mirror how he put his bumper up close to mine, his mouth working: What the hell kind of idiot was I to pass him, then slow down?

I waited until he swerved out to pass me, then I slammed the accelerator down.

Neither vehicle had much horsepower. But the little Toyota had enough to keep him from getting around me. A lone semi coming from the other direction forced him in behind me again. Once again, I slowed, watching his reaction in the mirror.

Now he was furious. Tomlinson and Ransom were out of sight, and there was a real possibility I'd just ruined his surveillance. Some idiotic tourist in a little white car. He laid on the horn, shot me his middle finger and swerved out to pass again.

We were on a long section of straightaway. The road had been built with fill dug by a floating dredge—typical of roads in the Everglades. There was a canal running along the eastern edge of the road, sawgrass and cypress domes beyond.

When he swerved, I swerved with him, forcing him off onto the shoulder, then accelerated, driving down the middle of the road so he couldn't pass again. I watched him charge up hard once more, until we were bumper to bumper, his expression contorted . . . and then I saw him lean and come up with something in his right hand.

A handgun.

That's what I was waiting for. I put as much distance as I could between our two cars. I was doing close to eighty and about three car lengths ahead of him when I mashed the Toyota's emergency brake to the floor. I felt the wheels lock, rubber screaming, and I turned the steering wheel a gentle quarter revolution to the right, which effectively pivoted the car 180 degrees—a "boot turn" in the language of combat drivers, taken from the days when bootleggers had to outrun the feds.

The driver of the Taurus did the only thing he possibly could to avoid hitting me—yanked the wheel of his car instinctively to the left, and I saw just the flash of his rear window and bumper as he went bouncing off the road and airborne through the guard rail, then into the canal, plowing a ton of water.

I stopped and backed until I was even with the Ford. It was floating trunk-high. I got out, using my car as a shield, then braced my right arm on the roof, the Sig Sauer pointed at the driver as he climbed out through the window.

He was shaken, his color not good. In Spanish, I yelled, "Show me your hands! Palms out!" Then: "Swim to this side. Now!"

He came climbing out on the bank with a water spaniel meekness. He was bigger than I'd expected. Younger, too. He had his hands over his head, trying not to slip in his soaked pants and leather shoes; he shook his head at me when I yelled, "Who sent you? Cordero?" thinking that if Cordero had sent him, I should shoot him, shoot him dead and leave him . . . then wondered if I could. Did I still have that dark and clinical little place in me that facilitated such extreme behavior?

But the man surprised me by saying in English, "No. Not Cordero. I don't know who hired me. I swear!" Then his expression became perplexed. "Wait, you're . . . you're *him*. The man I was supposed to be following. How . . . how . . . why aren't you in the truck?"

"I am. You're just having a bad dream, that's all."

"I didn't even see you back there."

"That's what you can expect to see when I'm tailing you."

His voice was shaking now. "I don't get it!"

"You're about to. In the kneecap. Every time you refuse to answer a question, bang, I shoot you in the kneecap. First question: Why the hell are you following me?"

He reached for his back pocket, and I leaned toward him, weapon extended, glancing quickly to the left and right: no cars coming.

"*Don't*. Don't shoot me. Please. What they told me was, if I somehow screwed up, if you figured out what I was doing, I'm supposed to give you this." He had his billfold out, and was taking a white note card from it.

"Who's they? Who're you working for?"

"My name's Romano."

"That's not what I asked."

"Okay, okay. I'm a private investigator from Lauderdale. Sometimes I do contractual work. For the government, for corporations, I'm not even sure who it was who hired me. It was all set up by phone. Here, maybe this will explain. I don't even know what it says."

I took the paper and saw that it was an envelope. I opened the envelope and read:

Doctor Ford,

In the event that you realize you're under surveillance and turn the tables, please don't hurt Mr. Romano or his coworkers. They are not in your league. I've hired him to provide me with information and to protect you if necessary. Friend or foe—remember that exercise?

The typewritten note was signed HH.

Friend or foe referred to a common instructional exercise used by state department and Secret Service types. On any important security assignment, where one or more people may be targeted for assassination, friendly surveillance is assigned without the knowledge of the potential target. It may unknowingly be assigned by more than one agency, so the trick is to figure out who the good guys are and who the killers are.

I said to Romano, "So tell me what you've seen. Have you noticed any other people watching me? Following me?"

He nodded his head, eager to please. "Yesterday, for sure. Three men in a white Chrysler that was rented out of Miami International. I checked it out."

"I was on the water most of the day yesterday."

"I know. I saw them watching you through binoculars."

"White or black? What color were they?"

"Two white, one a very light-colored black."

I crumpled the note and stuck it in my pocket. Touched the auto-uncock lever of the Sig, turned and walked back toward my rental.

"You're not going to go off and leave me, are you? My cell phone's in there ruined, my billfold, all my clothes. What'm I going to do about my car?"

I said, "You're asking my advice? Okay. Get in there and start bailing. And watch out for gators. You're entering the food chain, pal, and not exactly on the top rung."

I got back in my little white Toyota and drove away.

18

TOMLINSON SAID, "I thought you had to work in the lab, now here you are driving a rental car. You have some weird little crevices in that brain of yours, my friend. You make some odd behavioral choices." Then: "The old town's changed, hasn't it?"

Yep. Mango, what was left of the original, had certainly changed. Mango had once been a tiny clearing in a massive plain of marl and swamp. It was a collection of houses and docks on a weak curvature of mud flat that created a harbor, and the harbor curved away toward the charcoal gloom of Ten Thousand Islands, mangrove keys all in a maze, joined by water and shadow. They separated Florida's mainland from the Gulf of Mexico. Florida Bay was to the south, Key West seventy miles beyond, and nothing, neither house nor road, between.

Before these obvious changes, it wasn't a town, really. Not even a village. Mango used to be what was once known as a fish camp. It was a mangrove outpost: a row of peeling houses with rusted tin roofs built haphazardly, their impermanence uncontested, as if it were just a matter of time before a hurricane came and swept them away, or until roots and vines grew up through the floors, out the windows, and covered them.

Drive the winding mudflat road through seven or eight miles of swamp where the tide comes right up and floods across, then around a curve beneath coconut palms. Mango Bay rises out of the mangroves to the right. The village is on the left: streetlamps and houses on a low ridge of Indian mounds that face the water. The houses sit on squat pilings, the shell road separating them from the bay. There were also five houses built in the shallows, joined by individual boardwalks leading to the shore. They reminded me of my place on Sanibel.

Tucker had owned all those stilt houses at one time—fish shacks, he called them, but they were in much better shape now. In fact, all of Mango looked to be in better shape . . . modernized, anyway. The houses had been rebuilt, remodeled, repaired, and all of them had been painted or sided with aluminum, in Caribbean pastel colors, conch pink and coral and blue. Even the little store had been reopened, Homer's Sundries— only now it was a Circle K with a big plastic sign, cars parked in the shell lot, cars moving up and down the street. There looked to be a half-dozen new duplexes, too, all waterfront; a lot of money was being invested, with more being built down the shoreline, judging from the crane and cement trucks, all the construction noise in the distance. A busy place. Modern Florida had finally found Mango.

To Tomlinson, I said, "Yep. It certainly has changed. Except for this place."

Meaning Tuck's ranch house, the last house at the end of the road, built on the highest mound—a low gray shack with a tin roof and a sand yard cloaked by trees and Spanish moss. A fallen-down barn out back: hay and a couple of stalls; a little room with a cot and a hot plate—Joseph Egret's room, Tuck had called it.

I'd found Ransom and Tomlinson on the porch, waiting for the care-taker to come unlock the place.

Tomlinson was standing, looking out at the new houses, at the conve-nience store and a passing cement truck while Ransom moved from win-dow to window, looking in. "The contrast," he said. "Tupperware America and mudflat Florida. Obscene, man. Gives me the heebie-jeebies. You should never let them change this place. Ever."

I was impatient to leave, find out what Tuck had left—if anything—and get going, back to my lab. I said, "That's entirely up to Ransom." I watched her big, slow smile when I added, "This is her house now. Whatever she wants to do with it."

SILENCE HAS A museum quality in a house vacated by death. The wooden floors amplified the sound of our shoes as we walked inside; the grandfather clock made its familiar metronome noise from the corner near the fireplace.

Similarities to a museum didn't end there.

The man with the keys, John Dunn, told us, "Captain Gatrell wanted the house to stay just the way he left it. I think I mentioned that to you on the phone, Doctor Ford. Just after your uncle's death? So that's exactly what our owners' association has made every effort to do. Keep the place in good repair without changing the look of it. We owe him a great debt of gratitude. Captain Gatrell changed our lives. We've tried to honor his wishes to the letter."

They had succeeded. The place looked like Tuck had just walked down the street to buy chewing tobacco. In other words, the house was a mess. Clothes thrown on the floor, a couple of his prized cowboy hats hanging from the antlers of a mounted deer head. Dishes in the sink, books he'd been reading spread-eagle around the room, spit cups everywhere, but the big brass spittoon by his rocker, at least, had been cleaned. Bullet holes in the walls, too. Several. And a big, hand-painted sign nailed to a rafter:

GLADES SPRING WATER

FEEL FLORIDA FRESH

MANGO, FLORIDA

Dunn cleared his throat and chuckled to cover what might have been embarrassment. "Your uncle seemed to think . . . or have the belief that he had such a strong spirit that he . . . I mean, his ghost . . . no, his spirit, let's say. That his spirit would return to this house once he'd passed, so he wanted it ready to use and just the way he liked it after he died. Particularly the spit cups. He said he'd never had enough spit cups."

I had a vague recollection of John Dunn. Tuck had met him and several other men and women who lived in some gigantic trailer park off the Tamiami Trail. Somehow, Tuck had recruited them to move to Mango and help him fix it up, for which they received options to buy up some of Tucker's properties.

Ransom seemed delighted with the prospect of Tuck's ghost still hanging around. "That my daddy," she said, touching the Santeria beads she wore. "He a good man, so he have a good spirit. Someone to watch over me if'n I decide to live here. What you think, Mr. Tommy?"

Tomlinson was looking toward the ceiling, hands on hips, considering it. After a few moments, he said, "Definitely. He's here. Tucker Gatrell is definitely here. He has not left the building. If you want, we can hold a séance some night, invite him back and let the old gentleman speak through me. After all those shock treatments I had, I'm a hell of a good medium."

I said, "Another time. When you've rounded up a couple of space aliens, too. Mr. Dunn? Isn't there something you're supposed to give us?" Trying to hurry things along.

There was. It was another letter from Tuck, written on the familiar yellow paper, sealed in an envelope. Before he handed the envelope to me, though, he said, "Captain Gatrell's personal letter to me was very clear on this point. I am supposed to confirm that your sister is with you." He looked at Ransom, puzzled. "Your half-sister, I guess."

"She's my cousin, not my sister, but you can see from the photographs on the wall, she's the one Tuck meant."

There were lots of pictures, some framed, some just tacked to the rough wood walls. There were a couple of me, and several of Ransom. She never looked much older than in her teens. Another one I'd never seen was a photo of Tuck and Joseph Egret, a horse in the background. Tuck was wearing his favorite gray roper's hat, Joe a blue wind ribbon to hold his long hair. Another element in the Gatrell Museum.

Dunn had stepped to the wall, looking through his bifocals from one of the photos then back to Ransom. He smiled. "Young lady, you are a very beautiful woman. Handsome, I think that describes you even more accurately, and in a very feminine way. One of the most handsome women I think I've ever seen. I mean that."

Ransom did something similar to a curtsey. "And you a very nice-looking white gentleman. Got a nice little butt on you, Mr. Dunn."

The woman had a great gift for making male friends very quickly. Dunn had to be in his late seventies, but he was suddenly doing his best to look and sound younger. He made a waving motion with his hands. "What the hell, I think we can dispense with any more ridiculous red tape. I look in your face and I trust you—and it is a lovely face, so sweet and angelic—but there is one other thing your father—" He seemed to remember I was still there. "—that your uncle also wanted me to ask you. Is there any third party forcing you to come here? I have a feeling there could be that possibility."

Did he mean Tomlinson?

I said, "This is a good friend of mine. In fact, I think you two met a few years back."

"Actually, I was thinking of a couple of other people, no one that's here. A few days ago, a couple of black men—" He glanced at Ransom. "Sorry. Two *African*-American men came here asking about Captain Gatrell, where he lived, did his relatives ever come to visit his old house. Captain Gatrell once told me personally to keep my eyes open for . . . well, for men matching that description."

Ransom said quickly, "Did one of 'em got gold stars on his teeth, and the other was big as a cow?"

Dunn was nodding. "And accents. Accents very much like yours—not as lovely, of course."

Ransom ignored him. She looked at me, her eyes fierce. Said, "It them two no-account Rasta niggers again. They not done fuckin' with us, my brother. We see them come around again, what I'm gonna do is mix up the herbs and powders and drop a spell on them that'll make their prissy cocks shrivel up like raisins."

Tomlinson was suddenly very interested. "Really? I don't suppose there's some spell you know that does the reverse?"

Hers was a bawdy, lusty laugh. "Mr. Thomas, somebody done already dropped a double whammy of that spell on you judging by that big ol' thing you got swingin' between your legs." Then she turned back to Dunn who had paled slightly, and she said, "Thank you very much for them kind words. Now can we see that letter?"

Dear Duke,

If that witch bastard and his goat-humpers have forced you to come looking for what I took from him, and they're standing there holding a pistola on you, chew up this note and swallow before they can stop you. Unless you think they're gonna kill you for it, then let them have it. No amount of what I stole is worth you or Ransom dying.

If you get the feeling I am afraid of them people after what they did to me and to Rumer, you are right and I am man enough to admit that cold-blooded killers and filth such as them do scare me 'cause they ain't got no morals or conscience, so will do anything and it don't even cause them to blink. Which is why I'm making it not so easy to get what I left for you.

Just in case, I am going to tell you something only you would know. Then I'm going to tell you something else that only you would know. The first thing is, remember where my old dog, Gator, used to sleep? He's a good old dog though he has bit an asshole or two and he's probably gone now, dead like me and I hope he went out with a smile on his face. Right over his head was a place I used to hide cash money and such, things I didn't want some of the no-account people around Mango to steal from me. Go to that place and take a look. There's a nice little surprise for you there. Plus another letter. If the goat-humpers are with you, run for it right now.

Your Uncle, Tucker Gatrell

There was a postscript written in a different color of ink:

I'd meant to leave you six thousand dollars cash but had to spend it 'cause Joe and me need some traveling money plus to pay some vet bills.

After I'd finished reading, I handed the letter to Ransom and walked to the fireplace. Tucker had owned a big, rawboned Chesapeake that he adored, and the dog usually slept in front of the stone fireplace.

I leaned my weight against the mantelpiece and knelt to look at the rock. The fireplace had been made by stacking uneven layers of fossilized pink coral—coquina rock, some people called it—that had been quarried from Key Largo nearly a century before. As a child, I'd found those blocks fascinating because every close inspection revealed something not seen before. Imprinted on the limestone were miniature brain corals, staghorns and the fabricked impressions of sponges—all sorts of animals that had lived and died a thousand years or more before the first calendar was conceived. Something I also remembered about that fireplace was that a couple of the rocks slid out like heavy drawers and, behind them, Tuck would sometimes hide money or anything else he thought was valuable.

But which rocks?

Tomlinson said, "Secret compartments, man. That's what he's looking for. Ol' Tucker was a true romantic. I love stuff like this."

I was feeling around the edges of the rock with my fingers, trying to remember. I knew it was toward the top, but I wasn't quite sure where. "No secret compartments. Just sloppy workmanship. Tuck built the house himself, which is why it should be no surprise whatsoever."

High on the fireplace, off to the right, I felt one of the slabs move at my touch. It seemed to be in the right area. I wedged my fingers into the cracks and pulled . . . out came a section of stone that I nearly dropped, it was so heavy. I placed it gently on the floor and looked into the cavern its removal had created.

"Mr. Dunn? I don't suppose you have a flashlight?"

"Why, yes, I do. Got one out in the truck."

As he went out the screen door, I pulled out another section of stone. I could see a box or something set back there; I decided to wait for the light.

Yes, there was a small wooden box, heavily waxed, made out of some black and exotic wood. Probably something he'd picked up on one of his trips to Central America or Cuba.

I handed the box to Ransom, then reached in again. I removed what had the weight and feel of a weapon.

It was: Tuck's pearl-handled and engraved revolver. It had been wrapped in an oilcloth, mounted inside its holster, then wrapped again in more oilcloth. He was seldom fussy about the maintenance of anything he owned, but the revolver was in good condition. It was an old Smith & Wesson .44 long barrel, a weapon with sufficient firepower to bring down—in Tuck's words—"anything on two legs and most things on four."

I flipped the loading gate and spun the cylinder. Five of the chambers were loaded, the sixth empty—an old-time safety measure used particularly by men who rode on horseback.

I remembered Tuck saying more than once, "The only dangerous gun is a gun that's not loaded."

Not necessarily.

I pressed the ejector rod, punched out all five cartridges, dumped them in my pocket, then looked down the muzzle. Clean rifling, too.

I heard Ransom say, "My oh my, you don't believe Daddy Gatrell left us something nice now? I don't care a thing no more about that cash was supposed to be there."

She had the box open. She was holding up two more gold coins, one large, one small, similar to the ones she'd already showed me, but not the same. On these, the name of the king was Philip, and the dates were 1612 and 1640.

"He left us three silver coins, too. See there in the box?"

Tomlinson held up a lead-colored coin between his thumb and fore-finger. It was about the size of a nickel. He was squinting to read what was on it. "Interesting, very interesting. These coins, they were all struck between 1556 and 1598 . . . and let's see . . . they've got the Habsburg shield plus the legend. It's in Latin, it says 'Philippus II Dei Gratia,' which means 'Philip the Second by the Grace of God.' That's the way I translate it, anyway."

He stopped and turned the coin, showing it to Ransom. The kindly teacher sharing knowledge. "On the obverse . . . the back side, I mean, there's the Spanish cross with castles and royal lions in quarters, and the words, 'The King of Spain and the Indies.' " He handed the coin to her for inspection.

Ransom was beaming. She said to Dunn, "These two men I'm with, they about the smartest people you ever gonna meet. This one—" She used her chin to indicate Tomlinson. "He reads languages. Knows all about everything."

Tomlinson seemed pleased. "Oh . . . not really. The way I know is, I lived aboard in Key West for awhile. Did some work with dear old Mel Fisher when his people were salvaging the *Atocha*. So I learned a little about coins. These silver ones, they're called eight-reals—portions

of pieces of eight. Two pieces of eight are worth a gold escudo"—
he touched his finger to the smaller of the gold coins that Ransom held—
"and eight gold escudos equal a doubloon."

She was following along. "Why's the gold one perfect, very round, but
this silver one look like it made by a child?"

"The reals, they're irregular like that because they were made by cutting little chunks off bars of silver bullion and carved down 'til the
weight was right, then hand-hammered between engraved dies. Very
crude stuff. The mint was down in Ecuador, I think."

"And they worth a lot of money. A man in Nassau offered me three
hundred dollars apiece for the gold ones. Said even the little gold one,
he'd give me the same."

Tomlinson made a sound of derision. "Never trust that shyster, ever.
By weight, yeah, they might be worth something like that. But they're
worth twenty, maybe thirty, times their weight because they're so rare.
A doubloon in excellent condition, even the escudos—" He shrugged.
"—my guess is, if you had forty of them, you could sell them off carefully, find the right collectors, big money people, and you'd end up with
enough to buy a pretty nice house on Sanibel. If you had sixty of them,
you could buy an inexpensive place on Captiva." He shrugged again.
"That's about all I can tell you. Where they're from, how Tuck got them,
I have no idea."

I was beginning to have my suspicions, although I said nothing. Presumably, the coins had all been lost during transit somewhere between
South America and Spain, but they obviously were not from the same ship
nor the same shipwreck. They immortalized different kings from a variety
of dates. That suggested to me that Tucker had not gotten the coins from
some lucky diver who'd found a solitary wreck. He'd gotten them from a
collector, someone who had acquired them over a period of time.

Sinclair Benton, according to Ransom, had been a powerful man on

Cat Island for many decades. He'd sold his spells to the locals and they weren't cheap, so they had to pay for them with what they could. So make some rough calculations. For two and a half centuries, the Spaniards shipped gold and silver from the mines of South America to Spain. In those two hundred fifty years or so, they lost many dozens of ships throughout the Caribbean to poor navigation and storms. Over the passage of, say, thirty years, what are the chances that people on Cat Island and surrounding islands found the occasional Spanish coin or two while beachcombing or diving or hacking coral out of the reefs?

Of course they did. People are still finding gold and silver coins on the beaches of Florida, particularly places like Sebastian Inlet and Key West.

Okay, then multiply X number of lucky people by X number of accessible coins and you'd probably end up with a sizable number of available doubloons, escudos and reals. Or maybe Benton found the coins himself—listened to the fishermen, tracked down the rumored wrecks, and had his people work them. He could have found a little; he could have found a lot.

Ransom was beaming, very pleased with the knowledge of her new wealth. She reached into the box again and said, "Here you go, another letter he wrote to you. My brother, how can you not like a man who so thoughtful he always writing you notes?"

As she handed me the envelope, I said, "Yeah, he's really starting to win me over, that father of yours."

Dear Duke,

If you come this far, the witch bastard is probably dead and gone and not still after us, but he might not be dead and he might still be after us. So you got one more step to go. You will soon see why I don't want to take no chances. There ain't been much I done right in my life, and I want to do this thing right.

First thing I want you to do is go to the Estero River where them loony Koreshans thought they lived on the inside of the earth and built all them wooden buildings in what used to be jungle but ain't no more. Used to be a nice old lady there who took an interest in my papers and old pictures and such from my years as a famous hunting and fishing guide and all the famous people I showed how to fish and shoot. Many a times I kept my skiff at the Koreshan dock to fish the Estero River and them bars off Hendry Creek with Mr. Edison and Mr. Lindbergh and Harry Truman and Clark Gable, too.

I didn't trust them papers being around the ranch 'cause, as you know, this damn roof is likely to leak like a faucet come the rainy season and it do make paper and such rot.

The Koreshans had themselves what we used to call a music hall and that's where she put my stuff. It's all in one of them nice big wooden boxes I brought me back from British Honduras, stored under the stage where no one ain't likely to look. Walk inside and you'll see two wooden columns and this big black globe that shows stars on the outside of the earth, us living on the inside. Them Koreshans was loony but they did know how to build good buildings in a hard land. Who knows, you might get a smile out of seeing them old papers and pictures.

Second thing is, Duke, Joe and me, we got one more thing for you to do. Remember where it was you took off to after your mama and daddy died? You know the name of the river and so do I 'cause I had to hunt around for a week by skiff to find you. Just down from that river is a big long stretch of beach, which is where you had your camp set up, and behind there is a stand of royal palms and the stone pilings of a house that burnt down. Man name of Dr. Lunsford got control of some of the Ingraham property, built a little dock and airstrip and tried to raise cattle there, which Joe and me supplied, but the skeeters run us all off.

Cattle ranching down on Cape Sable, something else I failed at,
too.

Underneath one of the stone pilings, we buried a bottle that's got
a note in there for you. Joe cut an X into the top of the piling with an
old saw, so it should be easy to find and ain't going nowhere. Go find
it and I promise you won't be disappointed by your old uncle this
time.

After Tomlinson read the letter, he looked at me and said, "You know
what he's doing, don't you?"

We'd walked outside, putting some distance between Dunn and ourselves so we could speak privately. The three of us standing in the shade
of a big oak, Spanish moss hanging, Mango Bay holding blue light beyond, its islands undefined, ledges of black and gray.

"Taking one last opportunity to manipulate people," I answered. "He
could have trusted his attorney with the letters, the photos, the coins,
everything. But that just wasn't Tuck's way."

Tomlinson was shaking his head, his arm over Ransom's shoulder,
telling me I was wrong. "No. You don't see the pattern? It's for Ransom.
All of it. And you. What he's doing is making sure the daughter he never
really got to know sees the Florida he loved. Tucker had his quirks, I
don't argue that, but he was crazy about this country. That's what this is
all about. He figured out a way to get you two together, a way so you'd
have to take her around to the places he cared about, the places that made
him the man he was."

Ransom found that touching. I could see it in her expression as she
said, "You really think that it?"

"I'd bet on it. I didn't know Tucker well, but there was always a reason for his goofy ideas. Everything on separate levels. You think about it,
Doc, the man's whole life is a metaphor for all kinds of stuff. With some
people, their only attempt at art is the way they live their lives."

I had my hands on my hips, indifferent, not the least bit interested in hearing it.

Ransom sniffed and touched a finger to the corner of her eye. "Back when I was a little girl, I used to pray he'd come take me away. And when my sweet boy, Tucker, disappear in Horse Eatin' Lake, I prayed even harder. Now he done it. My daddy found a way to come take me." Then: "What that stuff about Koreshans mean? He talkin' about that crazy man who burned up with all them people awhile back?"

Tomlinson took the letter again, rereading it, as I explained that no, there wasn't a connection. At the turn of the century, Florida attracted—and continues to attract—odd religious splinter groups. The Koreshans had been led by a New York physician, Dr. Cyrus R. Teed, who convinced his gifted followers to come to Florida and found a New Jerusalem in the wilderness. They'd built a beautiful, functional little town on the banks of the Estero River. Teed had also preached celibacy, which is probably why his sect hadn't lasted beyond the lives of its followers.

Not that requirements of celibacy intimidated Tuck. Joseph Egret had once told me that my uncle kept a boat at the Koreshan docks because of all the love-starved women who lived in the female dormitory there. He'd pole his boat in quiet, at night, and leave a little lantern on for ladies watching from windows to see.

Tomlinson folded the letter. "Isn't there an Ingraham Bay down below Shark River? That whole Cape Sable area, it's beautiful. No roads, no houses for thirty, forty miles. That's where he wants us to go next."

I told him, "You two find the Koreshan music hall, I'll go to Shark River alone. I'll either rent a boat in Chokoloskee or run the Maverick down. Depending on the weather."

Chokoloskee is an island south of Everglades City. There's a boat ramp there, a few rental skiffs and a small marina.

I thought about it for a moment. How much delay should I allow the Colombians? There had to be sufficient time for logistics to be arranged.

I thought about the guy in the Taurus, the guy who'd try to tail me, telling me about the three men in the Chrysler. I thought about Dunn describing Clare and Izzy—not that there was any reason to expect Clare and Izzy to react, anticipate or understand, nor could I rely on their behavior. After a moment, I said, "Tomorrow afternoon, that's when I'll go. I'll head down there right after the guides leave and the fuel pumps are open."

"You don't want company? Amigo, it just so happens I got the whole weekend free. I'd love to go."

"Nope."

I am rarely so short with Tomlinson and he was taken aback. "You seem undecided—hah! Kidding, just kidding." Then: "What's the problem, Doc? You don't buy my theory that the old cowboy—Tucker I'm talking about—that Tuck came up with a way to get you two together. Ingenious. It really is. So you at least ought to take Ransom, plus it's been more than a year since I poked around Shark River myself. I wouldn't mind going back."

I was shaking my head, walking away. "Another time. I've got my reasons."

I listened to Ransom say, "See? Didn't I tell you something had him very scared? He a very frightened man, though he won't admit it," as I opened the door of my old truck, removed the cell phone off the dashboard, slipped it into my pocket.

19

THAT AFTERNOON, I finished work around the lab and made phone calls. I tried to contact Hal Harrington at the numbers he'd given me, but his secretaries in Cartagena, San Jose and D.C. told me he was away from the office. The secretary in D.C. said that he was not expected back until morning.

To each, I said, "Tell him that tomorrow I'll be leaving for Cape Sable, just below Shark River. I'll probably camp on the beach there. He can call me on the cell phone."

If they found the long message odd, they gave no indication.

I told the same thing to Lindsey, who did seem puzzled. "That sounds like the place you told me about. And you're going there without me? I'm jealous. I wish you could wait a week. Last night, when I was talking to him, my dad said he thought it'd be safe for me to be on my own, it wasn't likely the kidnappers would try again, but just give it five or six more days."

I explained to her that the trip wasn't recreational, it was family business, and that we'd go another time. We talked for a little while before I asked her if she knew where her dad was.

She said, "He's in Virginia. He'll be back in D.C. tomorrow," then I listened to her tell me about the skiing, how damn cold and boring it was up there when she wasn't on the slope, and that she wished she had my bear paws to warm her, or was back in Florida, lying in the sun on some deserted beach alone with me.

Then she told me she had to run, Big Ben and Little Ben, her bodyguards, were outside in the Range Rover, waiting to take her back to the lifts. The two of them were a hoot, especially Big Ben.

I said, "I'll call you in the morning before I leave Dinkin's Bay," making doubly certain she was clear about my schedule.

Twenty minutes later, I was inside South Trust Bank on Periwinkle. I made it just before they closed.

I found one of the managers, signed the log sheet, then went into the little room where she opened my safety deposit box and handed me an old leather attaché case, which I didn't open until I was back in the lab.

Crunch & Des lay in the window watching me with disinterest as I opened the attaché case and looked inside to make sure everything was there. I saw one folder labeled OPERATION PHOENIX and another with the words DIRECCION: BLANCA MANAGUA written on a label in red felt-tip pen, plus several others.

I returned all the folders to the leather case and put it in a garbage bag to keep it dry. Then I made myself busy readying my skiff for a long trip. I packed the starboard locker with water, ice, Diet Coke and beer.

I packed the port locker with canned beans, corned beef, and a couple of tinned hams—enough food for several days, plus my stout Loomis bait-casting rod with a fine old ABU reel loaded with twenty-pound test. I carry it for stopping big-shouldered fish around mangroves when I need to put food on the table.

I didn't know how long I'd be gone. I doubted if it would be more than two days, but I had no way of knowing for certain.

There is a saying I remembered from a month spent in Burma working with The King's Own Gurkha Rifles: *To catch a tiger, you must understand the behavior of goats.*

After packing tent, mosquito netting, jungle boots, Navy issue crew-neck sweater, watch cap and miscellaneous camping gear, I reloaded Tucker's old Smith & Wesson and placed it beneath the boat's console beside my Sig Sauer.

Even though I hadn't shot one in years, I'd have much preferred to have a rifle—something big bore with a first-rate scope.

I'D ALREADY SPOKEN with Ransom. She'd seemed bubbly, almost giggly. She told me about their visit to the Koreshan Unity. Something Tuck never anticipated had happened: The place had become a state park, completely fenced in with a guard gate, so she'd had to distract the nice, handsome ranger man while Tomlinson slipped into the Music Hall and found the hidden papers, right where Tuck had said.

Interesting papers, which she described. There were personal notes and letters, all to Tucker, from enthusiastic fishermen and hunters he'd guided and introduced to Florida's backcountry. The letters were signed by men such as Harry Truman, Dwight D. Eisenhower, Charles Lindbergh, Dick Pope, and Walt Disney. There were lots of photographs, too—all signed.

"Mr. Tommy, he tol' me some of these papers might be worth more than our coins. Not that we'd want to sell them, 'course. I'm just pointing out how Daddy Gatrell thought of his daughter and took care of her."

She also told me, if I didn't mind, that she and Mr. Tommy had gotten a room at the Naples Hilton to celebrate. He'd been telling her about something called a massage, an herbal wrap and a facial, womanly things she'd never heard of but wanted to try because, at her age, she said she wanted to try everything she could while she could.

She added, "If you not leaving for Shark River 'til tomorrow morning, why don't you pull in here and pick us up? Mr. Tommy, he say Naples is right on your way. I don't want you to make that trip alone, Doc. I got me a very bad feeling about what it is you doing. I touch my gris-gris bag, I touch my beads, and I get the really strong feeling someone gonna die."

I told her that I wasn't going to die no matter what her beads said—a subtle avoidance that she didn't catch—and to please put Mr. Tommy on the phone.

After a moment, I heard Tomlinson's voice say, "Doc? Wait 'til you see what it was the old bastard left for you two at the Koreshan Unity. These amazing letters and pictures. A handwritten letter from Lindbergh inviting Tuck to visit him in Hawaii. A letter from Walt Disney thanking Tuck for a great day fishing and his advice about where to build in Florida. There's this other letter—you won't believe who wrote it. This other letter—"

I said, "Hold it; be quiet for a second." Tomlinson was talking about one thing, but the nervous quality of his voice told me he was thinking about something else, which is why I cut him off. I said, "Tomlinson? Tell me something. Are you planning on sleeping in the same room with Ransom tonight?"

"Well, because of the prices and all; it's tourist season, you know . . . and we *are* at the Hilton. It was all kind of Ransom's idea because she wanted to be closer to Mango so we can stop back there in the morning and really take a look around. She's considering moving into Tuck's old place—can you dig that?—which is why I thought—"

Yep, he was nervous alright.

I interrupted again. "Please, please . . . spare me, okay? I know what's going on in that twisted and lecherous brain of yours. How many times have you told me that you'd never met an attractive woman in your life without immediately calculating the best way to get her into bed. Which is why you're not—repeat, are *not*—sleeping with Ransom tonight, damn it."

"Hey, amigo, as we both know, my you-know-what doesn't work worth a you-know-what—"

"I don't care about that. It's just not right."

Heard Tomlinson say, "Ransom? Would you excuse me for a moment?" Then, after a short pause, "Doc, I need to remind you of a couple of things. Ransom's a grown woman—a lot older than some of the women you date, by the way. She's been married and divorced. She's a mother. Call me a hopeless bleeding heart feminist, but I think she's capable of making her own decisions about who she sleeps with."

"Absolutely not. The only reason you're interested in her is because of the way she looks, that body of hers, and because you're hoping she knows some kind of island spell, Obeah I'm talking about, that'll make your equipment work. Which is bullshit, and I don't want her to be a part of something like that."

"Am I really hearing this?"

"You bet you are."

"I don't get it. Yeah, Ransom's spectacular, but not just because she's great-looking, man. It's because of her age, her personality. It's the whole far-out package. There's like this truly karmic gig going on between us, not the least of which is that we're both worried shitless about you. About what the hell kind of crazy, dangerous thing you are up to now."

"I'm not going to listen to this, Tomlinson. You two are not sleeping together. You just met! End of story."

"But why?"

"It's not obvious? I don't want you to sleep with her, damn it all, Tomlinson, because she's my—" I caught myself. I'd almost said because she was my sister. Instead, I said, "Because she's a blood relative, and the potential for complications is just too great. It would be like dating someone from the marina. And we both agree about the dangers of that."

"I'm sorry, I really am, Doc, but no promises," he said. "I just can't. The attraction's too strong, man. Very heavy vibes, which I think she feels, too. Ransom's one of the most beautiful women I've ever met; that's just the way it is. But I'll let you know."

Which really infuriated me.

After I hung up, I worked around the lab. I got everything I could packaged and mailed off.

I waited until an hour after dark to trailer the skiff behind my pickup, then I drove it south toward the Everglades, Mango and the islands beyond.

I PULLED INTO Everglades City at a little after 8:30 P.M. It was a half-moon night with stars. Everglades is a mangrove town built at the border of sawgrass and sea by a turn-of-the-century visionary and power baron. It was to have been the political seat of a great county. The village's fortunes ascended briefly, but isolation and swamp are formidable consorts, and it ultimately returned to being the outpost it was destined to remain.

Everglades had changed much, though, in just the last year or two—lots of new tourist facilities, several new restaurants and a billboard near the village circle advertising a trailer park on the narrow road to Chokoloskee. There were authentic Seminole souvenirs, gator tail sandwiches, birding tours and airboat rides, all the tacky, touristy standbys that are the historic mainstays of tacky, touristy South Florida.

Like Mango, the modern world had finally moved to within reach of Everglades City and begun the slow, osmotic process of change and homogenization.

I crossed the elevated river bridge and dropped down onto a slow boulevard of palms. The village has had the same streetlights since the 1930s, glass moon-globes on ornate iron stems. The streetlights were set apart at incremental distances, creating theatrical islands of light as I toured slowly through town. I was tempted to stop and have dinner at the Rod & Gun Club. I remembered, fondly, a nice lady I'd once overnighted with in one of the little cottages there. We'd spent it holding one another, nothing more, two friends providing comfort. One of the few and truly good ones. I remembered her good eyes and strong heart, and I wished her another private, silent farewell.

I make it a rule not to linger in sentimentality, however; I seem to have less and less tolerance for it. Tomlinson insists that the opposite is true. He says that I have grown both spiritually and emotionally since I opened the lab at Dinkin's Bay. He doesn't seem to understand that I don't consider that a compliment.

I decided not to waste time ordering dinner at a restaurant. I had canned goods in the boat, drinks, too. Instead, I turned back through town and stopped at the Circle K, where I loaded on more ice and fuel, then launched my skiff at the boat ramp.

The tide on the Baron River was ebbing. At idle, the black current swept me southward through the village and into the night. I stood at the wheel of my boat, big engine rumbling, and looked at the lights of the village. I could see people moving across scrims of windows, framed by leaves and vines, a micro-snapshot of lives being lived in this isolated Florida place.

Then, far off to the left, I could see the glow of Chokoloskee as I powered to plane across Chokoloskee Bay, running the flashing markers out Indian Key Pass, the moon following along behind me, its blue light strobing through the limbs of mangroves. The tops of the trees were individualized and set apart in starlight, a primeval canopy against the brighter sky. Then the mangroves thinned, fell away and disappeared so that it was like breaking some gravitational hold, and I was suddenly free, running straight into blackness and a horizon of stars.

When I was well offshore, clear of coral rock and oyster bars, I banked southwest. Sea and sky were lucent spheres joined at the horizon. I sledded across, down the surface of one sphere, then up the surface of another.

In a few minutes, I picked up the gloom of Pavilion Key, the westernmost of the Ten Thousand Islands, and an effective range to deep water.

Twenty miles or so beyond, I knew, was Shark River.

I stopped only once. I calculated that I was slightly south of Lostman's River. I took a whiz off the stern, looking up at the sky. No boats, no lights, nothing. The coastline was all darkness here. I might have been the only human being left on earth. I switched off the engine. I sat drifting there, in no hurry now. I stripped off my clothes and swung over the side, my only way to bathe for the next few days.

The February ocean was chilly, in the low seventies, nearly cold.

Back in the boat, I dried myself and checked the cut on my left arm. It seemed to be closing nicely. I squirted antibiotic cream onto gauze and taped it into place. Then I put on fresh clothes. I hadn't worn these clothes in so long that their use suggested ceremony. I put on camo BDUs, the dense Navy sweater over a T-shirt and the black watch cap.

Finally, I tied on my old and comfortable jungle boots before firing the engine and heading down the coast.

LOOK AT A map, and Cape Sable is the massive riverine promontory that forms the southwestern boundary of the Florida peninsula. It is uninhabited, isolated, seldom visited—many miles of beach fringed by strands of coconut palms, accessible only by boat. It is known for silence, mosquitoes and some of the most stunning sunsets on Earth.

There was good moonlight, but it was still too dark to see the stand of royal palm trees Tuck had mentioned, so I had to guess. I stern-anchored off Northwest Cape, and muled my gear up the beach. I pitched my red dome Moss tent, collected wood and built a pit fire for light and as a smudge to sweep some of the mosquitoes away.

Down on the Cape, mosquitoes are distressing in winter. In summer, they can be existential—a peppered cloud that swarms and attacks, a billion winged lives competing for mammalian blood.

With pants, sweater and headnet, though, I was protected, and worked away without much trouble. I wanted a big, public camp with lots of light and color, something easily seen from miles away. I thought about hiking up to Little Sable Creek to see if there was one of those tall, rope-straight mangroves growing there—a trunk adaptation associated with the Cape Sable area. I had the idea of putting up a little flagpole, something no one could miss.

I decided that seemed a little too much. If they wanted me, they would find me.

A frightening realization: Of course they would.

WHEN THE CAMP was complete, I began the more careful work of building a second, invisible camp. Because there was a chance I might need it, I took my folding entrenching tool and dug a hole in the hard sand large enough to hold me. I dug it deep enough that water began to seep in, then used my flashlight to find palmetto fronds to cover the thing.

The possible scenario was, if armed men approached my tent, I could lie on my back in the hole, wait until they'd passed, then surprise them from the rear.

Not a preferred plan of attack, but I wanted as many options available as possible.

When I was done with the hole, I walked inland a hundred meters or so to a border of trees. There were palms and Brazilian peppers—a noxious exotic—and a couple of huge black mangroves, too.

It was late now; the moon had drifted low toward the open Gulf of Mexico and by its light I saw, for the first time, the feathered crests of the royal palms that Tuck had mentioned, and that I also remembered from my first solitary visit to this place years ago as a boy.

A royal palm tree looks as if it is made from cement poured into an eighty-foot tube, then topped with a crown of fronds. Get up into one of those palms and you'd be able to spot any approaching boat miles before its arrival. Trouble was, I needed climbing hooks and a climbing belt to get up one of those trees. Worse, even the closest tree was too far from my false camp, and I didn't feel like moving all that equipment again.

I decided the black mangroves would be good enough and picked the stoutest, not the tallest, tree. I climbed until I was about twenty or thirty feet above the ground, then chose two strong branches that were about the right distance apart. Between those branches, I strung my good jungle hammock with its camouflaged roof and no-seeum-proof netting. Using sawed limbs, I also constructed a solid little platform big enough to hold me comfortably. Then I cut branches until I had a clear view of the beach camp, and used those branches to build a blind.

Back on the ground, I considered angles and distance. Years ago, with the Sig Sauer, I'd been able to shoot consistently and accurately up to about fifteen meters. I paced off the distance from the mangrove tree and built a makeshift lean-to on that spot. Also I constructed a small fire pit, then lit a pile of twigs and let it burn until it smoldered.

This had to be a convincing little outpost.

I thought I had everything I needed in my backpack but, of course, didn't. Twice I had to make the long walk to my boat to get something I'd forgotten. A typical camping exercise.

This, however, was not a typical camp.

I KEPT THE big fire burning for light. I opened a can of black beans and a small canned ham. Stuck them near the coals and made forays down the beach to collect driftwood for the fire. I had a stack of wood that was belt-high before I finally stopped to eat. I chopped ham into beans, and squeezed in the juice of one of the limes I'd brought. Sat back in the shadows, looking out across black water, eating, looking at the fire.

Driftwood makes the best of fires. It's saturated with sea salt and ocean minerals. The chemical combustion of those salts and minerals creates flames that burn translucent blue, green and violet—colors never seen in other campfires. Each piece of wood burns differently; each chunk creates its own prismatic display. Driftwood accurately translates the iridescent hues of Caribbean water into heat and flame.

As I sat there, my memory moved automatically and without conscious interest to that evening, years ago, after I'd loaded my little wooden skiff with camping gear and arrived alone at this place. I remembered my first view of the mangroves of Shark River. To a boy of eleven, they'd appeared massive, prehistoric—a black and green border at the Earth's end.

The river, too, seemed well-named. For water to suggest the presence of predators, it must be sufficiently dark and volatile to create swirling ambush points and unexpected drop-offs. It must have some depth to it, too, enough to shield that which lies beneath and thus demonstrate a potential for attracting creatures unseen—creatures that are unexpected, dangerous.

The second day of that long-ago camping trip, I'd baited a heavy boat rod with a live mullet and drifted on an incoming tide along the sheer mangrove wall. The mullet was the size of a bowling pin. I never expected that there was anything around big enough to hit it.

I was wrong. Within a few minutes, something below turned on the bait so hard that it nearly snatched the rod and me out of the skiff. Then it ran off a hundred yards of fifty-pound test line, pulling the skiff and me along behind like a ski boat before it popped the monofilament as if it were string.

I'd pitched my Scout tent on Shark Point. After hooking and losing that fish, though, I moved camp south to Cape Sable, miles from the river. Even then, I loved to swim open water, but the experience had done something to my confidence, to my sense of security above water and below. I didn't want to risk swimming again in a place that attracted animals so large and predatory.

Staring at the fire, I also thought about my mother. No longer able to recall her face from memory, I now remember her only from photographs. An attractive woman with strong cheeks and good eyes. By all accounts, she'd been a gifted amateur naturalist and one of the earliest advocates for a save-the-Everglades movement. She'd spent a lot of time lobbying hard up in Tallahassee.

I found it oddly comforting to know that just around the far curvature of Cape Sable was Flamingo, once an isolated fish camp, now headquarters for Everglades National Park. There, nearly hidden by mangroves, is a little brass plaque commemorating the founding of the park. My mother's name is there, second column, about midway down.

The last thing I did before climbing the tree and zipping myself into the hammock was re-anchor my boat. I anchored it bow pointed seaward, double-anchored, stern tied by a long line to a stake I drove into the beach.

Then I went for a quick swim. I swam out a couple hundred meters. There was a fresh wind blowing and I rode the waves up and down, the horizon all around me. From the crest of each wave, I could see the stars that form the Southern Cross.

The Cross was at eye level, afloat way, way out there at open sea.

Several times that night, I awoke to the sound of wind and to the niggling despair of old memories. Once I heard a powerboat come in close to shore and shut down abruptly. I thought I saw a light in the far distance. Thought I heard something going thud-thud-thud, like wood hitting wood.

I waited, watched, listened. Decided it was probably a pompano fisherman working the beach, banging his hull with a paddle to spook fish into his gill net.

Cordero or his hired helpers could not possibly have had time already to rent a boat or steal a boat and track me to Cape Sable.

I checked the cell phone to make certain it was still on.

Plenty of battery remaining.

If I had to stay there a few days, I could always recharge it from the adapter on my skiff.

I tried to call Harrington one last time. Got his voice mail. Didn't bother leaving a message. There was no need.

20

THEY CAME TO kill me the next day. They came blasting along the noonday beach, spraying white water against the blue of a February sky. Two men, both Caucasian, in a cabined, junky tri-hull that had an OMC outboard on the transom and faded block letters on the side: CHOKOLOS-KEE BOAT RENTALS.

That told me something. Gave me a little boost of confidence. It told me Cordero or his men were acting on last-minute information. Told me they hadn't taken time to get organized or to plan. They were eager—very, very eager to get the job done. They wanted to find me, make the hit, then get the hell out.

I'd been worried they'd come with a chopper. Maybe two. The drug people have plenty of money. If they'd sent a chopper after me equipped with the right kind of heat-sensing electronics, I wouldn't have a prayer.

It also suggested that they hadn't been tracking me personally. Someone had been passing them information.

I knew exactly who it was.

I was high above the ground on my little camouflaged platform watching them through my superb Zeiss binoculars. Hours before dawn, the wind had freshened from the north, blowing in a glittering high-pressure system. The seas were choppy; the sky had a crystal, Arctic resonance. The temperature dropped so abruptly that, by first light, it was too cold to sleep, so I climbed down from my hammock and stomped around until I got the blood circulating again. I used the binoculars to check the beach where I'd heard the boat the night before.

Nothing.

Because I was still cold, I stoked the big beach camp fire until it was roaring and boiled coffee, baking myself in the fire's heat, watching the horizon for boats.

There were a couple shrimp boats far out to sea, booms folded like wings. A speck of a sailboat, too, its canvas gull-white, motionless in the wind. Nothing in close, though.

Because I was confident I had the time, I took my entrenchment tool and hiked back through the sea oats and prickly pear cactus southward to the grove of royal palms.

It took awhile, but I finally found the remains of what was probably the Lunsford house, the place Tuck had described in his note. Partially buried in the sand were sheets of tin from the fallen roof and gray planks of clapboard. There was a rusted iron hulk being strangled by vines—a generator, perhaps—along with a small junkyard of pipe, porcelain, glass and wire. Out back were a couple of cattle skulls, too. Nearby were short chains of vertebrae growing out of the sand.

The stone pilings weren't hard to find. There were more than a dozen of them, much too heavy to move, spread out in a symmetrical, Stonehenge pattern.

Not stone, actually. In Florida, at the turn of the previous century, they'd made a dense cement out of local sand and crushed shell. Built all the houses up on knee-high stilts so air could circulate above and beneath. The cement was as hard and heavy as rock.

I don't know why I was so surprised to find that one of the pilings had an X cut in the top. Probably because Tucker had told me so many lies during his lifetime that honesty and accuracy even after death seemed out of character.

The cutting saw that Joseph had probably used was there, too, orange with rust, the wooden handle rotted off. It was strange to think that Joseph was the last person to have touched that handle.

I used my entrenchment tool and began to dig around the base of the piling. I watched a tiny scorpion crab away, its tail curled like a backhoe. I got down deep enough so that the silver sand turned gray with moisture when I finally hit something.

A second surprise: There really was a bottle.

I picked it up and studied the bottle in the sunlight. It was an old glass Hatuey beer bottle, the word Havana embossed on the bottom. Tuck had used a cork, and some kind of wax to seal it. Even so, I expected the paper inside to be a soppy mess.

It wasn't because he hadn't written this note on paper. He'd written it on a piece of buckskin brown cowhide that had been tanned soft as glove leather. He'd probably used a fountain pen judging from all the smearing.

I sat on the piling and read the note, then read it again. Read it a third time and began to laugh. The postscript from Joseph Egret was the funniest part. It read, "He's telling the truth, for once, Marion. If there was any way we could of gotten that box out, he would have lost it somehow by now or pissed it away, which he always had a way of doing."

I stood, still laughing, and said aloud, "You sly old son-of-a-bitch. Finally. You *finally* pulled one off."

Back at my mangrove camp, I tossed a rope over the limb of a nearby tree and tied the cell phone to it. Tied it close enough to the lean-to so that anyone approaching would see the little camp and make the obvious assumption, but far enough away so that I'd remain unseen, unexpected.

I studied the area carefully, considering my field of fire, then studied it some more. I finally decided that it was a good ambush point. A nice little predatory drop-off.

BY LATE MORNING, the sea breeze had begun to warm. By noon, I could feel the sun radiating through the canopy of mangrove leaves, but still I remained hidden away in my hammock or on the platform.

My Navy watch sweater became too hot, so I stripped it off and changed to an OD green T-shirt.

OD: olive drab.

I'd brought along *The Windward Road* to pass the time. A couple of journals, too. I'd alternately read for a few minutes, then check the horizon with my binoculars.

I saw several more boats far offshore, probably bound for Key West or the Dry Tortugas.

I had a Mako, then a Hewes flats boat sweep in close to the beach, trying to find some lee, on their way around the Cape to Flamingo.

Each time I saw a boat, my heart began to thud.

Then I did see them. Saw them pounding through waves a couple miles off, throwing big water, running way too hard for conditions.

It caught my attention.

I watched the boat dolphin right past my little place on the beach. Then watched it slow . . . stop . . . turn and began to vector shoreward.

They'd either seen the red Moss tent and the fire, or they were following some kind of direction finder.

As they drew closer, I identified the boat as one of the mass production tri-hulls that only non-watermen buy, and saw the name on the side— CHOKOLOSKEE BOAT RENTAL—and knew it had to be Cordero or his hirelings. I could also see that the OMC was burning way too much oil, blowing a cloud of blue exhaust as the boat banged its way through the waves. Then I could see the faces of the two men who stood behind the cabin windshield.

Both faces were familiar to me.

At the wheel of the boat was a man with a huge pumpkin-sized head and dyed, punkish hair—his hair was, appropriately, bright orange now instead of blue. I recognized him because he'd driven the smaller of the two Scarabs when Cordero's men had attempted to kidnap Lindsey.

Beside him was the man with the dark, Indio eyes set in a Castillian face; the man with the moustache and pointed goatee who'd tried his best to shoot me only a week ago.

They'd both come a'hunting, wanting a second chance.

They would have it.

I remembered the Lauderdale investigator who'd been tailing me—Romano?—remembered him telling me that he'd spotted three men on active surveillance, two white and one a very light-skinned black.

Where was the third?

I watched the two men closely through the binoculars, breathing evenly, but heart pounding. I saw that Goatee was holding something in his hand, staring at it intently. It looked to be like a little palm computer . . . yes, and he was wearing earphones, too. A computerized GPS link that was now undoubtedly locked onto the cell phone that Harrington had sent me—a device similar to something I'd used several times in the past; a high-tech surveillance system known by the code name of Glockenspiel and then, later, Triggerfish.

Beneath me and forty meters to my right, my cell phone began to ring—the first time I'd ever heard it ring. It rang so loud that I jumped, startled. It was a computerized melody that was familiar, yet my brain couldn't identify immediately. Then it did: The phone was playing the *William Tell* overture, the theme from the old television show *The Lone Ranger.*

Hal Harrington's strange little joke.

The phone continued to ring. Maddening. If Goatee and Orange were having trouble zeroing in on my cell phone's signature, they'd have no trouble now.

Through the binoculars, I watched Goatee began to gesture wildly toward my hiding place in the big mangroves. The boat was still half a mile off, but he seemed to be looking directly at me.

Had they seen the red tent? Yes . . . no doubt about it. I watched the tri-hull gain speed, porpoising through the surf toward the beach.

I touched my hand to the Sig Sauer on the platform beside me, a gesture seeking reassurance. No need for the sound arrestor here. As an emergency out, I'd placed Tuck's old .44, freshly loaded, on a plastic bag inside the little foxhole I'd dug. But my plan was to remain where I was, let them track the cell phone, then take them when they got into range.

I'd selected my ambush point. Now I'd wait for the electronic current to sweep them in.

But then I saw something that brought an ascending nervous spasm of nausea to my throat . . . something that also brought Tomlinson's old maxim freshly to mind: Want to make God laugh? Tell him your plans.

What I saw was the third man, the light-skinned black. An older man with curly, graying hair—maybe Cordero himself. He'd been in the cabin below and now stepped up onto deck. He was pulling something by the hair, then punching at something with his fists. I watched as he dragged Tomlinson out onto the deck and club him to his knees.

Then he dragged a second person onto the deck.

It was Ransom. I had to force myself to remain where I was, to keep watching, as he slapped her, making her move along.

21

IT WAS CORDERO. Had to be Edgar Cordero. Pure fury has an energy that's infectious, radiates, and the light-skinned man was in a rage.

I recalled a phone message from Harrington saying that Cordero had gone berserk, literally, prior to using a bat to beat a mother and child to death.

Now here he was, crazy with anger again.

I recognized it in the way he was brutalizing Tomlinson and Ransom. I could see it in the way his guy steered them hard toward shore, slowing only slightly, surfing down waves until the boat grounded itself on the beach, the hull lifting and heeling to starboard, spray pluming over the transom as first Goatee, then Pumpkin-head swung over the side into knee-deep water trying to steady the thing.

They either knew nothing about boats or didn't plan to stay long.

Then I watched Cordero shove Ransom backward over the side into the water and Tomlinson leap immediately to help her, lifting her to her feet in the slow surf, her tie-dye T-shirt, red and blue, clinging to her body, her expression dazed as she touched her own face experimentally, then looked at her fingertips. A familiar interrogative: Was her nose bleeding?

I was already climbing down the tree, not even thinking about it, the Sig in the back of my pants, checkered grip secure against my spine, my brain scanning to make sense of what I was seeing. I remembered saying to Tomlinson that I might rent a boat in Chokoloskee; remembered him pressing for us to make the trip together, then Ransom's dark assertion that they should not let me go alone.

"I've got a feeling someone's going to die," she'd told me, fingering her beads and her little bag of magic.

I'd done it. I'd put the idea of a rental boat into their heads and, somehow, the two groups had met on that tiny island and at that tiny marina. Ransom was a talker; so was Tomlinson. Both of them were easy sources of information; both easily followed. Both also easily overpowered.

I guessed that somewhere between here and Chokoloskee, probably hidden away in some small backwater, was a second tri-hull.

It was the boat Tomlinson and Ransom had rented before Cordero and his men had followed them, stopped them, then kidnapped them.

Halfway down the tree, I could still see the beach. I watched as Goatee, still holding the little palm computer, pointed toward the red tent. Saw Cordero make an impatient waving gesture with his right hand until the man with the pumpkin-sized head tossed him what looked to be an Uzi.

Under any other circumstances, it would have been an absurdly amusing sight: A distinguished-looking gentleman in gray slacks, black glossy shoes and an expensive dress shirt holding a submachine gun at waist level. I watched him as he ripped the top-mounted cocking handle back and fired into the tent, holding the trigger on full automatic, the muzzle climbing high enough to spray stray rounds into the trees near me as the nylon of the red tent shuddered.

Reflexively, I pressed myself against the mangrove's trunk, waiting. Then my ears strained in the abrupt silence of an empty magazine. I watched Cordero change magazines as Goatee walked cautiously to the tent, drew a nine-millimeter semiautomatic and fired several more rounds into it before he ripped the screen door open and peered inside. Then he kicked the tent and kept kicking it until the stakes finally pulled free, and the little red dome tumbled down the beach in the wind like tumbleweed.

I couldn't hear, then, what Goatee said to Cordero. But I heard Cordero's voice clearly as he grabbed Ransom and yanked her to his chest like a shield, then touched the barrel of the Uzi to her temple. I saw her jerk her face away from that hot flash arrestor as he called out in English, "You come out now or I kill your sister! You hear me? I blow her fucking head right off you don't come out!" Then he screamed my name: *"FORD!"*

Feeling numb, helpless, I dropped down onto the sand and walked toward the beach, hands high over my head.

I still had the Sig Sauer in the back of my pants. Why not? What was the worst they could do if they found it?

They were going to kill us all anyway.

I watched the expression on Edgar Cordero's face change when he saw me. Watched it change from rage to a slow demonic delight. He shoved Ransom roughly to the ground, absolutely focused on me, lifting the muzzle of the Uzi to chest level as he called, "So! The cockroach finally comes crawling into the sunlight! You are so seldom alone"—he turned and kicked Ransom viciously in the thigh—"that we brought you company! Does that please you, *cabrón*? How does it feel to see a member of your own family in pain?"

I'd never seen Tomlinson attempt violence. Now he did. He went charging at Cordero as if to tackle him, all arms and jeans and Hawiian shirt, but Goatee intercepted. Hit him behind the shoulders with the butt of his pistol once . . . twice . . . then kneed him to the ground.

I continued to walk toward the little group, my mind working frantically, seeing the white beach and broad ocean beyond them, their rental boat rolling beam to the waves now, my skiff bucking at anchor nearby.

I had to come up with something. I had to at least try.

The pit I'd dug was about twenty meters to Cordero's right. Still covered with palmettos, too. If Tomlinson or Ransom created some kind of diversion, maybe I could dive into the pit and come up firing. Take my chances because, the way things looked, it was the only chance we had. It might be even better to let Cordero's men disarm me first, give them a false sense of safety. Dive and grab Tucker's old revolver that I'd hidden in there. I could use the big .44 to take out at least one of them. Then, hopefully, in the confusion, get off a couple more shots.

"Come closer! I want to look into the eyes of the filthy scum who attacked my son Amador when he wasn't looking. Attacked him when he was not ready, like a woman fights!"

I kept walking. Watched as Cordero handed the Uzi to Pumpkin-head and, in Spanish, asked him for a knife.

I remembered Harrington saying that Edgar collected ears from his adversaries.

Kept them like trophies behind the bar to show his friends.

Now Cordero was walking toward me, opening the knife as he approached, his eyes glittering. I stopped, waited. I began to lower my hands, wanting to get into position to grab my pistol, but raised them again when Pumpkin-head poked the Uzi at me and yelled, "Hands up! I shoot!"

Edgar Cordero was a few inches shorter than me. He had a pocked face beneath carefully sculpted hair. He stood close enough that I could smell the cologne he wore and the metallic stink of nicotine. He stood there, face up, his eyes boring into mine as if we were two boxers at a weigh-in, and then he touched the knife to my cheek . . . then placed the blade on the top of my left ear. He was probably expecting me to flinch, but I didn't flinch because I knew there was no escaping what he was going to do.

I heard him say, "You attacked my son from behind, like a dog, and now he will never walk again."

Feeling the strange and eerie calm of total resignation, I replied, "Sometimes the only way to catch a coward is from behind."

I watched the man's face go momentarily blank . . . then contort with rage as, behind him, Ransom yelled, "Don't you hurt my brother!" and she lunged toward me . . . me feeling a searing pain in my ear as Edgar began to saw with the knife . . . and then I heard one booming gunshot . . . then a second gunshot as Ransom dropped to the sand.

Then, oddly and without reason, Cordero was on the ground near her, screaming, swearing in Spanish and holding his neck, which was gushing blood. Pumpkin-head was down, too. Motionless. He'd flung the Uzi far from him before burying his face in black sand.

What the hell had happened?

Goatee was suddenly in front of me, waving the pistol in my direction as he backed away toward the boats, yelling in Spanish, "What is doing this? Who is *there?*" but then he spoke no more as his head seemed to vaporize in a scarlet mist, his legs managing two more steps before his body collapsed near the water.

A microsecond later, I heard a third booming gunshot, the sound arriving long after the heavy grain cartridge, and I turned just in time to see a puff of smoke drift out of a royal palm canopy that had to be a half mile away.

"Doc, she's bleeding!" Tomlinson was on his feet, kneeling over Ransom, who had her face covered with her hands. There was lots of blood there and she wasn't moving.

I rushed to help, feeling a surreal and shuddering grief, but then she did move as Tomlinson lifted her, and Ransom stood shakily, hand still holding her bleeding nose. She was wide-eyed, trembling with shock, looking at Cordero who was now silent, eyes empty, staring at the sky, dead. Then she considered the other two faceless corpses before she touched fingers to her sacred beads and whispered, "God strike them dead, just like I pray for Him to do. It happened, my brother, it really happened. Don't be telling me no more about what ain't magic!"

In the distance, I could see a tiny figure dressed in ninja black climbing down the trunk of the palm. He had to be using climbing hooks and a belt from the way he moved. He was descending pretty fast.

I turned and said to Tomlinson, "Get in their boat and go. *Now.* They made you abandon the boat you rented, right?"

Not looking at me, looking at the dead men, he was shaking his head. "No, they got in our boat. Ours was a little bigger and seemed newer, so after they stopped us, they climbed aboard. I didn't know who the hell they were."

I said, "Perfect. Then get out of here. Fast! Go straight to the marina, get in the truck and drive back to Sanibel. And Ransom?" When she turned to me, I touched my hands to her shoulders and I hugged her close, patting her back, the only brotherly comfort I could offer. I whispered into her ear, "Promise me something. Don't say a word to anyone about what happened here. Ever. Will you promise?"

The frightened and bewildered expression on her face changed slowly to resolve. It was good to see, a verification of something strong and important. She said to me, "Not talkin' about this is what God already telling me to do."

I HELPED THEM get the boat off the beach, aware that the figure dressed in black was getting closer, ever closer. I kept telling them they had to hurry. I meant it. If they saw him, found out who it was, he would have to kill them. That's just the way it worked.

When Tomlinson and Ransom were safe, almost to the horizon, I turned and faced a man my size; a man in black nylon pants and a Navy watch sweater exactly like my own; a man wearing a black ski mask and carrying a Remington 700 sniper rifle with a cannon-sized Star-Tron Mark scope that I knew all too well.

"They're gone?"

I told him, "Yeah."

He looked at the three corpses before he looked at me. "I had to rush the first shot. Your long-haired pal was in my line of fire. Don't think I wasn't tempted to pop him, too. But why should I do your work for you?"

I said, "Nope, no way, you're wrong. It's no one's job anymore. We have an agreement." When he didn't respond, I added, "Remember?"

He was standing over Edgar Cordero. I listened to him tell me that he was sorry he'd had to use me as bait, but it was the only way to isolate the Colombian, get him on neutral turf, before he said, "Throat shot."

I felt like knocking the man on his ass, he'd cut it so close. Not that I knew he'd be there. I didn't. Then I watched him strip off his mask and hold out his hand to me as he said, "You're only the third or fourth Negotiator I've met. It's an honor."

I shook his hand, so much adrenaline in me that I was beginning to feel weak. I said, "You mean the third or fourth outside your own teammates, of course."

He smiled. Said, "Very insightful," as he nudged Cordero's corpse with the toe of his worn jungle boot. "This sick bastard would've found a way to kill Lindsey. It's the way he was. It's what he did. He'd gotten her scent and he hated me. Kill your enemy's children, his signature. He'd've never quit."

Then Hal Harrington reached into his pocket and handed me a handkerchief. "That's a nasty little cut you've got there on your ear."

I began to daub blood from the side of my face as he added, "The kind of guys my daughter usually dates, they've got tattoos and piercings, not scars."

22

WE BURIED THE three of them in the sand behind the dune where Harrington had hidden his rubber inflatable boat. We used our entrenching tools and buried the dead men deep. We spoke little, said less. I wanted no words nor exchange of information to be associated with the memory of dragging corpses and shoveling sand onto them.

Compartmentalization—something I'm very good at. Harrington had to be pretty good at it, too, and for obvious reasons.

Then we had our own private little ceremony. I tossed driftwood on the fire until it blazed. Got a couple of beers off the ice. We had a good talk, an enlightening talk. Discussed things and events that we both knew we could never discuss again. Ever.

At one point, he said to me, "What I'm seriously considering doing is going back to my home state and running for political office. The way this nation's going, we need to get involved and stay involved."

I told him that I found the idea of any of us going into politics unlikely.

He said to me, "Are you kidding? You didn't know? A few years back, one of us ran for a governorship and won. We're already into politics."

I said, "Him?" and then a name.

Harrington was nodding. "Exactly."

I stood there and listened to him laugh as he told me that he thought a cell phone that played the theme from *The Lone Ranger* was a nice touch. He laughed some more when he told me how he'd set up Cordero, fed him information about me, where I was, where I'd be. Charged him top dollar, too, as an anonymous informant. Made him send cash money to a post office box in Cartagena, and Cordero had paid it gladly, excited to be getting such excellent and dependable intelligence.

Then Harrington and I exchanged files. From a plastic sack, from my skiff, I handed him a thick folder labeled OPERATION PHOENIX, and another with the words DIRECCION: BLANCA MANAGUA written on the cover in red felt-tip pen.

I watched him leaf through all those papers before dropping them into the fire.

I took the book-sized dossier on me, the only one in existence—according to Harrington, anyway—and tossed it into the fire. I watched the pages burn and curl, the ink producing colors different from those in the flames from the driftwood; colors not so bright or pure.

Then I said to him, "What about Tomlinson? We *do* have an agreement."

From his backpack, Harrington handed me a sheaf of legal-size paper. Said, "This exonerates him. Just like you asked. It's based on the actual investigative report on the bombing at Coronado, but I had a few things changed here and there. It lays the blame on an entirely different group. Not Tomlinson's. According to this, he had absolutely nothing to do with it. Legally and officially."

As I read through the documents, Harrington added, "But he *is* guilty, you know. He probably played more of a role than either one of us realizes. You're the one who decided to let him live—why not let him live with the truth? Johnny Garvin was one of us, for Christ's sake. He was a friend of yours."

I neatened the papers with my hands before sliding them into my own backpack. I looked out at the Gulf: it was a little breezy but not bad. It'd be a nice run back to Everglades. "It was a long time ago and he's suffered enough," I told Harrington. "You keep forgetting something. Tomlinson's my friend, too."

EPILOGUE

ON A SLEEPY, summer-hot March afternoon, I trundled the pretty lady in her lacy red thong bikini around a forgotten curve of beach on Fernandez Bay, Cat Island, in the outer Bahamas. There, amid the sound of gulls and wind, I spread blankets in the sun while she hunted around for a shady place to stow our picnic lunch and cooler full of Kalik beer.

The sky was Bahamian turquoise. The bay silver. Cliffs behind us, copper.

Then I watched as she reached into her oversized straw purse, handed me a little brown bottle, shook her hair down long and blond, and she demanded of me, "Oil, you big lummox. I need sunscreen on all the hard-to-reach spots. But just the public places, not the private. We've promised to be on our best behavior, and so far, so good."

"I know, I know," I said, "and it hasn't been easy."

"Think of it as preventative medicine. Like you're a doctor. The oil, I'm talking about. I've been in snow country, remember, and neither of us wants me too burned to tour the island with your sister's junkanoo band tonight."

I said, "She's not my sister," as I watched the lady arch her back, hand searching up between her own shoulder blades, and then her bikini top made an elastic popping noise . . . and hung there momentarily before it dropped at my feet.

I was shaking my head. "Wait a minute. That's not fair. It really isn't. Plus, if someone comes around those rocks and sees us, they're going to get entirely the wrong idea."

"Sees us?" The woman laughed as she knelt, then made a purring feels-good sound as she lay belly-down on the blanket. "Who's gonna see us? Surely, you don't mean Tomlinson and Ransom. You didn't hear the noises coming from their cabana when we left? It was the same noise they were making all night long. Every time I woke up, anyway. They're going to be too tired to walk the beach. Probably too *sore* to walk the beach."

Two weeks earlier, back at Dinkin's Bay, I'd given Tomlinson the investigator's report exonerating him from the Coronado bombing. Told him it had been provided to me by friends who had to remain anonymous. As he read it, and he began to weep, I'd turned and walked away.

I told the lady now, "I think he's making up for lost time. Trying his best, anyway."

"Or celebrating," she said. "I don't blame them, either. A trip like this, they've got every reason to celebrate."

That was uncontestably true.

THE NOTE TUCK wrote to me, the one in the bottle, ink on leather, read:

I stole a box of gold from the witch bastard that was too big and heavy for me to hide or carry whole off the island so I had to sink it in a lake where no one goes and carry what coins I could out just a few at a time. The lake's called Horse Eating Hole and the idiots think it's got a dragon down there, which is why it's the safest place in the world fars that witch bastard Benton's concerned.

The directions that followed were detailed.

Even so, our first few days on Cat Island had not been without difficulties. The first thing I had to deal with was convincing Ransom that we needed to make peace with Izzy and Clare.

"Them two Rastamonsters?" she'd sputtered, "I'd sooner befriend a couple poison snakes. They always treat me so dirty, man. Call me a fat cow and worse before I decided to take my own body back."

Forgiveness, I told her—talk to Tomlinson about the importance of forgiveness. Plus, there was another consideration, too: If she didn't make up with Izzy and Clare, they could swear out papers and have the magistrate arrest her.

For Izzy and Clare, making peace meant returning the golden lion's head ring, along with ten thousand dollars cash. Izzy wasn't wholly satisfied. He kept hinting around that Ransom might have stolen more cash than that; maybe he hadn't counted the money right. But he was a victim of his own greed, and that was the final settlement.

Clare was particularly pleased by the ring. His broken nose still bandaged, he squeezed it onto his black pinkie finger, beaming, and said, "My brotheren, my brotheren, you make the Lion of Judah very happy this day, you give praise to the Holy Piby with what you just do. By your holy actions, I'm sayin'." He then whacked me on the shoulder fondly. "We be friends for all the time now, glory to God, 'cause this here the royal ring of Haile Selassie, the one belonged to King Solomon, who then give it to the Queen of Sheba, who give it to her son, Prince Menelik of Ethiopia. And that the way the ring be passed along for three thousand years 'til our Saint, Bob Marley, leave to be with Black Jesus."

He didn't seem upset at all when Ransom added with false innocence, "Yeah, an' it come all the way from New York, too."

Something I could not convince her to do, however, was to come with us to the lake that had taken her son. It was near Arthur's Town, forty acres or so of dark water, ringed with dwarf mangroves. The lake did, indeed, have a sinister appearance. In the low trees, wings spread like gargoyles, were dozens, maybe hundreds, of anhingas, or snake birds.

No other sign of life in a water space so black and luminous that it might have been the gigantic eye of something alive.

TOMLINSON AND I had to use machetes to hack a trail wide enough for the little inflatable we'd rented, plus SCUBA gear. Then we began the laborious, boring chore of using our anchor to sound the bottom. Tuck's note said the lake was really a limestone crater connected to the sea, the entire bottom no more than seven or eight feet deep until you found the crater, and then it plummeted to sixty feet.

That's where he said he'd dropped the box.

Even with the range marker Tuck had used and described—a large dead buttonwood on the western shore—it took us nearly an hour to find the hole. Then I rolled over the side, breathing easily through the borrowed regulator, and drifted down through the murk, not expecting the poor visibility to change, but it did. It changed abruptly at about forty feet. In one instant I was in water too black and dense to see my own hands. In the next instant, I pierced a chilling thermoclime and my head and face poked through a lens of crystal saltwater. Beneath me was an aquarium world of flaming coral colors—a demarcation so abrupt that I felt as if I was falling into a new and secret world from above.

There, by the mouth of a tiny cave, we found a sizable brass box, locked with a padlock, that was so heavy I had to rig it to an air bag to lift it.

Something else we found on the bottom near a second, larger cave was a child-sized human skull—almost certainly Ransom's son, the boy who'd refused to believe in superstition, and whose body was never recovered.

Drifting there, looking into the vacuous eye sockets, I had the startling realization that this boy had not only been a kindred thinker, he had also been my own flesh and blood.

I looked at Tomlinson. . . . He looked at me before holding an index finger to his regulator—*Sshhhh.* Let the child rest.

We did. We left him and never told Ransom. But first, I touched fingers to my lips, then touched his forehead. A private farewell to the nephew I never knew.

THEN THE FOUR of us sat alone in one of our two cabanas at Fernandez Bay, drinking champagne, whispering and giggling like conspiratorial children as we counted out 276 coins: sixty-one of them Spanish, gold and silver, the rest old British and French coins.

Ransom had looked at me teary-eyed and said, "We rich, my brother, we rich! Man, I'm gonna buy me a boat and live on Sanibel. Or maybe a house. Get me a TV and that red car, too!"

Now, though, as I applied suntan oil to the lady's long and lovely legs, old coins and considerations of wealth seemed not very interesting, nor even important. I found that—surprise, surprise—my hands seemed to have a mind of their own. They decided I couldn't just slather on the oil, it was only reasonable that I give her a body massage while I was at it.

Judging by the soft moaning sounds she made, the lady seemed to approve.

Once, she got up on her elbows, turned enough so I could see the milky, blue veins beneath the white skin of her breasts. I looked into her brilliant blue eyes as she asked, "You still sorry that your girlfriend couldn't make it?"

Meaning Lindsey Harrington who, over the phone, had stammered and stuttered at my invitation to Cat Island before she finally said, "Like, the thing is, Doc, I think the world of you. And you've, like, helped me a ton, you really have, and my dad approves, which is surprising as hell, but . . . but . . . well . . . remember me mentioning Big Ben, my body-guard? Now that Dad's let me out of prison, Big Ben and I've decided to go hang out in San Francisco for awhile. He knows an artist out there who does these, like, unbelievable tattoos."

As my hands worked their way up the lady's back to her strong shoulders, I said, "She's not my girlfriend. Girlfriends, I've decided, are a pain in the ass."

Which is when my friend, Dewey Nye, the former tennis great, got up on her elbows once more, laughing. She seemed to find that hilarious. She was laughing, then she was roaring. "Tell me about it, pal," she said. "Tell me about it!"

"On my window sill sit two pigeons, Major and Minor. They always sit there, looking at the papers and manuscripts on the desk inside. They know more about modern music than any two pigeons in the whole world and, for quite some time, their cooing has sounded like two-part inventions, slightly jazzed up with a lot of wrong basses.

"On the desk they see the merry pile of morning mail . . . sheets and sheets of letters, concert programs, posters, magazines—each of them full of adventure and excitement. The dean of Indiana University reports on the success of a new American opera whose world première he just gave with his students. Oak Ridge, a brand-new city, has a brand-new symphony, and there is a letter from its conductor, Waldo Cohn, atomic chemist, cello player, music fanatic. There are press reports on performances of an American opera from Stockholm, London, Berlin . . . a two-hundred-word telegram from Hollywood, which could have been, just as well, a gentle postcard.

"Bands in colorful uniforms march out of the papers, whirling, beautiful majorettes, cornet players with serious eyes. There comes a somber procession of participants in a fascinating lawsuit for infringement of copyright. Records of new American symphonies look out of scurrile covers.

"And composing has become a great contemporary pastime. There just doesn't seem anybody left in this great land who can read the Twenty-third Psalm, see a rosebud in June, woo a fair maid, or pass an ol' cotton, saw, wind, steel, wood, paper, or gin mill without breaking out in melody and mailing the result by registered post to a music publisher."